INVITATION TO THE PRINCE'S PALACE

BY
JENNIE ADAMS

AND

THE PRINCE'S SECOND CHANCE

BY
BRENDA HARLEN

D1150786

MILLS
BOON

Dear Reader,

Take one modern-day prince, add an everyday girl and an unconventional marriage arrangement, and watch the unanticipated romance unfold.

Invitation to the Prince's Palace is my first royal story, and I'm so excited to be exploring the fantasy of an everyday girl marrying literally the prince of her dreams.

One of my pleasures is to throw characters with differing backgrounds, histories and outlooks together and watch the sparks fly as they resist each other, fall for each other, and figure out how to overcome the odds to be together. I've particularly enjoyed writing Rikardo and Melanie's story. It has given me the chance to consider what it might be like for an ordinary girl to be swept off her feet and into a complete fantasy world—one she doesn't believe she deserves or would be able to live in. Watch her prince figure out how to convince her, and watch him come to believe that true love can indeed happen—even when it's the last thing he has planned!

I hope you enjoy the story of Australian cook Melanie Watson and her wonderful European prince, Rikardo Ettonbierre, as much as I enjoyed writing it.

With love from Australia,

Jennie

INVITATION TO THE PRINCE'S PALACE

BY
JENNIE ADAMS

First published in Great Britain 2012
by Mills & Boon, an imprint of Harlequin (UK) Limited,
Eton House, 18-24 Paradise Road, Richmond, Surrey TW9 1SR

© Jennie Adams 2012

ISBN: 978 0 263 89408 0

23-0212

Harlequin (UK) policy is to use papers that are natural, renewable and recyclable products and made from wood grown in sustainable forests. The logging and manufacturing processes conform to the legal environmental regulations of the country of origin.

Printed and bound in Spain
by Blackprint CPI, Barcelona

Australian author **Jennie Adams** grew up in a rambling farmhouse surrounded by books and by people who loved reading them. She decided at a young age to be a writer, but it took many years and a lot of scenic detours before she sat down to pen her first romance novel. Jennie has worked in a number of careers and voluntary positions, including transcription typist and pre-school assistant. She is the proud mother of three fabulous adult children, and makes her home in a small inland city in New South Wales. In her leisure time Jennie loves long, rambling walks, discovering new music, starting knitting projects that she rarely finishes, chatting with friends, trips to the movies and new dining experiences.

Jennie loves to hear from her readers and can be contacted via her website at www.jennieadams.net

For Kara

CHAPTER ONE

'YOU'RE here. I expected to have to wait longer.' Melanie Watson tried not to sound too desperately relieved to see the cab driver, but she *was* relieved. She'd been saving money to try to start a new life away from her aunt, uncle and cousin. She still didn't have enough, but tonight she'd experienced very clearly just how soul-destroying it truly could be to live among people who postured rather than accepted, who used rather than loved.

The family's gloves had come off and Mel had made the choice to leave now whether she was quite finan-cially ready, or not.

Mel had waited until her cousin had disappeared into her suite of rooms, and until her aunt and uncle had fallen into bed. She'd cleaned up every speck of the kitchen because she never left a job half done, and then she'd ordered a cab, left a note in her room, packed her life into suitcases and carried it to the kerb.

Mel tried to focus her gaze on a suburb painted in shades of silvery dawn. The sun would rise fully soon. The wispy chill would lift. Clarity and the new day would come and things would look better. If she could only stay awake and alert for that long.

She really felt quite odd right now, off kilter with an unpleasant buzzing in her head. She didn't exactly feel she might be about to faint, but…she didn't feel right, that was for sure.

'It's a nice time for a drive. It'll be really quiet and peaceful.' That sounded hopeful, didn't it? At least a little bit positive and not overly blurry?

With the kind of anonymity born of speaking to a total stranger, Mel confided, 'I'm a bit under the weather. I had an allergic reaction earlier and I didn't get to take anything for it until just now. The medication is having a lot stronger impact on me than I thought it would.'

She'd got the treatment from her cousin's stash while Nicolette had seen off the last of the wealthy guests. Maybe Mel shouldn't have helped herself that way, but she'd been desperate.

Mel drew a breath and tried for a chirpy tone that emerged with an edge of exhaustion. 'But I'm ready to leave. Melbourne airport here we come.'

'I arrived earlier than anticipated so I'm grateful that you are ready.'

She thought he might have murmured, 'Grateful and somewhat surprised' before he went on.

'And I'm pleased to hear your enthusiasm despite the problem of allergies. Might I ask what caused them?' The taxi driver's brows lifted as though he didn't quite know what to make of her.

Fair enough. *Mel* didn't know what to make of herself

right now. She'd fulfilled her obligations, had pulled off all the beautiful desserts and other food for the dinner party despite harassment from her relatives and cleaned up afterwards when the party had finally ended.

Now she really needed her wits about her to leave, and they weren't co-operating. Instead, they wanted to fall asleep standing up. Like a tram commuter after a big day's work, or a girl who'd taken a maximum dose allergy pill on top of a night of no sleep and wheezing and swallowing back sneezes and getting a puffy face and puffy eyes.

'My cousin bought a new perfume. She sprayed it near me and off I went. Apparently I'm allergic to gardenias.' Mel dug for the remnants of her sense of humour. She knew it was still in there somewhere! 'Just don't give me any big bunches of those and I'm sure we'll be fine.'

'I will see to that. And you are right. It is a good time for a drive. The Melbourne cityscape is charming, even in pre-dawn light.' His words seemed so serious, and his gaze focused on her eyes, then on the spot where the dimple had come and gone in her cheek as she made her small joke. Would the dimple have offset her red nose and puffy face? Somehow Mel doubted it.

Mel focused on him, too. It was difficult not to because the man was top-to-toe gorgeous. Tall, a little over six feet to her five feet four and beautifully lean. Mel blinked to try to clear her drowsy vision.

He'd spoken in that lovely accent, too. French? No, but something European, Mel thought, to go with his tanned skin and black hair and the almost regal way he carried himself. He had lovely shoulders, just broad enough that a woman could run her hands over them to appreciate their beauty, or lay her head to rest there and know she could feel secure.

He wore an understated, expensive-looking suit. That was a bit unusual for a cab service, wasn't it? And his eyes—they weren't hazel or brown but a glorious deep blue.

'I just want to curl up.' Maybe that explained her re-action to him because his broad shoulders looked more appealing by the moment.

'Perhaps we'd better get your luggage loaded first, Nicol—' The rest of the word was drowned by the double beep of a car's unlocking device. He reached for the first two suitcases.

She must have given her full name of Nicole Melanie Watson when she booked the taxi. Since going to live with her aunt and uncle at age eight, Mel had only been known by her middle name. It felt strange to hear the first one again. Strange and a little shivery, because, even hearing only part of the word, his accent and the beautiful cadence of his voice made it sound special.

Oh, Mel. For goodness' sake.

'It's a pretty set of luggage. I like the floral design.' Was *Mel* making sense? She'd rescued the luggage when her cousin Nicolette had wanted to throw it out, but of course this man didn't need to hear that. And *she* didn't need to be quite so aware of him, either!

'You wouldn't lose the luggage easily. The design is quite distinctive.' He cast her a sideways glance. 'You are quite decided about this?'

'I'm decided.' Had he had people try to scam him out of fares? Mel would never do that. She knew what it was like to try to live on a tight budget. Her aunt and uncle might be well off, but they'd never seen the need to do more than meet the basic costs of taking her in. Once she reached working age, they'd expected her to return their investment by providing cheap kitchen labour. For the sake of her emotional health, Mel had to consider any debt paid now. 'I won't change my mind.'

She glanced to where he'd parked and saw, rather than a taxicab, an unmarked car. The cab agency had said there was a shortage of cabs but she hadn't realised someone might come for her in their private car in their off-duty time. Wouldn't that be against company policy?

And the car was a really posh one, all sleek dark lines and perfectly polished. That didn't seem right for a cab driver, did it? How would he afford it? Mel frowned.

'Did you come straight from a formal dinner or something?' It must have been a really late night.

The words slipped out before she could censor them. The thought that followed worried her a little, but he'd have had sleep wouldn't he? He looked rested.

You'll be perfectly safe with him, Mel. It won't be like—

She cut the thought off. That was a whole other cause of pain for Mel, and she didn't want to let it in. The night had been tough enough.

'Most dinners I attend are formal unless I have a night with my brothers.' Rikardo spoke decisively and yet...his guest didn't look as he'd expected. She didn't...

seem as he'd expected. Her openness and almost a sense of naivety…must be because she wasn't feeling well.

He tucked the odd thoughts away, and tucked his passenger into the front seat beside his. 'You may rest, if you wish. Perhaps by the time we arrive at the airport your allergy medication will have done its job and you'll be back to normal.'

'I doubt that. I feel as though I've been felled by elephant medicine.' She yawned again. 'Excuse me. I can't seem to stop.'

He'd collected a drowsy and puffy version of Sleeping Beauty. That was what Prince Rikardo Eduard Ettonbierre thought as the airport formalities ended and he carried Nicolette Watson onto the royal private jet and lowered her into a seat.

She'd slept most of the way to the airport and right through the boarding process. The medication had indeed got the better of her, but she was still very definitely…a sleeping beauty.

Despite the puffy face she seemed to have held her age well since the days when she'd been part of his university crowd during his time in Australia. She'd been two years behind him, but he'd known even then that Nicolette wanted to climb to the heights of social success.

Though their paths had not crossed since those days, Nicolette had made it a point to send Christmas cards, mark his birthday, invite him as her personal guest to various events, and in other ways to keep her name in front of him. Rik had felt awkward about that pursuit.

He didn't really know what to say now, to explain his lack of response to all those overtures.

Perhaps it was better to leave that alone and focus on what they were about to achieve. He'd carefully considered several women for this task. In the end he'd chosen to ask Nicolette. He'd known there would be no chance he would fall for her romantically, and because of her ambitious nature he'd been confident she would agree to the plan. She'd been the sensible choice.

Rik had been right about Nicolette. When he'd contacted her, she'd jumped at this opportunity to elevate her social status. And rather than someone closer by, who might continue to brush constantly through his social circles once this was all over, when their agreement ended, Rik could return Nicolette to Australia.

'You should have allowed me to carry her, Your Highness.' One of his bodyguards murmured the words not quite in chastisement, but in something close to it. 'Even driving a car by yourself to get her— You haven't given us sufficient information about this journey to allow us to properly provide for your safety.'

'There is nothing further to be revealed just at the moment, Fitz.' Rik would deal with the eruption of public and royal interest in due course but there was no need for that just yet. 'And you know I like to get behind the wheel any time I can. Besides, I let you follow in a second car and park less than a block away. Try not to worry.' Rik offered a slight smile. 'As for carrying her, wasn't it more important for you to have your hands free in case of an emergency?'

The man grimaced before he conceded. 'You are correct, Prince Rikardo.'

'I *am* correct occasionally.' Rik grinned and settled into his seat beside Nicolette.

Was he mad to enter into this kind of arrangement to outwit his father, the king? Rik had enjoyed his combination of hard work and fancy-free social life for the past ten years. As third in line to the throne, he'd seen no reason to change that state of affairs any time soon, if at all. But now…

There were deeper reasons than that for your reluctance. Your parents' marriage…

His bodyguard moved away, and Rik pushed that thought away, too. He wasn't crazy. He was taking action. On these thoughts Rik turned his attention to the sleeping woman. Her hair fell in a soft honey-blonde curtain. Though her face still showed the ravages of her allergy problem, her features were appealing.

Long thick brown eyelashes covered eyes that he knew were a warm brown colour. She had soft pink lips, a slim straight nose and pretty rounded cheeks. She looked younger in the flesh than in the photo she'd emailed, than Rik had thought she would look now…

She sighed and Rik had an unexpected urge to gently kiss her. It was a strange reaction to what was, in the end, a business arrangement with a woman he'd never have chosen to know more than peripherally if not for this. A response perhaps brought on because she seemed vulnerable right now. When she woke from this sleep she would be once again nothing but the ladder-climbing socialite he'd approached, and this momentary consciousness would be gone.

The pilot commenced take-off. Rik's guest stirred, fought for a moment to wake. Her hand rose to her cheek.

'You may sleep, Nicolette. Soon enough we will take the next step.' He said it in his native Braston tongue, and frowned again as the low words emerged. He rarely spoke in anything but French or English, unless to one of the older villagers or palace staff.

Nicolette turned her head into the seat. Her lashes stopped fluttering and she sighed. She'd cut her hair too, since the emailed photo she'd sent him. The shoulder-length cut went well with the flattering feminine skirt and silk top she wore with a short cardigan tied in a knot at her waist. The clothing would be nowhere near warm enough for their arrival in Braston, but that would be taken care of.

Rik made his chair comfortable, did the same for his sleeping guest, and took his rest while he could find it. When Nicolette sighed again in her sleep and her head came to rest on his shoulder, Rik shifted to make sure she was comfortable, inhaled the soft scent of a light, citrus perfume, and put down the feeling of contentment to knowing he was soon to take a step to get his country's economy back on its feet, and outwit his father, King Georgio, at the same time. Put like that, why wouldn't Rik feel content?

'You had an uneventful flight, I hope, Your Highness?'

'Not too much longer and we'll be able to disembark, Prince Rikardo.'

Mel woke to voices, snippets of conversation in English and another language and the low, lovely tones of her taxi driver responding regally while something soft and light and beautifully warm was draped around her shoulders.

'What—?' Heart pounding, she sat up abruptly.

This wasn't a commercial flight.

There were no rows of passengers, just some very well-dressed attendants who all seemed to make her taxi driver the centre of attention in a revering kind of way.

Mel's allergy was gone. The effects of the medication had worn off. That was good, but it also meant she couldn't be hallucinating right now.

She had vague memories of sleeping…on an accommodating shoulder.

Yet she didn't remember even boarding a flight!

This plane was luxurious. It had landed somewhere. Outside it was dark rather than the sunshiny day she'd looked forward to in Melbourne, and Mel could feel freezing air coming in through the aperture where another attendant waited for a set of steps to be wheeled to the edge of the plane.

She should be feeling Sydney summer air.

Memory of that expensive-looking car rose. Had she been kidnapped? Tension coiled in her tummy. If anything was wrong, she'd left a note saying she was moving to Sydney. Her relatives might be angry to lose their underpaid cook, but she doubted that they would go looking for her. Not at the expense of their time or resources.

Breathe, Melanie. Pull yourself together and think about this.

The driver had asked her if she was 'sure about this'. As though they already had an arrangement? That would make it unlikely that she'd been kidnapped.

But they *didn't* have an arrangement!

Mel turned her head sharply, and looked straight into the stunning gaze of the man who'd placed her in that car.

She'd thought, earlier, that he was attractive. Now Mel realised he was also a man of presence and charisma. All those around him seemed to almost feel as though…they were his servants?

Words filtered through to Mel again. French words and, among those words, 'Prince Rikardo'.

They were addressing her driver as a prince?

That was easy, then, Mel thought a little hysterically. She'd fallen down a rabbit hole into some kind of alternative world. Any moment now she would sprout sparkling red shoes. *That's two different fairy tales, Mel. Actually it's a fairy tale and a classic movie.* Oh, as though that mattered! Yet in this moment, this particular rabbit hole felt all too real. And maybe there'd been a book first, anyway.

Stop it!

'You're fully refreshed? How are the allergies? You slept almost twenty-four hours. I hope the rest helped you.'

Did kidnappers sound calm, rational and solicitous?

Mel drew a breath, said shakily and with an edge of uncertainty she couldn't entirely hide, 'I feel a bit exhausted. The allergies are gone. I guess I slept them off while we travelled between Melbourne and…?'

'Braston.' He spoke the word with a slight dip of his head.

'Right. Yes. Braston.' A small country planted deep in the heart of Europe. Mel had heard of it. She didn't really know anything about it. She certainly shouldn't *be anywhere near it.* 'I'm just not quite sure— You see, I thought I'd be flying from Melbourne to Sydney—'

'We were able to fly very directly.' He leaned towards her and surprised her by taking her hand. 'You don't need to be nervous or concerned. Just stick to what we've agreed and let me do the talking around my father, the king.'

'K-king.' As in, a king who was the father of a prince? As in, this man, Rikardo, *was* a prince? A royal prince of Braston?

Stick with the issue at hand, Mel. Why are you here? That's the question you need answered.

'You are different somehow to what I have remembered.' His words were thoughtful.

'Remembered from our drive to the airport? I don't understand.' Her words should have emerged in a strong tone. Instead they were a nervous croak drowned by the clatter of a baggage trolley being wheeled closer to the plane.

Well, this was *not* the time for Mel to impersonate a scaredy frog waiting to be kissed into reassurance by a handsome prince.

Will you stop with the fairy-tale metaphors already, Melanie!

'You're nervous. I understand. I'll walk you through this process. Just rely on me, and it will be easy for both of us to honour our agreement.'

Mel drew a deep breath. 'Seriously, about this "agreement". There's been—'

'Your Highness, if you and your guest would please come this way.' An attendant waved them forward.

The prince, Rikardo, took Mel's elbow, tucked the wonderful warm wrap more snugly about her shoulders, and escorted her to the steps and down them onto the tarmac.

Icy wind whipped at Mel's hair and stung her face but, inside the wrap, she remained warm. Floodlights lit the small, private airstrip. A retinue of people waited just off the tarmac.

Mel had an overwhelming urge to turn around and climb back onto the plane. She might not be down a rabbit hole, but she was definitely Alice in Crazyland. None of this would have happened if she'd been completely herself when she ordered that ride to the airport and believed it had arrived. Mel would never take someone else's medication again, even if it were just an over-the-counter one that anyone could buy!

'Please. Prince…Your Highness…' As she spoke they moved further along the tarmac. 'There truly has been some kind of mistake.'

What could have happened? As Mel asked the silent question puzzle pieces started to come together.

If he'd called at the right address, then he had expected to collect a woman from there.

Her cousin had been in a strange mood, filled with

secrecy and frenetic energy. At the end of the dinner party, Nicolette had rushed to her room and started rummaging around in there. Had Nicolette been…packing for a trip?

Rik had said he'd arrived earlier than he'd expected to. That would explain Nicolette not being ready. Mel had thought that he'd called her by her first name of Nicole, but it could have easily been 'Nicolette' that he said. She and her cousin looked heaps alike. Horror started to dawn. 'It must have been Nicolette—'

'Allow me to welcome you on to Braston soil, Nicolette.' Rikardo, *Prince Rikardo*, spoke at the same time. He stopped. 'Excuse me?'

Oh. My. God.

He'd mistaken Mel for Nicolette. Mel's *cousin* had made some kind of plan with this man. That meant Rikardo really was a prince. Of this country! As in, royalty who had made an arrangement with Nicolette.

Mel, the girl who'd worked in her aunt and uncle's kitchen for years, was standing here in a foreign country with an heir to the throne, when it was her cousin who should be here for whatever reasons she should be here. How could the prince not realise the mistake? Surely he'd have seen that Mel wasn't Nicolette, even in dawn light and with Mel affected by allergies? Just how well did this prince know Nicolette?

Yes, Mel? And how many times has Nicolette become furious when one of her acquaintances mistook you for her when they called at the house?

'Unless we're in the public eye, please just call me Rik.' He hustled her into the rear of another waiting car and climbed in beside her. A man in a dark suit climbed into the front, spoke a few words to the prince in French, and set the vehicle in motion.

The prince added, 'Or Rikardo.'

'You probably have five given names and are heir to a whole lot of different dukedoms or things like that.' Mel sucked up a breath. 'I do watch the news and see the royal families coming and going.' She just hadn't seen this particular royal. 'The most famous ones. What I mean is, I'm not an overt royal-watcher, but I'm also not completely uninformed.'

Which made her sound like some kind of overawed hick who wouldn't have a clue how to behave in such august company. Exactly what Mel was! 'Please... Prince...Rik...I need to speak to you. It's urgent!'

'We have arrived, Your Highness.' The words, spoken in careful English, came again from the driver.

He'd drawn the car to a whisper-quiet halt and now held the door open for them to alight. Rikardo would get out first, of course, because he was, after all, a prince.

A burst of something a little too close to hysteria rose inside Mel's breast.

'Thank you, Artor, and also for speaking in English for the benefit of our guest.' Rikardo helped Mel from the car. He glanced down into her face. 'I know you may be nervous but once we get inside I will take you to our suite of rooms and you can relax and not feel so pressured.'

'S-straight to the rooms? We won't see anyone?' Well, of course they would see people. They were seeing people right now. And what did he mean by *their* suite? 'Can we talk when we get there? Please!'

'Yes, we will talk. It shouldn't be necessary at this late stage, but we will discuss whatever is concerning you.' He seemed every inch the royal as he said this, and rather forbidding.

Mel's stomach sank even further. She hadn't meant for this to happen. She hadn't meant to do anything other than take a taxi to the airport. She had to hope it would be relatively easy to fix the mistake that had been made.

Rik whisked her up an awe-inspiring set of steps that led to a pair of equally stunning studded doors. As they approached the doors were thrown open, as though someone had been watching from within.

They would have been, wouldn't they? Mel glanced up, and up again, and still couldn't see the ending of the outside of this enormous palace. Parts of it were lit, other parts melted into the surrounding darkness. It looked as though it had been birthed here at the dawn of time. Mel shivered as the cold began to register, and then Prince Rik's hand was at her back to propel her the final steps forward and inside.

Voices welcomed their prince. Members of the royal retinue of staff stood to attention while others stepped forward to take the prince's coat, and Mel's wrap.

How silly to feel as though the small of her back physically held the imprint of the prince's fingers. Yet if he hadn't been supporting her Mel might have fainted from the combination of anxiety and feeling overwhelmed by the opulence.

The area they entered was large, reaching up three levels with ornate cornicing and inlaid life-sized portraits of royal family members fixed into the walls. A bronze statue stood to one side on a raised dais. Creams and gold and red filled the foyer with warm resplendence. It would be real gold worth more than an entire jewellery store.

'Welcome to the palace.' Rik leaned closer to speak quietly into Mel's ear.

'Thank you. That is…' Mel's breath caught in her throat as she became suddenly very aware of his closeness.

She'd laid her head on his shoulder, had slept the hours of the flight away inhaling the scent of his cologne. On some level of consciousness, Mel knew the pace of his breathing, knew how it felt to have him sleep with his ear tucked against the top of her head. The feel of the cloth of his suit coat against her arm, his body warmth reaching her through the fabric.

For a moment consciousness and subconscious memory, nearness and scent and whatever else it was that had made her aware of him even initially through a fog of medication, filled Mel. She forgot the vital need to explain to him that he'd made a mistake and she had, too. She forgot everything but his nearness, and the uneven beat of her heart.

And then Prince Rikardo of Braston spoke again, softly, for her ears only.

'Thank you for agreeing to help me fulfil my father's demands and yet maintain my freedom…by temporarily marrying me.'

CHAPTER TWO

'THERE'S been a terrible mistake.' Rik's bride-to-be paced the sitting room of his personal suite. Tension edged her words. One hand gestured. 'I don't belong here. I'm not the right girl. Look at all this, and I'm—'

'You won't be staying here all that long.' Not for ever. A few months... Rik tried to understand her unease. She'd been fully willing to enter into this arrangement. Why suffer a bout of cold feet about it now? She'd stepped into his suite, taken one glance around and had launched into speech.

'This is an interlude,' he said, 'nothing more.' And one they'd agreed upon, even if she hadn't yet signed the official contract. Rik's aide had the paperwork in a safe place, but it was ready and waiting, and Nicolette had made it clear that she was, too. So what had changed?

She drew a shuddery breath. 'This is gilt and gold and deep red velvet drapes and priceless original artworks and cornices in enormous entryways that take my breath away. This is more than a rabbit hole and a golden pumpkin coach and a few other fables meshed together. This is—' Her brown-eyed gaze locked with his and she said hotly as though it were the basis of evil: *'You're a prince!'*

'My royal status is no surprise to you.' What did surprise Rik was how attractive he found the sparkle in her eyes as indignation warred with guilt and concern on her lovely face. He'd never responded this way to Nicolette. He didn't want to now. This was a business arrangement. His lack of attraction to Nicolette was one of the reasons he'd chosen her. It would be easy to end their marriage and walk away.

So no more thoughts such as those about her, Rik!

'But it is a surprise. I mean, it wouldn't be if I'd already read about you in a magazine or something and I certainly completely believe you.' Shaking fingers tucked her hair behind her ear.

She didn't even sound like the woman he remembered. She sounded more concerned somehow, and almost a little naïve.

A frown started on his brow. He'd put down her openness, the blurting of a secret or two to him when he collected her, to the influence of the allergy medication. But that had worn off now. Suspicion, a sense of something not right, formed deep in his gut. He took a step towards her, studied her face more closely and wished he had taken more notice of Nicolette's features years ago. Those freckles on her nose—? 'Why do you seem different?'

'Because I'm not who you think I am,' she blurted, and drew a sharp breath. Silence reigned for a few seconds as she seemed to gather herself together and then she squared her shoulders. 'My full name is *Nicole Melanie* Watson.'

'Nicole...'

'Yes.' She rushed on. 'I'm known as Melanie and have been since I went to live with my aunt, uncle, and cousin *Nicolette* when I was eight years old. *Nicolette* would fit right in here. I've tried to figure this out since I woke up in your private jet and realised I wasn't at Sydney airport about to get off a plane there and go find a hostel to stay in while I searched for work because I could no longer stay—'

She broke off abruptly.

Sydney airport? Hostel? Search for work? There was something else about her statement, too, but Rik lost the thought as he focused on the most immediate concerns.

'I am not certain I understand you.' His tone as he delivered this statement was formal—his way of throwing up his guard. 'Are you trying to tell me—?'

'I think you meant to collect Nicolette and you got me by mistake. I don't see what else could have happened. When you said my name before, I thought you said Nicole, not Nicolette. I thought I must have given my full name when I ordered the taxi.'

'If what you say is correct...' Rik's eyes narrowed. Could this be true? That he'd collected the wrong woman? 'I haven't seen Nicolette for a number of years, just a photo sent over the Internet. I thought when I collected you that you'd changed and that you looked younger than expected. If you are not Nicolette at all—

Do you look a great deal like your cousin?' He rapped out the words.

'Y-yes, at least a fair amount. And I sound like her. It really annoys her. Acquaintances do it all the time when they come to the house. Mistake us for each other, I mean.' The woman—Melanie—wrung her hands together. 'This is all just a horrible mix-up. I was zonked out on medication, and waiting at the kerb for my ride to the airport to start a whole new life and you took me instead of taking Nicolette, who probably should have been waiting but she's never on time for anything, and you said you were early.'

Horror came over her face. 'Nicolette will be *furious* at me when she finds out what's happened.'

'It is not up to your cousin to take out any negative feelings on you if a mistake has been made.' A thought occurred to him. 'While I thought you were your cousin, you…mistook me for a taxi service?'

'I didn't know then that you were a *prince*!'

Did his lips twitch? She sounded so horrified, and Rik had to admit the idea of being mistaken for a cab driver was rather unique. His amusement faded, however, as the seriousness of the problem returned to the forefront of his thoughts. He didn't notice the way his face eased into gentleness as he briefly touched her arm.

'I'm sure there'll be a solution to this problem.' He bent his thoughts to coming up with that solution. He had planned all this, worked everything out. And after a long flight to get to Australia from Braston…he'd collected a cousin he'd never heard of, who had no idea of his marriage plans, the bargain Rik had struck with his father, King Georgio, or the ways in which Rik intended to adhere to that bargain but very much on his terms.

If he couldn't straighten this all out, his error could cost him the whole plan, and that in turn could cost the people of Braston who truly needed help. Rik held himself substantially responsible for that need.

'It's kind of you not to want to blame me.' She spoke the words in a low, quiet tone and gazed almost with an edge of disbelief at him through a screen of thick dark lashes.

As though she didn't expect to be given a fair hearing, or she expected to be blamed for what had happened whether she was in the wrong or not.

'There's no reason to blame you, Nicol—*Melanie.*' For some reason, Rik couldn't shift his gaze from the surprised and thoughtful expression in her eyes.

She looked as though she didn't quite feel safe here. Or did she always carry that edge of self-protectiveness, that air of not knowing if she was entirely welcomed and if she could let down her guard?

Rik had lived much of his life with his guard firmly in place. As a royal, that was a part of his life. But he knew who he was, where he fitted in the world. This young woman looked as though she should be happy and carefree. She had said she'd been about to start a new life. What had happened to make her come to that decision? To leave her family at dawn with all her suitcases packed?

Had Nicolette contributed to that sudden exit on Melanie's part?

You have other matters to sort out that are of more immediate concern.

Rik did, but he still felt protective of this young woman. She'd suddenly found herself on the other side of the world in a strange place. A little curiosity towards her was to be expected, too. He'd collected a stranger. Naturally he would want to understand just who this stranger was.

He would need her help and co-operation to resolve this problem, and she would need his reassurance. 'This doesn't have to be an insurmountable difficulty. If I can get you back out of the palace, keep you away from my father and create a suitable story to explain that bringing my fiancée home took two trips...'

'It seems such a strange thing to do in the first place, to marry someone for a brief period knowing you're going to end the marriage. Why do it at all if that's the case? How well do you know my cousin?' The words burst out of Mel as she watched Prince Rikardo come to terms with the problem of a girl who shouldn't be here, and one who should be and wasn't.

She felt overwrought and stressed out. What would happen to her plans now? Mel needed to be in Sydney looking for work. Not here suffering from a case of mistaken identity.

And then she realised that she'd just questioned a prince, and perhaps not all that nicely because she *did* feel worried and uneasy and just a little bit threatened and scared about the future. 'I beg your pardon. I didn't mean that to sound disrespectful. I guess I'm just looking for answers.'

'Your cousin is a past acquaintance from my university days in Australia who has kept in touch now and then remotely over the years since.'

So he didn't know Nicolette closely, had potentially never really known her. But he'd said he intended to marry her, albeit briefly. Mel's mind boggled at the potential reasons for that. Nicolette had hugged the secret close. Maybe she'd been told she had to? What was in it for Mel's cousin?

Well, even if it were to be a brief marriage, Nicolette would for ever be able to say she'd been a princess. Mel's cousin would love that. It would open even more doors socially to her. That left what was in it for Prince Rikardo?

'This must all seem quite strange to you, to suddenly find yourself here when you thought you were headed for Sydney, wasn't it?' His voice deepened. 'To start a new life?'

'I did say that, didn't I? When I thought you were a taxi driver and blabbed half my life story at you.' She drew a breath. 'I also meant no insult by thinking that you were a taxi driver.'

'None was taken.' He paused.

Did he notice that she dodged his question about starting a new life? Mel didn't want to go into that.

'Let me get the wheels in motion to start rectifying this situation,' he said. 'Then we'll discuss how this happened.'

For a blink of time as he spoke those words Mel saw pure royalty. Privileged, powerful. He would not only fix this problem, he would also have his answers.

He'd said he didn't blame her, that it wasn't her fault. But Mel couldn't be as self-forgiving. She should have realised something was amiss. There'd been signs. An unmarked car; a driver not in uniform; even the fact that he'd tucked her in the front of the cab beside him rather than expecting her to get in the back. Of course he would demand his answers. Had she really thought she would get off without having to face that side of it?

Would she in turn learn more of why he'd chosen her cousin for this interaction? 'Yes, of course you'll need to set wheels in motion, to contact Nicolette and sort out how to get her here as quickly as possible. I'm more than willing to simply be sent to Sydney. You can put me on any flight, I don't mind. I don't need to see my cousin again.' She didn't *want* to see Nicolette again and be brought to account for all of this, and for choosing to leave the family without a moment's notice, because Mel *wouldn't* go back.

What did Prince Rikardo see in Nicolette?

He didn't have to see anything.

Or maybe he liked what little he knew of Mel's cousin and they could conduct this transaction between them and perhaps even become firm friends afterwards. Nicolette could be charming when it suited her. There'd been times over the years when she'd charmed Mel. Not lately, though.

Mel searched Rikardo's gaze once more. Though his mind must be racing, he didn't appear at all unnerved. How could he portray such an aura of strength? Did it come as part of his training in the royal family? An odd little shiver went down her spine and her breath caught.

What would it be like, to be a prince such as Rikardo Ettonbierre? Or to be…truly in Nicolette's shoes, about to marry him, even if briefly?

Are you sure that his strength is simply a result of his position, his royal status, Melanie?

No. There was something in Rikardo Ettonbierre's make-up that would have demanded those answers regardless, and got them whether he'd ever been trained to his heritage, or not. That would have shown strength, not uncertainty, no matter what.

'We will make all the necessary arrangements. If we do it quickly—' Rikardo strode towards a phone handset on an ornate side table. He lifted the phone and spoke into it. 'Please ask my aide to attend me in my suite as soon as possible. I have some work for him to do. Thank you.' He had just replaced the receiver when a knock sounded on the door.

'That's too soon to be my aide,' he murmured. 'It will be our dinner. You must be hungry.'

The door opened. Members of staff entered bearing covered dishes. Aromas filled the room and made Mel realise just how long it had been since she'd eaten.

'The food smells delicious.' She'd always *cooked* the meals, not had them brought to her on silver salvers. 'I have to confess I *am* quite hungry.'

'That is good to hear.'

Rather than from Rikardo, the words came in a more mature yet equally commanding voice. The owner of that voice stepped into the room, a man in his early sixties with black hair greying at the temples, deep blue eyes and the power, by his presence alone, to strike dumb every staff member in the room.

Mel hadn't even needed that impact to identify him, nor the similarities to the prince. All she'd needed was one look at Rikardo's face, at the way it closed up into a careful mask that covered and protected every thought.

The king had just walked in.

This was the worst thing that could have happened right now. They'd needed to keep her, Melanie, out of sight of this man. Mel's breath froze in her throat and her gaze flew to Rik's. What did they do now? She caught a flash of a trapped look on Rikardo's face before he smoothed it away.

Somehow that glimpse of humanness opened up a wealth of fellow feeling in Mel. She had to help Rik out of this dilemma. She didn't even realise that she'd thought of him as Rik, not Rikardo.

The king's gaze fixed on her, examining, studying. He'd spoken to her. Sort of. Mel didn't know whether or not to respond.

'Indeed, Father, and it is fortuitous that you are here.' Rik stepped forward. He didn't block his father's view of Mel, but he drew the king's attention away from her. 'I would like a word with you regarding the truffle harvest, if you please.'

The older man's eyes narrowed. He frowned in his son's direction and said: 'It *pleases me* to know my future daughter-in-law will eat a meal rather than pretend a lack of appetite to try to maintain a waif-thin figure.'

Waif-thin figure?

Mel worked in a kitchen. She might have been underpaid, but she'd never been hungry. Was it usual for kings to speak their minds like this?

There was another problem, though. Even Mel, with her lack of understanding of royal protocols, could guess that it wasn't appropriate for Rikardo not to introduce her to his father, even if the king had surprised them in Rik's suite.

Should she introduce herself? Why hadn't Rikardo done that?

Because you're not who you should be, Melanie. How is he supposed to introduce you without either telling the truth or lying? Neither option will work just at the moment.

And anyway, why don't you interview all the kings you're on a first-name basis with, and collate the responses to discover a mean average and then you'll know whether they all speak bluntly?

She wasn't thinking hysterically exactly, Mel told herself.

Just don't say anything. Well, not anything bad. Be really, really careful about what you say, or, better still, stay completely silent and hope that Rikardo takes care of this. Didn't he say earlier if you came across his father to let Rik do all the talking?

Yes, but that was before he realised Mel wasn't Nicolette. His father didn't know that, though, and now the king had spotted Melanie. Not only spotted her but spoken to her and had a really good look at her. And if she didn't respond soon, the king might think—

'Your Highness.' Mel sank into what she hoped was an acceptable style of curtsy. She tried not to catch the older man's gaze, and hoped that her voice might pass for Nicolette's next time.

Rikardo had mistaken Melanie for Nicolette. But she'd been puffed up with allergies then. Rikardo strode towards the door of his suite.

At the door, he turned to face Mel. 'If you will excuse us? Please go ahead and eat dinner.' He asked one of the kitchen staff to let his aide know they would speak after Rikardo finished with the king. From outside, Rikardo called in another member of staff. 'Please also show my guest her rooms.'

In about another minute, the king would be out of here. Mel could stop holding her breath and worrying about what she might reveal to the king that could cause problems for when Nicolette arrived.

Mel glanced into Rikardo's eyes and nodded, acknowledging that he intended to leave.

Rikardo swept out of the room and swept his father along with him, even if he was the king.

Melanie thanked the staff for the delivery of the meal. She felt their curious gazes on her, too, and she would have liked to strike up a conversation, to ask what it was like to work in the kitchens of a palace. Instead, she kept her gaze downcast and kept the interaction as brief as she could.

The rooms she would use were lavish. Mel could barely take it all in.

And then finally she was alone.

So she could sit at the royal dining table in Prince Rikardo's suite that had its own guest suite within it, and eat royal food while she waited for the prince to have his discussion with his father about truffle harvesting. She hadn't known the country grew truffles.

But that wouldn't be all of the conversation and it would no doubt be difficult for the prince, but then Rikardo would come back here and tell Melanie his plans, and somehow or other it would all be all right.

Mel turned to the dining table, looked at the array of dishes. She would eat so at least she had some energy inside her to deal with whatever came next.

It *would* be all right. Rikardo was a prince. He would be able to make anything right.

CHAPTER THREE

Rik stood by the window in the sitting area of his suite. Early sunlight filtered across the snowy landscape of mountains and valleys, and over Ettonbierre village below. Soon people would begin to move around, to go about their work—those who *had* enough work.

He had once liked this time best of all, the solitude before the day's commitments took over. Today, his thoughts were already embroiled and his aide already on his way to Rik's suite to discuss yet another matter of urgency. The past two years had been problem after problem. Rik's marriage plans had been part of the solution, or so he had believed. Now...

He had spoken to his father last night. It hadn't been the greatest conversation he'd ever had; it had taken too long, and at the end of it he had known the impossibility of trying to bring Nicolette out here now to pass her off as his fiancée.

Really he'd known that from the moment Melanie had told him he'd collected the wrong girl. Too many people had seen her. Then Rik's *father* had seen her. She had tried not to be too noticeable, too recognisable. But the king *had* noticed. Right down to the three freckles dotted across the bridge of her nose.

Rik had whisked his father out of his suite. He'd bought a little time to come up with a solution before his father formally met his fiancée. But in the end there *was* only one solution.

A soft knock sounded on the outer door of his suite. Rik strode towards it. He didn't believe in the edict that a prince should not do such menial things as open doors to his staff. He and his brothers all worked on behalf of the people of Braston one way or another, so why wouldn't they open a door?

And now you all have a challenge to fulfil. The prize is that your father will come out of his two-year disconnection from the world around him, caused by the queen moving out and refusing to return, and co-operate to enable the economy here to be healed.

'Good morning, Prince Rikardo.' His aide stepped into the room and closed the door behind him. 'My apologies for disturbing you at this hour.'

'And mine for disturbing you late last night.' Rik gave a wry twist of his lips. 'To examine an emailed photograph, no less.'

And the passport of Nicole Melanie, which had been handled by one of his retinue of attendants when they arrived at the airport with his guest deeply asleep.

Nicole, not Nicolette. Only Rik could have spotted that mistake and he'd been otherwise occupied at the time.

'But with a purpose, Your Highness. It is unfortunate that the two women do not look enough alike to ensure we could safely swap them.' Dominico Rhueldt drew a breath. 'I have carried out your wishes and transferred the funds from your personal holdings to the bank account of Nicolette Watson, and ordered the set from the hand-crafted collection of the diamond jeweller, Luchino Montichelli. It will be delivered to Nicolette within two days.'

The man hesitated. 'Your Highness, I am concerned about the amount of money going out of your holdings towards relief to the people. I know they are in need—'

'And while I have the ability I will go on meeting needs, but that doesn't fix the underlying problems.' Rik sighed. It was an old conversation. 'Nicolette. She is happy with this…buy-off?'

A gift of baubles and a cash injection in exchange for her acceptance of the changed circumstances, and her silence.

Though Rik's question referred to the woman he'd organised to briefly marry, he struggled to shift his thoughts from the one he'd carried onto a plane recently.

He glanced at the closed door of his guest suite. Last night when he'd got back, he'd tucked the covers over Melanie. She'd been curled up on the bed in a ball as though not quite sure she had a right to be there. Sleeping Beauty waiting to be woken by a kiss.

The nonsense thoughts had come to him last night. A result of tiredness and the suppression of stress, Rik had concluded. Yet the vision of her curled up there was still with him. The desire to taste softly parted lips, still there. He'd been absorbed in Braston's problems lately.

Perhaps it had been too long since he took care of those other needs.

His aide rubbed a hand across the back of his neck. When he spoke again, his words were in French, not English. 'Nicolette acknowledged the payment and the order of the diamond jewellery as her due as a result of the changed circumstances. She accepts the situation but it is good, I think, that she will be unaware of any other plans you may intend to implement until such time—'

'Yes.' If 'such time' was something Rik could bring about.

'The other matter of urgency,' his aide went on, 'is unfortunately, the truffle crop.'

Rik swung about from where he'd been half gazing out of the windows. One search of Dominico's face and Rik stepped forward. 'Tell me.'

'Winnow is concerned about the soil in one of the grove areas. He feels it looks as it did last year before the blight struck again.'

'He's tested it? What is the result? We were certain we'd prevented any possibility of this happening this year. The crop is almost ready for harvest!' Rik rapped the words out as he strode to his suite. He stepped into the walk-in closet and selected work wear. Khaki trousers, thick shirt and sweater, and well-worn work boots. A very un-princely outfit that his mother would have criticised had she been here to do so. Rik started to shuck clothes so he could don the new ones.

His aide spoke from a few feet away. 'Winnow is doing the testing now.'

'I will examine the soil myself and speak with Winnow.' Rik laced his boots and strode into the sitting room.

'Your guest?' Dominico also glanced towards the closed door of the guest suite. 'Shall I wake her? Inform her of your immediate plans?'

'Allow her to sleep on while she has the chance. She had a long and difficult day before we arrived here. Please ask, though, that Rufusina be prepared to go with me to the groves.'

Melanie heard these words faintly through a closed door. She shifted in the luxurious bed, opened her eyes to a canopied pelmet draped above her head, and remembered curling up for just a moment while she waited for Prince Rikardo to return from speaking with his father. Now she was under the covers. Still in her clothes, but as though someone had covered her up to make sure she'd be comfortable. And that was Rik's voice out there, and it sounded as though he was about to go out.

Who was Rufusina?

'I'm getting up.' The words emerged in a hoarse croak. She cleared her throat, sat up, and quickly climbed out of bed. And called more loudly. 'Prince— Your Highness—I'm awake. I'm sorry I fell asleep before you got back last night. I'll be out in five minutes. I won't keep you waiting.'

Only after she called the words did Mel realise how they might have sounded to members of staff if any were out there with him, and, given he'd just spoken to someone, they probably were.

Heat rushed into her face, and then she felt doubly silly because she hadn't meant the words in that way, and the staff wouldn't care anyway, surely. And Rikardo would send her back to Australia today so none of this would be her problem for much longer.

Mel stopped in her headlong dash to the bathroom and wondered where the burst of disappointment had come from.

From being in a real live palace for a night and having to go home now, she told herself. And perhaps just the tiniest bit because she wouldn't have the chance to get to know Rikardo better.

'That's *Prince* Rikardo to you, Melanie Watson, and why would he want to get to know you? You're a cook. Not even a formally qualified one. You're not even in his realm.' She whispered the words and quickly set about putting herself together so she wouldn't keep the prince waiting.

Well, she *was* in his realm—literally right now. But in terms of having anything in common, she didn't exactly fit here, did she? No doubt he would want to speak to her sooner, rather than later, to tell her how he would get rid of her and how soon Nicolette would arrive to make everything as it was supposed to be.

That would be fine. Mel would co-operate fully. She only wanted to be sent home so she could get on with her life! Preferably avoiding contact with Nicolette in the process.

Outside in the sitting area, Rik's gaze caught with his aide's. 'I cannot be in two places at once right now. It would be rude to abandon Melanie now that she is awake, but breakfast must be offered, and I need to get to the groves.'

'Permit me to suggest a picnic breakfast for you and your guest after you have attended the groves. It would be easily enough arranged.' Dominico, too, glanced at the closed door of the guest suite. 'You might have a nice, quiet place in mind?'

Rik named a favourite place. 'That would be convenient to speak to Melanie there and see if she can find her way clear—'

'I hope I didn't keep you waiting.' The guest in question pushed her suite door open and stepped into Rik's sitting room.

Rik's head turned.

His aide's head turned.

There were appropriate words to be uttered to help her to feel comfortable, to extend grace. Rik wanted to do these things, to offer these things, but for a moment the words stuck to the back of his tongue as he gazed upon the morning face of Melanie Watson.

Soft natural colour tinged her cheeks. She'd tied her hair back in some kind of half-twisted ponytail. Straight falls escaped to frame the sides of her face. She wore a long, layered brown corduroy skirt trimmed in gold, brown ankle boots with a short heel and rubber-soled tread, and a cream cashmere sweater. In her hands she held a wool-lined coat. Her lips bore a soft pink gloss and she'd darkened her lashes with a touch of mascara.

Her clothing was department or chain store, not designer. The hairstyle had not come at the expense of an exclusive salon or stylist but thanks to a single brown hair tie and a twist of her hands. Yet in those five minutes she had produced a result that had knocked Rik out of his comfort zone, an achievement some had striven for and failed to achieve, in various ways, in decades of his life.

'You look lovely.' The inadequate words passed across his lips. A thought quickly followed that startled him into momentary silence. He wanted his brothers to meet her.

Maybe they would, if either of them were around today. And maybe Melanie would be on her way back to Australia before any chance of such a meeting could occur.

He stepped forward, lifted her right hand in his, and softly brushed her fingers with his lips. 'I hope you slept well and feel rested.' He introduced his aide. 'Dominico assists me with all my personal and many of my business dealings.'

In other words, his aide could be trusted utterly and was completely aware of their situation. At the moment, Dominico was more aware than Melanie.

Rik truly did need to speak with her, to set all matters straight as quickly as possible. He hoped that Melanie might co-operate to help him but it was a great deal to ask.

So much for your arrogant belief that you could outwit your father, still get all that you want, and not have to pay any price for it aside from the presence of a fiancée here for a few months.

Rik had collected the wrong woman and created a lot of trouble for himself.

So why did he feel distracted by the feel of soft skin against his lips? Why did he wish that he could get to know Melanie?

He pushed the thoughts aside. There was work to do. A truffle crop to bring to fruition disease-free, and a woman to take to breakfast. 'Will you join me for a walk outdoors? I need to attend to some business and then I thought we might share a picnic breakfast. I know a spot that will be sheltered from wind and will catch the morning sunshine. We can speak privately and I can let you know the outcome of my discussion last night with my father.'

'A—a picnic breakfast would be lovely, but is it all right for people to see me?' Her balance wobbled just enough to make him think she might have been about to curtsy to him. 'I'm sorry I wasn't still awake when you finished speaking with your father last night. It would have been okay to wake me up. I must have crawled under the covers.'

She hadn't. Rik had tucked her in. Had paused to gaze at a face that seemed far too beautiful. He suspected it had occurred to her that he might have tucked her in. The flush in her face had deepened.

Rik realised he still had hold of her hand. He released it and stepped back. 'It will indeed be fine. You are dressed well for the conditions. Shall we?'

Rikardo led Melanie through corridors and along passageways and past vast rooms with domed ceilings. Everywhere, staff worked with silent efficiency, going about their day's tasks.

Without making it seem a big deal, he explained that

she never needed to curtsy to anyone but his father or mother, and to them only in certain formal circumstances.

'Am I likely to meet your mother this morning?' Mel glanced about her and tried not to let an added dose of apprehension rise.

Rikardo shook his head. 'No. The queen is away from the palace.'

'Well, thank goodness for that, anyway,' she blurted, and then grimaced.

But Rikardo merely murmured, 'Indeed,' and they fell silent.

In that silence, Melanie tried not to let her mind boggle at the thought that she was walking through a palace beside a prince, and feeling relieved not to be about to meet a queen, but it all did feel quite surreal. Rikardo nodded to a staff member here or there. He'd said it was fine to be seen out with him by anyone they came across, so Mel would take that at face value. He'd obviously come up with some explanation for her presence.

'The kitchens here would be amazing.' She almost whispered the words, but she could imagine how many staff might work there. The amazing meals they would prepare. Mel felt certain the royal staff wouldn't have cake plates thrown at their heads as her cousin had done to her that final night.

Rikardo turned to glance at her. 'You can see the kitchens later if you wish.'

Before she left for the airport. Mel reminded herself deliberately of this.

'I didn't know that Braston grew truffles. I probably should have known.' She drew a breath. 'I've never cooked with them. My relatives loved throwing dinner parties but they were too—'

She bit the words back. She'd been going to say 'too stingy' to feed their guests truffles.

'Truffles have been referred to as the diamonds of the kitchen. Along with tourism they have represented the main two industries for Braston for some years now.' Rik stepped forward and a man in liveried uniform opened the vast doors of the palace and suddenly they were outside in the morning sun with the most amazing vista unfolding all around.

'Oh!' Melanie's breath caught in her throat. Everywhere she looked there were snow-capped mountains on the horizon. A beautiful gilded landscape dotted with trees, hills and valleys and sprinkled with snow spread before them. 'I didn't see any of this last night. Your country is very beautiful. I'm sure tourists would love to see it, too.'

'It is beautiful, if small.' Pride found its way into Rikardo's voice. 'But much of Europe is, and there are countries with more to offer to travellers. I would like to see an improvement in the tourist industry. If my brother Anrai has his way that will also happen very soon.'

Melanie liked his pride. Somehow that seemed exactly as it should be. And also the warmth in his tone as he referred to a brother. That hadn't been there when he'd spoken about the king or the queen, and, even if she'd only met the king briefly and had tried not to catch his attention too much, Georgio did seem to be a combination of forthrightly spoken and austere that could strike a girl as quite formidable.

You could handle him. If you managed yourself among your aunt and uncle and cousin for that many years and held onto your sense of self worth, you can do anything.

It hadn't hurt that Mel had set up a back-door arrangement and sent lots of cakes and desserts and meals out to a local charity kitchen to be shared among the masses. Her relatives never had caught on to that, and Mel had had the pleasure of giving away her cooking efforts to people who truly appreciated them.

Well, that life was over with now. Over the past year or so the family had forgotten to give her the kind moments that had balanced the rest. They had focused on the negative, and Mel had started saving to leave them. Now she just had to get back to Australia and to Sydney so she could start afresh.

It would be all right. She'd get work and be able to support herself. It didn't matter if she started out with very little. She pushed aside fears that she might not be able to find work before her meagre savings ran out.

Instead, she turned to smile at Rikardo. He looked different out of doors and in profile in these surroundings, more rugged somehow.

Face it, Mel. He looks attractive no matter what light you see him in, and each new light seems to make you feel that he's more attractive than the last one. And that moment of shared consciousness when she first stepped into his sitting room this morning. Had she imagined that?

Of course she'd imagined it. Why would a prince be conscious of…a kitchen hand? *A cook.* Same difference. They were both worlds away from being an heir to a kingdom.

'We commercially grow black truffles here.' Rikardo spoke in a calm tone. 'If you are not aware of it, truffles have a symbiotic relationship with the roots of the trees they grow under.'

'In this case oak trees,' Melanie murmured while she tried to pull her thoughts together. *Was* he calm? If so, his threshold for dealing with problems must be quite high. 'That's what they are, isn't it?'

Her glance shifted below them to the left where grove upon grove of trees stood in carefully tended rows. 'I'd heard that truffles could be grown commercially in that way. I think in Tasmania—'

'That's correct, and, yes, they are indeed oak trees.' He'd taken her arm, and now walked with her towards a grouping of …

Outbuildings? Was that a fine enough word for buildings within the palace grounds? There were garages with cars in them. Sports cars and other cars. Half a dozen at least. They all looked highly polished and valuable. They would go very fast.

Did the sun go in for just a moment? Mel turned her glance away. A man drove past them in one of the vehicles. Rik raised an arm as the driver slowed and tooted the horn before driving on. 'That is Anrai.'

'I thought he resembled you in looks.' Except Rikardo was far more handsome. And having her arm held by him made Mel way too conscious of him.

Small talk, Mel. You're supposed to be indulging in polite, get-to-know-you-but-don't-be-nosy-about-it small talk. 'How many brothers do you have?'

'Just the two, both older than me and busy trying to achieve their own plans—' He broke off.

A worker walked towards them, leading…a pig with a studded red collar around its neck. When the animal saw Rikardo, it snorted and almost pulled the worker over in its enthusiasm to get to the prince.

Rikardo looked down at the animal and then turned to Mel. 'This is Rufusina. She is a truffle hog and will be coming to the groves with us this morning.'

'*This* is Rufusina?' For some reason Melanie had pictured a gorgeous woman in an ankle-length fur-lined coat with long flowing brown hair. Maybe the woman had known Rikardo for ever and had secretly wanted to marry him herself.

Can we say overactive imagination? Well, this was the perfect setting for an imagination to run wild in! Mel tried to refocus her thoughts. 'She's a very interesting-looking truffle hog. She looks very…'

Porcine?

'Very intelligent,' Mel concluded.

'I am sure that is the first thought that comes to all minds.' For the second time since they'd met, Rikardo's lips twitched. Though his words laughed at Mel just a little, they laughed at Rufusina, too, for there was a twinkle in his eye as he watched the hog strain at her leash to get to him, and succeed.

Rikardo then told the hog to 'sit' just as you would say to a dog. The pig planted her haunches and cast an adoring if rather beady gaze up at him. She got a scratch behind each ear for her trouble. Rikardo took the lead.

They were at the groves before Mel had come to terms with her prince having a pet pig, because, whether he'd said so or not, this animal had been raised to his hand.

Mel would guarantee it. She could *tell*. They arrived also before Mel could recover from the beauty of Rikardo's twinkling eyes and that hint of a smile.

And what did Mel mean by '*her* prince' anyway? He certainly wasn't! She might have him for a few more hours, if that, and all of which only by default anyway because she'd been silly enough to think he was a cab driver.

Later, after she'd been returned to Australia, she could write her story and send it in to one of those truth magazines and say she'd spent a few hours with a royal.

She wouldn't, of course. She wouldn't violate Rikardo's privacy in that manner.

Today, in the broad light of Rikardo's…kingdom, Mel couldn't imagine how she'd mistaken him for anything other than what he was, whether she'd been over-tired and overwrought and under the influence of an allergy medication or not.

It wasn't until they reached the actual truffle groves that Mel started to register that Rikardo seemed to have somehow withdrawn into himself as they drew closer to his destination. She wasn't sure how to explain the difference. He still had her arm. The pig still trotted obediently at his side on its lead. Rikardo spoke with each person they passed and his words were pleasant, if brief.

But Rikardo's gaze had shifted to those rows of oak trees again and again, and somehow Mel *felt* the tension rising within him as they drew nearer.

'Winnow.' Rik greeted a spindly man in his fifties and shook his hand. 'Allow me to introduce my guest, Miss Watson.'

So that was how Rik planned to get around that one. But would that be enough? Because for all the people that mistook Mel for her cousin, plenty more…didn't.

'Do you have the results of the soil test, Winnow? Are we infected again with the blight?'

This time Mel didn't have to try to hear the concern in Rikardo's tone.

'The test shows nothing, Prince Rik.' The man stopped and glanced at Melanie and then back to the prince. 'I beg your pardon. I mean, Prince Rikardo.'

'It's fine, Winnow. We are all friends here.' Rik dipped his head. 'Please go on.'

Winnow pulled the cap from his head and twisted it in his hands. 'The test shows nothing, but last year and the year before…'

'By the time the tests showed positive, it was too late and we ended up losing the crop.'

'Yes. Exactly.' Winnow's face drew into a grimace. 'I cannot prove anything. Maybe I am worrying unduly but the soil samples that I pulled this morning do not *look right* to me.'

'Then we will treat again now.' Rikardo didn't hesitate. 'Yes, it is expensive and a further treatment we hadn't planned for will add to that expense, but our research and tests show that enough of the treatment will keep the blight at bay. If you have any concern whatever, then I want the treatment repeated.'

The older man blew out a breath. 'I am sorry for the added expense but my bones tell me—'

'And we will listen.' Rikardo clapped the man on the back. 'Order the treatment. I will draw funds for it.'

From there Rikardo examined the soil samples himself, and took Rufusina into one of the groves to sniff about. Mel didn't fully understand the process. The older Winnow kept lapsing into the beautiful local dialect as he spoke with Rikardo.

It was worth not being able to understand, to hear Rikardo respond at times in kind. She felt as though she'd heard him speak to her in the same language but she must have imagined that. In any case it was very lovely, a melodious harmony of tones and textures.

'We will take breakfast up there, if you are agreeable.' Rikardo pointed to a spot partway up a nearby mountainside. He'd handed the truffle hog over to Winnow, who was about to put her to good use in the groves before seeing her returned to her home. And with an admonishment to ensure the pig didn't run off, as she was apparently wont to do on occasion.

But right now...

There was a natural shelving of rock up high where a bench seat and table had been set into it. The view would be amazing. 'Oh. That would be lovely.'

They began the climb. 'The truffles. Will they be okay?'

'I hope so. We've had two years of failed harvests. That has resulted in a devastating financial blow to the country's economy while we searched for a preventative treatment that would work without affecting the quality of the truffles.' He led her to the bench seat and table.

Opposite was a mountain with large sections covered in ice. Mel sat, and her glance went outward and down, over groves of trees and over the village named after the royal family. 'There must be so much rich history here. I'm sorry that there have been difficulties with the truffle industry. From Winnow I gather you play a key role in this truffle work?'

'I run the operations from ground level to the marketing strategies.'

Mel's gaze shifted to the village below. 'You must care about the people of Braston very much.'

'I do, and they are suffering. Not just here and in Ettonbierre village, but right across the country.' He drew a breath. 'I had planned that we should eat while I led up to my request but perhaps it is best to simply state it now and then explain.'

Mel's breath locked in her throat. Rikardo had a request of her? She glanced again at the scene below. Rikardo led a privileged life compared to the very ordinary ones playing out down there. There was a parallel to her life with Nicolette and her cousin's parents. But there was also a difference.

Rikardo seemed willing to go to any lengths to help those who depended on his family for their livelihoods. 'What can I do to help you? To help…them?'

'You are kind, aren't you?' It wasn't a question, and

he seemed as concerned by it as he was possibly admiring of it. 'Even though you don't know what I may want.'

Mel lowered her gaze. 'I try to be. What is it that you need?'

'If it is at all possible, if it's something you can do without it interfering unreasonably with your life or plans and I can convince you that you will be secure and looked after throughout the process and after it, I would like to ask you to take Nicolette's place.' Blue eyes fixed on her face, searched.

'T-take her place?' She stuttered the question slightly.

If Mel had peered in front of her in that moment, she felt quite certain she would have seen a hole. A rabbit hole. The kind that Alice in Crazyland could fall down.

Or leap into voluntarily?

'Just to be clear,' Mel said carefully, 'are you asking *me* to be the one to temporarily marry you?'

CHAPTER FOUR

'I know a marriage proposal must seem quite strange when you expected to be sent back to Australia today.' Rik searched Melanie's face.

He felt an interest and curiosity towards her that he struggled to explain.

And an attraction that can only get in the way of your goals.

He couldn't let that happen. And right now he needed to properly explain his situation to her. That meant swallowing his pride to a degree, something he wasn't used to doing. Yet as he looked at the carefully calm face, the hands clenched together in the folds of her skirt as she braced herself for whatever might come next, it somehow became a little easier.

At worst she would refuse to help him.

That would be a genuine 'worst', Rik. You need her help, otherwise you'll end up locked into a miserable marriage like that of your parents, or unable to help the people of Braston at all because this plan of yours has failed.

'May I be plain, Melanie?'

'I think that would be best.' She drew an uneven breath. 'I feel a little out of my depth right now.'

She would feel more so as he explained his situation to her. He had to hope that she would listen with an open mind.

'The arrangement that I made,' he said carefully, 'was to bring your cousin over here and marry her a month later.'

Melanie responded with equal care. 'You indicated that would be a temporary thing?'

'Yes.' He sought the right words. 'The marriage was to end with a separation after three months and Nicolette would then have been returned to Australia and a quick divorce would have been filed for.'

'I see.' She drew a breath and her lovely brown eyes focused on his blue ones and searched. 'You didn't intend to let your father know those circumstances until after the marriage, I'm guessing? What did you hope to gain from that plan?'

'Aside from my brothers, Nicolette, and my aide, no one was to know of the plan.' He'd intended to outplay his father, to get what he wanted for the people without having to yield up his freedom for it. 'This plan probably sounds cold to you.'

'It does rather reject the concept of marriage and for ever.' Melanie sat forward on the bench seating and turned further to face him. Her knee briefly grazed his leg as she settled herself.

The colour whipped into her cheeks by the cold air around them deepened slightly. That…knowledge of him, that awareness that seemed to zing between her body and his even when both of them had so much else on their minds…

Is something that cannot be allowed to continue, Rik, particularly if she is willing to agree to the business arrangement you're asking for with her.

'In my family, many lifelong marriages have been made to form alliances or for business reasons.' He hesitated, uncertain how to explain his deep aversion to the idea of pursuing such a path. 'That doesn't always result in a pleasant relationship.'

Melanie's gaze searched his. 'It could be quite difficult for children of such a marriage, too.'

'It's not that.' The words came quickly, full of assurance and belief as though he needed to say it in case he *couldn't* fully believe it?

Rik had his reasons for his decision. He was tired of butting heads with his father while the king tried to bully him to get whatever he wanted. His father needed to acknowledge that Rik would make his own decisions. That was all. 'There have been myriad problems in the past couple of years.

'The first year the truffle crop failed it was difficult.' People relied on the truffle industry for their survival. 'Around that same time, my mother, the queen, moved out. That was an unprecedented act from a woman who'd always advocated practical marriages and putting on a good front to the public, no matter what.'

Melanie covered her surprise. 'That must have caused some complications.'

'It did. For once my father found himself on the back foot.'

'And you and your brothers found yourselves without a mother in residence. I'm sorry to hear that. It's never pleasant when you lose someone, even if they choose to leave.' A glimpse of something longstanding, deep and painful flashed through her eyes before she seemed to blink it away. 'I hope that you still get to see her?'

'I see my mother infrequently when there are royal occasions that bring us all together.' Would Mel understand if he explained that his contact with his mother hadn't changed much? That the queen had never spent much time with her sons and what time she had spent had been invested in criticising their clothing, deportment, efforts or choices in life? Better to just leave that alone.

'My parents died years ago.' She offered the confidence softly. 'I went to live with Nicolette and my aunt and uncle after that happened.'

He took one of her hands into his. 'I'm sorry for your loss.'

Dominico had informed him of some of these things this morning after the security check the aide ordered on her came through. The invasion of Melanie's privacy had been necessary, but Rik had refused to read the report, asking only to be told 'anything that might matter'. Though he had to protect himself, somehow it had still felt wrong.

'Thank you.' She gently withdrew her hand, and folded both of them together in her lap.

She went on. 'You've explained about the truffle crops failing, how that's impacted on your people. One year is a problem but two years in a row—'

'Brought financial disaster to many of our truffle workers.' And while Rik pursued every avenue to find a cure for the blight to the truffle crops, his father had denied the depths of the problem because he was absorbed in his anger and frustration over his queen walking out on him.

'On top of these issues, the tourist industry also waned as other parts of Europe became more popular as vacation destinations. Tourism is Anrai's field. He has the chain of hotels and the country certainly still gets a tourist market, but when there is so much more to do and see just over the border…'

'You have to have something either comparable, or totally unique, to pull in a large slice of the tourist market.' Melanie nodded her head.

'Exactly. Our country needs to get back on its feet. My brothers and I have fought to get our father to listen to the depth of the problems.' They'd provided emergency assistance to the people out of their own pockets as best they could but that wasn't a long-term solution. None of them had endless supplies of funds.

In terms of available cash, nor did the royal estate. It had what it had. History, a beautiful palace and the means to maintain it and maintain a lifestyle comparable to it for the royal family. Their father oversaw all of that, and did not divulge the details of what came and went through the royal coffers. It was through careful investment of a shared inheritance that Rik and his brothers had decent funds of their own.

'Despite these difficulties you came up with a plan.' Mel searched Rikardo's face. Her heart had stopped pounding in the aftermath of his remarkable request, though even now she still couldn't fully comprehend it, couldn't really allow herself to consider it as any kind of reality.

It was Alice down that alternative universe hole again, yet it wasn't. He truly wanted her to marry him. For practical purposes, to outwit his father, and just for a few months, but still…he wanted her to marry him.

She started to find it hard to breathe again. 'And somehow your plan involved trading off a brief marriage for sorting out the country's economic troubles.'

'Yes. My father has pushed all three of us to marry. I think we all have expected that Marcelo would have to do that whether he wanted to or not because he is the eldest. It is part of his heritage.'

Mel nodded. 'I thought when I came here, well, I guess I was so overwhelmed by it all that I didn't stop to think that everything might not be rosy just because there's a palace filled with amazing things. Just because you're a prince doesn't mean everything is easy for you. Or for your brothers, either.'

'My brothers and I went to our father in a concerted bid to get him to listen to the seriousness of the problems the people are facing and with our plans for addressing those problems. Leadership reform is also desperately needed, and that is something Marcelo has been working to achieve for some years now.' Rikardo drew a breath. 'Our father finally did listen. We got our concessions from him.'

His tone became even more formal as he went on. 'But that agreement came at a cost. In return for agreeing to requests that will help us protect Braston's people from further financial hardship, his demand was that we each marry within the next six months.'

'To ensure that the family carries on?' Mel asked the question and then wondered if she should have.

Even as a king, did Georgio have the right to push his sons to marry if they didn't feel ready? If they didn't want to? For Rik to go to such lengths to avoid the institution, he must have some deep-seated reasons. Or did he just not want to be bullied? That was reason enough, of course!

Mel might not ever fully understand, and for some reason she felt a little sad right now. Her gaze shifted to the cliff face opposite. Two men were near the top, tourists or locals with rappelling equipment.

Mel had to navigate *this* discussion. And Rik's explanations did help her to start to understand what was at stake, at least for the people of Braston.

Could she decide to just walk away when the futures of so many people hinged on Rik meeting his father's demands? When him bringing her here by mistake could have ruined those plans? If she hadn't been on the street filled with allergy medication…

Whether she'd meant it or not, her actions had contributed to this current problem, and if there was no other way to fix it…

But it's such a big undertaking, Mel. Marriage, even if it is only for a few months! And there'd be publicity and a dress and so much else, and you'd be fooling Rik's father the whole time and then he'd realise he'd been fooled and be very angry.

Yet Mel knew that Rik would protect her; that he would make sure his father didn't bring any of his wrath down on Mel's head. Rik wouldn't *allow* that anger to have its head. 'When it ended you would send me back to Australia, to Sydney. I wouldn't be exposed to the aftermath here.'

'And because we'd give an interview when we dissolved the marriage and let the magazines and tabloids have that, I would hope you wouldn't attract much media interest when you went home.' His gaze searched hers. 'I would direct them towards me and ask you to do the same. At worst there might be some photographs and speculation about you in the newspapers over there for a brief time.'

That was to be expected when such an event had happened, but if all the information were already given, surely the papers wouldn't care much once they realised Mel wasn't going to talk to them, and the split had been amicable? 'That shouldn't be so bad.' The whole thing wouldn't be too scary if she decided to do it. Would it?

She reached for the picnic basket that sat ignored on the table before them, and hoped that Rik couldn't see the tremble in her fingers. 'Would you like coffee? Something to warm your hands around?'

'Thank you.' His gaze, too, shifted to the men on the nearby mountain peak before it returned to Mel. 'I should have unpacked the basket and made it all available to you the moment we got up here.'

The thought of a prince unpacking breakfast for her horrified her but she bit back her words about it and instead, served the food and coffee for both of them.

When she set his plate in front of him, he caught and held her gaze.

'I know what I'm asking isn't easy. I made this plan because I do not feel I can marry, truly…permanently.' He hesitated. 'The demonstration of that institution within my family—'

'Has been about as warm as what I've seen in Nicolette's family.' Mel bit her lip, but that was her truth and there didn't seem to be much point in avoiding saying it now.

They started on their food. There were eggs cooked similarly to a quiche but without the pastry base. Small chunks of bread dipped in fragrant oil and herbs and then baked until they were crisp and golden. Grilled vegetables and fruits and a selection of pastries.

'What you've asked me to do *is* unexpected.' Stunningly so. 'But I ended up here, you can't swap me for Nicolette, and if I don't agree, the game is up with your father and you either have to marry someone for real and stay married to her, or your father won't grant you the "concessions" you asked for.'

'I'm afraid I didn't allow for collecting the wrong woman outside Nicolette's home, but that is not your fault.' He frowned and sipped his coffee. 'It's important you don't make your decision based on guilt. A mistake happened that was out of my control, and yours.'

She did feel at least partially responsible, but Mel kept that thought to herself and instead took a small bite of a tasty grilled vegetable before she went on. 'I'd like to know what the concessions are that your father has agreed to.'

'I am determined that the truffle crop this year will not fail.' Rikardo set down his knife and fork and turned to face her. 'When it flourishes, I'll need a spectacular marketing idea to get buyers back onside to buy our product. Many of them have lost faith because of the blight that struck our crop two years running.'

Mel, too, set down her utensils. 'What is this marketing idea?'

'On the palace grounds there are truffles that grow naturally.' Rik's gaze shifted to where the palace sat in splendour in the distance. 'For centuries those truffles have been eaten only by royals. It probably sounds rather archaic but—' He shrugged and went on.

'These truffles are particularly fine. If buyers are given the chance to obtain small quantities of them in exchange for purchasing commercial quantities of our regular truffles, I believe they will jump at the opportunity.'

'What a clever idea.' Melanie spoke without hesitation. 'People will go nuts for a chance like that. I can also imagine that you might have had a job on your hands to get the king to allow you to use those truffles.'

'Correct. My father tends to adhere to a lot of the old ways and does not want to consider change.' Georgio was strong, stubborn, unbending. Rik preferred to take the strengths he'd inherited from his father, and turn them to better purpose.

As for Melanie, she looked beautiful and innocent and wary and uncertain all rolled into one as she sat beside Rik on the bench. Yet she also seemed well able to think with a business mind, too, and her eyes shone with genuine encouragement for him as she heard his plans for the truffle marketing.

Would she agree to help him out of the corner he'd got himself stuck in? Did he even have the right to ask that of her?

'I don't want to harm you through this agreement, Melanie.' That, too, had to be said. 'I have asked for your help, but if it is not something you can do, you do not have to give it.'

'But you want to help your people.' Her gaze turned to meet his, and held. 'You chose Nicolette because you weren't…romantically attached to her or anything like that, didn't you?'

'I did. That allowed the situation to remain as uncomplicated as possible.'

'It would be easy to end the marriage and get on with what you really wanted to do with your life afterwards.'

He dipped his head. 'Yes.'

'I'm not ready to consider marriage yet. The real thing, I mean.' Even as Melanie spoke the words, a part deep inside her whispered a question. Did she believe she would ever be ready? Did she even feel she had the right—?

What did she mean by that? Of course she had the right, and she would still have the right if she married Rikardo and they then divorced. Melanie pushed the strange question aside.

And she thought about all those people subject to circumstances beyond their control, just trying to get on with their daily lives. People in a lot of ways who would be just like her. Not royal people, but everyday people who simply needed a bit of a hand up.

Mel could do this. She could be of help. She could make it so Rikardo didn't have to lock himself into a long-term marriage he didn't want. Maybe later he would find someone and be able to be happy. The little prick she felt in her chest must have been hope that he would indeed find that happiness.

'I'll do it.' Melanie spoke the words softly, and said them again more forcefully. 'I'll do it. I'll marry you so you can make your plan work. I want to help you.'

'You're quite certain?' Rik leaned towards her as he spoke.

'I am. I'm totally sure.' And in that moment, Mel was. She could help him. She could do this to make up for him not being able to marry her cousin.

'Thank you, Melanie.'

'You're welcome.' Her face softened and the beginnings of a smile came to her lips. Her gaze moved to *his* lips and suddenly she had to swallow because something told her he was going to kiss her as part of that thank you.

She thought it, and her breath caught, and then he did.

Rik's lips brushed hers in a soft press. His hand cupped her shoulder, and even through layers of cloth Mel felt that. Registered that as she received a kiss from a prince.

That was why it felt so remarkable. It had to be the reason—a kiss from a prince to thank her for agreeing to help him out of a tight corner.

Yet Melanie didn't feel as though a prince was kissing her. She was being kissed…by a man, and it felt wonderful in a way no kiss had before.

In that moment her response was completely beyond her control. Her mouth softened against his, gave itself to his ministrations before her thoughts could catch up or stop her. If those thoughts had surfaced, would the kiss have ended there, with a simple brushing of lips against lips? A simple "thank you" expressed in those terms? Because that was indeed what Rik had set out to do.

It had to have been and yet somehow, for Mel at least, it had become something very different.

Mel closed her eyes. For a moment she forgot she was on a mountainside in Europe with a royal prince, seated at a table with a picnic breakfast spread before them and the most amazing scenic vistas on all sides.

She forgot that it was chilly here but that the sun shone and they were sheltered from the wind. A man was simply kissing her and she was kissing him back and that man had a pet truffle hog he'd named and whom he doted on, even though he tried very hard to hide the fact. He cared for his brothers and for the people who lived in his country, and she'd liked him from the moment she'd thought he was a gorgeous cab driver come to take her away to the airport so she could make her way to Sydney.

'Rik.' She'd slept on his shoulder and blabbed at him when she wasn't quite sensible, and, despite all the smart things she should be thinking right now, the kiss felt right.

'Hmm?' He whispered the half-question against her lips.

Mel didn't know whether she said it, or thought it. She simply knew the words.

Kiss me again.

CHAPTER FIVE

I would kiss you for ever and it would not be enough.

Rik thought the words inside his mind, thought them in his native language. Thought them even though they could not possibly be true and he must simply be swept up in gratitude and relief.

Yet deep within himself he knew that now, in this moment, Melanie would welcome the prolonging of this kiss. His instincts told him this. The way she yielded petal-soft lips to him told him this.

It was that thought of her willingness that finally prompted him to stop something that he should not have started in the first place, and that he hadn't expected would make his heart pound. He, who rarely lost his cool over anything, had been taken by surprise by kissing a slip of a girl up high on a mountainside.

'Thank you...' Rik released Melanie and drew back, and for a moment couldn't think what he was thanking her for.

For rescuing him. The prince was being rescued by the same generosity that he'd felt in Melanie's soft lips.

You are on dangerous ground with this thinking,

*Rikardo. If she is kind, then she is kind and that is some-
thing indeed to be appreciated. But the awareness of
each other—that cannot be, and it cannot go on.*

He shouldn't have touched her. Arrogantly, he hadn't
known that doing so would be such a stunning thing.

The kiss had been startling in its loveliness. It wasn't
a manly description. But with Melanie it felt exactly
right to describe it in this way.

Melanie was startling in her loveliness, and that came
from the generous way she gave of herself.

He'd meant only to touch her lips with his, should
perhaps not have considered even that much. Rik would
like to say that he'd expected not to feel any attraction
to Melanie, that he had expected to feel as indifferent
towards her as he had felt towards Nicolette, but he'd
known it would be different.

Yet he had kissed her, and had ended up shocked and
a little taken aback by just how much he had enjoyed
that kiss. Her response to him had felt unrehearsed and
open. That, too, had added to her appeal.

Maybe she had simply wanted to kiss a prince.

In many other circumstances, Rik would have accepted the thought and yet Melanie had agreed to help
him for no reason other than out of generosity to try to
help others. She hadn't asked him what she would get
out of the arrangement. She'd wanted to hear the problems and then she'd made a decision based on what she
felt she could do to help.

'I guess we just sealed the bargain.' Her words held
a tremor. She turned to the picnic basket and started to
carefully repack it. 'We should probably get back. Now

that we've made this decision, your father will want that official meeting. That's assuming he can fit me into his schedule. I imagine royal families are very busy and I certainly wouldn't presume—'

'It will be all right, Melanie.' She was fully back into 'dealing with a prince and a promise and a royal family' mode and in feeling out of her depth, though she had valiantly jumped into this for his sake.

And for the sake of the people of Braston.

Did that mean she *hadn't* thought of Rik in that light as they kissed? That he had simply been a man kissing a woman, and she a woman kissing a man? Had his impact on her come completely from Rikardo the man, not from him being the third prince in line to the throne of Braston?

It wasn't a question that should even have mattered. Rik had accepted that women were attracted to his title first, sometimes to the man within, second, but always that first was there.

Perhaps some of his questioning came from the relief of knowing he hadn't blown his chance of avoiding being locked into a miserable marriage as part of his bargain with his father.

Melanie's gaze meshed with his. 'Are *you* quite sure you want to do this? I want to help you and help the people of Braston, but in the end what you do has to be really what you want.'

'I'm sure.' He got to his feet and lifted the picnic basket. 'We may not get much done today other than the meeting with my father if he is available, but Dominico will want to get the ball rolling on a few things.'

Melanie agreed. Now that she had committed to marrying Rikardo, she wanted to get things moving.

She didn't want to stop and give herself too much time to think about the next month and the three that would follow it.

That might have been rather easier for her before they shared that kiss. Mel stumbled slightly on the uneven ground. She didn't want to think about the kiss, either! Her heart still beat hard from its impact.

'I have you.' Rik's hand shot out and grasped her arm.

And I have received the most moving kiss I've ever experienced.

Not that Mel *had* a great deal of experience. Her life with the family had kept her busy. Oh, she'd dated here and there with men that she met out in her 'normal' world. At the fresh produce store, or once it was the delivery guy from the local butcher's shop. There hadn't been a lot of time or opportunity.

There is always the time and the opportunity if you want it enough.

Well, now there was a prince.

No, there wasn't. Not like that. She wasn't dating Prince Rik. She *was* going to marry him, but that was for an agreed purpose that had nothing to do with romance. Right. So she was safe from getting any of the wrong kind of ideas about him or anything like that.

Why then, with Rik's hand on her arm, and the memory of a kiss still fresh in her mind and stamped on her lips, did Mel feel anything *but* safe?

From what? Falling for him? That would be insane.

Much more than falling down a rabbit hole or wearing sparkling magic shoes that would take her anywhere.

So focus on getting back to the palace to start this process that will help lift the country's economy. Rather than thinking about kisses, you should think of how you can find out as much as possible about truffle crops so you really can be of help to Rik for the short time you're here.

'Do you have books about truffle cropping in the palace?' She glanced towards the prince.

Yes, *the prince*! That was what Rik was, and Mel mustn't forget it. And since when had she started to think of him as Rik?

He said you could.

And if you have a shred of self preservation left, then you should address him as 'Your Highness' or something equally distancing, in person and in your thoughts.

'I have books at the palace and also at my personal home up in the mountains.' He glanced at her, and then up and beyond her to where those two tourists had found their way to what to Mel looked like a sheer wall of ice.

Rikardo had a second home in the mountains?

Well, duh, Mel. He's got to be about thirty and he's a prince. Did you think he'd still live permanently in a couple of rooms in the palace? Even if those rooms were quite glorious and added up to more like a small house. 'I'd like to look at the books, if that would be okay. I'd like to learn more about the industry.'

She might not be able to do anything to help with the problems they'd had, but if Rik planned to harvest truffles from the royal grounds that, too, would be rather special. Maybe there were records about that, as well.

'The kitchen staff would have special truffle recipes, wouldn't they? Maybe handed down through the centuries? I'd love to see those!' Mel tried hard to walk normally and not lean into him. He still had hold of her arm and her silly response receptors wanted to melt into his side as though they had every right just because he'd kissed her.

He might be marrying Mel, but he was doing that to help him *avoid* a committed relationship.

And Mel was marrying him to help him out, and she didn't need to add the complication of being attracted to him to *that* mix. So it was just as well they'd shared that kiss and put it behind them. They could get on with the business end of things now.

As if it will be that easy, Mel. What about the wedding preparations? The fact that his father will think the two of you want to marry for real?

'I need to have the right things to say to your father!' The words blurted out of her with a panicky edge she didn't anticipate until it was too late to cover it up. 'That is, I don't want to be unable to answer any questions he might ask about how we met, how long we've known each other, that kind of thing.'

'We met through your cousin Nicolette when I was at university in Australia. Six months ago we came across each other on a computer forum and we've been chatting online and on the phone ever since.' He turned his head and deep blue eyes looked into hers. 'I wanted you for my princess. You are calm and pleasant and I felt

I could spend the rest of my life with you. It's not the entire truth, but it's as close as we'll get.'

'Okay. That will work. I know the years that Nicolette was at university, though I didn't attend myself.' There was one other issue, though. 'What's my story? Why did I say yes?'

Before he could answer, she shook her head. 'If your father asks me that question, I'd rather tell him that I will do everything in my power to be as supportive of you as I possibly can in all the time we're together.'

He dipped his head. 'Then stick to that. Commitment to me is implied in such statements. My father should find that more than acceptable.'

'Wh-what will be expected…otherwise?' Mel asked the question tentatively, and she didn't want to be tentative. She needed to know, therefore she was asking. She straightened her spine. 'When we're married, will we be in your suite as we are now, or…?' Despite the straighter spine she couldn't quite bring herself to put it into words.

His gaze met hers. In it was steadiness. 'For the sake of appearances we would be sharing my room and…bed at first. This is something that can be managed with a little creative imagination without needing to cause you undue concern. Just for the look of things, you understand?'

'Just—just part of our overall practical arrangement. Yes. I understand totally. That's very sensible.' Mel tried not to stutter the words, tried to sound mature and au fait with the situation and what it might entail. They might be sleeping together at the start—her mind tried to boggle and she forced it not to—but they wouldn't be *sleeping together*. Not, well, you know. Not like *that*. She drew a breath. 'Right. That's okay, then. We can make that work.'

'We will, Melanie, so do not worry.' His words again held reassurance.

And Mel…relaxed into that reassurance.

They were at a turn in their downward descent where the two mountainsides faced each other when a cry ripped through the air, shattering her composure and bringing Rikardo to an abrupt stop.

'Damn. What's the man doing? He's tangled in his equipment!' Rik dumped the picnic basket and strode towards the source of the cry.

Mel followed, and after a few moments managed to spot what Rik had already seen. A man dangled against that icy outcrop. It was one of the two men she'd seen earlier. The other—Mel couldn't see.

'Stop, you fool!' Rik spoke the words aloud but they were too far away for any hope that the man might hear them.

Even so, Mel echoed the sentiment.

The prince let out a pithy curse. 'If he keeps trying to get loose, he'll drop to the bottom.' He didn't slow his pace, but he turned to glance at her. 'There's no one anywhere near except us. I've rappelled that section many times. I have to see if I can help while we wait for a rescue team to get here.'

He already had a cell phone out, and quickly called for assistance and explained the situation and that he would see what he could do until the rescue team arrived.

Mel could hear someone at the other end insisting the prince must not go anywhere near the dangerous situation, before Rik said, 'Get help here as quickly as possible' and ended the call.

She bit back the inclination to ask him if he *would* be safe enough. 'What can I do, Rik?'

'Keep yourself safe. Do not follow the path I take. Follow the path that's cut into the mountain and you'll reach the same destination. It will take longer, but I'll know you are not at risk. When the rescue team starts up the mountain, point them to where I am.' He strode ahead confidently.

Mel followed at the best pace she could manage. Each moment counted and Rik quickly got ahead of her, and then cut a different path towards the ice-bound cliff. After a few minutes she could hear him shout to the man first in English, and then in French. The conversation continued in French, and Mel could only guess what was being said.

She struggled on, determined to reach Rik and be of help if she could. She was within shouting distance herself when she looked back and saw the rescue team starting up the mountain. Mel waved to them and pointed to Rik's location, and got a wave back from the leader of the team.

Mel kept going, and then there was the man, dangling in mid-air, and Rik saying something sharp and hard to a second man at the top of the cliff before taking that man's unused equipment and kitting up.

The third prince of Braston was over the edge in a breathtakingly short time. Mel didn't go any further, then. She wasn't sure she could have if she tried. Instead she stood frozen in place, completely unable to breathe as all the concern for his safety that she'd pushed back rushed to the surface and threatened to overwhelm her.

She bit back the instinct to call out, 'Be careful.' Considering what he was doing, he would already be at the bottom of the cliff if he weren't taking care.

Nevertheless, what followed made Melanie's blood chill. She'd never watched ice rappelling. It looked risky, and it was obvious from the way he tried to control his slip that Rik didn't have the right boots on his feet for the job.

The stranded man, despite Rik's instructions that even Melanie could tell were to stay still and wait whether they were in French or not, continued to tug and pull at the tangle he was in. Did he *want* to end up at the bottom of the mountain?

'Your Highness, you must wait for us!'

'Please, Prince Rikardo, you must come away from there!'

The words were called as the rescue team came close enough to see what was happening, but it was too late. If Rik didn't do something about this man, he would kill himself. Panic had the man in its grip. The second man showed no apparent interest in proceedings, sitting there with a blank look on his face.

Had Melanie looked like that when she'd taken that medication and faded into sleep?

He's taken some kind of illicit drug, Mel. You've seen

*enough of that in Melbourne to recognise it. No doubt
Rik recognises it, too.*

'You have to make sure that second man doesn't
interfere with what Rik's doing or do anything stupid
himself.' She spoke the instruction to the head of the
rescue team as they drew close. 'He's under the influence of something. It's likely that both of them are, because Rik's struggling to get the stranded one to listen
and stop fighting to get free.'

Rik had rappelled out beside the man. He couldn't
untangle him, but he was trying to calm him. At his own
risk! Even now the man reached for Rik with clawing
hands!

'Oh, please, be careful,' she whispered.

She didn't notice that she'd called him Rik as she
spoke to the rescue team, or that she'd spoken as though
she had every right to that authority. Mel didn't care.

The next ten minutes felt like a lifetime. When
the man was hauled up, Rikardo followed. He moved
with confidence. Mel had made her way to the top and
wanted to grab him once he got up there and…

Shake him? Check that he was unharmed?

Kiss him a second time?

'All is well, though I have asked the team to take
both men to the nearest hospital and have them checked
over, drug tested and, if need be, charged by the police.'
Rik's words were spoken across a very calm surface.

But beneath that calm must be all the anger over the
stupidity of those two men.

'Your Highness…' One of the rescue team approached.

'I am well and unharmed but you must excuse me now,' Rikardo said with respect, and firmness.

And then he stripped out of the equipment he'd commandeered, took Mel once again by the arm, and started down the mountain with her.

Mel walked at his side. 'I'm so glad you knew what to do up there. I'd like to see you do that properly one day, with all the right equipment, because I think you would be amazing at it.'

I'd like to see you do that properly one day...
Melanie's words rang in Rik's ears as he put his Italian sports car through its paces on the way to his mountain retreat home.

Her words were a salve to the anger he'd bitten back over the stupidity of those two men. Had they *wanted* to get themselves killed? The other one, when questioned, had said he was waiting for his turn to go out 'alone' and that ice rappelling was 'easy, man'.

The man had been so far gone that he hadn't even comprehended the danger his friend was in. Well, they were both safe now.

Rik let the thoughts go and turned his attention to his driving. He'd held back until he reached the private road that led to his home. This road, he knew better than the back of his hand, every turn, just how much he could give behind the wheel to release the pent-up energy that came from that stressful rappel in someone else's untested equipment. He'd needed this.

He's going too fast. Mel couldn't get the thought out of her head. Her logical mind understood that Rik had control of the car. It was clear he knew this road well. The road itself was wide with plenty of room for dual traffic and yet it was a private road. They hadn't seen any other cars and she guessed they were quite unlikely to do so.

All of this made infinite sense. The paralysing fear inside Mel did not make sense. Her fingers curled into the edges of her seat. Her heart pounded with a mixture of apprehension and the need to get out of this situation at any cost.

'Please stop.' The words whispered through her clenched teeth, whispered so quietly that she didn't know how Rik could have heard them.

All Mel knew was that she wanted out of this car. Now.

'Melanie.' A voice tinged with remorse broke through her fear. The car began immediately to slow and Rik said, 'I'm sorry. I didn't realise you were uncomfortable.'

It's all right. I'm fine. There's no need to slow down or stop.

In her mind, Mel entertained these polite thoughts. But her instincts were in a very different place. She struggled to breathe normally, to not throw her door open and try to get out. The reaction was so intense and so deep that it completely unnerved her. She couldn't speak, couldn't think clearly, didn't know what to say to him, didn't understand why she had ended up feeling like this.

Within moments the car moved much more slowly and fingers wrapped firmly around the hand nearest to him. 'Do you need me to stop the car completely, Melanie? My house is less than a minute away and I'd rather get you there if possible.'

The roaring in her ears started to recede but Mel was still a long way from calm. Her fingers tightened around his. 'I don't know what came over me. I feel stupid for the way I've reacted.'

'You are certainly not stupid.' Rik spoke these words softly as he drew the car to a stop in front of his mountain home. The place was maintained for him, but did not have permanent staff. They would be alone here, and he was glad for that now to give Melanie a chance to recover.

Whatever had happened during the trip had affected her deeply, and he felt she would benefit from space and not having to deal with anyone new just for the moment.

Had the panic come on because of all the pressure he'd put on her? It was a lot to ask a woman to become his temporary princess, to work with him to fool his father into believing the marriage was intended to last a lifetime.

It was a lot for her to find herself here under confused circumstances let alone the pressure Rik had added to that load for her.

You must take care of her. Give her time to calm down.

He got out of the car, opened her door for her and took her hand to help her out. His home was chalet-style, built of log and with a sharply pitched roof. Large windows gave beautiful views from every part of the home and were one-way tinted for privacy. Rik doubted that

Melanie noticed any of it. Her face was sheet-white and the hand he held within his trembled.

'Let me get you a hot drink, Melanie.' He led her inside and to a comfortable leather sofa in the living room.

'Thank you. It is a bit chilly, isn't it?' Melanie sank onto the sofa and didn't argue about who should be preparing the beverages.

Rik didn't waste time, and quickly returned with coffee for both of them. He took his seat beside her. 'This will take the chill away.'

The rooms were centrally heated, but she'd clearly had a shock. It would take time for her body to return to a normal temperature.

Rik had brought that shock about. He had put too much on her. Bringing her to Braston with her waking up from a long sleep to discover she was in the middle of Europe instead of in Sydney. He'd asked her to replace her cousin and briefly marry him. Had piled all the worries about the country onto her, and then had left her to cope with her concern for him while he rappelled onto an icy cliff in dangerous circumstances to deal with a man who didn't want to hear reason, and another who could have added more trouble to the mix.

To cap it off, Rik had come up here to get away from things, and the speed of his driving had frightened her enough that she hadn't been able to even tell him what was wrong.

As Melanie sipped her coffee and colour began to come back into her face Rik set his drink down and turned to her. 'I am sorry that you were afraid during the drive up here.'

'You weren't to know that I would react like that. I didn't know it myself.' She forced her gaze about the room before meeting his eyes. For the first time since leaving the car, she seemed to see her surroundings.

Maybe that, too, helped her, because she said valiantly, 'It was worth the trip. This is a lovely home and the views are amazing. And I feel much better. I'm sure I won't have that kind of problem again.'

'I am pleased that you're starting to feel better. What happened to you? Do car trips always make you uneasy?'

Back in Australia, she'd checked when he collected her from outside Nicolette's home that he felt fresh enough to drive. Rik hadn't thought anything of it.

'That's the first time I've been in a sports car. They go very fast.' As she seemed to consider what had happened she frowned. 'I don't understand this myself. I don't drive, but I'm not usually the type to panic unnecessarily, and with hindsight I *know* that you had control of what you were doing.

'I'm just sorry that I spoiled the drive for you,' she said. 'You obviously needed an outlet after dealing with those two foolish men and keeping your calm so well, both before and after.'

Rik *had* needed that outlet. Sometimes keeping his cool came at a cost to his blood pressure!

'I felt like telling them off myself for being so stupid,' she added hotly, 'and I wasn't the one who had to risk life and limb to go out and stop that first man from falling to his death!'

Maybe if she learned to drive herself, she might feel better informed and more confident to assess the skill of other drivers when they were behind the wheel.

They were side by side on the sofa, and Rik became very conscious of that as they fell silent and gave their attention to their drinks.

After a moment, she spoke with a slight teasing tone in her voice. 'You make very good coffee. Is it allowed, for a prince of the realm to do such tasks as make coffee?'

'And do them well?' He shrugged his shoulders. 'I think in today's world it is, and I would go hungry and thirsty up here if it weren't.'

She was a plucky girl. Resilient. The thoughts came to Rik and lodged. He couldn't help but admire her for that.

'Do you think I could have a tour while we're here?' she asked. 'I'd love to see the rest of your home.'

'Absolutely.' Rik got to his feet and held out his hand to help Melanie rise.

He was getting in the habit of that, of reaching for her hand far too often…

But you will need to do things like that to make the upcoming marriage plans seem realistic to your father.

Even though Georgio would not expect it to be a love match, he would still expect such demonstrations.

'The meeting with my father has not yet been arranged. I think it can wait for a little longer yet.' Rik drew a breath. 'I'd like some time to restore a better mood before I tackle that talk, to be honest.'

'Then I'm glad I asked for the tour.' Mel melted the moment Rik confessed his need to prepare for the talk with his father. And she truly did feel so much better now. 'We can stay here as long as you want. It's a beautiful place.'

Rik was good company and they'd just sort of got engaged, so why shouldn't they stay here for a bit, if they wanted to? She could use the time to ask a few questions about how they would work their way through the next few months, too.

'I'll need a wedding dress.' Visions of past royal marriages scrolled through her mind. 'Something very simple that won't cost the earth.' She turned to Rik. 'How do we pull off a wedding in a month?'

'With a really good wedding planner, and, as you've already realised, with the most simplified plans possible.' He started towards the rear of the house and said firmly, 'Now let me show you the rest of my retreat, and all the views. I think they're worth seeing.'

They were, and Mel looked out of floor-length windows at some very lovely scenery before Rik toured her through the rest of his home. It was surprisingly humble. Well, not humble. It was a delightful four-bedroom chalet-style home but it certainly wasn't, well, a palace.

'I love this place,' she blurted. 'If it was me I'd be up here all the time. Normal-sized rooms, calm atmosphere, no one to tell you what to do.'

'You've just worked out the secrets of my attraction to this home.' He smiled and led her into the final room.

It was an office, with a desk and computer and shelves of books about… 'Oh. Can I look at some of those? Do you have ones that show what the truffles look like when they're harvested? History books? Anything about the *royal* truffles? Cooking? The growth process from beginning to end and the uses of truffle hogs?'

'Yes to all of that. And I trained Rufusina under the tutelage of Winnow. There is a photo album.' Rik brought out the photo album and a selection of books and before Mel knew it she was nose down in some gorgeous pictures, and some very interesting information. He didn't have cookbooks, but he told her that some of the old recipes were still produced at the palace and described some of the dishes.

'Truffled turkey. I'd like to cook that.' Mel thought back through her cooking career. 'The closest I've come to cooking with truffles is using truffle-flavoured oil a few times.'

Rik's brows lifted. 'You had a career as a cook?'

'Yes, working for my aunt and uncle.' Mel glanced at him through her lashes. She'd thought he would have known that already.

They were seated with her on the swivel chair, and him leaning back against the corner of the desk in his office. It wasn't a large room, and as she let herself register the cosiness, his closeness, Mel suddenly became breathless. 'I cooked for them for years. Cakes and desserts were my speciality, but I cooked all the meals, including for dinner parties. They liked to schmooze wealthy—'

She coughed and turned her attention back to the

books. 'These are wonderful resources. It's an intri-
cate industry. You've done well to get the black truffles
growing commercially here.'

'Not so well in the past two years.' Rik glanced up
and towards the windows.

The frown that came to his face made Mel follow
his glance.

She hadn't noticed the change in atmosphere, but
now she saw it. 'I didn't know it had started snowing.'

'Yes.' He got up from the desk. 'Why don't you se-
lect what books you'd like to bring back to the palace
when we return, while I see what's in the kitchen that
we can have for our lunch?'

Not that Mel minded either way and it wasn't as
though Rik were trying to trap her into spending time
with him here. He'd probably enjoy the time away from
the palace while he could, but would have been just as
content to be up here by himself.

Something in his expression still made her ask. 'How
long do you think it will snow?'

CHAPTER SIX

IT SNOWED all that day. When darkness fell, Rik closed the curtains throughout his chalet home and turned to face Mel.

While Rik appeared completely calm Mel couldn't say the same. She stood rather uncertainly in the middle of the living room.

With the prince. Up here in his chalet where he'd just made the decision that they wouldn't be leaving until morning. So they would be here. All alone. Together. For all that time.

'It won't matter too much?' She asked the question in a deliberately businesslike tone that somehow managed to emerge sounding chatty and confiding and breathless all at once. Mel forged on. 'That you can't get back tonight, I mean?'

Even despite the tone, Mel would have said she did well, that the question was at least focused on whether he might have problems because he couldn't attend to duties at the palace tonight.

Yes. That was a good way to put it. 'Your duties—?' Really, she felt quite relaxed about this whole situation.

After all they were just staying in a different location for a night. She'd slept in a bedroom within Rik's suite of rooms last night, which was rather intimate when you thought about it, and that hadn't bothered her.

Not even when you leapt out of bed the next morning because you could hear him speaking just outside your closed door? Because you wanted to get through the shower and look your best for him before he saw you? Because you hadn't been entirely certain whether he'd pulled the covers over you the night before when you might not have looked your best?

'It won't matter at all. I gave Dominico another quick call while I was outside checking the snowfall. He'll take care of anything urgent until I get back tomorrow morning.' His cheek creased as he gave a lopsided and quite devastating smile. *He* didn't seem at all concerned or put out by their circumstances.

Which was great, of course.

That was exactly how Mel would feel in a moment when she finished pushing away these silly thoughts about being up here alone with him and how that might impact on the rest of the evening. It must be because he had kissed her on the mountainside earlier. Or because they'd spent the afternoon poring over truffle books and photo albums that showed many shots of Rufusina being trained by Rik and Rik laughing in some of the shots.

Perhaps it was also because she would be pretending to be engaged and then married to him.

'We'll end up holding hands and kissing...' Somehow the words were attached to the blood vessels in her face.

Heat swept upwards from her neck and rushed into her cheeks.

'Yes,' Rik said in a deep voice. 'At times we…will.'

Rikardo. Prince Rikardo. You'll end up holding hands and kissing Prince Rikardo.

Oh, as though putting it in the correct words made it any better!

Even the reminder didn't hold the weight it should have, and Mel just didn't know what to do about that. Something had happened when he took her hand and got her out of the car and brought her inside and made her a hot drink and set to work to help her get past the ridiculous fear she'd experienced.

He acted just like your dream idea of a very ordinary man, showing a sensitive side while still being very, very strong and being wonderful and appealing and all the things you might want—

But Mel didn't want a man. Well, not for a long time. Not like that in the way of settling down together and falling in love so she ended up vulnerable. She wasn't ready for that! The thought burst through, and was somehow linked to her earlier panic while trapped in the speeding car with Rik.

Maybe she just felt panicky at the moment, full stop.

Maybe she needed to focus on right now because this was enough of a challenge, thanks very much!

Rikardo wasn't an ordinary man anyway. Mel couldn't afford to forget that.

Not while reading truffle books and smiling over Rufusina photos. Not while kissing him on a mountainside because that had been a kiss to seal a bargain.

It might have blown her away, but he'd just kissed her and that had been that. Probably checking to make sure he could make it look believable any time they had to repeat the exercise over the next month and the months after that.

How many times might they...?

Mel's heart tripped.

She contemplated turning into a contortionist so she could kick herself for being so silly. The next months would be businesslike as often as possible. That was what they would be. Now what had they been saying? 'Evening in. Yes. That'll be fine. The only thing that matters is that it doesn't interfere with other plans of yours. The treatment in the truffle groves—has that been done today or do you need to be there to supervise it? That's the one thing I didn't ask about while we studied those books.'

'Winnow has supervised the treatment today. He knows what to do, and Dominico organised payment to cover it.' He brushed this aside as though it were irrelevant.

Not the treatment part, the money part. Was it? Mel hadn't got the impression that the money would come out of some endless royal coffer. If that could happen then Rik wouldn't be stressing over getting the people out of financial trouble to the degree that he was. He'd said that there needed to be reform.

Her eyes narrowed. Had he paid for that treatment himself somehow? Out of money that perhaps shouldn't be invested in that direction because it was for his personal use or he'd earned it himself? She knew so little about him and she wanted to know…everything?

Purely because Mel preferred to understand the people she dealt with!

'We'll treat tonight as an evening off,' he declared. 'If the remainder of this month is very busy, we can remember that we at least had a few hours to—how do you say it? "Veg out and do nothing."'

'Why, yes.' A delighted laugh escaped Mel. She couldn't help it. The sound just flew out. Mel also couldn't drag her gaze from that crease in his cheek, or from the sparkle in his deep blue eyes.

So she gave in and let herself enjoy the moment. It wasn't as though Rik would want to spend the entire night kissing her senseless just because they were alone.

Just because he'd kissed her once already. Just because he was the best kisser she'd ever been kissed by and there would be times in the public eye, at least, when he would kiss her again. Just because he made her want to don sparkly shoes *and* leap into a rabbit hole.

'If we're having a night in,' a night of not kissing each other, 'then I guess we just need to work out how we want to spend our time.'

'Not reading about truffles.' This too was said with a smile.

Oh, she could fall heavily for that smile. She wouldn't, though. Not when she'd reminded herself that she was doing this to help him, and help the people of Braston, and because she'd ended up here by mistake and there weren't a lot of other options for him now, like none at all really, and she could afford the time and effort to help. Did it really make any difference whether she started her new life in Sydney this week or four months from now?

'I think I've taken in as much information about truffles as I can manage for one day, but I'm pleased to know more about the industry. It's obviously really important—to—to people here.' She'd almost said that it was important to Rik, and that was why she'd wanted to understand.

That wouldn't be the key reason, of course. She wanted to be supportive of Rik's efforts. She'd made the commitment to marry him for that reason. But she wasn't obsessing over learning all about his life and work or anything like that.

Are you sure about that, Melanie? Because you seem mightily interested in him, really.

Yes, she was sure! And no she was not ridiculously interested! She was helping to fix a problem that she was partially responsible for creating in the first place. She was no more interested than she should be.

'It's a fascinating industry,' she said in the most dampening tone she could muster. 'The truffle industry. But perhaps we could pass the time this evening some other way?'

Like snuggling on the sofa?

No. Like…well, she didn't know. Cooking? Playing on the Internet?

'How do you feel about television?' Rik indicated the large screen in the corner of the room. 'I have a selection of DVDs I've not yet got around to watching.'

'Watching DVDs would be…' *Smart. Sensible. Safe?*

Better than thinking about kissing the whole night? 'A good idea. I don't mind a good comedy, but I'll watch most things.'

They sat on the floor in front of the DVD cabinet going through choices until she found episodes of an Australian comedy show she hadn't yet watched. 'Oh, you have this series! I've only ever seen a few episodes but it's supposed to be brilliant!'

So they sat side by side on the sofa with popcorn that Rik made in the microwave, and sodas from his fridge, and watched comedy episodes until Mel had giggled so many times that she'd forgotten to feel self-conscious at all in Rik's presence. Instead she had become totally enamoured of the rich, deep rumble that accounted for *his* laughter.

And she forgot to guard against letting herself be aware of him as an attractive appealing man and not a prince who should be held at arm's length because she was only here for a few months and he was marrying her so he could avoid any kind of commitment to a woman, even if Mel didn't know why he seemed to need to do that as much as he needed to. They were almost through the evening, anyway.

So why are you almost holding your breath, Mel, as though waiting for something to happen?

'Goodnight, Mel.' Rik walked Melanie to the opened doorway of her bedroom.

They'd watched their comedy episodes. Mel had paid more attention than he had. Did she feel it the way that he did? This compulsion that ate at him to draw closer, know her, use every avenue and every moment to learn more of her and to let her learn more of him? And a coinciding physical consciousness that seemed to fill the air around them with a charge of electricity just waiting for one small spark to set it ablaze?

Why did this woman make him feel this way more than any other had? Rik didn't want to admit that to himself, but he forced the acknowledgement.

Then admit that you desire her, and that the desire is as much about her personality as it is about her physical appeal.

He'd spent this evening with her and he'd thought about how different their lives were and mad thoughts had come through his mind about bridging the gaps.

Look how well longevity and sticking together had worked for his father and mother. The queen had walked out, had done the one thing Rik and his brothers had never expected. She had turned her back on what she had treated as the core of her duty. And now neither parent would discuss the matter with their sons.

Rik turned his thoughts back to the present.

At times today Mel seemed to have almost forgotten that Rik was a prince. He'd…liked that. But now was not a good time for him to forget the arrangement they'd made. He needed this to work. To be distracted by her beauty and appeal was not the right thing for him to do, to be distracted mentally and in *liking* her so much, even less smart because it spoke of an emotional awareness that couldn't happen. Rik could never trust…

'Good—goodnight, Rik.' She said the words quietly, almost tentatively.

With a question in their depths?

Her small hand came to rest on his forearm and she reached up and briefly kissed his cheek. 'I'll see you in the morning and I'll be ready for whatever needs to be done to help get your temporary marriage plans started, or just to keep out of the way if you need to work in the truffle groves tomorrow.'

Rik searched her face and saw the determination to do the right thing, to dismiss him and her awareness of him at one and the same time. To remain Melanie here and Rikardo there and never the two should cross over their lines.

He saw all that, and he *felt* what was inside her. A very different compulsion that he felt, too, that made him want to lean in and replace that pseudo-kiss with the real thing. To know for himself if the last kiss had been some kind of strange fluke. If her lips would taste as good a second time.

'Sleep well.' He turned and started for his room at the end of the short corridor. 'I will see you in the morning. Thank you for your company this evening. I…really enjoyed it.'

And with that, Prince Rikardo Eduard Ettonbierre of Braston went to his room, stepped inside and shut the door firmly behind him.

Only then did he lift his hand to allow his fingertips to lightly trace where her lips had pressed to his cheek.

It was perfectly fine for him to find Melanie likeable, and to still marry her, end the marriage short months later, and get on with the single life that he wanted, and *needed* to maintain.

He *would not* be marrying for real.

Rik sighed and dropped his hand. For now he needed to prepare for bed.

Tomorrow was a new day and no doubt a new set of challenges.

CHAPTER SEVEN

'I WOULD like to present to you my fiancée, Nicole Melanie Watson.' Rik spoke the words to King Georgio formally, and as though the other impromptu meeting had never occurred. 'My fiancée is known by her middle name of Melanie.'

If the occasion had been less formal, Mel might have smiled at Rik's tweaking of history to suit himself. But this was not that kind of moment. Mel curtsied.

'I am pleased to meet you, Melanie.' Georgio took her hand and air-kissed above the fingers and, while doing so, searched her face. After a moment he gave a slight nod and indicated a setting of leather lounges and chairs to the left.

They were in what Rik referred to as one of the 'great rooms'. It was a large area, and could have felt intimidating if Mel hadn't walked in here determined *not* to be intimidated.

Mel and Rik had made their way down the mountain this morning. He'd driven at a gentler pace and Mel had remained calm until they were almost at the palace.

Nervous anticipation had set in then but Mel felt that was justified.

'Let us get to know one another a little, Melanie,' Georgio said as they all took their seats.

Rik sat on one of the sofas beside Mel. He seemed deeply resolved this morning. Last night, when she'd thought he would kiss her at her door, kiss her *properly*, Melanie had thought he might feel as confused and tempted and aware of her as she did of him. But of course that was quite silly. He might have wanted to kiss her. But that didn't mean his emotions were engaged.

Not that Mel's were!

Concentrate on the king, Mel. This is not the time for anything else.

'Melanie and I first met through a cousin of hers.' Rik added a few details.

When the king nodded, Mel bit back the urge to heave a sigh of relief. But she also had to handle her share of the conversation. 'I admire Rikardo, and the work that he does for the people of Braston. I want to be as supportive of that as I possibly can.'

'That is good.' Georgio's glance shifted from Mel to Rik and back to Mel again. 'And what did you do before you agreed to marry my son?'

'I worked as a cook.' It might not have been a glamorous job. It would probably sound even less glamorous if she admitted she had done that for little money, working for her relatives to earn her right to a sense of belonging.

Note to self, Mel. You never did earn that right and you waited too long to get yourself out of that situation.

A similar set of rites was being played out in this room between Rik and his father.

She turned the highest wattage smile she could muster towards King Georgio. 'My history is humble, I suppose, but there's nothing to be ashamed of in coming from everyday stock.'

'If that "stock" has an appropriate history attached to it.' Georgio's eyes narrowed. 'My son will run a check. I will see this report for myself.'

Like a police-record check or something?

No, Mel, it will be a lot more detailed even than that.

She tried not to bristle at the thought, and at the king's emotionless declaration. As though he did this all the time and would have no hesitation in eliminating her like a blot from Rik's radar screen if she didn't come up to standard.

It didn't actually matter whether Georgio liked her or approved of her or not, provided she could marry Rik so that Rik could carry out his plans.

I still don't like it. My family history is my business. I don't want it exposed to all and sundry.

'Dominico already ran the check.' Rik clipped the words off. 'You may take Melanie at her word, Father. There is nothing in her history to justify the need for you to view the report.'

Mel stiffened inwardly for a second time.

Rik leaned close to her and said softly, 'I'm sorry. It was necessary. Dominico gave me a very light summary of the report.'

Much of Mel's agitation subsided. 'I don't have anything to hide. I just don't like the idea...'

'Of your privacy being invaded.' The twist to his lips was ironic.

Somehow that irony helped Mel to let the matter go.

Georgio straightened slightly in his chair. 'I could order a search of my own.'

A chill formed in the edges of Rik's deep blue irises. 'But I think you will agree there is no need.'

For a moment as father and son locked gazes the room filled with the powerful clash of two strong wills. It occurred to Mel then that there were matters within such families that were very different from 'regular' life. Yes, Rik had ordered a search of her life and history. No, she hadn't liked hearing that. But if Rik hadn't done the search, his father would have ordered it. At least this way Mel wasn't exposed to Georgio reading the entire report.

A moment later Georgio glanced away. Rik had won that round, it was done and the conversation moved on to more general topics.

Rik raised the matter of the truffle harvest. Mel sat quietly listening, but she remained aware of Georgio's examination.

No way would he have accepted a switch between her and her cousin. He was too observant.

So you've done the right thing, Mel, by agreeing to help Rik. And Georgio is a strong-willed man and very set in his attitudes. You're helping Rik to avoid being pushed into a long-term loveless marriage for the wrong reasons, too.

'You have done well this morning, Melanie. I'm proud of you.' Rik spoke the words and then realised it perhaps wasn't his place to feel such an emotion in the rather personal way that he did towards his fiancée right now. She wasn't marrying him for real reasons. She was doing this to help him and she understood that it would all end a few months from now.

Tell her what the buy-off will be in exchange for her assistance.

The thought came, and Rik…pushed it aside once again, for later. He would take care of Melanie, would ensure that she got good assistance to start her on her way with her new life in Sydney when she returned to Australia. When the moment was right to bring the topic up, he would do so. He…felt that she would know inherently that he would…take care of her.

Rik used a key to unlock the door to a small room. 'There will be a number of rings you can choose from for your engagement ring.'

'From the family h-heirlooms?' Mel's footsteps faltered in the doorway.

For a moment Rik thought she might back out of the room, refuse to enter. 'They are not all heirlooms,' he said, 'but yes.'

She drew a deep breath, threw her shoulders back and continued into the room. 'It's probably a good idea to use something from the family's stock of jewellery. The ring can be given back when we're finished, and it won't have cost you anything. We need to find one that fits and doesn't need adjusting, and that you wouldn't choose if you were—'

Doing this for real.

The words echoed unspoken in the room.

The practicality of her determined attitude made Rik want to smile, and yet when they stepped fully into the room and he saw the spread of jewellery that Dominico had laid out for them, a strange feeling swept over him. His gaze shifted from piece to piece until he found a ring that he felt would suit Mel. A ring that he would have chosen for her if their circumstances had been different?

There *were* no different circumstances possible, either now or in his future. Yet to Rik in this moment—

He lifted a ring with a platinum band. The three diamonds were Asscher cut to reflect light off the many facets. The stones were perfectly round, and set with the larger of the three diamonds raised higher than the two to its left and right. Because the ring was simple and the setting not as high as some, the size of the diamonds did not leap out as it might have.

The platinum band would suit Melanie's colouring; the setting would look beautiful on her finger. It was a ring he could enjoy seeing on her for decades.

Well, it would do for the time being. He lifted the ring. 'This was not an engagement ring, but a dress ring of my grandmother that she had fashioned for her later in her life. Her fingers were small and delicate as yours are. I do not know if she ever even wore it. She was rather indulgent when it came to such creations. I…feel the ring may suit you.'

'Oh.' Melanie didn't even glance at the remaining jewellery. And when Rik took her hand gently in his and slipped the ring onto her finger, she caught her breath. Her gaze flew to his. 'It—it fits perfectly. Just as though—'

'Just as though,' he murmured, and there, in the quiet of a small room filled with valuable jewellery that Melanie had been hesitant to go anywhere near, Rik lifted her hand and kissed the finger upon which his engagement ring now rested.

'Just as though we were a real engaged couple, I was going to say.' She whispered the words and glanced down at the ring. 'I didn't expect it to look—'

Right. She hadn't expected it to look right. Rik didn't need her to finish the sentence to know that was what she'd meant to say. He hadn't expected it either. Nor had he expected the sudden sense of well-being and destiny that swept over him when he placed the ring on her finger.

Was he getting in over his head with her somehow despite his determination to treat this as a business transaction? Had he allowed some attitudes and thoughts to slide in wrong directions because, if he hadn't, then how had he ended up with such unexpected feelings in the first place?

Rik should have been sorting out the answers to those questions. Instead he leaned towards her and somehow his arm was around her, drawing her close.

This time when he kissed her it was he who lost himself in a moment that should not have been, lost himself in the taste and texture and the giving of Melanie's lips as he kissed her until he had to break away or—

It would all feel far too real?

You cannot let it become that way, Rikardo. Melanie

*is a sweet girl, but she never will be more than a means
to an end. You will never marry permanently, not for
real and not for love, and not to lock yourself for ever
into a loveless marriage.*

He would never trust such an emotion as 'love'
within that institution. Not when his parents hadn't
managed even to love their sons let alone each other.

'I have something else that I wish to show you this
morning.' Rik escorted her from the room. Away from
a room full of the beauty that should go with emotion
and dreams and the love of a lifetime, but had it ever
existed within his family? There was that old legend,
but …

Rik increased his pace.

'Th-thank you for the beautiful choice of ring, Rik,'
Mel said softly as they stepped out of doors and started
along an outside pathway that led between vast stretches
of snow-covered grounds.

On her finger, the ring felt light and comfortable. It
fitted perfectly and maybe that was what disturbed Mel
so much. That and the fact that *Rik* had chosen it out of
a dazzling array of royal jewellery. Rik had wanted her
to wear *this* ring, and then he'd kissed her. It was the
second time they'd sealed their agreement with a kiss,
and each time became more difficult to treat as just a
meeting of lips against lips.

What kind of state would she be in by the time he
kissed her on the wedding day?

'I should not have kissed you like that.' His glance
meshed momentarily with hers.

Had he read her mind? Considering the messy con-fused state of the thoughts in there, she hoped not!

Rik went on. 'Our arrangement is not for…that kind of purpose and I should have remembered.'

'Well, it was probably because we'd just been with your father and working so hard to make sure that all went well.' She gave a laugh that sounded just a bit forced. 'We got a little too carried away in our roles but it was only for a moment. It probably barely left an impression, really.'

Her words were just making this worse! She bit her lip. Mel glanced about them and her gaze fell on a small piece of machinery ahead. 'That's an interesting-looking vehicle.'

Rik followed Melanie's gaze.

She was wise to change the topic. He was more than happy to work with her in that respect, though his glance did drop again to her hand where the ring sat as though it belonged there, and then to her soft lips, which had yielded so beautifully beneath his just mo-ments ago. He wanted to kiss her again. Kiss and so much more.

Not happening, Rik.

And yet his instincts told him that the kisses they'd shared had been far more than instantly forgettable to her.

To him, too, if he were honest.

'This is an all-weather buggy.' He explained that Winnow had taken the vehicle out of storage and made sure it was in working order. 'In first gear it doesn't drive any faster than a person can walk. It's easy to handle. All you need to do is steer and make it stop and start. It will drive on snow and it can handle rough terrain but there are plenty of paths here to drive it on. Our appointment with the wedding planner is not for another hour. I thought I might show you how to work this while we wait.'

Her gaze flew to his. 'You want me to drive it?'

'I thought it might be a good way for you to start to be able to get around more while you're here.' In truth there were a dozen ways he could ensure that Melanie could move around the area, and for the most part Rik expected to be with her anyway. Even so...

'I don't drive cars.' She said it quickly, and then tipped her head to the side and looked at the buggy, and back at Rik. 'I've never really had any interest in learning.'

'This is not a car.' He watched her face, and took a gamble. 'But if you don't feel that you can try it—'

Her chin went up. 'Of course I'll try it. That would be like saying I didn't want to try riding a skateboard or making some new dish in the kitchen.'

She was a plucky girl, his Melanie, Rik thought. Before he could pull himself up on the possessive manner of wording that thought, Melanie stepped forward and did an at least passable job of feigning delight at the idea of learning all about the buggy.

'First I will demonstrate.' Rik sat in the driving seat with Melanie beside him and showed her the controls. They were on castle grounds in an area where the worst that could happen was they ended up off the path. He got the buggy moving, explaining as he drove, and then, when he felt Mel was ready, Rik simply got out of the seat and started walking beside her. 'Slide into the driver's seat.'

Mel slid over and gripped the wheel. A moment later she was steering the buggy grimly.

He guided her along, helping her to master steering around corners and stopping and starting. After a few minutes Mel didn't need his help, and even asked if he would get back in with her so she could increase speed to a higher gear.

Finally her hands unclenched and she gave the first hint of a smile before she stopped the buggy and turned to look at him.

'Well done,' he praised. 'I am glad you have been able to do this, Mel.'

'It was fun. It's such a long time since I've completely enjoyed anything that resembled vehicle travel. All the way back to when my parents used to take me every Sunday and we'd go…' Her expression sobered and she frowned as though trying to remember something.

Though she tried to conceal it, sadness touched her face. She climbed out of the buggy. 'I don't remember what we used to do. They…died in a car crash.'

His hand wrapped around her fingers, enclosing her. He wished he could warm her heart from that chill. He wanted to do that for her so much. 'I am sorry—'

'It's all right. It was a long time ago.' Her words relegated her pain to the past. But her fingers wrapped around his…

A member of the palace staff approached to let Rik know that the wedding planner had arrived. The moment ended, but the tenderness Rik felt for Melanie grew inside him.

Duty. He had to attend to his duty.

Rik dipped his head. 'Please tell the planner we will be with her shortly.'

'Yes, Prince Rikardo.' The man walked away.

Melanie turned her gaze towards Rik and drew a deep breath. 'This is the next phase, isn't it? We have to convince this planner that we're doing this for real, even if we do want a simple, quick, trouble-free arrangement.' She seemed to think about what she'd just said, and a thoughtful expression came over her face. 'You must have chosen a great planner, if the woman believes she can achieve that, in a month, for a royal wedding of any description.'

Rik drew a slow breath as his gaze examined her face, flushed with the success of learning to drive the buggy, and her expressive eyes that had clouded when the topic of her parents had come up.

Perhaps he should ask Dominico for a proper look at that report after all. It might tell Rik more about Melanie's background.

Only to help understand her, he justified, and then frowned because, of all reasons he might read the report, wasn't that the most personal and therefore to him, at least, the most unacceptable? 'Dominico seems to believe this planner will be up to the task. Let us go see how she fares with our requests.'

CHAPTER EIGHT

'You have made very rapid plans, Rik.'

'Are you sure you want to marry so quickly? Our father might still have given us what we wanted if we all became engaged and then spoke to him again about the arrangement. That way you could have held off from actually marrying until closer to the six-months mark. Things might have changed by then.'

The words came to Melanie in two different male voices as she went in search of Rik. It was four days later and she'd woken to find her breakfast waiting for her, and Rik already gone to the palace grounds to oversee the harvesting of the first of the special truffles.

'It won't make any difference whether I marry soon, or marry after many months. You know this. Our father will not change his mind or soften his expectations.'

Rik didn't explain the reason for his statement—the brief nature of the intended marriage—and Mel didn't know if he'd told his brothers the truth about it as yet or not. But did his voice sound oddly flat *because* he knew this fact?

She must be imagining it.

You and your over-inflated ego are imagining it together, Mel.

'Good—good morning, Rikardo.' Mel spoke to make her presence known. Not because she minded her impending marriage to Rik being discussed, but because it wasn't right to eavesdrop, even if she hadn't meant to.

'Melanie. I am glad you're awake and have found us.' Rik stepped forward. He touched her hand and gestured to the two men standing to their left. 'These are my brothers, Marcelo and Anrai.'

'Hello. I'm pleased to meet you both.' The words emerged in a calm tone before Mel stopped to remember that she was being introduced to two more princes.

Rabbit hole. Sparkly shoes. Do I look good enough for this occasion, and why didn't I address him as Prince Rikardo or Your Highness?

She drew a breath.

'It is a delight to meet you, Melanie. Our brother has told us about you.' The older man bowed over her hand and managed to make the gesture seem relaxed and European rather than princely and…royal. 'I am Marcelo.'

The first in line to the throne. The brother who would most of all be expected to marry and stay married, whether he wanted to or not. He was dark like Rik, a little taller, and his eyes were such a deep inky blue, they were almost black.

'I am Anrai.' The second brother smiled a killer smile, shook her hand, and stepped back as though content to observe proceedings from this point. His hair was a lighter brown, thick and with a slight wave. It flopped over his forehead and drew attention to sparkling pale blue eyes.

Mel had dismissed him as not as handsome as Rik. She could now see that he would actually be a quite stunning lady-killer, but he still didn't appeal to *her*. She only had eyes for—

'Hello.' Mel tried to smile naturally and not feel overwhelmed by being surrounded by these three very royal men. It wasn't until she glanced at Rik's face that she realised she'd placed herself so close to his side that they were almost touching. Not because she felt intimidated but because…

Well, she couldn't explain it, actually. What she did realise was that she'd been allowing herself to think of Rik more as a man, and less as a prince. At least this meeting had given her that reality check. And it was nice to meet his brothers. 'Have any of the truffles been dug out yet?'

A snort from behind them drew Mel's attention. She turned her head and there was Rufusina. The pig had a quilted coat on and a keen look in her eyes, as though she was sitting in apparent obedience waiting for something.

'Rufusina's obviously champing at the snout,' Mel observed. 'What's the hold-up?'

'There's no hold-up—' Rik started.

'We were just deciding how best to go about the extraction,' Anrai added.

Marcelo's brows formed a vee. 'It is the most stupid thing to wait for a sign from—'

Rufusina lifted her snout, sniffed the air once, and then again.

Rik said under his breath, 'Wait for it.'

Anrai's shoulders stiffened.

The truffle hog sniffed the air a third time and trotted to a group of trees.

'*Now* I will go in there.' Anrai followed Rufusina's rapidly receding form. 'But only because I think she knows where the best truffles are. It has nothing to do with anything else.'

'Marcelo?' Rik turned to his older brother.

'I was not concerned in the first instance.' The oldest brother followed Anrai. 'All the truffles on the palace grounds are exceptional, as has been proved in years past. That is all that matters.'

Rik turned to Mel. 'Would you care to be present while Rufusina does her work and finds us the choicest truffles?'

'I would love to be there.' Mel's curiosity was tweaked. Just what had that "rite of passage" been about? And to be present while such wonderful foods were lifted from their resting places? Imagine *tasting* such a wonderful, rare indulgence!

Rik took her arm and started towards a grove of trees that looked very old. 'It is an exciting moment.'

'Apologies, Melanie, for walking away.' Anrai rubbed the back of his neck with his hand. 'Once the pig sniffs the air three times—'

'It will guide the prince to truffles that are the choicest, and that are possessed of the power to make his deepest hopes come true.' Marcelo said the words with a dismissive twist of his lips. 'You must forgive us, Melanie. We are being foolish this morning, but Rikardo—'

'Asked nicely if you would both like to be present for this event.' Rik jumped in with the words that were almost defensive.

Mel thought about her rabbit hole and the sparkly shoes and how out of place she'd felt when she arrived here, and how different this world was from anything she had ever known. And she looked at three big, brave men who had hovered at the edge of a grove of trees and refused to shift until...

'A magic truffle hog unlocks the key to safe passage, and perhaps to the granting of your wishes?' The words came with the start of a smile that spread until it almost cracked her face in half.

She could have laughed aloud. Mel could have done a lot of things. But then she looked properly at the grove of trees and thought about age and history. Three princes *had* all come to participate in this ritual. Rufusina *had* lifted her nose and sniffed three times and then trotted over here with purpose. Mel sobered. 'How old is the legend? Are there bad aspects attached if you don't do things the right way?'

'Centuries. None of us have ever come near the harvesting of these truffles until now. It's usually left to our staff, but I wanted to oversee it this time.' Rik didn't seem offended by her initial amusement. He did seem a little uncomfortable having to explain the situation. 'The legend is more to do with prosperous lives, and making the right choice of marriages and so on. But I am only concerned with getting good truffles for my overseas buyers.'

'Yes. That is no doubt the priority.' Mel bit back any further smiles. She turned to the others and said to all three of them, 'I'm grateful to have the chance to see this, and I hope to get a good look at the truffles themselves when they're harvested.'

Winnow approached as Mel made this statement.

The three princes were all about business after that. It was strange to stand back and watch these three privileged men go about digging bits of fungus out from beneath beds of rotting leaves. Rufusina did her thing, and Rik praised her for being a good hog, at which the pig sort of…preened, Mel thought fancifully, and checked her own feet to make sure they hadn't sprouted those sparkly shoes while she was daydreaming.

'This one looks good, brother. And smell the pungent odour.' Anrai handed a truffle to Rik.

Rik examined the truffle. 'It is good. Take a look at it, Melanie.'

Before Mel could blink, the truffle had been dumped into her hands. She didn't know much about truffles. Not in this state, but that didn't stop her from wanting to cook with them, to discover if they were indeed as fine as it was claimed, to revere the opportunity to hold this piece of life and privilege and history. 'Will they be enough for your marketing plans, Rik?'

She didn't notice the softness in her tone, didn't see the look exchanged between Rik's brothers as Rik bent his shoulders to protect her from the wind that had sprung up as he answered her question.

'I hope so, Mel. I very much hope so.'

They gathered the truffles. Some were sent with Winnow to be prepared for travel. Rik placed the others in a basket, thanked his brothers for their presence and saw them on their way, and then turned to Mel. 'Shall we have that peek at the kitchen that you mentioned?'

'Y-yes. I'd like that.' Mel liked it even more that Rik had remembered that small comment of hers from days ago.

They made their way to the kitchens. Rik introduced Mel to the staff and somehow, even though she'd always been on the other side of things in this environment, he made it comfortable and easy. Enough that when he had to excuse himself to attend to other matters, Mel accepted the invitation to remain behind and observe as the staff prepared the midday meals.

'I'm almost afraid to taste,' Melanie murmured as Rik removed the cover from the last dish.

They were in his suite. He'd asked for their meal to be sent here, and wasn't that what people would expect of a newly engaged couple—to want every moment alone? Yet Rik knew that he'd chosen to dine with Melanie here because *he* wanted to keep her to himself more than he perhaps should.

The legend talked of sharing the first meal prepared with the truffles, that the prince must share the tasting process...

He pushed the fanciful thoughts aside. This was a matter of practicality. And perhaps of giving Melanie a moment that she might not otherwise experience. 'Each of the dishes have been enhanced with the addition of the truffles.'

'The kitchen staff said there are different opinions about actually cooking the truffles.' Mel had listened with interest to the discussion about that in the kitchens earlier. She'd learned so much! 'The risotto and the duck dishes both smell divine.'

'Before we start on those, I would like to give you the chance to sample the first truffle in very simple form.' Rik lifted a single truffle from a salver. His fingers shook slightly. He steadied them and lifted his gaze to hers.

It was just a legend. Foolish stuff.

The prince prepares the truffle and offers it to his bride.

Mel drew a shaky breath as though she perhaps, too, felt the air change around them, almost as though it filled with anticipation as she yielded her palate to his ministration...

He shaved transparent slices of truffle onto the pristine white plate. The butter knife slid through creamy butter. Just the right smear on each sliver, a sprinkle of salt crystals.

Rik held the first slice out to her. Soft pink lips closed over it, just touched the tips of his fingers as her eyelids drifted closed and she experience her first taste of...a legend.

'It's almost intoxicating.' Her words whispered through her lips. 'The permeation of the scent, the beau-

tiful texture. I can't even describe how amazing…I feel
as though I've tasted something sacred.'

She couldn't have rehearsed those words if she'd
tried. Rik took his own slice of truffle, unbelievably
pleased in the face of *her* pleasure.

They moved on to eat the other dishes. Melanie experienced each new taste with curiosity and perhaps
with a little awe. Rik shared her pleasure and knew that
it renewed his own. He couldn't take his gaze from her
mouth. He wanted to lean forward and taste the flavour
of the truffle, of salt and butter, from the inside of her
lips.

It was just a legend.

But Melanie Watson was not a legend. She was a very
real woman, and Rik…desired her in this moment, far
too much.

They left for France that afternoon. Mel settled into
her seat on the family's private plane and observed,
with some wonder, Rik's calm face. 'I don't know how
you do it.'

'Do what?' He glanced out of the window at the scud-
ding clouds beneath the plane's belly before he turned
his gaze to her and gave her all of his attention.

'Remain so calm in the face of being chased all the
way to the plane by a wedding planner waving colour
swatches and bits of lace and begging for fittings and
a decision on the choices for the table settings.'

'We gave her the answers she needed.' A slight smile
twitched at the corners of Rik's mouth. 'And perhaps

next time she won't wear those kinds of heels for running.'

'I could learn a thing or two.' Melanie had taken to the wedding planner. 'She's doing her best to make things easy for us while we fly all over Europe showing buyers what they'll be missing out on if they don't make an order this year for Braston truffles.'

'In truth we're only going to Paris.' There was a pause while Rik looked into her eyes, and while he registered how committed she had sounded to his country's industry as she spoke those words.

'It's still more exciting than almost anything I've done.' Melanie returned his glance.

How did he do that? Make it seem as though the whole rest of the world suddenly faded away and it were just the two of them? Mel would be hopeless at truly being married to him. There'd be photos through the tabloids all the time of her making goo-goo eyes at him when she didn't realise she was doing it.

Um, where was she?

She would not, anyway. An unguarded thought here or there, or coming to realise that he was a good man and one she could admire, hardly equated to a Rufusina-like devotion to the man.

And you just compared yourself to a truffle hog, Mel. I don't think pigs wear magic slippers. 'Magic trotters, maybe,' Mel muttered, and snapped her teeth together before anything even sillier could come out.

'I hope the marketing trip is successful.' For a moment Rik dropped his guard and let her see the concern beneath the surface. 'There's no room for failure in my plans, but I still…'

Worry?

'All the kitchen staff said the truffles were the best ever. I have nothing to compare to, but I thought they were stunning.' Mel was glad she'd spent the time in the kitchen while Rik finalised plans for their trip.

He'd sprung it on her just as though they were taking a walk around the corner. "Oh, and by the way we're leaving for Paris this afternoon, I'll have the staff pack for you."

She'd let that happen, too, and hadn't even tried to oversee what got put in the suitcases. Melanie Watson, cook, had stayed clear and let the palace staff pack her things for a trip to Paris.

'I'll help you in any way I can, with the marketing efforts.' Mel didn't know if she could do anything. Did being his fiancée count?

Her glance dropped to the ring on her finger. Every time she looked at it, it seemed to belong there more than the last time. It had seemed to be made for her from the moment Rik lifted it from a bed of black velvet and placed it on her finger.

What was happening to her? She was losing the battle to keep her emotional distance from him, that was what. There was no point saying she only cared about the people of Braston, or only admired him because he cared about their futures. Mel did feel all those things, but they were only part of what she felt for him.

Face it, Mel. Somehow you got caught in your own

feelings towards him and, instead of getting them under
control or stopping them altogether, they've grown more
and more with each passing day.

CHAPTER NINE

'I AM interested, you understand. Braston black truffles have been a high-standard product.' The owner of the group of elite Parisian restaurants spoke the words to Rik with a hint of regret, but as much with the glint of good business in his eyes. 'It is just with your truffles being totally off the market for two years I have found other supply sources.'

This was the fourth restaurant owner they'd seen since they arrived in Paris. The others had come on board, but something told Mel this one might be a harder sell.

They were inside the man's home, seated at a carved wooden dining setting. At the end of the table, a wide glass vase held a bunch of mixed flowers. The moment they walked into the room, Rik's gaze had examined the arrangement.

He'd been checking for gardenias, Mel had realised, and her heart had been ridiculously warmed by the gesture on his part. There were none, but that bunch of flowers looked particularly pretty to her now.

'The blight to our crops was tragic, but we are back

on our feet and, as you can see, the commercial truffles are the same high standard.' Rik lifted one of the truffles he had placed on an oval plate in the centre of the table, took up a stainless-steel shaver and shaved thin slices from the black shape.

As the older man examined the truffle slices, and Mel recalled the almost spiritual moment of trying her first truffle with Rik, he went on.

'I know at this time of year you would be sourcing truffles. I'd like to see Braston truffles back on the menu at your restaurants.'

At his feet was a travel carrier containing more truffles, and from which he had unpacked the plates and shaver as well as a beautiful small kitchen knife with a gold inlaid handle.

'And I'd like to put them there, but—'

'I have an added incentive that may sweeten the deal for you, Carel.' Rik spoke the words quietly.

'And that is?' Carel was the last on their list.

It was almost nine p.m. now and they had been fortunate that the man rarely worked in any of his kitchens these days, preferring to visit as suited him, so he'd been more than happy to meet with Rik at his home.

The incentive of the truffles harvested from royal grounds had worked well with the other restaurant owners. They'd all placed orders for commercial truffles so they could also obtain some of the other truffles. Mel wondered if Carel would be as willing to be convinced. Middle-aged, and ruthlessly business focused, this man was much harder to read than the others.

A surge of protectiveness of Rik rose in Mel's breast.

He shouldn't have to beg for anything. He was, well, he was a prince! And yet that description was not the first one that had come to Mel's mind. Rik was good and fair and hardworking and dedicated and his care for the people of his country ran so deep that she knew it would never leave him. He deserved to be respected because of what was inside him.

Carel tipped his head slightly to the side. 'We have already discussed pricing and you certainly do not plan to give away—'

'Braston's truffle crops at a price that won't help my people get back on their feet?' Rik said it softly. 'No. And deep down I know you would not respect such a gesture if I made it.'

The older man was silent for a moment before he dipped his head. 'You are correct.'

'How would you feel about a complimentary gift of some of the truffles grown on the palace grounds?' Rik watched Carel's face for his reaction. 'To go with your order, of course.'

Mel watched both their faces.

'There are legends surrounding those truffles.' The older man's glance moved to Mel before it returned to Rik and he asked with the hint of a smile, 'Do I need to ask whether you harvested the truffles yourself? I am assuming you have brought them with you to show?'

'You do not need to ask, and I have brought them.' Rik's answer was ironic and guarded all at once.

Before Mel could try to understand that, Rik drew another white rectangular plate out and placed just one truffle on it.

Carel leaned forward to look.

Rik shaved the truffle, allowing the wafer thin slices to fall onto the plate and the pungent aroma to rise.

What exactly did that legend stand for? Mel made a note to find out when they got back to the palace.

'The aroma is muscular with a particular rich spiciness I have never encountered.' Carel lifted one of the slices to examine the texture, and colour.

He looked, he inhaled, and after a long moment he put the truffle slice down. 'I do not know. I'm not convinced that the royal truffles will equate to anything exciting enough on the plate. If I agreed to your offer, I would want to be sure that the truffles were a good enough selling point in terms of taste, not only legend.'

'And yet they *are* the stuff of legends,' Rik said with a hint of the same spark.

This was the business dance, and both men were doing it well.

'Indeed.' The older man dipped his head. 'That is undeniable and an excellent marketing point. But I would be using them at my restaurants for the most expensive dishes only on a very limited basis. They would have to live up to and beyond expectation in all ways.'

'They do. They would!' The words burst out of Mel. She touched the edge of one truffle slice with the tip of her finger and caught and held Carel's gaze. 'These truffles have a flavour and scent you'll never find anywhere else. The texture is beautiful. They provide the most stunning enhancement to the dishes they're used in or when eaten by themselves.'

'This is quite true.' Rik's gaze softened as he glanced

at Melanie's face. She wanted so desperately for this trip to be successful, for him to obtain all the markets for his truffles that he had set out to recapture. 'But I understand Carel's point, too.'

Rik appreciated Mel for that investment in him. It seemed a bland way to describe the warm feeling that spread through his chest as he acknowledged Melanie's fierce support of his efforts. It *was* a bland description, but Rik wasn't at all sure he wanted to allow himself to examine that warmth, or try to know exactly what it might mean.

'For me, I do not have the evidence of this truth.' Carel again smelled and examined the truffle and its slices. 'I am sure my chefs would like to try cooking with these, but they are busy at the restaurants—'

'*I'll* cook them for you!' Melanie got out of her chair. 'Right here and now.'

If Carel had given any indication that he wouldn't allow it, no doubt Melanie would have immediately stopped. But the older man simply watched with a hint of appreciation on his face as Melanie fired up on Rik's behalf. Carel waved a hand as though to say: By all means go ahead.

Rik had to push back a bite of possessive jealousy as he realised the older man was…aware of his fiancée as a woman.

Surely this doesn't surprise you, Rik? Every man would notice her beauty. How could they not?

Melanie stepped into Carel's open-plan kitchen. It was immediately apparent that she was at home in this environment. A chopping board sat on the bench.

She glanced towards the refrigerator. 'May I use anything, *monsieur*?'

Carel smiled. 'Yes. Anything.'

Mel took chicken breast, salad greens and dried raspberries, and then selected a bottle of red wine. Finally she retrieved salt and pepper and cashews and a long thin loaf of bread from Carel's pantry.

Rather than the kitchen knives available to her, Mel walked back to where Rik sat at the table. She took the gold-handled knife from where it rested near Rik's right hand.

As she did so she touched his shoulder briefly with her other hand. 'For luck.'

He didn't know whether she meant the knife, or the touch. Perhaps both.

'Your fiancée has pluck.' The Frenchman spoke the words quietly as he sat back to watch Melanie take control of his kitchen. 'I shall eagerly observe this.'

A half-hour later, Mel drew a deep breath and carried the chicken salad to the table. The meal looked good on the plate, colourful and versatile, full of different textures with the thin slices of truffle heated through and releasing their gorgeous aroma. The wine reduction made a beautiful sauce. The thick slice of bread coated with beaten egg yolk, the lightest combination of chopped herbs and grated sharp cheese and lightly toasted made a perfect accompaniment.

Even so, the proof would be in the taste, not only the visual appeal. Mel placed the dish before her host and brought the other two servings for Rik and herself.

Minutes later, Carel put down fork and knife and

lifted his gaze. He spoke first to Rik. 'The truffles are better than anything I have ever tasted. Cooked in the right way, and served with a little royal legendary on the side, these will be highly sought after at my restaurants this season. I am happy to place my order with you.'

'Thank you.' Rik dipped his head and cast a smile in Mel's direction. 'And thanks to you, Melanie, for this meal. You are a wonder in the kitchen. I did not realise just how skilled you are.'

'I would have you in any of my kitchens, Melanie.' Carel's statement followed Rik's.

And while Mel basked in Rik's surprise and the fact that he'd obviously enjoyed the meal, she had to be judicious about it. 'I have to confess that I watched the truffles being prepared at the palace today and learned all I could from the process.'

She turned to smile at the Frenchman. 'Thank you for your compliment.'

'In truth it is a job offer.' The man's gaze shifted between Mel and Rik. 'Any of my restaurants, any time. Permanent work, good wages and conditions. You would be more than welcome. Not that I suggest you would be available…'

Mel was more "available" than the man realised. She said something that she hoped was appropriately appreciative but non-committal. Carel didn't know that she and Rik wouldn't remain together as a couple, so she couldn't exactly have asked the man to hold that thought for a few months.

Plus there'd be work permits and all sorts of things, and when this was all over Mel would need to be back in Australia. She tried valiantly not to let those thoughts spread a pall over Carel's acceptance. Conversation moved on then. Mel sat back and let Rik lead those topics with their host. And *she* tried to gather her calm, and not think too much about the future. Not tonight. Not here in Paris. Not while she felt…vulnerable in this way.

'I hope you will excuse us if we leave you now,' Rik said twenty minutes later.

They had shared a second glass of wine with Carel but it was getting late. 'It is time for us to return to our hotel.' He thanked the man again for his business, and then he and Melanie were outside.

'I would like to stroll the streets before we go back to our hotel.' He turned to examine her face. 'Are you up to a walk?'

'That would be…I would like that.' Her response was guarded. She hoped he couldn't hear that within her words. Beneath it there was too much delight, and that made her feel vulnerable. 'I'd like to see a little more of P-Paris by night.'

'Then I will get our driver to drop us a few blocks away from our hotel.' Rik did this, and they made their car trip in silence before they got out to walk the rest of the way.

The hotel Dominico had booked for Rik was in a beautiful part of the city. At first Melanie felt a little stilted with Rik, but he linked his arm with hers and told her the history of the area, pointing out buildings. And using the night and this moment to enjoy her closeness?

Dream on, Melanie Watson!

'I never thought I would see places like Paris, and Braston.' Melanie turned her face to look into his. 'It's very beautiful on your side of the world.'

'It is…' His gaze seemed to linger on her eyes, her mouth, before he turned his glance back to the buildings around them. 'We have some time in the morning. Is there something you'd like to do?'

'I would love to see some markets.' Mel tried to keep her enthusiasm at a reasonable level. She did. But the chance to explore Paris, even a small portion of it. How could she not be excited? 'A peek at some local colour?'

'Then we shall find markets tomorrow,' Rik said and tucked her more closely against his side. For a moment he felt, not resistance, but perhaps her effort to maintain what she considered to be an appropriate mental and emotional distance?

He should resist, too, but tonight…he did not want to. And so he walked calmly until he felt her relax against his side, and then he took the pleasure of these moments with her in peace, away from expectations and work commitments and other things that went with being… who he was.

'I am enjoying being anonymous with you right now, Melanie.' His voice deepened on the words, on the confession. He couldn't hold the words back.

'Sometimes I forget that you're a prince.' She almost whispered the words in response, as though they were a guilty secret. 'You make extraordinary things seem everyday and normal. Then I forget who you are and just—' She broke off.

Treated him as a man?

Dangerous territory, Rik. The next step is to believe she likes you purely because of you and not your title, and then there would be a woman seeing the man first.

If Rik allowed himself to form any kind of attachment to that woman it could be difficult to let her go when the time came.

He had to do that, and he had no proof that she liked him in any way particularly. Other than kisses, and could he really say those kisses meant all of these things?

You don't have the faith to look for anything else. You've allowed your upbringing to taint your outlook, to stunt what you will reach out for.

In an attempt to refocus his thoughts, he turned his attention back to their visit to Carel. 'You said you'd been a cook, but I did not know you had such skills as you displayed tonight. You won Carel over to placing that order.'

Rik's compliments warmed Mel. 'I enjoyed cooking with the truffles tonight, and I'm so relieved that Carel liked the dish. I took a risk. I wondered if you might have felt I stepped out of line.'

Mel searched his face. 'I—I could just as easily have *lost* you that deal!'

'I do not think so.' Rik gave a slight shake of his head. 'He was too enamoured of you from the first moment. The job offer he made…'

'Was flattering but it's out of the question, isn't it?' She didn't make a question out of it. Well, it wasn't one! 'I've signed on to help you, not to try to set myself up to cook in a Paris restaurant the day after our m-marriage ends.' Mel crossed her fingers and prayed that Rik hadn't heard that slight stumble when she'd referred to that last bit.

'You are very faithful, Nicole Melanie Watson.' Rik shifted his arm and instead caught her hand in his.

His fingers were strong and warm and familiar, and Mel couldn't stop from curling hers around them.

Rik's eyes softened as he smiled at her. 'That is rare and I admire you for it very much.'

They continued their walk in silence, just strolling side by side as though they had all the time in the world. As though they didn't have a *care* in the world.

But underneath, tensions simmered. If everything were so comfortable and unthreatening, why did Mel's heart beat faster with each step they took? Why did a sense of hope and anticipation mix with her awareness of Rik and make her want their walk never to end, and yet at the same time make her want to return to the hotel because she hoped against hope…

That he would kiss her goodnight again? That this night would never end? That it would end for her in his arms? All such foolish thoughts!

'Here we are.' Perhaps he felt it, too, because he swept her into the hotel without another word.

And it seemed as though time warped then because they were at the door of their suite before she could draw a breath, and yet she remembered the endless silent moments in the lift, just the two of them, wishing she could reach out to him, wishing she had the right…

Face it, Mel. You're starting to care for him. To care

for Prince Rikardo Ettonbierre of Braston. Caring as though you might be...

Caring for a man who was a good man, but also a prince, and that meant he was not any man for her because she was an everyday girl.

Mel didn't know what she was thinking, what she hoped for!

Except for a kiss from...a prince?

No. A kiss from Rikardo. That was what she wanted and needed. He *was* a prince, but he could have been the boy next door and she would have wanted that kiss just as much.

You are in trouble, Mel. Big, big trouble because you can't fall for him!

The scent of brewed coffee met them as they entered the suite. A glass bowl with fruits, a bottle of wine and chocolates sat on the low coffee table near the sofa and chairs, and, in the small kitchenette, a basket held fresh baked croissants. The lights were turned down. The suite looked ready to welcome lovers.

Mel's breath caught in the back of her throat. They weren't, of course. There were two bedrooms. It wasn't as though she and Rik—

'The coffee smells good. Just the ticket after that walk in the night air.' Mel stripped off her coat and followed her nose to the kitchenette. She felt she did really well at acting completely normal and unconcerned.

Except she should have dodged the idea of coffee altogether, said goodnight and headed straight for her room rather than prolonging this. What if Rik thought she'd done that so they could take advantage of this romantic scene? What if he thought she was angling for more of his company for that reason?

'You don't need to have any, of course,' she blurted, and then added, because that could have been taken as rather ungracious, 'but I'll pour you a cup if you like, and if you're hungry I can get you a croissant.'

'Coffee would be welcome.' He briefly glanced at the food items and away again. 'I do not think I will spoil the memory of that meal just now.'

Mel found two cups. She got them out of the cupboard and filled them with steaming liquid, and was proud that her fingers didn't tremble.

There was an enclosed balcony, beautifully warm and secluded with stunning views. They took their drinks out there and stood side by side soaking in the ambiance of the city lights.

They weren't touching and yet Mel felt so close to him, so aware of him. How was she supposed to walk away at the end of this arrangement without…looking back and wishing?

If wishes were horses then beggars would ride. Wasn't that the saying? She wasn't a beggar, but she was also not the princess who lived around the corner from the prince. She and Rik weren't on an even playing field; they never would be. Mel needed to remember that. She had to remember who he was, and who she was.

'I am pleased with this evening's efforts.' Rik set his empty coffee cup down on the ledge, took hers and placed it beside it. 'I've regained four key markets.

There are others to chase but those are smaller and can be done out of Braston over the next couple of weeks.'

'You've taken a big step towards getting the people back on their financial feet.' There was pride in her voice that she couldn't hide. In the soft night light Mel looked into his face and knew that her happiness for him must show. 'You've earned the right to feel some peace.'

'You have played a part in my peace.' He spoke softly, with a hint of discovery and perhaps acceptance in his voice. 'And I should keep my distance from you. I know it, but I do not want to do it.'

Her breath quivered in her throat. 'What is it that you want to do?'

'This.' Rik leaned in and claimed her lips with his.

'Melanie.' Rik breathed her name into her hair. Her face was pressed against his chest. He had kissed her until they were both breathless with it. He wanted to kiss her again, and with his fingertips he gently raised her chin.

Her eyes glowed, filled with softness and passion for him. She'd told him there were times when she had thought of him as a man, not a prince. Rik wanted that acceptance from her now, for her to see him as Rikardo, regardless of what else there might be in his life. For once he simply wanted to be a man to a woman.

He drew her soft curves more securely into his arms and breathed the scent from the side of her neck and let his mouth cover hers once again. Tongues caressed and a low moan sounded. His, and a warning bell began to register in the back of his mind not to do this because there was naivety in the way she yielded to him, as though she was new to this, as though perhaps she wasn't particularly experienced…

'What are we doing?' Melanie spoke in a low tone. She drew back. Shields rose in her eyes, concealing her reaction to him, protecting her. 'This—this isn't the same as before when there was a reason to kiss me. It doesn't matter about Paris, about the romance of being here. I shouldn't have let myself be tempted. I shouldn't have looked for that—'

Her words were disjointed. Discomfort filled her face, and Rik…wished it didn't have to be that way, but hadn't he set them up for exactly this? He'd made his choices. 'I should not have stepped over this line, either. It was not a smart thing to do.'

He wrestled with his own reactions. He'd wanted to take, conquer, claim—to stamp his ownership on her and possess her until she was his and his alone. That urge had bypassed all his usual roadblocks.

'I have never—' He stopped himself from completing the sentence. Instead he tried to turn his attention to tomorrow. 'You must go to bed now, get some sleep ready for our visit to the markets.'

Her eyes still held the glaze of the moments of passion they had shared, but they also held confusion, uncertainty, and unease. She searched his face and Rik saw each emotion register as she found her way back to here and now and…to who they were and to remembrance of the arrangement they shared. *He* should have never forgotten that arrangement, yet when he was near her he couldn't seem to remember even the most basic of principles, of sticking to his word and to their goals.

'Thank you for showing me a little of Paris this evening, and for allowing me to take part in your talks with the restaurateurs.' Her chin tipped up. 'Goodnight, Rikardo. I hope you sleep well.'

CHAPTER TEN

'THANK you for finding these markets for me to see.' Mel let her gaze shift from one market stall to the next as she and Rik walked through them. Somehow that felt much easier than looking the prince in the eyes.

They'd kissed last night and she'd withdrawn. Did he know how far she had stepped over the line within herself by entering into that kiss? Mel was too close to falling dangerously for…a prince. She couldn't do that. She had to be businesslike about her relationship with Rik, even if their surroundings or circumstances felt very romantic or extraordinary.

No matter what, Mel. You have to keep your distance inside yourself no matter what. So treat this outing as an outing. Nothing more and nothing less.

She drew a breath and forced her gaze to his. 'Thank you for making time for us to come here.'

'You are welcome, Melanie.' His tone, too, sounded more formal than usual.

And were his shoulders held a little more rigidly?

Mel tried very hard after that, to focus only on the moment. The markets were a treasure trove of local clothing, some new, brand name and quite expensive but with equally much vintage and pre-loved. It was the latter that appealed to Mel.

'You are sure you don't want to look at the branded items?' When they arrived here Rik had pressed what felt like a very large bundle of currency into Mel's hands, and instructed her that she was not to leave empty-handed.

That, too, had felt awkward. Ironically, not because he had wanted to give her this gift but because they had both let their fingers linger just a little too long, and then quickly withdrawn.

Mel's thoughts started to whirl as they had last night in the long hours of courting sleep that wouldn't come. A part of her wanted to find a way to get him to care for her truly. *That* was the problem.

He didn't, and he wouldn't. Not today, not tomorrow or next week or next month or in any number of months. At the end of their time together he would send her away from him fully. How much more did she need to think about it before she accepted that fact? Accepted that a few kisses in the heat of the moment in a beautiful city didn't mean all that much to a man who could kiss just about anyone, anywhere and any time?

Mel drew a slow breath. She forced air into her lungs, forced calm into her inner turmoil. And she cast her glance once more about the market and kept looking until the blur of colours turned once again into garments piled on tables, and she spotted a pretty skirt and moved closer to look…

'I'd like to buy this one.' It wouldn't break the bank.

In fact, it was ridiculously cheap. But it was exactly what Mel would wear, a long, beautifully warm tan suede that fell in an A-line cut. A memento of Paris. That thought, too, was bittersweet. 'It should fit me, but even if it doesn't I can take it in.'

She held out the rest of the money. 'Thank you for giving me this gift. I'd like to browse a little longer and then I'll be ready to go.' She hoped her words were convincing and didn't sound as strained as she felt.

'You must keep that to spend any time you wish.' Rik pressed the money back into her hands, and waited for her to tuck it away in her purse.

As the days passed after Paris, Melanie showed her strength by being the perfect fiancée to Rik. No one, not his brothers and not his father, could have said that she wasn't fully supportive of him, utterly committed to him.

Not in love with him, perhaps. That kind of acting would be a stretch, but the rest yes. She maintained her role beautifully. She showed no stress. She seemed perfectly content as she forged ahead making plans for their marriage, liaising with all those involved in the preparations as the days slid closer to the first of the three wedding rehearsals. But beneath the surface…

Rik was not content. He couldn't forget holding her in his arms in Paris. He, who had grown up trained to live by his self-control, had felt that night as though he teetered on the brink of losing it. He had longed, *longed deep down inside*, to make love to her but Melanie had broken away.

'You behaved like some smitten, lovelorn—' He bit the words off before he added fiancé. It was already bad enough that he was talking to the walls as he walked along. He *was* Melanie's fiancé. Just not in any normal sense of the word.

Their first rehearsal was tomorrow and he did not feel prepared. Perhaps things were just moving too quickly for his comfort, for him to feel that he possessed that control that he needed to have. All would be safe in Melanie's capable hands. Instinctively he knew this. Provided the actual marriage day went ahead, anything else would not overly matter anyway...

Rik made his way to the kitchen. The palace always had kitchen staff on call. He could have got one out of bed to make him a cup of coffee or a sandwich or to bring him pickings from the refrigerators, but he would rather forage for himself. At least it would pass some time until he managed to nod off, and Mel would be safe and sound asleep in *her* bed while Rik wrestled his demons.

That was part of his insomnia problem, knowing Mel was so close and he couldn't touch her. Mustn't touch her. He strode to the double doors of the palace kitchen and pushed with both hands. Before he even opened them, the scent of fresh baking hit him.

Why would anyone be baking at this time of night? Baking up a storm, he realised as his gaze lit on an array of cakes and cookies spread on the bench.

Something tickled the back of his mind, and was lost as he realised *who* was doing the cooking. 'Mel—'

'Rik! Oh, you startled me.' The cake plate she held

in her hands bobbled before she carefully set it down
and placed a lid over it.

'I had permission.' Her words were almost defensive. 'I needed some time in the kitchen. It's what I do
when I need—' She cut the words off, waved a hand.
'Well, never mind. I'm almost done here, anyway. All
I need to do is leave the kitchen sparkling. It's almost
there now.' Mel turned to wipe down a final bench top.

She had dark smudges under her eyes. Was Melanie,
too, more disturbed than he'd realised since their trip to
Paris despite her valiant efforts to support him? Was she
also feeling tortured and struggling with her thoughts?

Leave the cleaning up for the staff.

Rik wanted very much to say the words. He bit them
back because it seemed important to her to leave the
kitchen as she had found it. Aside from those cakes and
cookies.

'The staff told me these could be used tomorrow.'
Mel gestured towards the food items. She went on to
mention some need for the foods.

Rik only half heard the explanation, because he was
looking at those smudges beneath her eyes.

'I don't suppose you're hungry?' She gestured towards a chocolate cake covered in sticky icing. 'It's
probably the worst thing to do, but I thought I'd eat a
piece and maybe—'

'Relax for a while?' He didn't know what she'd
planned to say, but to Rik, standing in the kitchen in
the middle of the night unable to sleep, with Melanie
obviously also unable to sleep, it made perfect sense

to use his insomnia to try to at least help *her* to relax. 'Why don't we take it back with us?'

Mel hadn't expected Rik to walk in on her cooking splurge. He was the reason for it, so maybe it would be good to spend that time with him. Perhaps then she would be able to shake off the feeling of melancholy and impending loss that had become harder and harder to bear as each day passed.

You'd better smile anyway, Mel. He doesn't need to see your face and start wondering what your problem is.

In truth Mel didn't *know* what the problem was. She'd hoped that cooking would shake the answer loose but it hadn't.

'I guess we can make coffee in our suite?' It was only after she said the words that she realised she'd referred to the suite as theirs as though she had every right, as though she had as much ownership of it as Rik did.

'I put a pot on before I left.'

His words made her realise that, while he'd caught her cooking in the middle of the night because she couldn't sleep, he must have had similar problems otherwise he wouldn't have been wandering the corridors and making pots of coffee when normal people would be asleep in their beds.

Mel put pieces of cake onto plates and loaded them onto a tray, which Rik promptly took from her hands. One final glance around the kitchen showed that the staff would have nothing more to deal with than delivering the goodies tomorrow morning, and Mel would try to be available to help with that.

The smell of brewed coffee met them as they stepped into the suite. It reminded Mel of Paris, of being held in his arms and kissed.

'Did the suede skirt fit, or did you have to alter it?' Rik's words made Mel realise that he, too, was remembering.

Her breath hitched for a moment. She forced her thoughts away from the reaction. She'd got through day after day doing the same. Each time any unacceptable thought tried to raise its head, Mel pushed it away. Surely no one would be able to tell just how often she thought about Rik, about those moments? How she longed for them all over again? 'The skirt fits perfectly. I'm planning to wear it tomorrow, actually.'

For the festival being held in the town. Rik hadn't spoken of it, so Mel didn't know what his role of involvement would be, if any. And the kitchen staff had told her that the event itself would be a low budget affair.

That didn't mean it couldn't be fun, though, and it was an unusual theme. Mel at least wanted to take a look. All of which was trivia, really, and yet there were times when trivia felt a little less emotionally threatening than the rest of life!

They sat side by side on the sofa eating cake and sipping coffee. A very ordinary, normal thing to do except for the fact it was after midnight, and this was Rik's suite of rooms, and they were engaged and yet in the truest sense they really weren't.

She blurted out, 'The wedding planner supervised

a fitting of the gown this afternoon. I won't wear it to the first rehearsal tomorrow, of course, but…'

How did she explain what she couldn't understand herself? Just how much that fitting had taken from her emotionally and she couldn't say why because it was just a dress in the end, and the wedding wasn't going to be real, and Mel *knew* all of this.

Mel didn't want to think about why. 'Well, it's a beautiful gown. I'm amazed at how quickly it's being created.' She drew a breath and tried to make light of it as she went on. 'Have you been fitted for your suit?'

'Yesterday.' He glanced towards her. 'I've left you to handle the bulk of the work for this wedding while I attended to other things. I should have supported you better.'

She leaned towards him, shook her head. 'You've been all over the country checking on the truffle harvesting, making sure the orders are going out in perfect condition. That's so important.'

'And that's your generosity shining again.' He lifted his hand to the side of her face. 'You have a tiny dot of cake batter right there.' His fingertip softly brushed the spot.

Mel closed her eyes. Oh, it was the stupidest thing to do but it was what his touch did to her. She melted any time they were close.

'It's there, isn't it?' The feather-light touch of lips replaced his fingertip against her cheek. He kissed the spot where her cooking efforts had made their way onto her face, and then he sighed softly and pressed his cheek to hers. 'All the time that need is there. I do not know why.'

That was as far as he got, because he turned his head to look into her eyes, and Mel turned her head to look into his eyes, and their lips met.

The fire ignited. Immediately and utterly and Rik's arms closed around her and Mel threw hers around his neck and held on. She didn't know if she could have let go if she'd wanted to. This was what had been troubling her. This was what she'd tried to think about and figure out.

Her thoughts formed that far, and then they became action. Her mouth yielded to his, opened to him even as she took from him. She sipped from his lips and ran her tongue across his teeth.

Everything was pleasure, and somehow all of those feelings seemed to have caught themselves in a place deep in her chest where they swirled and twined and warmed her all at once. Rik was the warming power. Everything about him drew her. Mel didn't want to resist being drawn.

'I don't want to leave this, Mel.' His words echoed her thoughts, and he used the diminutive of her name, and Mel loved that.

'I don't want to leave it, either, Rik.'

'Do you understand what will happen?' His words were very deep, emotive and desirous and almost stern all at once.

'I do.' If there was any hesitation in her words it was not because of uncertainty in that decision. 'This—this is new for me.'

Please don't stop because I've admitted that.

'But it's what I want, Rik. I—I have no doubts.'

'I do not want to consider doubts, either.' Rik's words were strong, and yet the touch of his hand was so gentle as he stroked the side of her face, her neck. 'I will cherish you, Melanie. I will cherish you through this experience.'

That made it right for her. It just…did. The tiny bit of fear that had been buried deep down, that she might not know what to do or how to please him, evaporated. He would guide her. Mel could give this gift and share the gift of his intimacy in return. She wanted that. She *needed* it, though she did not understand why that need held such strength.

Rik took her hand and led her to his bedroom. Mel managed to register that the room was similar to her own but with a more manly tone, and then Rik drew her into his arms and kissed his way from the side of her neck to her chin and finally to her lips as their bodies pressed together and Mel didn't notice anything more about the room.

This felt exactly right. That was what Mel thought as her hands pressed against his chest, slid up to his shoulders and she let herself touch his muscular back through the cloth of his shirt. Yet that was not enough. 'I want—'

'What do you want, Melanie? Tell me.' He encouraged her to put her need into words.

And maybe he needed to hear that, too, for her to tell him.

'I need to touch you. I need to feel your skin beneath my fingertips while you're kissing me.' She almost whispered it, but he heard and he guided her hand to the buttons of his shirt.

It was all the permission that Mel needed, and, though she trembled inside, her fingers slipped each button free until his chest was revealed and she could touch his bare skin. 'You're so warm.'

'That is because you are in my arms.' He shrugged out of the shirt and then he gave all of his attention to her and to this exploration that they shared moment-by-moment in giving and receiving and discovering and finding.

When he laid her on the bed, Mel looked into his eyes and though her thoughts and feelings were blurred by passion, impossible to define, every instinct told her. 'This is what I've needed. I know it's right. I want you to make love to me, Rik. Just to share this together, the two of us without thinking about anything else.'

Rik cupped her face in his palm. 'And so it will be.'

Melanie blossomed beneath Rik's ministrations. She was beautiful in every way, and he told her in English and French and told her in the old language of Braston, words that he had never uttered to another woman as he led her forward on this journey.

He hesitated on the brink of claiming her. 'I am sorry that there will be pain. If you want me to stop—'

'No.' Mel let the word be a caress of her lips against his. A sigh inside her. A whisper of need that she gave from her heart, and that was terrifying because Mel couldn't bring her heart to this. That was far too dangerous a thing to do. 'Please don't stop, Rik. I...don't think I could bear it if you did.'

There *was* pain, but she held his gaze and the tenderness in his eyes, the expression that seemed akin to awe as he bent to kiss her lips again, allowed her to release that pain, to let it pass and to trust in him to lead her forward.

He did that, and then there was only pleasure and she crashed suddenly over an incredible wave and he cried out with her, the most amazing experience Mel had ever experienced, and the most powerful, knowing that she, too, had brought *him* to *this*.

Afterwards he held her cuddled against his chest as their breathing slowed. A deep lethargy crept up on Mel. She tried to fight it, to stay alert, to even *begin* to figure out what happened now or what she should say or do. There was so much and she didn't know how to find understanding but she knew she didn't regret this, could never regret it.

But what did it mean to him, Mel? What did it mean to Rik? Is there any possibility now—?

Mel could have been embarrassed, but they had shared this. How could she now feel anything that even resembled such an emotion? There was no room inside her. She was filled with other emotions, inexplicable to her right now, and overwhelming because what they had shared had been overwhelming. She shivered, wishing for his warmth, and then he was there, drawing her close.

He tucked her chin into his chest and she felt tension

drain from him, too, and wondered what his thoughts might be.

'Sleep, Melanie. You need it right now more than you know.' He stroked his fingers through her hair.

Mel slept.

CHAPTER ELEVEN

'IF I'D remembered this festival was on today I'd have left the country.' Marcelo's face pulled into a disgruntled twist.

'Oh, I don't know. Is it so horrible having the opportunity to flirt with lots of lovely local women?' Anrai dug his brother in the ribs.

Marcelo didn't crack a smile. 'It is if they then want to marry you!'

Anrai, too, now grimaced. 'I forgot that from last year.'

'And the year before and year before and year before,' Marcelo said beneath his breath. 'You need to stop being such a flirt, Anrai. It will catch up with you one day. Anyway, we had to be here. Rik's first wedding rehearsal is later today.' Marcelo turned to Rik. 'Can you believe the marriage is only a week away?'

'No.' Rik glanced at his brothers, heard the sibling teasing. He might even have wanted to join in, if there'd been any space left in his thoughts or emotions right now for anything other than the woman he'd held in his arms last night.

It was just one week before their marriage.

They had spent just one night in each other's arms.

He should not have let that happen but it had and now he did not know what to do, how to go forward. So many thoughts and emotions swirled, and Rik…did not like to feel out of control, confused, uncertain of his path and yet all he could do was continue because… nothing had changed when in a way…everything had. But nothing at the core of him, nothing of how he was. Of his parents' traits within him.

Nevertheless, Rik needed to find Melanie. The marriage *was* only a week away. They did have a rehearsal this afternoon and…he didn't know if he had irreparably messed things up with Melanie.

And even now you wish you could take her again into your arms.

Rik tried to force the thoughts aside. They were of no use to him, a line crossed that must not be crossed again. He glanced around him. He and his brothers were in Ettonbierre village, and, yes, there was a festival on today.

Rik had forgotten all about it. So had Anrai and Marcelo who'd both only arrived back at the palace late last night and had walked out with him this morning intending to meet a man to discuss tourism plans for the region.

All three brothers had plans and goals. All three relied on the success of each other to allow them to achieve those goals. The prize was recovery for a struggling country, the cost to be their freedom if Anrai and

Marcelo could not also figure out ways to avoid their father's insistence that they lock into lifetime marriages.

Rik tried to dismiss the thoughts. He looked around him. This festival was what Melanie had cooked for in the middle of the night. Just a few hours ago, and then Rik had found her in the kitchen and taken her back to his suite. She'd mentioned the wedding rehearsal. She had probably been worrying about it and that had prompted her cooking spree. And then perhaps other thoughts had pushed those worries aside for a time as they…made love.

And those thoughts had now given her new concerns? Of course they would have. They had given Rik fresh concerns, fresh questions. He had to keep her with him and keep both of them to their agreement. He hoped last night would not have undermined that goal. That was the only *clear* path Rik could define. Surely the only one that mattered, so why did reminding himself bring a sense of loss rather than the sense of eventual freedom it should?

Every thought brought Rik back to the same thing. He and Melanie had made love. That *had* changed things. He'd felt as though his world had shifted alignment and Rik couldn't figure out why he felt that way or what it meant.

He'd woken at dawn with Melanie curled in his arms and a sense of rightness that had quickly changed when the reality of what they had done stabbed him in the chest.

How could that have been a smart decision on his part? Melanie had been innocent and had allowed passion to sway her judgement, but Rik was experienced and should have known not to let this happen.

Not when there was no future for them, no future when their involvement was based on a situation that he had set up to avoid becoming tied down in a relationship. He couldn't bear to perpetuate his family's emotional freeze-out into another generation, to be the one turning the cold shoulder to his partner and receiving the same in return. To have his children asking themselves why they were not fit to be loved.

No. He could not carry that legacy forward.

When he woke this morning and thought of all that, remorse and confusion and a lot of other emotions had set in. Melanie was a giving girl. She would be kind. She would definitely care for her children.

But Rik...could not match those traits. He'd eased away from Melanie and got up. Showered, dressed, told himself he needed to think and that he would wait for her to wake and then they would...

What? Somehow sort themselves out so that last night didn't have the impact on them that it already had done?

She'd been a virgin. She'd given him a beautiful gift. That could never be undone now and even with all his concerns, Rik felt that he *had* been given that beautiful gift, the gift of Melanie in all of who she was, and he didn't begin to know what to do now because he hadn't planned for this and he had nothing to give in return of equal or acceptable value.

A confronting thought for a man who always set out to be in charge of his world, who had been raised into position and privilege and must now acknowledge that in this, he lacked.

'I just want to find Melanie.' He frowned. 'There are a lot of people around. She is the fiancée of a prince now, and shouldn't be unattended without at least two bodyguards with her.'

Rik totally overlooked the fact that he had encouraged Melanie to move about the palace grounds and surrounds using the small buggy vehicle, and had believed she would be perfectly safe where members of the palace staff would never be too far away or the villagers would know she was a guest at the palace.

But the festival would bring tourists and strangers. Anything might happen.

And your protectiveness of her is out of proportion to your ability to let her into the core parts of you that you withhold from the world.

But not from his brothers?

That was different. It was all that he had. Care for his brothers and for the people of Braston. He could not bring normal love and caring feelings to a marriage.

'Hate to point it out to you, brother, but *we* don't have any bodyguards with us.' Anrai raised his brows. 'You're sounding very serious considering the temporary nature of your arrangement with Melanie. Much as I think she's a wonderful girl,' his brother added.

'She is.' Rik didn't notice the tightening of his mouth as he spoke, the flash of warring emotions that quickly crossed his face. Instead his gaze scanned the crowds, searching as he missed the surprised and thoughtful gazes his brothers exchanged before they gave nods of silent decision, told him they needed to find their contact and get on with their meeting, and gave him the space to make his search.

Rik glanced around the crowded village square. There were colourful rides for children to play on, stalls out in the open selling home produce and hand-sewn items. A kissing booth, another to have your romantic future read, another for chemistry tests to find potential matches.

The fair had started out as a proposal day centuries ago as a means for men to woo their potential brides with offers of a fowl or a pig as a dowry. Today it had turned into an opportunity for the folk of Ettonbierre village to let their hair down for a day, for children to play and young men and women to flirt with each other, ask each other out.

He didn't want Melanie anywhere near this.

The jealous, protective thought came from deep within Rik. He had no right to it but still it came. A moment later he spotted her and he strode towards the small group gathered outside the food marquee at the edge of the town square.

'It's very flattering of you to say that to me, and yes I guess it would be fair to say that I am a guest of Prince Rikardo at the palace at the moment.' Mel spoke the words as she tried to edge away from the small crowd that had gathered outside the food tent.

She tried to sound normal, polite and not as deeply confused and overwrought as she felt this morning. Pretending calm until she started to feel it was a method that had worked for her after their trip to Paris. Surely it would work again now?

After Paris you were recovering from a kiss. Last night you made love with Rik. The two aren't exactly on a par. 'I'm really not at liberty to discuss that any further at this time.'

Though Rik had assured her none of the villagers would recognise the ring she wore as her engagement ring, Mel tucked her hand into her skirt pocket just in case, and was proud that she'd managed to think clearly enough to consider that need.

In that same thrust to find some sliver of normalcy in the whirl of her emotions she'd delivered all the cakes she could carry to the fair. She had stepped outside the catering tent intending to take a quick look at the festival before heading back to the palace.

Rik had been out on the grounds somewhere when she had first woken up. She probably could have gone looking for him, but what would she have said? She'd needed a moment to try to clear her head before she faced him.

You wanted more than a moment. After all that you shared with him last night you had no idea how to face him. Why downplay it, Mel, when it's all you can think about and every time you do think about it, you can hardly breathe for the mix of feelings that rushes through you?

She'd fallen asleep in his arms, more drained emotionally and in every way than she had understood. And had woken alone, only to realise she was not alone because doubt had come to rest on her shoulder to whisper in her ear. Doubt about his feelings in all of this. Doubt that she had any right to expect him to *have* any feelings about it. Just above the other shoulder lurked despair. Mel didn't want to acknowledge that, but…

She and Rik had shared something. It had been stunningly special to Mel, but that didn't mean it had been any of that to Rikardo. To the prince. How could it have been?

You managed to forget that little factor last night, didn't you? That he's a prince and you're a cook and his path is carefully set and doesn't include any kind of emotional commitment to you.

'If you change your mind while you are here…' The man in front of her gave an engaging smile and handed her a piece of paper with his phone number on it.

Proposal Day. The festival had a history. Mel had heard it all from the kitchen staff. But nowadays it was a chance for people to get to know each other, date or whatever. Mel wouldn't have been interested before. Now that she'd made love with Rik, she felt she could never be interested in any other man, ever again.

The man turned away. There were two others. Mel managed to quickly send them both on their way. She needed to get out of here, to make her way back to the palace and maybe during that solitary walk she would gather up all the pieces of herself and get them back into some kind of working order. Maybe she could hole up in her room for the entire day to complete that task. Would that be long enough?

It will never be long enough, Mel. You know what's happened.

The thought was so strong, so full of conviction. It forced her hand, and realisation crashed over her, then, whether she was ready for it or not.

She'd fallen in love with Rik. It was the answer to why last night had moved her emotions so deeply that she had wondered if she would ever be the same. The answer was no, she never would.

Because "everyday girl" Melanie Watson had fallen in love with Prince Rikardo Ettonbierre of Braston.

It should have been a moment of wonder, of anticipation and happiness. Instead, devastating loss swept through her because last night had been the total of any chance to show her love to him in that way. A moment that shouldn't have happened.

In return, Rik had made no promises. Not at the start of their marriage agreement, and not last night. He'd given in to desire. That wasn't the same as being bowled over by love so that expressing those feelings was imperative.

Mel was the one who had foolishly given her heart. Well, now she had to get back on her feet somehow. She had to get through marrying him and walking away, to do all that with dignity when all she would want to do was beg him to keep her, to want her, to not reject her or abandon her or punish her for—

What did she mean, punish?

And today there was the first wedding rehearsal. How could she get through that?

'Melanie. What are you doing here? Why were you talking to those men?'

Rik's words shook her out of her reverie, stopped

a train of thought that had started to dig into a place deep down where she had hidden parts of herself. But the interruption did not save her from her sense of uncertainty and panic. That increased.

She glanced at him. Oh, it was hard to look and to know what was in her heart.

Please don't let him see it.

That one glance into his face showed austerity, as though he had stepped behind shields, had taken a fortified position.

In that moment he really resembled his father…

Rik had told her he couldn't buy into a cold relationship. He'd been so against the institution of marriage. He…hadn't believed in love.

Mel had thought that was because he'd been hurt, had seen his parents in a loveless relationship. But looking at him now, seeing that capacity to close himself off when she needed so very much for him to…let her in…

Last night was not the same for Rik, as for you. And whether or not he is like his father, you have to accept what he told you at the start. He won't ever love you, Mel. Not ever.

That attitude must make it much easier for Rik to deal with things like arranging this marriage and knowing he would be able to walk away from it later. It wasn't his fault that he'd asked her to help him. He had the right to try to protect his interests, and he'd wanted to help the people of Braston. His father had put him in an impossible position.

And now you have allowed yourself to end up in one, by falling for him.

All she could do was try to match his strength. She stared at the face she had come to cherish far too much in the short time she had known him, and prayed for that strength.

'Rik. I...' She didn't know what she wanted to say. What she should try to say.

'I was concerned. You may not be safe here, Melanie.'

If his frown showed anything but attention to her presence here at the fair, Mel couldn't discern it.

He went on. 'You are all on your own.'

Oh, she knew that more than well, though she realised that Rik meant it literally in this case.

A thousand moments of trying to escape wouldn't have got her any closer to feeling ready for this. For facing the feelings that had overcome her, and for facing him. She loved him. Deep down in her heart and soul, all those feelings had formed and intertwined and she had no choice about it.

How could Mel combat that? How could she take what had happened last night, and put it in some kind of perspective somehow so that she could contain these feelings, get them under control and then somehow make them stop altogether when it just wasn't like that now?

How could she marry him, live as his...princess but secretly in name only, let herself become more and more familiar with him with the passing of each day and then leave at the end of a few short months and get on with her life as though none of this had happened?

Those pretty, sparkly shoes were nowhere to be found right now.

'I came out to deliver some of the cakes that I baked last night for the festival.' Her words held a tremor and she cleared her throat before she went on. She didn't want that tremor. She couldn't allow it. She just couldn't. He mustn't detect how shaken she felt and perhaps figure out why.

Rik wanted a single life, not to be bound in the very relationship that he'd asked her to help him avoid. The knowledge lanced through her, of how utterly useless it would be to hold out any hope that their circumstances might change.

So press on, Mel. You can do it. One step after another until you get there.

'I wanted a look at the festival.' There. A normal tone, a normal topic of conversation.

A bunch of unspoken words filling the air between them.

She tightened her lips so they wouldn't tremble. 'I thought it might be interesting, and I didn't want the kitchen staff to have to bring all the cakes and cookies themselves.'

'And you had men lined up to ask you out.' His words held no particular inflection.

So why did Mel believe she could hear possession in them?

Because you are engaged to him, but for a purpose, Mel. That's all it is.

They might have been keeping their marriage plans secret from the masses for as long as they could possibly manage, but that wouldn't mean he would be happy to see her out being asked on dates by local men. 'I didn't expect that to happen. I just stepped out of the food tent.'

'I know. I saw.' Rik suppressed a sigh as he searched his fiancée's eyes, her face. She looked overwhelmed and uncertain, shaken to the core.

He blamed himself for that. And into that mix he had brought a burst of jealousy that was completely inappropriate.

'I should have waited for you this morning.' Whether he'd known what to say to her, or not, Rik should have waited. A prince did not avoid facing something just because he did not know how to manage a situation. 'Winnow called early and I went—'

'It's all right.' She touched his arm, and quickly drew her hand away as though the touch had burned her.

Remorse pricked him afresh. Remorse and a confusion of feelings? He pushed the impression aside. There were no warring feelings, just resolve and the need to try to ease them through this so they could go forward. Rik straightened his shoulders.

Melanie gestured in front of them. 'I've probably wasted your time, coming to look for me, too. Let's head back. I'm sure you have a lot of things that you need to do before the—the rehearsal later.'

'There is nothing that cannot wait until then.' But it was good that Melanie would come back with him now. For the first few minutes until they got free of the fair and started on the path back to the palace, Rik let silence reign.

Once they were alone, he slowed his pace. 'We need to talk, Melanie. About last night.'

'Oh, really, I don't think there's any need.' Every defence she could muster was immediately thrown up. She tipped her chin in the air. 'It's just—it was—we have our arrangement! Last night wasn't—it happened, that's all but it doesn't need to make any difference to anything. Nothing needs to change. Really I'd prefer to just forget all about it.'

'But that is not possible.' And even though he knew it should not have happened, Rik did not want...to deny the memory or to let her think— 'I don't want you to imagine that I took what we shared lightly,' he began carefully. 'It was—'

'Lots of people sleep together for lots of different reasons.' She drew a shuddery breath. 'We did because we did. We were...a little bit attracted to each other and maybe we were...curious. Now that curiosity is set to rest it doesn't have to happen again.' Her words emerged in stilted tones but with so much determination.

She was saying all the things that Rik himself believed about their situation. Not dismissing what they had shared, but doing all she could to put it in an appropriate context. This was what he would have tried to do himself, so why did her response make his chest feel tight? Make him want to take her in his arms again and try mend them through touch when touch had brought them to this in the first place?

They rounded a bend in the road. The palace came into view.

Rik barely looked ahead of them. He could only look at Melanie. Guilt that he had caused her this unease vied with feelings of...disappointment and...loss within him.

How could that be so? He must only feel relief, and…
the need to reassure her.

So get your focus back on the goal, Rik. It's as important now as it was at the start.

It was. In her way, Melanie was right. Nothing about any of that had changed. Nothing at the core of him, either. Nothing of what he needed, of what he could give and…what he could not give.

So do what you can to reassure her, Rik, both for now and for later.

'I will look after you for the short term of our marriage, Melanie.' A rustle sounded around a bend in the path and he briefly wondered if Rufusina had got loose again before the thought left him for more important ones. 'You will lack for nothing. I will provide everything you might want, and when you go back to Australia afterwards—'

'I don't need anything extra from you. I still have all the money you gave me while we were in Paris. That's more than enough to see me back to Australia.' Her words were protective, proud. 'I can take care of myself once I've finished being your temporary princess. All that matters is that you've held onto your freedom, and you've got the things you needed—'

'What is this? What is going on here?' King Georgio appeared before them on the path.

Not Rufusina on the loose and foraging.

But Rik's father, becoming angrier by the moment as what he had just heard sank in.

'What trickery have I just heard, Rikardo? I did not say that you could marry temporarily. You must marry permanently!' His gaze shifted to Melanie and further suspicion filled it.

Before the king could speak, Rik took a step forward, half shielding Melanie with his body. 'This situation is of my making, Father. You will not question Melanie or accuse her about any of this.'

'Then you will explain yourself.' Georgio's words were cold. 'And this will not be done standing in the middle of a walkway.'

Security people had gathered in the king's wake.

'You will attend me appropriately, inside the palace. You will not keep me waiting.' Without another word, the older man walked away.

Rik turned to Melanie.

'All your plans, Rik.' Concern and unease filled her face. 'He looked so angry.'

'I must speak to him now, try to get him to understand.' He hesitated. 'You will wait for me?'

'I'll wait in our—in the suite until you can let me know what happened.'

With thoughts churning, Rik took one last look at the woman before him, and turned to follow his father.

CHAPTER TWELVE

I AM stunned.

Rik thought the words silently as he walked towards the grand historic church where he and Melanie were to today rehearse the marriage ceremony. Stunned almost to the point of numbness by what his father had just revealed.

He needed to speak to Melanie now more than before, and when he stepped through the doors of the church, she broke away from the small group of people gathered near the front of the large ancient building, and rushed to his side.

'I couldn't wait for you any longer.' She said the words in a hushed whisper. 'Dominico came to get me and I couldn't tell him anything was wrong. Is—is the wedding off now? What happened? What did your father say?'

Beyond them, Anrai and Marcelo waited, along with the priest and various others expecting to participate in this marriage ceremony next week.

Another brother could be standing there.

'This will shock you, as it did me when my father revealed it, and I would ask that you not tell anyone until I can speak to Anrai and Marcelo.' Rik drew a slow breath. 'The reason that my father pushed so hard for marriages is because there is an older brother, a love child to a woman in England. Two years ago this man discovered his true identity. He's been trying to gain a position in the family through my father since.'

'Is—? That isn't sounding like good news to you?' Melanie's hand half lifted as though she would press it over her mouth before she dropped it away again.

'His existence is the reason my mother left, and he has now gained access to copies of our family law and worked out that he can try to claim ascendancy and, with it, Marcelo's position, rights, and work. If Marcelo is married, his position is safe, but until we are also married, Anrai's and mine…are not.'

'In other words he doesn't really belong within the family.' She said it quietly. 'He's not wanted.'

'He is not royal born.' Rik said it carefully. 'Whether he will find a place within the family, at this stage I do not know. I would like to meet him and discern for myself what manner of man he is and go from there. I would not reject a brother, but I also would not welcome a threat to the security of my country and people.'

'That's fair.' She seemed to relax as she said the words.

Rik went on. 'The old laws—this is part of why Marcelo wants to bring change. This is not merely so we can all maintain our positions. It is to keep the people of the country safe as well.'

'Why would this man push for a position that

shouldn't rightly be his? Surely he must realise that he can't just walk in and take someone's place?'

'My father has no doubt contributed to the man's anger and frustration by refusing to acknowledge him at all when he should have done so many years ago.'

'Well, you can take care of your part in it. You're marrying me. You can say you've been married then. Your position will be safe!'

All but for one vital thing. 'I must *remain married*, Melanie. My plan to marry you and then end the relationship afterwards will not work for this.'

'What—what will you do?' She searched his face and her eyes were so deep and so guarded as she began to realise how this new situation had raised the stakes. 'You'll need to find someone else. You'll need to start looking right away. Someone you can make that kind of commitment with. There must be *someone* you could accept in that way.'

The priest cleared his throat noisily at the front of the church.

Rik's brothers cast glances their way that were becoming more than curious.

Of all settings and times, this had to be about the worst but at least as Rik had informed Melanie of the basics of the issue his thoughts had cleared. He knew exactly what he needed, now, and from whom, but could he yet again convince her?

'You want me to be the one, don't you?' The words came from between lips that had whitened with shock. 'You want me to be married to you permanently?'

'We are already together. I would provide for your

every need. You would live a privileged life, want for nothing.' It would resolve problems, not only for Rik, but also for Melanie. 'You would never again have to fend for yourself, and later if you wanted a child I would…allow it.'

There were other words that tried to bubble up, but Rik needed to protect himself in this—

Her glance searched his face before it shifted to take in the church, the people waiting for the rehearsal to start. 'I can't do it. Not even for the people.' She whispered the words before she added more strongly, 'I've tried hard in my life and I've never rejected people even when they've rejected me, but I won't line up for another lifetime of that.

'I blamed myself for losing my parents in that car crash. I thought after that I didn't deserve happiness, to be alive when they weren't, but that was grief talking. I do deserve happiness. I deserve better from you.'

Melanie turned on her heel and ran from the church.

CHAPTER THIRTEEN

'I'VE made the biggest mistake of my life.' Rik spoke
the words to Marcelo as his brother drove them towards
the country's small international airport. He felt sick
inside, close to overwhelmed and very, very afraid that
he might have lost his chance with Melanie for ever by
stupidly trying too hard to protect himself and by being
too slow to realise…

Rik had lost valuable time searching for Melanie out
of doors. He'd thought she must have run to their spot
on the mountainside, or perhaps back to Ettonbierre
village to lose herself in the crowd there.

As he'd searched, knowing his brothers were also
looking, Rik had begun to panic. In her distraught state,
what if something happened to Melanie? And all that he
had locked down inside him and tried to deny since he
and Melanie made love had begun to inexorably make
its way to the surface and demand to be known.

'She will not leave the airport.' Marcelo offered the
assurance without taking his glance from the road. 'If
need be, the flights will all be delayed until we get there.
Dominico will take care of it.'

That was a privilege of position that, in this moment, Rik was willing to exploit without compunction. It was Melanie's reaction when he caught up with her that concerned him.

'I have used Melanie without considering how she might feel. Not respected her rights and emotions.' He shook his head. 'I asked her to remain permanently married to me as though she should be grateful for all the privileges she would receive as part of the family.'

'Such as being in a loveless marriage for life?' Marcelo's words were not harsh, neither teasing, but a statement of understanding of things that he and Rik had never discussed about their upbringing.

'I wanted to avoid that at all costs.' Why hadn't Rik understood sooner that his drive to pull Melanie into exactly that long-term relationship had not been fuelled merely by the need to protect his position and that of his brothers, in the knowledge of this unknown brother? It had been driven by need of *Melanie*. And yet he felt no warmth towards this unknown man. 'I cannot find soft emotion in my heart for him, Marcelo. Even now when I realise how I feel about Melanie—'

'One thing at a time,' Marcelo advised. He drew the car to a halt in a no stopping zone in front of the airport. 'We all need to get to know this man. Good luck, brother.'

Rik met Marcelo's gaze as he threw the car door open. 'Thank you.'

Rik drew a deep breath and strode quickly into the airport terminal.

* * *

I'm not going to feel guilty about the money.

Melanie thought this as she twisted her hands together in her lap. She'd packed all her luggage, half dreading that Rik might appear at any moment. Then she'd summoned palace staff to carry it all downstairs and put it in the cab she'd ordered. A real cab this time, with no mix-ups.

She'd bought an airline ticket to get back to Australia. The flight wasn't going directly there. She'd asked for the first one that would get her out of the country and she'd used the money Rik had given her that day in Paris, to pay for it.

It was almost time, just a few more minutes and she would be able to board the plane, and…fly away from Braston, and from Rik, for ever.

Her heart squeezed and she forced her gaze forward. Other people in the boarding lounge talked to each other or relaxed in their chairs, at ease with themselves and their plans. Mel just wanted to…get through this. She felt she was letting down the people, but Rik would find someone else. Prince Rikardo Eduard Ettonbierre of Braston would not struggle to find a woman willing to marry him for life.

Mel couldn't be that woman. Not without love.

'Melanie!'

At first she thought she'd imagined his familiar voice, a figment within her mind because her heart hurt so much. It was going to take time to get past those raw emotions and begin to heal.

Could she heal from falling in love with Rik?

'Mel. Thank goodness you're here.' Rik appeared in

front of her. Ruffled. Surprisingly un-prince-like with his tie askew and his suit coat hanging open. *Real*.

Mel shot to her feet. She wasn't sure what she intended to do when she got upright. Run? Faint? Throw herself at him and hope against hope that he would open his arms and his heart to her?

Get real, Melanie Watson. You're still a cook and he's still a prince and he doesn't love you and that's that.

'I don't have a glass slipper.' His words were low.

And confusing. 'I—I don't understand.'

Words came over the airport speaker system. French and then English. Her flight was being called. Mel had to get on the flight. She glanced towards the gate, to people beginning to go through. Her heart said stay. Her survival instincts said go. Go and don't look back because you've done that "love people and not be loved in return" thing and it just hurts too damned much to do it again. 'I have to go, Rik. I paid all your money to buy the ticket. I can't buy another one.'

'I will buy you another ticket, Mel.' He lifted his hand as though he would take hers, and hesitated as though uncertain of his welcome. 'If you still want to go.'

Oh, Rik.

'Please. I left out something very important when I asked you to marry me.'

'Another bargaining chip?' She hadn't meant to say it. She didn't want to spread hurt, or reveal her heart. Mel just wanted…to go home and yet, where was home now? Could home be anywhere when her heart had already decided where it wanted to be? 'I didn't mean that.'

'You had every right to say it.' Rik gestured to a room to their left. 'There's a private lounge there. Will you give me a few minutes, Mel? Please? You will still be able to make this flight if you want to, or a next one. Anything you want, but please let me try—'

'All right.' She led the way to the room, pushed the door open and stepped inside. Somehow it felt important to take that initiative. To be in charge even if she was agreeing to stall her plans to speak with him.

It was a small room. The lounge suite was quintessential airport "luxury". Deep red velvet with large cushions all immaculately kept. There were matching drapes opened wide and a view of runways with planes in various stages of arrival and departure.

All Mel could see was Rik's blue eyes, fixed on her brown ones, searching as though there was something that he desperately needed to find.

'This isn't a fairy tale, Rik. I know you're a prince but to me you'll always be a man first. You'll be Rik, who I—' Fell in love with. She bit back the words.

'No. There is little of the fairy tale about current circumstances and I confess I was shocked by my father's announcement of a secret brother.' Rik did take her hand now, and led her to a lounge seat.

Somehow they were seated with her hand still held in his and far too much of a feeling of rightness inside Mel's foolish, foolish heart. 'I hope that situation can be worked out so that nobody loses too much.'

'I do not know what is possible. I have not had time

to get all the facts together, let alone think of how to act on any of them.' For this moment Rik brushed the topic aside. 'Melanie, I asked you to marry me permanently—'

'But deep down even though you have to do it, you don't want to be tied in a relationship like that, and I… can't do it when—' She ground to a halt.

'When I offered all those things that don't matter to you, and nothing else? They never have.' One side of Rik's mouth lifted in a wry, self-mocking twist. 'Everything that makes me a prince, that might appeal, doesn't matter to you. I was too slow to think about that, and too slow to understand why I needed so much for you to agree to help me anyway.'

Was it care that she saw in his eyes? Mel didn't want to hope. Not now. Not when she'd made up her mind to go and that was the only solution. 'You'll find someone, Rik. You'll be able to marry and hold onto your job. I'm sorry it will have to be for all your life. I'm sorry for that.'

Each word tightened the ache in her chest. Each glance at him made it harder to keep the tremor out of her voice.

'The thing is, all that has changed for me, Melanie. It has changed because I fell in love with you.' His words were low. Raw.

Real? Mel frowned. Shook her head. There was no allergy medication to blame now. Nothing but a hope and sense of loss so deep that she was afraid she'd heard those words only inside her, afraid to hear them at all, and so she denied. 'No.'

'The moment I took you into my arms and made love to you, I fell in love with you.' This time when he said it, emotion crowded *his* face. 'Please believe me that this is true.'

Mel had never seen that emotion, except…lurking in the backs of his eyes when he held her last night…

Could she believe this? Could Rik truly have fallen in love with her? 'You're a prince.'

'As you said when we first met.' He inclined his head. His eyes didn't twinkle, but memory was there.

'I'm a cook. From Australia.' A commoner with no fixed abode. 'I didn't even know how to curtsy properly.'

Do you really love me, Rik?

Could he really love *her*, Nicole Melanie Watson? 'You said you would never love.'

'I didn't know there would be you, and that you would come to live, not only at the palace, but that you would move into my heart.' He took both her hands into his.

She glanced down. 'The ring! I meant to leave it in the suite.'

'*Our* suite. I am glad you didn't take it off.' He touched the diamonds. 'It is made to be there.' His gaze lifted to hers. 'I know I am asking for another leap of faith, and if you cannot find anything in your heart for me then I will accept it, but I am hoping against all hope that you will agree to give me a chance to show you how deeply I have come to love you.'

'I want to, Rik.' Oh, she wanted to do that with all of *her* heart. 'If you truly love me—'

'I do.' He didn't hesitate. Conviction filled his tone. 'If you can learn to love *me*, I will be the happiest man in the world.'

'That was what you meant about the glass slipper.' She hadn't realised that he wanted to make her his princess truly, in every way. 'I'm a practical girl, Rik. I like cooking and I lost my parents and grew up trying to be loved and my aunt and uncle and Nicolette didn't, and I promised myself I would never be hurt like that again.'

But she'd opened her heart to Rik and he…loved her. 'Are you sure? Because I don't know how you could have overcome all that. You were so firmly fixed that you wouldn't be able to have that kind of relationship.'

'I thought I was incapable of experiencing those feelings. Love, commitment.'

'Your upbringing harmed you.' Mel didn't want to hurt him with the words, but they were part of *his* history, of who he was.

'We have both experienced hurt at the hands of family.' There was regret and acknowledgement, and love shining in his eyes openly for her now. 'But you have set all of my love free.'

Mel believed it then. She let go of the last doubt and took her leap of faith. 'I fell in love with you, too, Rik. I thought I was going to help you to solve a problem and then go back to Australia. Instead I wanted to stay with you for ever, but when you asked me—'

'I stupidly didn't realise what those feelings inside meant.' He drew a breath that wasn't quite steady. 'I thought I'd lost you. I couldn't bear that thought.' Again his fingers touched her ring as he drew her to her feet with him and held both her hands. 'Will you marry me next week, Mel? Give me a chance to show you every day for ever how much you mean to me?'

'Yes.' Melanie said it and stepped into his arms and, oh, it felt right. So, so right, to be in Rik's arms, in the prince's arms, where she belonged. There were no sparkly shoes. She wasn't down a rabbit hole. She had simply…come home to this man of her dreams. 'Yes, I will marry you next week and stay married for ever, and love you every single day while you love me every single day.'

Mel knew there would be hurdles. She was marrying a prince! But she would give all of her heart to him and now she knew that she could trust it into his love and care.

He glanced out of the window and smiled. 'You've missed your flight. Let's go…home and start counting the days until next week.'

'The wedding planner is going to be relieved that she doesn't have to start all over again.' A smile started on Melanie's face and she tucked her arm through Rik's and they left the room and made their way out of the airport to a car parked and waiting for Rik. The keys were in it, just as though it had been brought for him and left specially.

Well, it would have been, wouldn't it? Mel thought. After all, he was a prince.

And Melanie Watson, cook, was marrying him.

For now and for ever.

And that seemed exactly right.

EPILOGUE

'THERE is nothing to be nervous about.' Anrai spoke the words to Melanie as they made their way towards the rear-entry door of the church. 'And thank you for allowing me to be the one to escort you for this occasion.'

Melanie drew a deep breath and glanced at her soon-to-be brother-in-law from beneath the filmy bridal veil. Excitement filled her. This was the moment that she and Rik had worked towards, and that now would be the fulfilment of very new and special dreams for them. 'You know that I love him.'

'Yes. He is lucky. I do not profess to hold similar hope for myself, but I am glad that you have found each other.' Anrai's words were warm, accepting, and then the doors were thrown open and music started and they began the long walk to the front of the church.

Soft gasps filled the air as guests saw the beautiful gown, the train that whispered behind her. A hint of lace. Tiny pearls stitched in layers. A princess neckline for an everyday girl about to become that princess.

Mel's glance shifted to one row of seats in the church. To her uncle, and aunt, and her cousin. Her gaze meshed with Nicolette's for a moment. Nicolette looked attractive in a pale pink chiffon gown. But today the attention was all for Melanie.

For a moment Mel felt a prick of sadness, but she couldn't make her cousin see that love came from within, was a gift so much more important than any material thing.

It was Nicolette who looked away, who couldn't seem to hold her cousin's gaze any longer.

And then there was Rik at the front of the church, waiting faithfully without glancing back until Anrai arrived with Mel on his arm and passed her hand to Rik's arm, placing it there as Mel's father would have done if he'd been here.

Warmth spread through Mel's chest as she looked into her prince's eyes and saw the love and happiness there and somehow she thought her parents might have been watching. She felt their love and warmth, too.

'Dearly beloved…' The priest began the service.

And there before God and his witnesses, Nicole Melanie Watson married Rikardo Eduard Ettonbierre, third prince of Braston.

He *did* have several titles and various bits of land.

His wife-to-be *was* a wonderful cook.

And they were still working on the agreement about who got ownership of any of Rufusina's offspring should the hog ever choose to bless them with a litter.

But Rik and Mel were happy today, and they would remain happy. And Rufusina's offspring were a whole other legend…

* * * * *

THE PRINCE'S
SECOND CHANCE

BY
BRENDA HARLEN

First published in Great Britain 2012
by Mills & Boon, an imprint of Harlequin (UK) Limited,
Eton House, 18-24 Paradise Road, Richmond, Surrey TW9 1SR

© Brenda Harlen 2011

ISBN: 978 0 263 89408 0

23-0212

Harlequin (UK) policy is to use papers that are natural, renewable and
recyclable products and made from wood grown in sustainable forests. The
logging and manufacturing processes conform to the legal environmental
regulations of the country of origin.

Printed and bound in Spain
by Blackprint CPI, Barcelona

Dear Reader,

Gabriella Vasquez and her "Dear Gabby" column were originally created to introduce an online read story. She was only supposed to be a promotional tool, not a heroine. I certainly had no intention of giving her a story of her own.

But as Gabby wrote her columns, there was a common thread in her responses to readers—an animosity towards the prince regent's cousin, Cameron Leandres. And who could blame her? In the original series, he tried to usurp the throne from Prince Rowan and he put the moves on Prince Marcus's girlfriend—and almost every other female in sight.

Still, Gabriella's aversion to the prince seemed deeply personal, and I began to wonder: what could have happened to make her dislike him so much? And I began to worry: could I make this prince into a hero? Because obviously there was some kind of history between these two characters…and it was a story I needed to tell. *The Prince's Second Chance* is that story—I hope you enjoy it!

Best,

Brenda Harlen

Brenda Harlen grew up in a small town surrounded by books and imaginary friends. Although she always dreamed of being a writer, she chose to follow a more traditional career path first. After two years of practicing as a lawyer (including an appearance in front of the Supreme Court of Canada), she gave up her "real" job to be a mum and to try her hand at writing books. Three years, five manuscripts and another baby later, she sold her first book.

Brenda lives in southern Ontario with her real-life husband/hero, two heroes-in-training and two neurotic dogs. She is still surrounded by books (too many books, according to her children) and imaginary friends, but she also enjoys communicating with "real" people. Readers can contact Brenda by e-mail at brendaharlen@yahoo.com.

In memory of Catherine Elizabeth Witmer
~writer, reader, reviewer & friend~

Chapter One

"Do you have a minute?"

It wasn't every day that Cameron Leandres looked up from his desk to find Rowan Santiago, his cousin and the prince regent of Tesoro del Mar, standing in the doorway of his office.

"Of course," Cameron said, because he couldn't imagine responding in any other way to the ruler of the country. "But not much more than that—I'm meeting with the Ardenan Trade Minister at nine-thirty."

"Actually, that meeting has been…postponed," Rowan told him.

Cameron frowned. "No one told me."

"I just got off the phone with Benedicto Romero."

He immediately recognized the name of Ardena's king and waited silently, apprehensively, for his cousin to continue.

"He's furious about this morning's paper and threatening not to renew our trade agreement."

"I skimmed the front section," Cameron said. "I didn't see anything that would impact our negotiations."

"Did you check the society pages?" The prince regent tossed the paper onto his desk.

The photo and the headline battled for his attention, but it was the bold words that won out: *Prince Cameron Adds New Notch to His Bedpost?*

It was a mockery of the headline that had run on the front page only a few days earlier, *Prince Cameron Adds New Title to His Portfolio*, announcing that he'd been named the country's new Minister of Trade. He didn't want to know what *this* article claimed, but his eyes automatically began to skim the brief paragraph.

Apparently his new responsibilities on the political scene haven't curbed the prince's extracurricular activities. In fact, just last night the prince was spotted at Club Sapphire making some serious moves on the dance floor—and on the King of Ardena's youngest daughter.

Cameron clenched his jaw, holding back the vehement curse that instinctively sprang to his lips. He glanced at the photo again, recognizing the woman who had plastered herself against him on the dance floor.

"I didn't know that she was the king's daughter," he said, ruefully acknowledging that truth wasn't much of a defense.

"The king's seventeen-year-old daughter."

Cameron dropped his head into his hands, and this time he didn't manage to hold back the curse.

"Did you sleep with her?" Rowan asked bluntly.

"No!" Maybe he shouldn't have been shocked by the question, but he was. And while he might have told anyone else that it wasn't their business, he couldn't say that to the prince regent. They both knew his actions reflected on his office.

He was relieved to be able to assert his innocence in this situation, because even if he hadn't guessed that the woman in the photo was underage, he had known that she was far too young for even a serious flirtation. While he hadn't always been discriminating in his choice of female companions, he was thirty-six years old now and long past the age where he was easily seduced by a warm body and willing smile.

"I was there with Allegra de Havilland," he explained, naming his frequent if not exclusive companion of the past six months, "and this girl—she only said her name was Leticia— came up to me on the dance floor while my date was in the ladies' room. We didn't even dance for two minutes. When Allegra came back, she and I left."

His cousin nodded. "Then there's no reason to believe that this can't be salvaged."

Cameron didn't know how to respond. His cousin had taken a chance on him six years earlier when he'd first appointed him to his cabinet, after Cameron had done everything in his power to undermine Rowan's position. At the time, he'd suspected that Rowan was subscribing to the old adage "keep your friends close and your enemies closer" and he couldn't blame him for that. But over time, as they'd worked together on various projects, they'd developed a mutual respect for one another. And Cameron would forever be grateful to his cousin for giving him the chance to be something more than a worthless title in the history books.

When he finally spoke, it was only to say, "I regret that this has caused a problem with the king."

Rowan nodded. "You need to be extra cautious and remember that, as a royal and a member of public office, everything you say and do is subject to media scrutiny."

"Do you want my resignation?" He held his breath, waiting for his cousin's response.

"No, I don't want your resignation. You've been an asset to this administration."

Cameron exhaled. "Do you want me to talk to the king?"

"No," Rowan said again. "I've invited him to join me for lunch. Hopefully I can smooth things over with him then."

Cameron refused to consider what the repercussions might be if his cousin failed. Rowan hadn't been born for the position he was in, but he'd stepped in without missing a beat when Julian and Catherine, his brother and sister-in-law, were killed in a fluke explosion on their yacht.

Maybe Cameron had resented Rowan's appointment back then, because he'd felt that he was just as qualified and capable of doing the prince regent's job. But over the past half-dozen years, he'd realized that he didn't want those duties and responsibilities, even on an interim basis. And he regretted that his own actions—however inadvertent—were making his cousin's job more difficult.

"I also contacted *La Noticia*," Rowan continued. "Because I was annoyed that Alex would run such a headline without at least giving us a heads-up."

Alex Girard was the society columnist for the local paper whose fair and objective reporting had earned him several invitations to the palace and the opportunity to write exclusive stories about the royal family. Now that Cameron thought about it, it wasn't only out-of-character for the reporter to launch an attack on a member of the prince regent's cabinet but potentially detrimental to his own career.

"As it turns out, Alex didn't have anything to do with the story. He's out of the country for a couple of weeks so the society pages are being covered by another staff writer—Gabriella Vasquez."

Cameron should have guessed that. Not that she'd always hated him. In fact, there was a time when they'd been extremely close. But that was long before she'd become "Dear Gabby" and started using her column to vilify both his character and his activities. And while her references to him had always been unmistakable, she was usually more subtle in her condemnation. Now she'd apparently taken the gloves off.

And he was prepared to do the same.

* * *

Gabriella wasn't surprised when she received the summons to her editor's office, but she did feel the tiniest twinge of guilt when she saw Allison Jenkins—one of her oldest and dearest friends—rubbing her forehead, as she often did when a major headache was brewing.

"You wanted to see me?" Gabriella said.

The editor looked up. "I'm sure you know why."

"Since there wasn't anything particularly controversial in my 'Dear Gabby' column this week, I'm guessing this is about the 'Around Town' segment."

"Would you also like to take a guess as to how many phone calls I've received this morning? Or how many emails have flooded my inbox?"

Gabriella's own office computer had actually been so over-loaded with incoming messages that it had crashed, but she was unconcerned. Everyone knew that the newspaper business was suffering and anything that increased circulation—as her contribution to the society pages had done exponentially—couldn't be a bad thing.

"So put your big girl panties on and deal with it," Gabriella said. "That's why they pay you the big bucks."

Alli shook her head. "You're not even sorry."

"Why should I be? I didn't write anything that wasn't true."

"You may have created an international scandal," her editor warned.

"*I* wasn't dirty dancing with the King of Ardena's underage daughter," she pointed out.

"They were dancing," Alli repeated. "There is absolutely no evidence of anything more than that."

"I never said that there was."

"No," her boss agreed. "But your text implies that the prince is a seducer of virgins."

Gabriella knew that he was, but she didn't intend to admit

that to her boss. "Royal headlines sell papers," she reminded Allison.

"And we get a lot of inside news because we've worked hard to establish a good relationship with the palace."

"Do you really think anyone at the palace even noticed an article buried in the middle of page twelve?"

"I don't think it, I know it," Alli told her. "Because one of the multitude of phone calls that I received was from Prince Rowan."

Gabriella swallowed. "The prince regent called you?"

"And he wasn't very happy."

"Then I'll apologize for putting you in an awkward position," she said. "But I can't apologize for what I wrote. Prince Cameron uses his title and his charm to lure women into his bed and innocent girls should be forewarned."

"Then take out a public service announcement with your name on it but don't use this newspaper to pursue what is obviously a personal vendetta."

Gabriella felt the sting of that reprimand because she knew there was some truth in her boss's words. When Alex Girard had asked her to cover the celebrity watch while he was on vacation, she'd had mixed feelings about the request. For the better part of sixteen years, she'd been careful to steer clear of anyone connected with the royal family. Of course, that hadn't been too difficult for a commoner who didn't move in the same circles they did.

But this new assignment would require Gabriella to seek them out, to go to the places they were known to frequent, to rub elbows with their friends and acquaintances. Of course, the assignment was broader than the royal family, but everyone knew that the Santiagos and the Leandreses were the real celebrities in Tesoro del Mar.

"For Monday's paper, I wrote about the prince regent's picnic at the beach with his family. Tuesday, I covered Princess Molly's book launch and her reading at the library. Yesterday,

I was out of town interviewing the Hollywood elite who are filming a romantic comedy in San Pedro. In fact, I didn't even want to go to Club Sapphire last night, but I got a tip that 'several people of note' were going to be there, so I went."

"Who else was there?" Alli wanted to know.

"Most of the Hollywood contingent," Gabriella admitted.

"Why didn't you get any pictures of them?"

"Because I already have a ton of photos that were taken during the interview sessions."

Alli dropped her head into her hands. "Are you trying to give me an ulcer?"

"I did my job," Gabriella said.

"Which you could have done just as effectively by concentrating on the visiting actors—what they were wearing, what they were drinking, who was hooked up with whom."

"And ignoring the prince's presence?" Gabriella challenged.

"It would have been enough to reference the fact that Prince Cameron was there," her editor insisted.

"With the king's daughter," Gabriella reminded her.

"I'm going to end up with an ulcer and a pink slip," Alli muttered. "But at least I'll have you to keep me company when I'm unemployed."

"I didn't cross any lines."

"Tell that to the legal department when we get slapped with a libel suit."

"It's not libelous if it's true," Gabriella insisted.

"But the truth is often a matter of opinion, isn't that correct, Ms. Vasquez?"

Gabriella recognized that voice. Even after more than sixteen years, the smooth, sexy tone hadn't faded from her memory, and her breath caught in her throat as she spun around to face the door.

Cameron.

"This day just keeps getting better and better," Alli grumbled, but not so loudly that the prince could hear.

Gabriella didn't see her friend move—she couldn't seem to tear her eyes from the man lounging indolently against the doorjamb—but she heard the chair slide and knew that Alli was rising to her feet in deference to the man at her door. She would probably even curtsy.

Gabriella refused to do the same. She wouldn't bow and scrape to this man. Not now, not ever again.

But she couldn't deny that seeing him made her heart slam against her ribs, and while she was determined to play the scene out coolly and casually, her knees had gone just a little weak.

He hadn't changed much in sixteen years. His hair was still thick and dark and slightly tousled, as if he couldn't be bothered to tame it. His golden-brown eyes were further enhanced by thick, black lashes and bold, arched brows. His perfectly-shaped and seductively-soft lips were now compressed in a firm line, the only outward sign of his displeasure.

He was dressed in a charcoal-colored suit with a snowy white shirt that enhanced his olive skin and a black-and-silver patterned tie. But in his case, it was the man who made the clothes rather than vice versa, and not just because he was a royal but because of the supreme confidence he wore even more comfortably than the designer threads on his back.

On closer inspection, she realized that there were some subtle signs of the passing of time: a few strands of gray near his temples, laugh lines fanning out from his eyes, but certainly nothing that detracted from his overall appearance.

His shoulders seemed just as broad as she remembered; his body appeared as hard and lean. He'd always known who he was, what he wanted, and he'd never let anything—or anyone—stand in his way. He was as outrageously sexy and devilishly handsome as ever, and she'd never stood a chance.

"Do you think we could speak privately in your office?"

Cameron asked her, his tone as casual as his posture—and in complete contradiction to the anger that she saw glinting in the depths of those hazel eyes.

Gabriella lifted her chin. "I don't have an office, I have a cubicle. Not all of us are handed cushy jobs with—"

"You can use mine," Alli interrupted hastily, shooting daggers at Gabriella as she moved past her on the way to the door. "I have to get to a meeting with the marketing director, anyway."

"Thank you," Cameron said, inclining his head toward her.

Gabriella had no intention of thanking her boss. She was feeling anything but grateful at the prospect of being stuck in Allison's tiny little office with a man who had always made her feel overwhelmed in his presence. But she squared her shoulders, reminded herself that she wasn't seventeen years old anymore, and faced him defiantly.

In the more than sixteen years that had passed since he'd dated Gabriella Vasquez, Cameron hadn't forgotten about her, but many of the details had faded from his mind. Facing her now, those details came flooding back, washing over him in a powerful wave that left his head struggling to stay above water.

When they'd first met, her hair was a tumbling mass of curls that fell to the middle of her back. Now, the sexy sun-streaked dark tresses grazed her shoulders and the shorter style drew attention to her face, to the dusky gold skin, cocoa-colored eyes, long, inky lashes, and soft, full lips that promised a taste of heaven.

His gaze drifted lower. From her full, round breasts to a narrow waist and the subtle flare of slim hips and down long, lean legs. His hands ached to trace the familiar contours as they'd done so many years before, and he had to curl his fingers into his palms to resist the urge to reach for her.

But even more than her physical attributes, what had attracted him was that she had spirit and spunk—even when she knew she was outgunned, she didn't surrender. From the first time they met, she'd been a challenge—and an incredible pleasure. He pushed aside the memory, firmly slammed the door on the past.

"Sixteen years is a long time to hold a grudge, wouldn't you agree?" he asked her.

"I would," she said easily. "And while I realize you may find this difficult to believe, the page twelve article wasn't about you."

He snorted, confirming his disbelief.

"The 'Around Town' section of the newspaper covers celebrity sightings and rumors. I saw you at the club with Princess Leticia and it seemed obvious to me that royalty hooking up with royalty would make some pretty good headlines."

"So it was just about selling papers?"

"That's my job," she said pleasantly.

"Why don't I believe you?"

She shrugged. "I've been writing an advice column for *La Noticia* for twelve years—my editor could confirm that fact, but you scared her away."

He felt a smile tug at the corners of his mouth, but refused to give into it. "Maybe because your editor has more sense than you do."

"Maybe," she agreed.

"You don't think I could have you fired?" he challenged softly.

Her eyes flashed, but her tone remained even when she responded. "I'm sure you could, but then I would have to sue for unlawful termination and all the gory details would be revealed, putting far too much importance on one little article."

His gaze narrowed. "That 'one little article' may result in

the King of Ardena walking away from a trade agreement that has been in place for more than fifty years."

"That would be unfortunate," she said, "but hardly my fault."

"You implied that I seduced his daughter."

"Did you?" She held up her hands. "Sorry. Forget I asked. I don't want to know and it's none of my business."

He gritted his teeth, but before he could respond, the ring of a cell phone intruded.

"Excuse me," she said, turning away from him to check the display on the slim instrument he hadn't realized was in her hand. Frowning, she connected the call. "Sierra?"

He couldn't hear what the caller was saying, but judging by the way Gabriella's face paled, the news was not good.

He was more than a little annoyed with her, irritated by her easy dismissal of him, and furious about the headlines she'd manufactured. So why did seeing the obvious distress on her face bother him? Why did he wish she would turn *to* him rather than turn away?

Gabriella's hands were unsteady as she closed the phone. The call had obviously shaken her, but when she turned back to him again, her face was carefully composed.

"As fascinating as this conversation has been," she said lightly, "I have to go."

"We're not done here, Gabriella."

She lifted her chin in a gesture that intrigued him as much as it irked him. "If you have any other concerns about the job I'm doing, take them up with my editor."

He let her brush past him and head out the door, and he tried to ignore the regret that gnawed at his belly.

There was no point in wishing that he'd handled things differently sixteen years earlier, no point in wondering where they might be now if he had. He'd been given more than enough second chances in his life; he couldn't expect another one from Gabriella.

And even if he wasn't still royally ticked about her creative reporting, she'd made it more than clear that she had no interest in him whatsoever. Not that he was entirely sure he believed her claim. Because if she truly didn't have any feelings for him, why did she continue to target him in her column? Why had she written a headline that she had to know would get his attention?

I did my job.

Her words echoed in his mind and he wondered if it really was as simple as that. Maybe he only wanted to believe that she'd never forgotten about him because he'd never forgotten about her.

They'd dated for only a few months, and although he'd dated a lot of other women both before and after his brief affair with Gabriella, no one else had ever lingered in his mind the way she had done.

She'd been both naive and inexperienced—and not at all his type. But there was something about her innocence that tugged at him, something about her purity and sweetness that had thoroughly captivated him.

She hadn't been similarly entranced. While a lot of women had wanted to be with him because he was a prince, Gabriella had seemed more intimidated than impressed by his title— and determined to keep him at a distance. But he'd never been the type to take a detour just because someone had set up a roadblock, and that was an aspect of his personality that hadn't changed in the past sixteen years.

No, Gabriella, he thought as he followed her path out the door. *We're not even close to being done.*

Chapter Two

Gabriella was still shaking as she exited through the automatic doors and stepped into the bright sunshine, but she knew it wasn't Sierra's phone call alone that was responsible for her distress. Learning that a child was in the hospital would be enough to send any parent into a panic, but hearing her daughter's voice had reassured Gabriella somewhat. Of course, she wouldn't be completely reassured until she'd held Sierra in her arms, so she unlocked the door and sank into the driver's seat, anxious to get to the hospital to do just that.

She tried to put Cameron Leandres out of her mind as she drove, but her thoughts were torn between worry for her daughter and worry for herself—and the secret she'd been holding on to for sixteen years.

It was her own fault. She should have realized that there would be repercussions if she continued to taunt him in print. But she'd been so angry with him for so long, and when she'd seen him at the club, up close and personal for the first time in so many years, she'd been overwhelmed by memories and emotions. And then she'd seen him dancing with the young Ardenan princess, and she'd recognized the look on the teen-ager's face when she'd gazed up at the prince because she'd once looked at him exactly the same way.

And for just a little while, Cameron had looked back at Gabriella as if she was the center of his world, and she'd let herself believe that she could be. She'd deluded herself into trusting that he truly cared about her, that she actually mattered to him. She wasn't the first woman to make that mistake, and she certainly hadn't been the last, though that knowledge didn't lessen her heartache in the slightest.

But that was a long time ago, and she was over him, wholly and completely. And if her heart had done a funny little skip when she'd seen him standing in the doorway of Allison's office, well, that wasn't really surprising. He was still an in-credibly attractive man and any woman would have responded the same way. In fact, she'd be willing to bet that even Alli's cynical heart had gone pitter-patter. Not that she was going to question her editor about it. In fact, if she never again heard his name from her friend's lips, it would be too soon.

But just as she pulled into the hospital parking lot, her phone beeped to indicate an incoming text message. She drove into a vacant spot and checked the display.

where r u? r u with the prince? i came back to my office and u both were gone and i picked up some pretty heavy vibes btwn the 2 of u.

So much for thinking she might be able to avoid the topic, but it was easier to lie to her friend when she didn't have to look her in the eye. So she texted back:

I got a call from Sierra. She was in a fender bender with a friend. I'm at the hospital now, will check in with you later.

Then she tucked the phone in her purse, put both Allison Jenkins and Cameron Leandres out of her mind, and went into the hospital.

"Sierra Vasquez?" she said to the nurse behind the desk.

"First room on the right, third curtain on the left."

"Thank you."

She found her daughter exactly where the nurse had indicated. She looked so small and pale on the narrow hospital cot, the fluorescent yellow cast on her arm a bright contrast to the pale green sheets on the bed. Her heels clicked on the tile floor as she crossed the room, and Sierra's eyes flicked open.

"Hi, Mom."

"Hi." She brushed a dark curl off of her daughter's forehead and touched her lips to the pale skin there. "You told me you weren't hurt."

"I'm not," Sierra said. "Not really. And I didn't want you to freak out."

"Do I look like I'm freaking out?"

Sierra's lips tilted up at the corners. "I know when you're freaking out, even when no one else does."

"Well, it's a mother's prerogative to worry about her child." She pulled a chair up beside the bed. "How's Jenna?"

"Not a scratch. Her mom came and got her already. Mrs. Azzaro wanted to wait to see you, but she had a deposition or something that she had to get back to court for."

"I'll call Luisa tonight," Gabriella said, and took Sierra's hand in hers. "So what happened?"

"A cat ran across the road. Jenna swerved to avoid it and ended up hitting a lamppost."

"I didn't even know Jenna had her license," she noted.

"She got it three weeks ago," Sierra admitted.

"And her parents let her drive to school?"

"Probably the first and last time."

"Probably," Gabriella said. "Although I'm sure Don and

Luisa are just as relieved as I am that no one was seriously injured."

"I wish I could say the same about the car."

"Cars can be fixed," Gabriella said.

"Speaking of fixed," Sierra said. "Why are you all fixed up today?"

Gabriella glanced down at her matching skirt and jacket. She'd always told Sierra that one of the greatest advantages of working from home was being able to work in her pj's. Not that she usually did so, but she also didn't dig "the good clothes" out of the back of her closet or torture her feet in three-inch heels except for rare visits to the newspaper offices.

"I had a meeting with my editor this morning."

Her daughter's brows rose.

"Don't ask," Gabriella told her.

"I'm sorry if I dragged you away from something important," Sierra said.

"Nothing is more important than you." She put her arm across her daughter's shoulder, hugged her carefully. "And I don't think I need to point out that this accident wouldn't have happened if you'd been at school, where you were supposed to be."

"I had a free period, Mom."

"During which you're supposed to do your homework or study."

"Jenna wanted to get a new pair of shoes for her date with Kevin tonight and there was a sale…" her explanation trailed off when she caught the look on her mother's face. "Okay, I won't leave school property again without getting your permission first."

"And to make sure you remember that, you're grounded for a week."

"A week?" Sierra squawked indignantly.

"Are you angling for two?" Gabriella asked.

Her daughter sighed. "Okay—a week."

Gabriella stood up again. "Now I'm going to find the doctor to get you out of here, then we'll go rent some movies and spend the night—"

"You're not staying home with me tonight, Mom."

She frowned. "Why not?"

"Because Rafe's flying in for the weekend, and he said he was going to make reservations at L'Atelier." Sierra frowned at her. "You forgot, didn't you?"

"No," she denied, although not very convincingly. But she hadn't forgotten so much as she'd pushed the information to the back of her mind, not nearly as excited about Rafe's plans as her daughter seemed to be.

"This could be the night," Sierra continued, "and I'm not going to be the one to screw things up for you."

She didn't need to when Gabriella was perfectly capable of screwing things up entirely on her own, and probably would. But she wasn't going to think about that now. She wasn't going to worry about what might or might not happen with the American businessman who had started dropping hints about the future he wanted for them together.

"Honey, Rafe and I can have dinner another time. I don't want you to be alone tonight."

"Paolo could come over to watch movies with me."

Gabriella raised her eyebrows. "And I certainly don't want you alone with your boyfriend."

Sierra rolled her eyes. "I didn't expect we would be alone—Grandma will be home, won't she?"

Still, she hesitated.

"I only broke my wrist," Sierra said. "That's no reason for you to break your plans with Rafe."

"Rafe will understand."

Sierra sighed. "Mom, he's going to ask you to marry him tonight."

"He didn't tell you that, did he?"

"No, but I'm not an idiot. An impromptu visit, dinner at L'Atelier, something important to discuss…"

No, her daughter definitely wasn't an idiot. And Gabriella knew she should be pleased that Sierra obviously liked and approved of the man her mother had been dating for the past year and a half. Of course, everyone liked Rafe. He was a wonderful man—handsome and successful and generous and giving, and Gabriella cared for him a great deal. But marriage?

She was almost thirty-four years old and she'd lost her innocence a long time ago, but she was still relatively naive and inexperienced. She'd fallen head over heels in love only once, when she was barely seventeen years old, and her life experiences after that had been very different from most other girls her age. She'd survived first love and first heartbreak, but it had taken her a long time to put the pieces of her shattered heart back together.

While she'd long ago abandoned her girlish dreams of walking down the aisle, she'd believed that her heart was sufficiently mended that she could fall in love again. But as wonderful as Rafe was—and he truly was—something still held her back.

She refused to let herself think about what that something— or who that someone—might be.

Cameron didn't feel like going out. After being ambushed by the underage princess at Club Sapphire the night before, he wanted only to stay home, far away from the prying eyes of the paparazzi.

Maybe he was getting old. Since his thirtieth birthday, more than six years ago, he'd started to think that he wanted more than an endless parade of interchangeable women through his life. Spending time with friends and family members who were happily married had further convinced him that he wanted that same kind of close connection with someone—someday. But it seemed that he could never stay with any one woman long enough to allow that kind of closeness to develop. Or maybe he'd just never met the right woman.

When Michael's daughter was born, Cameron had become even more aware of the emptiness of his own life. The realization that he wanted a family wasn't just unexpected but shocking, considering how screwed up his own family had been.

His father—Gaetan Leandres—had been a farmer by birth and by trade and he'd been content with his lot in life, at least until he'd had the misfortune of falling in love with a princess. They'd married against, and possibly to spite, her father's wishes, and they'd had three children together. Cameron believed that Elena had loved her husband, but when Gaetan had died and left her alone, she'd suddenly resented everything that she'd given up to be with him.

So she'd tried to pass her dreams and ambitions on to her children. Michael, her firstborn, had always known what he wanted and had refused to let her manipulate him. Marissa, her youngest child and only daughter, had mostly escaped Elena's attention by virtue of her gender. So it was almost by default that she'd focused her efforts on her second son.

And Cameron, still looking for his own place and purpose in life, had been much more susceptible to his mother's manipulations. As a result, he'd done some things he wasn't proud of, hurt a lot of people who never should have been hurt, and walked away from the only woman he'd ever loved.

Walked away? His lips twisted wryly. No, what he'd done was push her away—so forcefully and finally that she'd never wanted to look back. And Cameron had never let himself look back, either. He'd never let himself admit that he might have made a mistake, that every woman he'd been with since had been little more than a pale substitute for her.

Until today when, for the first time in more than sixteen years, he'd found himself face-to-face with her again.

Gabriella Vasquez—the only woman who had ever taken hold of his heart.

He closed his eyes, as if that might banish her image from his mind. He didn't want to think of her now, to remember what they'd once shared, to imagine what might have been. There was no point. Gabriella was his past and he had to look to the future.

Not that a status-conscious socialite like Allegra was a woman he could imagine being with for the rest of his life. But hopefully a casual meal with his frequent companion would generate some positive publicity to counteract all the negative headlines of last night's fiasco at Club Sapphire.

And there would be publicity—of that he had no doubt. Gone were the days when he only had to worry about card-carrying members of the media shoving cameras in his face—now they hid in the shadows and used telephoto lenses. And even if no paparazzi were around, there would be someone with a camera in a cell phone eager to snap a shot.

He arrived at Allegra's condo at seven-fifteen, knowing she would keep him waiting at least fifteen minutes. He didn't usually mind, but for some reason, he found the delay tonight more than a little irritating. When Allegra swept into the room, however, he couldn't deny that she was worth the wait.

She was wearing a sheath-style dress of emerald green that molded to her slender frame and enhanced the color of her eyes. Her long, blond hair was styled in a fancy twist that was both sexy and sophisticated. Round emeralds surrounded by diamonds glittered at her ears and a matching pendant dangled between her breasts.

"I'm sorry I kept you waiting," she said.

"You look lovely," he said, his response as automatic as her apology, though probably more sincere.

"Would you like a drink before we go?" she asked, gesturing toward the well-stocked bar in the corner.

He shook his head. "We have reservations at L'Atelier and if we don't leave now, we'll be late."

"L'Atelier?" Her eyes lit up and her lips curved as she tucked her hand in his arms. "Aren't you full of surprises tonight?"

When they were seated at one of only a half-dozen tables in the exclusive upper-level dining room, Cameron ordered a bottle of Cristal because he knew it was Allegra's favorite.

During the course of the meal, they sipped the champagne and talked about nothing of importance. When the waiter cleared away his empty plate and the remnants of Allegra's coq au vin—because she never did more than sample her dinner—a flash of color near the doorway caught his eye.

A swirling red dress wrapped around luscious feminine curves. A tumble of dark curls that grazed sexy shoulders. A low, throaty laugh that shot through his blood like an exquisite cognac.

His breath caught; his throat went dry.

No, it couldn't be.

Then she turned, and his heart actually skipped a beat.

It *was* Gabriella.

He didn't recognize the man she was with, but he didn't really take a good look. He couldn't tear his eyes off of the woman who had preoccupied far too many of his thoughts since their encounter earlier that morning—the same woman who had haunted his dreams for far too many years.

She looked absolutely stunning. Sensual. Sexy. Seductive.

The return of the waiter with their dessert dragged his attention back to his own table. He noticed that Allegra was frowning slightly, obviously displeased by the wavering of his attention but reluctant to say anything about it.

He reached across the table for her hand, and she smiled at him. She was always quick to forgive and forget—and willing to disregard troublesome newspaper headlines. It was unfortunate, he thought, that he wasn't even close to falling in love with her.

"Allegra—"

She leaned forward, her eyes bright and filled with anticipation. "Yes?"

He drew in a breath. "I think we should take a break."

She blinked. Once. Twice. "*Excuse* me?"

He couldn't blame her for appearing shell-shocked. He had no idea where those words had come from. And yet, now that he'd spoken them, he felt an immense sense of relief—and more than a little bit of guilt.

"You brought me here tonight…to dump me?"

"No," he said. "I didn't plan— I mean, I'm not dumping you."

Her eyes filled with tears, but she valiantly held them in check. He breathed a silent sigh of relief, grateful that she wasn't the type of woman to make a nasty scene.

"It sure sounds that way to me." Her voice was cool and carefully controlled as she pushed her chair away from the table. Then she picked up her champagne glass and tossed the contents in his face. "You son of a bitch."

So much for thinking she wouldn't cause a scene, Cameron thought, as he wiped up the Cristal with his linen napkin.

Gabriella had escaped to the ladies' room for a moment of quiet to catch her breath and settle her nerves. As she'd readied herself for her date with Rafe, she'd worried about Sierra's prediction. When they'd arrived at the restaurant and been led to the upper level, her apprehension had increased.

She knew there were about half a dozen tables in the exclusive dining room, but the arrangement and décor were such that the diners at each table had the illusion of complete privacy. There were tall columns and lush greenery, soft lights and romantic music, and just walking into the scene had her stomach twisting into knots. Because in that moment, she knew that Sierra was right—Rafe had brought her here tonight because he was going to ask her to marry him, and she didn't know how she would respond to that question.

She considered calling her daughter and begging Sierra to call *her* with some trumped-up emergency that required Gabriella to immediately return home. The only reason she didn't make the call was that she knew she couldn't count on Sierra's complicity. Her daughter clearly thought it was a good idea for Gabriella to marry Rafe and wouldn't understand her hesitation. A hesitation that had led her to hiding out in the ladies' room rather than facing a perfectly wonderful man who wanted to spend his life with her.

As she was reapplying her lip gloss, the door to the ladies' room flew open. When a weeping woman flung herself onto the chaise lounge and buried her face in her hands, Gabriella realized that some people had bigger problems than she did.

She dropped the lip gloss back into her purse and glanced around, but the spacious room was otherwise empty. So she plucked a handful of tissues from the box on the counter and went to the sitting area, lowering herself to the edge of a chair facing the distraught woman.

Wordlessly, she offered the tissues.

The blonde lifted her head, looked at her through beautiful, tear-drenched eyes.

Gabriella barely managed to hold back a shocked gasp.

It had been awkward enough to imagine that she'd been trapped in the washroom with a broken-hearted but anonymous stranger. But she knew who this woman was—she was Allegra de Havilland, Prince Cameron's consort.

As quickly as Gabriella identified the woman, she also recognized that the juiciest headline of her career was in the palm of her hand.

Chapter Three

She immediately pushed the thought aside, ashamed that she would consider—even for a second—capitalizing on someone else's pain for the purpose of advancing her career. It wasn't as if she aspired to take over Alex Girard's "Around Town" column, after all, she was just having some fun with it while her colleague was on vacation. But it would be cruel to exploit Allegra's obvious heartache for a headline. So Gabriella didn't ask what the callous prince had done, she only asked, "Do you want me to call you a cab?"

The gorgeous heiress dabbed carefully at the mascara streaks under her eyes. But instead of answering Gabriella's question, she said, "I thought things were moving along nicely, that we were moving toward being exclusive."

"Men are usually a few steps behind women when it comes to relationships," Gabriella said lightly.

"I could have handled it if he said he needed more time, but he said we should take a break, spend some time apart."

Gabriella winced, understanding how harshly those insensitive words would slice through a heart that was filled with love. On the other hand, they weren't nearly as cold as the words—and the fistful of cash—he'd once thrown at her.

"Everyone warned me that he was a snake," Allegra continued, "but I didn't believe them. I didn't want to believe them, because he was always so considerate and charming."

Calling Cameron Leandres a snake was an insult to snakes, but Gabriella kept that assessment to herself, knowing that it would do nothing to ease Allegra's pain.

"After almost six months, he's suddenly changed his mind about what he wants?" Her eyes filled with tears again. "I want to hate him. There's a part of me that does hate him. But a bigger part really does love him." She dabbed at the streaks of mascara again, then her eyes suddenly went wide. "I'm so sorry—you must have a husband or a boyfriend or someone waiting for you—"

"It's okay," Gabriella assured her. "He won't mind."

"He must be a real prince of a guy," Allegra said softly.

She smiled at the irony. "He really is."

"Then you're a lucky woman."

Gabriella nodded. "So what are your plans for the rest of the night? Are you going back to your date—" she deliberately didn't use Cameron's name or title because she didn't want Allegra to know that she'd guessed his identity "—or do you want the maitre d' to call a cab for you?"

"I can't go back out there. I threw my champagne in his face."

Gabriella nearly choked trying to hold back a laugh. "Then you don't have to," she assured the other woman. "You wait here, and I'll come back to get you when your cab has arrived."

"You're being very kind," Allegra said gratefully.

"I've been where you are," she said, then, taking in the luxurious surroundings, she smiled wryly. "Well, not exactly.

But I've had my heart broken before, so I can relate—at least a little—to what you're feeling right now."

She took a quick detour to where Rafe was seated, to let him know what she was doing before she tracked down the maitre d'. She tried to apologize for the interruption of the romantic evening he'd planned but, Rafe being Rafe, he understood.

After she watched Allegra's cab pull away, she turned— and came face-to-face with Prince Cameron Leandres for the second time that day.

"I can just imagine the headlines that are scrolling through your mind," he said, a definite edge to his voice.

She smiled, unable to resist taunting him. "I doubt that you can."

"Why don't you give me a chance to tell my side of the story?"

"Because I'm not interested in anything you have to say." She started to move past him, but he caught her arm.

The jolt of heat that shot through her veins in response to the contact was as unwelcome as it was unexpected. As low as her opinion was of him, she had to wonder what it said about *her* that the briefest touch could send her pulse racing. Except that her heart had been pounding even before he'd touched her—even before she'd seen him standing there. It was as if she was hardwired to respond to this man as she'd never responded to anyone else before or since their long-ago affair.

But while she couldn't deny her instinctive reaction to him, she had no intention of letting him know the effect he had on her. Instead of yanking her arm from his grasp, as she wanted to do, she simply looked at his hand and lifted her brows, deliberately cool and unaffected.

His fingers uncurled, his hand dropped away. "Of course not," he said sardonically. "It's just about selling papers, right?"

"That's my job," she reminded him, then moved past him to return to her date.

But she was obviously more flustered than she wanted to admit, because as soon as she got back to the table, Rafe was on his feet, his brow furrowed with concern. "Are you okay?"

She forced a smile. "Yeah. It's just been a really long day."

"I ordered pizza," he told her.

She glanced up, startled. "Pizza?"

"From Pinelli's," he explained. "We can pick it up on the way back to your place."

"But—"

He touched a finger to her lips, silencing her protest. "We'll do this again some other time," he promised her.

"I'm sorry."

And she *was* sorry that she'd ruined the mood he'd so carefully set—but she was also relieved that he wouldn't be getting down on one knee tonight.

"Don't be," he said, and brushed his lips against hers.

The gentle kiss was as steady and reliable as the man who kissed her. There was no startling jolt of awareness, no unexpected surge of heat, nothing she couldn't handle. And Gabriella was glad for that. She didn't ever want to feel out of control again.

Rafe tossed more than enough cash on the table to pay for the bottle of champagne they'd barely touched and compensate the waiter for the tip on the hefty dinner tab he was missing out on as a result of their premature exit. Then they picked up two extra-large cheese and pepperoni pizzas on the way home, to share with Sierra and Paolo and Katarina, Gabriella's mother who had canceled her own plans in order to stay home and chaperone the young couple.

In the comfort of her home, surrounded by family, Gabriella found herself relaxing again. And when Rafe said that he was going to call it a night, she exhaled a silent sigh of relief as she walked him to the door. Obviously her suspicions about his intentions tonight had been off-base. As she'd told Allegra, women usually started thinking about commitment before men and Rafe was obviously happy with the status quo.

Or so she thought until he pulled a small, square box out of his jacket pocket.

Her eyes went wide, her breath caught, and she felt a fine sheen of perspiration bead on her brow.

Rafe chuckled, but the sound was strained. "Honestly, Gabriella, I've never known another woman who would blanch at the sight of a jeweler's box."

She swallowed, forced a smile. "I don't like to be predictable."

"No worries there." He flipped open the lid, and her eyes dropped back to the box with the same combination of fascination and trepidation that compelled passersby to gawk at the scene of an accident.

"Wow," she said, and swallowed again.

"I've had this ring for a couple of months now. I brought it with me tonight because I thought—I'd *hoped*—you might finally be ready to wear it." He closed the lid again and pressed the box into her hand. "But I know you're not, so I'm only going to ask you to hold on to it until you are."

She looked up at him, hoping he knew how truly sorry she was that she couldn't take the ring out of the box and put it on her finger. And hoping, just as desperately, that someday she would be ready.

It was with more than a little apprehension that Cameron unfolded his newspaper the next morning. Seeing nothing on the front page that was cause for concern, he turned the page. By the time he got to the "Around Town" section, he was mentally drafting his resignation, certain that nothing he could say or do would save his political career after Gabriella

Vasquez had pried all the intimate details of his latest failed relationship from his obviously unhappy ex-girlfriend. But the headline at the top of the page—*American Actress Storms Off Set*—gave him pause.

Although he didn't usually read the gossip columns, he forced himself to do so now, to ensure that he wasn't somehow to blame for the actress's behavior.

He skimmed several paragraphs about the drama that had taken place during filming of a romantic comedy in San Pedro, and then he found his name at the bottom of the page.

In other news: a rep for native supermodel Arianna Raquel has confirmed that the twenty-four-year-old is expecting her first child with Russian composer, Pavel Belyakova; and Prince Cameron and long-time girlfriend Allegra de Havilland were spotted dining at L'Atelier Friday evening.

He turned the page, looking for more. But that was it— barely a footnote at the very bottom of the page.

He exhaled a sigh, as surprised as he was relieved, and even more curious.

It was the curiosity that led him to track her down at her home and ask, "Why?"

Gabriella stared at him, appearing as surprised by his presence at her door at this early hour as by the inquiry.

"What are you doing here?" she demanded, completely disregarding his question to ask her own.

There was something in his tone that warned him she wasn't just surprised that he was there but…scared?

No, he was obviously misreading the situation. As she'd already proven that her pen was mightier than his sword, she had nothing to fear from him.

He shrugged. "I wanted to talk to you, but I didn't want

to have another conversation where we'd be surrounded by reporters."

"How did you know where I lived?"

"I called your editor." He'd expected a downtown address and had been surprised to find himself driving toward the outskirts of the city. He'd been even more surprised to pull up in front of a modest but well-kept two-story home on a quiet cul-de-sac.

It was a house made for a family, and it made him wonder if Gabriella had one. It wasn't unreasonable to expect that she'd married and had children at some point over the past sixteen years, even if she still looked more like a centerfold fantasy than a suburban mom.

He cut off his wandering thoughts before they could detour too far down that dangerous path, but cast a quick glance at her left hand and found that it was bare.

As bare as the long, slender legs that seemed to stretch for miles beneath the ragged hem of cutoff shorts she wore low on her hips. As bare as the sexy, curve of her shoulders peeking above the neckline of her peasant-style blouse. As bare as—

Gabriella's soft groan drew his attention back to their conversation. "You called Alli? Thanks. As if I didn't get enough of an interrogation after your appearance at the office yesterday, now you contacted her for my home address."

He cleared his throat, suddenly uncomfortably aware of her nearness, of the soft feminine scent that had always clouded his senses when he was near her. "I didn't realize that would be a problem."

"As if that would matter to you," she muttered.

"Can I come in?"

"No."

Her response—immediate and definitive—had him lifting his brows. "Do you really want to take the chance of someone spotting me standing on your doorstep?"

"If you didn't want to announce your presence to everyone on the street, you should have driven something a little more inconspicuous than an Aston Martin." But she did, reluctantly, step away from the door so that he could enter.

Of course, she didn't move any farther into the house than the foyer, and she faced him squarely, arms folded across her chest. The open-concept design allowed light to spill into the entranceway from the east-facing windows, and it surrounded Gabriella now, giving her an almost ethereal appearance. Although the dark scowl on her face spoiled the illusion somewhat.

He glanced around, appreciating how the sunny yellow walls complemented the terracotta floor. Her furniture was simple in design and neutral in color, with bold splashes of turquoise, lime and purple used as strategic accents.

"Nice place," he told her.

"Thank you," she responded stiffly. "But since I don't think you stopped by to compliment my décor, why don't you tell me why you're really here?"

"Because I can't figure you out."

"I don't know why you'd bother to try," she told him.

Her tone was dismissive, and yet, he couldn't forget the flare of awareness he'd seen in her eyes when he'd touched her arm the night before, confirming that she'd felt the same jolt that had shaken him to the core.

It had been like that between them since the first time they'd met. But he wouldn't have expected that there would be anything left of that long-ago connection, not after so many years, and especially not considering the way their relationship had ended.

He'd been young and scared of the feelings he had for her, and he'd treated her badly. He had no excuse for his behavior—and no reason to expect that she'd forgiven him, which made the absence of any mention in the gossip column of his argument with Allegra all the more puzzling.

"You could have completely skewered me in today's paper," he noted.

Her brows rose. "Because you stomped all over some poor woman's heart? That's hardly news."

"I didn't realize how badly I'd stomped on yours," he said.

She waved a hand dismissively. "Ancient history."

"Is it?" He took a step closer, watched her eyes narrow, darken.

"Yes," she said firmly.

But he could see the pulse point at the base of her jaw, and it was racing.

"I never forgot about you, Gabriella. And I don't think you forgot about me, either."

"How could I when your face is plastered on the tabloids on an almost daily basis?"

"You're not going to give me an inch, are you?"

"I've already given you a lot more than I should have." She slipped past him and reached for the handle of the door. "Now I have things to do and I'd really like you to go."

But he wasn't ready to leave. Not yet. "Who was the guy you were with last night?"

"Newsflash," she said. "I'm the reporter, you're the object of the public's curiosity. Therefore, I get to ask the questions and you get to smile and look pretty."

"Who is he?" he asked again.

She sighed. "Rafe Fulton."

The name didn't mean anything to him, but he wanted to know more than the man's identity—he wanted to know what the man meant to her. "Boyfriend?"

"Yes."

He frowned at that, but before he could say anything else, footsteps sounded overhead.

Gabriella's gaze shifted to the stairs. "You really have to go now."

He didn't particularly want to hang around to meet the boyfriend, but he was baffled by Gabriella's sudden and obvious desperation to get him out the door. Was her boyfriend the possessive type? Would he disapprove of her having a conversation with another man? Would he—Cameron's blood boiled at the thought—take out his displeasure on Gabriella?

"Gabriella—" He reached for her hand, found it icy cold.

She tugged her hand from his grasp, wrenched open the door. "Please, Cameron. Just go."

The footsteps were coming down the stairs now. Not the heavy tread he'd anticipated, but light, quick steps.

"What's for breakfast, Mom? I'm starving."

Cameron froze, his mind spinning.

Mom?

"I'm making French toast as soon as Gram gets back from the market with the eggs," Gabriella called, then hissed at him, "Please go. I don't want to explain your presence here to my daughter."

Daughter.

She wasn't trying to get rid of him for the benefit of an angry husband or possessive lover, but because she didn't want him to meet her child.

Except that the voice he'd heard didn't sound like that of a pre-schooler or even a pre-teen, but more like that of an adult.

"Mmm, I love French toast," the voice replied.

And then she stepped into view and he saw that his assessment had been right. Gabriella's daughter wasn't a little girl, but a young and stunningly beautiful woman with her mother's dark tumbling curls and distinctly feminine curves. She was dressed similarly to her mother, too, in shorts and a T-shirt, with the addition of a sling around her neck to help support the arm that was encased in a neon-yellow cast.

Except for the cast, looking at her was like looking at Gabriella sixteen years ago, and the realization nearly knocked him off of his feet.

"Whoops." The girl stopped in mid-stride when she spotted Cameron standing in the foyer beside her mother. "Sorry—I didn't realize you had company."

"It's okay," Gabriella said pointedly. "Cameron was just on his way out."

He ignored her, focusing instead on her daughter, who was eyeing him with unbridled curiosity.

As she drew nearer, he saw that the child's eyes were lighter than her mother's—more hazel than brown.

More like the color of his own eyes.

His gaze flew back to Gabriella.

She tilted her chin, as if daring him to ask. But he didn't need to ask.

In that moment, all of the pieces fell into place.

A long-ago conversation. Tear-filled eyes looking to him for answers. Desperate panic. Fierce denials. Reassurance. Relief.

He'd worked hard to forget her, to forget what they had been to one another, but she hadn't been able to forget. She'd lived with the reminder of their long-ago affair every day for the past sixteen years.

The girl standing in front of him was that reminder.

Gabriella's daughter was his daughter, too.

Mi Dios. He was a father.

As his gaze lingered on the beautiful young woman, he couldn't help but think: *Lord, help us both.*

Chapter Four

"Hey, aren't you—" Sierra's sleepy brain woke up in time to halt the impulsive flow of words. She had almost asked her mother's visitor if he was one of the royals, but thankfully she realized how ridiculous the question was before she embarrassed herself by asking it.

She shook her head but still couldn't shake the feeling that she recognized him from somewhere. "Sorry, for a minute I thought you looked…familiar."

"I am Cameron Leandres," he said, and bowed.

Sierra held back a snicker.

Was this guy for real?

Then the name clicked, and her head suddenly felt so light, she thought that she might faint.

"Then you are—ohmygod—you're *Prince* Cameron?"

"I am," he agreed, in the same casual tone.

Sierra's gaze flew to her mother, who seemed neither surprised nor impressed by this revelation.

Of course, her mother worked in the newspaper business

and she'd been covering the "Around Town" section while Alex was on vacation. She knew everyone in the country who was newsworthy. Obviously she would have recognized him immediately. But that still didn't explain what the heck the guy—the *prince*—was doing in her house. And wouldn't Jenna just die when she heard about this?

"And you are obviously Gabriella's daughter," Prince Cameron noted.

"Sierra Vasquez," she responded automatically, wondering if she was supposed to bow or curtsy.

She glanced at her mother again, as if for guidance, and noticed the stiffness of her posture, the deepening of the faint lines that bracketed her mouth. Whatever had brought this member of the royal family to their door, it was apparent to Sierra that Gabriella wasn't pleased by his presence.

"It's a pleasure to finally meet you, Sierra." The prince's comment drew her attention back to him and further piqued her curiosity.

Before she could say anything else, her mother interrupted.

"Thanks for the information, Your Highness," Gabriella said. "I'll be sure to pass it along to Alex when he returns from his vacation."

"There's no need for such formalities between old friends, Gabriella," the prince chided.

Old friends?

Sierra felt her jaw drop.

She turned to her mother, noted the spots of color that rode high on her cheeks, a telltale sign that she was either embarrassed or angry. Because she used to rub elbows with royalty? Or because she didn't want Sierra to know that she used to rub elbows with royalty? It made her wonder how long her mother had known the prince—and just how close they used to be.

Curiosity was eating away at her, but she didn't dare ask her mother those questions. At least not right now.

"What happened to your arm?"

It was the prince who spoke again, his tone was casual and friendly, as if he was unaware of the tension in the room. Or maybe he was just unconcerned about it.

She glanced cautiously at her mother, because she knew Gabriella was still angry about the events of the previous day. "Car accident."

He frowned. "You can't be old enough to drive."

"Your Highness—" Gabriella began to interject again, with obvious impatience.

"Not yet," Sierra responded to his statement. "My best friend was driving."

"I hope no one was badly injured."

She shook her head, lifted her arm slightly. "This was the worst of it."

The crunch of tires on gravel was unmistakable through the open window, evidence that her grandmother had returned from the market.

"Go help with the bags, Sierra," her mother said.

It was obvious that she was being sent out of the room so that her mother could finish her conversation with the royal visitor in private, and Sierra was itching to know why. What business had brought the prince to their home? And why was her usually composed and level-headed mother so obviously flustered by his presence?

"I think you're forgetting which one of us has the broken arm," she responded, hoping for a brief reprieve.

"Now," Gabriella snapped.

Sierra's brows lifted in response to the unexpectedly sharp tone. Her mother was definitely unnerved, and as much as she wanted to hang around and hear the rest of the conversation between them, the sound of the back door opening prompted her to do as she was told.

* * *

Gabriella breathed a silent sigh of relief when Sierra finally exited the room. She knew she'd only been granted a brief reprieve, that her daughter would have plenty of questions for her later. And she would face them later. But right now, she had to face the prince, who wasn't likely to be nearly as patient nor understanding as Sierra.

"So how old is she?" Cameron asked.

Gabriella crossed her arms over her chest. "My daughter is none of your business."

"Unless she's my daughter, too."

He'd kept his voice low, his tone even, but she couldn't resist glancing toward the doorway through which Sierra had disappeared to confirm her daughter was not within earshot. "She's not."

"How old is she?" he asked again.

She lifted her chin. "Fifteen."

"When's her birthday?"

"What gives you the right to barge in here and ask me all these questions?"

"Her birthday," he said again.

Her reply wasn't a date but a directive, and he responded to her crude words with a casual lift of his brows. His unruffled demeanor only irritated her further. Of course, he could afford to be cool—he didn't have anything to lose.

"Look, Your Highness—"

"I don't remember you ever being as hung up on my title then as you seem to be now," he mused.

She hadn't even known he had a title when they first met. If she had, she probably would never have got up the courage to even speak to him. But to her, he'd just been one of a group of college kids who regularly came into the restaurant on Friday nights. Maybe he was a little more handsome than the others, a little more charming. And he was the only one whose smile made her heart beat faster.

Even not knowing that he was royalty, she'd known that he was out of her league. Not just because he was older and more sophisticated, but because it was obvious that his family had money while her family worked for those with money. If Gabriella wanted to go to college someday, as she'd intended to do, she would have to earn the money to pay for her education. Which was how she ended up serving wood-oven pizzas and pitchers of beer to spoiled frat boys like Cameron and his buddies.

"Obviously I wasn't as discerning then as I am now," she said coolly.

"Ouch," he said, but smiled after he said it.

It was the same smile that had always made her knees a little bit weak. So easy and natural, so completely charming and utterly irresistible—at least to a seventeen-year-old girl. But she wasn't seventeen anymore and there was too much at stake to let herself to succumb once again to his considerable charms.

"*Cameron.*" She used his name this time, and was rewarded with another smile.

"Isn't that much better, *Gabriella?*"

His pronunciation of her name was as sensual as a caress, and she felt something unwelcome and unwanted stir inside of her. "What would be much better," she told him, "would be for you to leave so that I can enjoy the rest of the day with my family."

"But we have so much to catch up on," he insisted.

Despite the casual tone, she knew the words weren't an invitation but a threat.

"Another time," she offered.

"You're only delaying the inevitable," he warned her.

She knew that might be true. But she also knew that "the partying prince" had a notoriously short attention span, and she was confident that he would soon forget about her and Sierra and this impromptu visit entirely.

"I'll be happy to meet with you at a mutually convenient date and time," she lied.

"All right," he finally said. He pulled a BlackBerry from his jacket pocket and scrolled through some data, no doubt checking his calendar. "Next Saturday afternoon. Two o'clock in front of the Naval History Museum."

"I'll have to check my schedule," she told him.

His gaze narrowed. "Next Saturday at two o'clock," he said again. "If you're not there, I'll come back here. And I won't leave until all of my questions have been answered."

"I'll be there," she agreed, because she knew that she had no choice. And because she was hoping that, at some point in the coming week, something more important would come up and he would forget.

Gabriella knew *she* wouldn't forget. Because nothing was more important to her than her daughter—and keeping the secret of Sierra's paternity.

Cameron didn't want to wait a whole week to get the answers he sought. But he wasn't entirely sure he trusted Gabriella to tell him the truth, and he knew that if he had some time, he could uncover some of the answers himself.

By Thursday afternoon, he had the most important one. As he stared at the copy of the birth certificate in his hand, his gaze focused on the date that confirmed his suspicions. Sierra Katarina Vasquez was born on June fifteenth—nine months after the weekend he and Gabriella had spent together on the northern coast. Which proved that Gabriella's beautiful fifteen-going-on-sixteen-year-old daughter was also his daughter, even if the father was listed as "unknown" on the registration of her birth.

The sight of that single word had filled him with burning fury. He was as stunned as he was incensed that she would deny the role he'd played in the creation of their child. But his anger faded almost as quickly as it had built, as snippets of a long-ago conversation filtered through his memory.

They'd had the occasional stolen moment together over the period of a few months, and then one glorious extended weekend at Cielo del Norte. When he'd dropped her off after their brief holiday was over, he'd promised that he would call her—but he never did. In fact, several weeks passed before he saw her again, before she tracked him down.

He remembered the exact moment he'd spotted her standing beside the stone archway that guarded the entrance to his campus residence. His initial surprise had been replaced by pleasure, then guilt and regret.

He wanted to go to her, to take her in his arms, to tell her how much he'd missed her. Because he had, and every time he'd thought of her, he'd felt an aching emptiness deep inside. But he'd made up his mind—he was too young to get seriously involved with any one woman—and he'd been sure that, in time, he'd get over her. So instead of going to her, he walked right past, as if he didn't even see her.

He'd thought she would take the hint, that she would turn away. But she'd raced across the field, chasing after him.

"Cameron, wait."

He couldn't pretend he hadn't heard her, so he halted, and tried to look vaguely puzzled. "Hi, uh, Gabriella, right?"

Her eyes—those beautiful, fathomless dark eyes that haunted his dreams—went wide, her face drained of all color. But then she firmed her quivering lip and lifted her chin. "Yes, it's Gabriella," she told him. "We spent a weekend together at the beach last month."

"Yeah," he nodded, as if only now remembering. As if the memories hadn't preoccupied his every waking thought and haunted his every dream since he'd said goodbye to her. "It was a good time."

She hesitated, as if she wasn't sure what else to say to him.

Then she tilted her chin another fraction and met his gaze dead-on. "I think I might be pregnant."

He couldn't see his own face, but he would have guessed that it was even whiter than hers now. He took an automatic step in retreat. "No. No way."

"I don't know for sure," she admitted, her gaze sliding away from his now. "But I thought you should know."

He shook his head. He didn't want to know. He didn't want to believe it was possible. They'd been careful. He was always careful. Except for that last morning. He'd realized that he'd run out of condoms, but he'd thought that it would be okay—he'd convinced her that it would be okay—just one time.

"When—" he managed to clear his throat, but his mind remained fuzzy "—when will you know…for sure?"

"I can pick up a test…on my way home."

He nodded and reached into his back pocket for his wallet. He didn't even count out the bills—he just pulled out all the money that he had and thrust it toward her.

She stared at the money in his hand, her eyes filling with tears.

"Just take it," he said. "In case you need anything."

She knocked the money out of his hand and turned.

"Gabriella."

"Don't worry," she said, her usually warm voice colder than he'd ever heard it before. "I don't need anything from you."

Then she'd walked away, but the tight, panicky feeling that had taken hold inside his chest didn't go away, not for a long time. But as the days turned into weeks and the weeks into months and he didn't see her or hear from her again, he'd been relieved. He'd assumed that she'd made a mistake, that she hadn't been pregnant. Now he knew otherwise.

In retrospect, he could hardly blame her for refusing to name him on her child's birth certificate. If anything, he should thank her. Because at twenty years of age, he hadn't been ready to be a parent. He didn't imagine that Gabriella had been any more ready than he, but she'd taken on the responsibility, anyway. She could have terminated her pregnancy or given the baby up for adoption, but she'd done neither. She'd given birth and raised their child on her own.

Maybe not completely alone, since it seemed that her mother had stood by her. But as far as he knew, she'd never even attempted to contact him again. Not once in the past sixteen years had she tried to get in touch with him to let him know that he was a father.

He knew he couldn't blame her for that. And yet, when he looked at the young woman who reminded him so much of Gabriella when he'd first met her so many years before, he couldn't help but resent having been excluded. Not just excluded but explicitly disavowed by that one little word: *unknown*.

And what would have been different if she'd named him on the child's birth certificate?

He instinctively winced in response to the question that echoed in the back of his head. Even now, more than sixteen years later, he couldn't pretend that everything wouldn't have spun out of control. There would have been a media circus, at the very least. As soon as anyone had seen his name on the birth certificate, the existence of his illegitimate child would have been in the headlines. And he would have responded the same way he'd responded to every scandal that he'd faced: with bald-faced, blatant denials.

He would have been instructed by his royal advisors to deny even the possibility that he was the father of Gabriella's baby. If there had been any proof that she'd spent the weekend at Cielo del Norte with him, then he'd produce a dozen more witnesses to testify to the fact that they weren't alone. She would have been portrayed as a girl of loose morals who'd gotten herself into trouble and was looking for a quick payoff by claiming he'd been with her. And if she'd tried to force the issue by demanding a paternity test, well, the Leandres name and money were more compelling than science.

Yeah, he was still mad at Gabriella Vasquez, but he figured his residual anger couldn't begin to compare to hers.

She'd had sixteen years to resent who he was and what he'd done—how was he ever going to make up for that?

Chapter Five

Gabriella never considered not showing up at the museum. She didn't dare disregard Cameron's threat about returning to her home, and if they were going to have it out about Sierra she wanted to do it somewhere else. But a full week had passed since he'd knocked on her door, and she did let herself hope that he had forgotten about this meeting, that he'd forgotten about her daughter.

Her daughter.

She repeated the words to herself, a soft whisper that couldn't be heard by anyone else, and found solace in them.

Sierra was *her* daughter. From the very beginning, Gabriella had known it would only be the two of them, that they would have to make their own way together. Cameron had made his feelings very clear and if Gabriella had let herself imagine that he might change his mind once he'd had a chance to think about the possibility of their baby, the princess royal had disabused her of that ridiculous notion.

Her own mother had been stunned when Gabriella told her

that she was pregnant. Worse, she'd been disappointed. Gabriella had seen it in her eyes, and it had shamed her. Her father had passed away when Gabriella was only ten years old, and her mother had taken on a second job after his death in order to ensure they didn't lose the house they'd always lived in. It hadn't been easy for Katarina, working two jobs and trying to be both a mother and father to her only daughter, but she'd always been there for Gabriella.

When Gabriella started showing an interest in boys, Katarina had sat down with her and talked to her about love and lust, impressing upon her the importance of respecting her body so that others would, too. Gabriella had assured her mother that she had no intentions of falling in love or falling into bed with anyone. She had plans for her life. She wanted to go to college and build a career before she even considered getting seriously involved.

And then she'd met Cameron. Prior to the first time he walked into Marconi's Restaurant, Gabriella hadn't realized that lust could race through a woman's body with such intensity, making her want with such desperation that there was no thought or reason. She'd tried to resist, but she'd been so completely inexperienced and totally unprepared to withstand his easy charm.

Or maybe she hadn't tried as hard as she should have, because even then she'd thought it was more than lust. She'd convinced herself that she was in love with him, and she'd believed him when he'd said that he was in love with her. And though her mother's warnings had echoed in the back of her mind, she didn't think there was anything wrong with two people in love making love.

It hadn't taken her long to realize she'd been duped, by her own hormones as much as his words.

But that was a lot of years ago—and she was a different woman now.

A woman who glanced at her watch for the tenth time in half as many minutes. It was almost two o'clock.

She shifted her gaze to the crowd of people who were milling around the entrance, but she didn't see Cameron anywhere. Maybe he wasn't going to show up. Maybe—

"You look like you're ready to bolt."

His voice, deep and warm and tinged with amusement, came from behind.

Gabriella whirled around, her heart pounding furiously against her ribs. "Not before two-oh-five," she assured him.

He smiled, his teeth flashing white in contrast to his tanned skin, and her knees went weak. Silently she cursed him, then cursed herself louder and harder.

"Where's your entourage of bodyguards?"

"I'm flying beneath the radar today," he told her.

She didn't see how that was possible. Even as casually dressed as he was, in well-worn jeans and a faded Cambridge University T-shirt with a battered Baltimore Orioles baseball cap on his head, there was something about him that made him stand out from the crowd. Although he dwarfed her five-feet-four-inch frame, he was probably just about six feet tall, and he was more slender than muscular. But his shoulders were broad, and he carried himself with a confidence that edged into arrogance. He was the type of man who would never go anywhere unnoticed, and the realization made Gabriella wary.

"The museum closes at three," she told him, anxious to commence and conclude this unwanted meeting.

"I didn't actually plan on going inside," he replied.

She frowned. "Then why are we here?"

"I thought we could take a walk." He offered his arm to her.

Gabriella only stared at him. "In the middle of downtown on a Saturday afternoon?"

His lips curved again, and her heart pounded.

"Are you worried about what the gossip columnists might say if we're seen together?" he teased.

"I'd think you should be the one to worry," she said, unable to deny that being seen with the prince made her uneasy. Because his baseball cap really wasn't much of a disguise.

He just shrugged. "I stopped letting rumors and innuendo bother me years ago."

She wished she could say the same thing, but the truth was, she'd always hated the idea of anyone talking behind her back, spreading gossip and lies. She only had herself to blame for the worst of it. By refusing to name the father of her baby, she'd given people reason to talk, to speculate, to sneer.

"Gabriella?"

She pushed the painful memories aside. "Where are we walking to?"

"The harbor front."

It would be even busier down by the water, but maybe that was his plan—to hide in plain sight. So she fell into step beside him, grateful that she was wearing low-heeled sandals. She'd changed her clothes four times before she'd left the house—not because she wanted to impress him but because she wanted to ensure that she didn't give that impression.

"Have you had lunch?" he asked her.

"I had a late breakfast." Truthfully, she'd barely nibbled on the omelet her mother had made for her, because her stomach was tied up in knots in anticipation of this meeting.

"We could pick up some sandwiches at The Angel and take them to the park for a picnic."

"I wouldn't have taken you for the picnicking type," she said.

"A lot changes in seventeen years."

"True enough," she agreed.

"Although you look the same," he noted. "Aside from some subtle changes. Your hair's a little shorter, your curves are a little fuller, but you still knock the breath out of me every time I see you."

"And you still have all the best lines," she retorted.

"You don't believe it's true?"

"I learned a long time ago not to believe any words that come out of your mouth."

A muscle in his jaw flexed. "I guess I can't blame you for that," he finally said.

Gabriella didn't respond. She'd promised herself that she wouldn't let him get to her, that no matter what he said or did, she would remain cool and unruffled. But after less than ten minutes in his company, she was feeling decidedly uncool and extremely ruffled.

He paused on the sidewalk outside of the café. "Proscuitto and provolone with mustard?"

She was surprised that he remembered. She'd thought it was only a coincidence that he'd chosen to stop at The Angel. She wouldn't have expected him to remember that they'd been there together once before—stopping in for provisions on the Friday afternoon before they'd stolen away for the weekend. Not only had he remembered that they'd stopped at this café, but he'd remembered what she'd ordered.

But as he'd pointed out, they weren't the same people now that they were then, and she'd changed a lot more than he could imagine. "Turkey and Swiss with mayo."

"Iced tea?"

She nodded. While he ducked inside the café, she waited outside, watching the crowd.

When Sierra was little, Gabriella would often bring her down here on weekends. They would browse through the little shops that lined the waterfront and eat sandwiches in the park, throwing their crusts to the ducks that paddled in circles around the pond. Then they'd walk a little farther, and she'd hold tightly to Sierra's hand as she said a silent thank-you to the playboy prince who lived in the fancy house that was just barely visible at the top of the hill, because he'd given her the greatest gift in the world. Then they'd go back to Lorenzo's for some lemon ice before they headed home.

She smiled at the memory, the smile slipping as she re-membered that Sierra still loved to spend Saturday afternoons at the harbor front, though she usually preferred to do her shopping with Jenna and Rachel now. Gabriella had a moment of panic then, when it occurred to her that she might run into her daughter here in town. She wasn't sure what Sierra's plans were for the day, but she figured it would be just her luck to meet Cameron downtown in order to avoid him seeing Sierra again—and then running into her anyway.

"Gabriella?"

Her breath caught in her throat, but she chided herself for the instinctive reaction. The deeply, masculine voice obviously didn't belong to her daughter. As she turned to respond, the initial sense of relief was replaced by guilt and remorse when she found herself face-to-face with Rafe.

Cameron walked out of the café with a paper bag in hand and a smile on his face. He wasn't sure he could explain his good mood. He'd been furious beyond reason when he'd re-alized that Gabriella had given birth to his child and never bothered to tell him about his daughter, and even if he thought he understood why she'd kept that information to herself, he knew it was going to take them both some time to get past all of that history.

But he also knew that he wanted to get past it. He wanted to get to know his daughter, he wanted Sierra to know that he was her father, and he wanted a second chance with Gabriella—a first chance for the three of them to be a family.

Family. The word made his chest feel tight. At first, he'd thought his reaction was panic at the idea of being tied down to one woman and her child, but the more he thought about it, the more he'd realized what he was really feeling was a yearning. A yearning that had been stirring inside of him since he'd seen her standing in her boss's office.

Or maybe the yearning had been there for the past seventeen years. Maybe that was why he'd never had a long-term relationship with any one woman—because he'd never gotten over Gabriella. Because he couldn't help but compare every other woman he'd been with to her, and no one had ever measured up.

He shook his head, banishing the ridiculously romantic notion from his mind. He'd barely been twenty years old when they'd had their brief affair so many years ago and he hadn't been pining for her since. Truthfully, he'd hardly even let himself think about her during the intervening years. But when he'd realized she was the author of the offending "Around Town" column, he'd grasped the excuse to track her down. Yes, he'd been frustrated and angry—but he'd also been curious. He'd wanted to see her again, to find out what she'd been up to over the past seventeen years, and he was curious to know if there was anything left of the chemistry that had always sizzled between them.

There was still sizzle—and a whole lot of baggage that he never could have anticipated. But he wasn't going to worry about that today. Right now, he just wanted to spend a pleasant day with Gabriella, to learn about his daughter and convince her mother that he wanted to be part of her life again.

And maybe, if he was lucky, he might have a chance to test the potency of that chemistry. He pushed open the door, his smile fading as soon as he saw that Gabriella wasn't alone.

She was with a man, holding his hand, and the man was smiling at her in a way that left Cameron in no doubt about the fact that they'd been lovers. Maybe they still were. His fingers automatically curled into fists, and it was only when he heard the crinkle of the paper bag that he remembered it was in his hand.

"Ready, Gabriella?" His tone was deliberately casual.

She started and turned, her cheeks flushing with color. He thought she tried to tug her hand from the other man's grasp, but he held on, his smile looking a little strained now.

"Oh. That was quick," she said.

He lifted a brow, silently questioning.

"Cameron, this is Rafe Fulton. Rafe, this is Cameron."

He offered his hand, not because he felt compelled by social custom but in order to force the other man to release his hold on Gabriella, as he finally did.

"It's a pleasure," Rafe said, although the look in his eyes warned that it was anything but.

"You're American," Cameron noted, immediately picking up on the accent.

"That's right," Rafe agreed.

"New York?" he guessed.

The other man nodded. "Although I seem to spend more time traveling than I do at home these days."

"Rafe's in international banking," Gabriella explained.

"Is that why you're in Tesoro del Mar?" Cameron asked him.

"That's the reason I first visited Tesoro del Mar almost two years ago," Rafe told him, then shifted his gaze to Gabriella. "But not the reason I keep coming back."

The flush in Gabriella's cheeks deepened. "Cameron and I have some things—business—to discuss."

"Then I'll leave you to your…business," Rafe said, taking a step back. "And I'll look forward to seeing you at seven."

She nodded.

"Busy day for you today," Cameron mused, as the other man walked away.

"You picked the date and time for this meeting," she reminded him.

"I guess I did," he agreed. "I didn't realize your boyfriend would still be in town."

"Would it have made a difference if you did?" she challenged.

"No," he admitted, and began heading toward the park.

Gabriella fell into step beside him. When they found a vacant picnic table in the shade, he spread a couple of paper napkins on top before setting out their food. She opened her iced tea, took a long swallow.

Cameron took a bite of his sandwich, although his appetite had diminished. "How serious is it?"

She frowned. "What?"

"You and Rafe," he clarified. "How serious is it?"

"Is that why you wanted to see me today—to talk about my relationship with Rafe?"

Actually, that was the absolute last thing he wanted to talk about. "No—I wanted to talk about what you're planning for Sierra's birthday."

Every muscle in Gabriella's body went completely still. "What are you talking about?"

"It's June fifteenth next week," he pointed out to her. "I just assumed you'd be having a party for the big occasion."

Her cheeks paled, but her gaze never wavered. "As a matter of fact, I am."

He nodded. "A girl's sixteenth birthday is a special occasion." Then, when Gabriella remained silent, he pressed on. "It is her sixteenth birthday, isn't it?"

"Obviously you already know the answer to that question."

"Birth registrations are a matter of public record," he reminded her.

"Her age doesn't prove anything," she said.

"No," he agreed. "But I imagine a DNA test would prove plenty."

She wrapped up her untouched sandwich, her appetite obviously gone. "Do you really want to subject yourself to the sort of scandal that would entail?"

"Maybe the better question is: do you want to subject Sierra to that sort of scandal?" he challenged. "Because I'm not the one denying that she's my daughter."

She rose to her feet, facing him across the table. "You have no right—"

"I think the courts would agree that I have plenty of rights," he assured her.

Her eyes filled with tears. "You bastard."

"Actually, *my* parents were legally married when I was conceived."

"Which just goes to prove that having both a father and a mother isn't a guarantee of anything," she snapped.

"You never did pull your punches," he mused.

She stormed away. He abandoned the remnants of their lunch to follow her into a stand of trees.

"What do you want from me?"

He wasn't sure there was a simple answer to that question, so he only said, "I want a chance to know my child."

"Why?"

"Because she's my child."

Gabriella didn't waste any more breath trying to deny it. When she spoke again, it was only to say, "She doesn't know you're her father."

"Maybe it's time that she did," he told her.

Her gaze flew to his—her dark eyes filled with anger and frustration. "What gives you the right, after sixteen years, to make that decision?"

"How about the fact that, for sixteen years, I didn't know I had a child?"

"You didn't want to know," she reminded him.

He couldn't deny that was true, at least in the beginning. But the situation was different now, and he had no intention of continuing to deny his relationship to Sierra. "When is her party?"

"You're not invited."

"That wasn't what I asked," he said mildly.

She huffed out a breath. "Saturday night. Eight o'clock. And you're not invited."

"Where?"

"Cameron—"

"At your house," he guessed.

"Yes," she admitted. "It's a surprise and you're not invited."

"Do you really think you can keep me away?"

"I think you should be able to see the potential for disaster if you show up. It only took Sierra a few minutes to figure out who you are and once her friends realize you're royalty, well, there will be pictures of you all over the internet before the birthday candles are even lit."

"I might be more inclined to appreciate your concern if you weren't responsible for so much of my bad press of late."

"Honestly, I don't care what kind of photos or videos the kids snap of you. I *do* care how your presence at the party might impact Sierra. What possible explanation could you give for being there?"

"Other than the truth, you mean?"

She glared at him. "Other than that."

"I'll be your date," he suddenly decided.

"I don't think so."

"I'm sure you could accept that more easily than explaining to all of the guests that I'm the birthday girl's father."

She folded her arms across her chest. "And how am I supposed to explain to my daughter that I'm dating someone other than my fiancé?"

He frowned at that. "You and Rafe are engaged?"

"Yes," she told him, but her defiant gaze flickered away.

"Then why aren't you wearing his ring?" he demanded.

She blinked, as if startled by the question. "It's, uh, it's a little big, so I've decided not to wear it until I've had a chance to get it adjusted."

"Really?" He considered her explanation for a moment, then shook his head. "If he was serious enough to buy a ring, he'd make sure it was the right size so he could slide it on your finger as soon as you said 'yes.'"

She didn't respond.

"Or maybe that's the real reason you're not wearing it," he continued. "Because you haven't said 'yes.'"

"My relationship with Rafe isn't any of your business."

"It is when you keep using it as a roadblock between us."

"There is no 'us,'" she said again.

He hadn't seen her in more than sixteen years, so her statement was hardly unreasonable. And yet, something about her adamant tone irked him, made him want to prove differently. Unable to think of any words that might convince her, he kissed her instead.

Chapter Six

Gabriella had all kinds of reasons for not ever wanting to see Cameron Leandres again, and only one for acceding to his request: Sierra. She'd thought—desperately hoped—that she might convince the prince that he had no reason to believe her daughter was also his. She hadn't let herself think of her own feelings. Or maybe she hadn't believed that she could have any feelings for the man who had broken her heart so many years before. But the moment his lips touched hers, she knew that she'd made a very dangerous miscalculation.

Because in that first whisper-soft brush of his mouth against hers, she was catapulted back in time. It was as if everything she was feeling was new and unfamiliar and all-encompassing. She hadn't just been a virgin when she'd met Cameron, but an innocent in far more ways than she'd realized—completely unprepared for the depth and breadth of the emotions and desires that he brought to life within her. But she'd been an avid pupil of his experienced seduction, an eager participant in their lovemaking.

This was only a kiss—and should have been simple enough for Gabriella to resist. But she had never been able to resist Cameron. She'd known from the beginning that a relationship between them could never work out—his family was blue-blood, hers was blue-collar—but she'd somehow got caught up in the romantic fantasy, anyway. She'd let herself hope and dream, and she'd had her heart shattered.

Afterward, she'd convinced herself that what she'd felt with him hadn't been all that she'd remembered. That it was only an unfortunate combination of teenage hormones and inexperience that had made her behave so recklessly and impulsively. She'd found some solace in that, and a certain amount of relief that she'd never felt so out-of-control with any other man. Not even the man who'd asked her to marry him.

But suddenly, hidden in the shadows of the trees, she was feeling it all again. The same desperate, burning need; the same fiery, raging desire. And she was no more prepared for the feelings now than she'd been when she was seventeen. As his lips moved over hers, demanding rather than coaxing now, she responded, giving him all that he wanted, showing him all that she wanted. His fingers tangled in her hair and he tipped her head farther back, deepening the kiss. Her lips parted, their tongues met, desires tangled.

He nibbled on her bottom lip, murmured some words that her swirling mind couldn't begin to decipher. Then his hand slid up to her breast, his thumb brushing over the crest, and she whimpered low in her throat.

She knew this was wrong—being here with him, kissing him, wanting him. But she couldn't seem to help herself. She couldn't stop her heart from pounding, her blood from pulsing, or her body from yearning. But she could hate him for it. And she did.

She pulled away, her eyes burning with tears that she refused to shed. Not for this man. Not ever again.

He cupped her chin, forced her to meet his gaze. "You're not going to marry that American."

"Whether or not I marry Rafe has nothing to do with you."

"If you were really in love with him, you wouldn't have kissed me back."

"Kissing you only proved to me how lucky I am to have Rafe," she retorted.

He stepped closer, his gaze dark and foreboding. "You should be careful about throwing his name in my face," he warned. "Especially when your lips are still warm from mine."

She tilted her chin, met his stare evenly. "Don't worry. It won't happen again."

"Don't make promises you can't keep," he warned her. "But putting that aside for now, it is you who has a decision to make."

"What decision is that?" she asked warily.

"Whether to uninvite your American friend to Sierra's birthday party so that I can be your date—or to introduce me to our daughter as her father."

Of course, they both knew what her decision would be. She'd spent the better part of sixteen years protecting Sierra from the publicity that would be generated by the truth of her paternity, and she had no intention of subjecting her daughter to the headlines now. "I guess I'll see you next Saturday at eight."

Cameron understood why Gabriella was concerned about the media discovering the truth about Sierra's paternity. While being a royal entitled one to many perks, the status also came with restrictions—one of which was the inability to talk about personal issues without worry that confessions would end up on the front page of the morning newspaper. Experience had taught Cameron that the only people he could trust to keep his secrets were his family, so when he and Gabriella parted ways after their lunch in the park, he drove toward his brother's house in the exclusive gated community of Verde Colinas.

Michael and his wife had lived there happily for thirteen years, and when Samantha died almost two years earlier, Cameron had expected that his brother would want to move out of the home they'd shared together. But Michael had no intention of going anywhere, and only those family and close friends who had known him when Samantha was alive knew how much of a toll her death had taken on him. Their sister, Marissa, had contacted Cameron several times over the past few months, hoping that he would have some advice or insights on how to reach Michael, to make him see that he still had family who cared about him and—most importantly—a daughter who needed him.

Their efforts had been unsuccessful, but Marissa remained optimistic. "I'm sure he just needs time," she'd said to Cameron during a recent conversation. "Samantha was such a huge part of his life for so many years—it can't be easy to get over that kind of loss."

Cameron wouldn't know. He didn't think he'd ever been all the way in love. In fact, the closest he'd ever come had probably been with Gabriella, and that was too many years ago to even count. Since then, he'd mostly avoided personal entanglements, and—Allegra's dashed hopes aside—most of the women he dated knew he wasn't looking for anything serious or long-term.

He'd had more than a few women claim to be in love with him over the years, but he knew that what they really loved was being with a prince. Too often the words had been followed by a request—"I love you and I miss you so much when you're gone. Maybe this time I could go to Australia/Bermuda/China with you." Or a demand—"If you loved me, you would get me tickets to the concert/talk to someone about that parking infraction/buy me that condo at the waterfront."

That was a favorite of his mother's tricks—playing the affection/demand card to get what she wanted, and it had taught Cameron that everyone wanted something from him.

Everyone except his sister, he realized, when Marissa answered the door. She was the one person who always gave so much more than she ever asked for. She led him into the kitchen now and immediately began to make a pot of coffee.

"Michael's not here?" he guessed.

She shook her head. "He's at the office."

He heard music coming from the other room, and he peeked around the corner to see his twenty-one-month-old niece spinning in circles to the music.

"On a Saturday?" he responded to Marissa's statement about his brother's whereabouts.

"He said something about a big project outline he had to finish," she explained.

"And you're here watching Riley again," he guessed.

"The nanny only works until six and not at all on weekends, so I've been helping out when I can," she admitted.

As if on cue, the little girl raced into the room. She halted when she saw Cameron, then smiled shyly before she lifted her arms to her aunt.

Marissa scooped her up with one arm and an ease that revealed she'd done the same thing countless times before.

"How often is that?" he asked.

His sister shifted the child to her other hip, and shifted her gaze away from his.

"Marissa?" he prompted.

"I've moved into the spare room downstairs," she admitted.

"You've moved in?"

She shrugged. "It got me out of Mother's house."

"I'm sure she had something to say about this arrangement," he noted dryly. The princess royal always had an opinion, especially when it came to her children.

"I don't even know if she's realized I'm gone," Marissa told him.

He frowned but didn't argue her claim. It was a well-known fact that Elena paid scant attention to her only daughter, choosing to focus her energies and ambitions on her two sons. Both he and Michael had disappointed her in that regard, making Cameron wonder if their mother might have made a mistake in disregarding her daughter's potential. Except that his sister was too pure of mind and soft of heart to fall in with their mother's machinations, which was one of the reasons that he'd come to her now. Because she was also too loyal and sweet to judge the brother who had made more mistakes than he cared to admit.

"She hasn't come around here in a while," Marissa continued, rubbing the baby's back. "I think she's finally realized that Michael may never forgive her."

"For what now?" Cameron asked.

"For convincing Samantha to get pregnant—in order to ensure the continuation of the Leandres line."

And it was as a result of complications that arose during childbirth that Samantha had lost her life.

"Then, when the baby was born, Mother didn't want to have anything to do with her."

"Because she was a girl," he guessed, pouring himself a cup of the freshly brewed coffee.

She nodded.

"Then I guess there's no reason that I should feel compelled to share my news."

"What's your news?"

"That she has another granddaughter."

Marissa gaped at him. "You're a daddy?"

He smiled as he nodded. "I can't imagine her calling me

'daddy,' though, considering that she's almost sixteen years old."

His sister sank into a chair. "A teenager."

He nodded again.

"I can't believe it."

"I'm still getting used to the idea myself," he admitted.

"You didn't know?"

"Not until a few days ago."

"Are you...sure?" she asked hesitantly.

"That she's mine, you mean?"

Now it was Marissa's turn to nod.

"Yeah, I'm sure. If for no other reason than that Gabriella tried so hard to deny it."

"I'm assuming Gabriella is the mother."

"She is," he confirmed. "Gabriella Vasquez."

"Oh, this just keeps getting better and better," Marissa said, amusement evident in her tone. "And it certainly explains why the columnist always seemed to have a chip on her shoulder where you were concerned."

"Don't tell me you read that drivel."

His sister's chin went up. "It's not drivel, it's interesting. And while she strikes me as a very savvy lady, I do have to wonder how and where the two of you ever hooked up."

"She was a waitress at Marconi's," he admitted. "And from the first moment I laid eyes on her, I was seriously smitten."

Marissa's brows rose. "How did I not know any of this?"

"You were away at school at the time, and we weren't together for very long," Cameron explained.

"Long enough, obviously," she remarked dryly.

He couldn't disagree with that.

"So what went wrong? What did you do that prevented Gabriella from telling you that she was pregnant? Because I know that you have your faults, but I also know that you wouldn't walk away from your responsibilities."

He stared into the mug of coffee cradled between his hands

and wondered what he'd ever done to deserve her loyalty. "I think she tried to tell me, but I didn't want to hear it. I was young and scared and I'd just been subjected to another of our mother's endless lectures about the duties and responsibilities of being royal and—"

"And you let her come between you and the only woman you'd ever loved," Marissa told him.

He frowned. "I was twenty years old. What did I know about love?"

"You probably knew more then than you do now—because you've spent the past sixteen years trying to forget about her."

"You're such a hopeless romantic, Mar."

"Because I can believe in love even though I've never experienced it myself?" she challenged.

"Because you believe that the chemistry that draws a man and a woman together is based on elusive emotion when the reality is that the male-female attraction is founded on lust rather than love."

"Lust flares hot and bright and burns out quickly," she told him. "Love endures."

"And you know this how?"

"It's obvious—at least to me—that you still have feelings for Gabriella Vasquez, even after all this time. The only question now, big brother, is what do you intend to do about those feelings?"

It was a question that Cameron couldn't begin to answer.

When Gabriella returned home, it was to an empty house. Not wanting to think about Cameron or Rafe or the million things she had to do before Sierra's birthday party the following weekend, she decided to spend some time working on her column instead.

Unfortunately, the first letter she opened proved that escape from her own problems was impossible.

Dear Gabby,

My boyfriend of two years recently asked me to marry him and although I'm now wearing his ring, I'm not sure that I'm ready to make that kind of lifelong commitment. I said "yes" when he proposed because I do love him and because I figured a long engagement would give us both the time we needed to be sure that we want to be together forever.

But he insists that he doesn't want to wait, that he wants to start our life together right now. He says that if I really love him, I'll marry him.

I do love him, but I'm only twenty-one. He insists that he's ready to settle down and has warned that if I'm not ready to start a life with him, he'll find someone else who is.

Should I set a date or bide my time?

Signed,

Muddled about Marriage

The email address from which the letter had been sent clearly identified "Muddled" as the VP of a local telecommunications company, a title that carried more prestige than power and was granted to her upon graduation from college by the president—her father—only a few months before his death. Now, less than a year later, her twenty-first birthday celebration had been big news because it meant unrestricted access to her trust fund.

Gabriella considered for a moment, wondering if this additional information would impact the advice she intended to give "Muddled," and decided that it would not. Even if the letter writer wasn't an heiress and her fiancé wasn't so obviously a fortune-hunter, her response would be the same: ditch the jerk *now* before you're stuck with him forever.

Of course, she was a little more subtle in her formal response.

Dear Muddled,

If you're not sure that you're ready to make a lifelong commitment, then you're definitely not ready and your fiancé shouldn't be pressuring you and he definitely shouldn't be issuing ultimatums.

If he loves you, he will wait, and if he finds someone else while he's waiting, then he obviously isn't as committed to you as he claims to be—and if that's the case, it's much better to find out before you speak the vows that will tie you together.

If he continues to pressure you, then you should set a date—to move on with your life without him. Because if you let him propel you down the aisle before you're sure that it's what you want, you'll find yourself standing at the altar and kissing a frog!

Good luck,
Gabby

Gabriella re-read the letter and her response, then clicked to save it on her computer. She felt comfortable with the advice she was giving to the young woman, but as she lifted her gaze to glance at the clock above her desk, the light blue box on the shelf caught her eye and she sighed.

"Muddled" was right to be concerned—she was young, she'd barely had a chance to experience life and shouldn't be rushing to tie herself down—especially when she had reason to suspect her boyfriend's motivations. Gabriella had no similar excuse.

She was almost thirty-four years old and she'd known Rafe for two years. He was handsome, charming, intelligent, successful and wealthy, and she'd been attracted to him from the beginning. So why was she hesitating?

She lifted the box down from the shelf and opened the lid, blinking at the flash of white fire that seemed to erupt from within. The ring was truly dazzling—a three-carat heart-shaped diamond in a platinum bezel setting—and she was sure it had cost Rafe a small fortune.

He hadn't pressured her, but she knew that her almost-fiancé had believed it was only a matter of time until she took the ring out of the box and put it on her finger. Gabriella wasn't so certain.

What if I'm never ready?

But, of course, she hadn't actually spoken those words aloud. She hadn't dared ask the question that might have alerted him to the reality of her emotional scars. She'd been too afraid that he would walk away from her forever. And though she wouldn't blame him if he did, she wasn't ready to lose him. She couldn't commit to spending the rest of her life with him, but she didn't want to live her life without him, either. She didn't want to be alone.

She carefully—almost cautiously—took the ring out of the box and slipped it onto the third finger of her left hand. It fit perfectly, as Cameron had correctly assumed it would, but it felt heavy. Part of the sensation was a direct result of the size of the rock, but she knew that it felt a lot heavier than it really was, that it was the weight of expectations that felt so cumbersome when she put the diamond on her finger. With a sigh of sincere regret, she put the ring back in the box.

She'd hoped that she could wear it someday, but she knew now that it would never happen. She'd thought her heart was sufficiently mended that she could fall in love again, but as wonderful as Rafe was, something had always held her back. After the kiss she'd shared with Cameron in the park, she knew that it wasn't something but some*one*. And she knew that she would have to tell Rafe the truth about her feelings.

She was still at her computer, staring unseeingly at another reader letter, when the doorbell rang. She automatically rose to respond to the summons, surprised to find Rafe on the step.

"It can't be seven o'clock already," she said, wondering how she could have lost track of so much time.

"It's not," he admitted. "But I decided I couldn't wait until then to see you."

She moved away from the door so that he could enter. He stepped into the entranceway, but didn't go any farther.

"Something's wrong," she guessed.

"I've decided to go back to New York. Tonight."

Her throat was suddenly tight and dry, so that she had to swallow before she could ask, "Why?"

"Because as long as you're still hung up on Sierra's father, you're never going to be able to make a commitment to me."

She dropped her gaze, felt her cheeks flush, but she had to ask, "How did you know he's Sierra's father?"

"It wasn't anything obvious," he assured her. "It certainly isn't as if she looks like him—it was more the way he was looking at you. And the way he looked at me when he saw me with you, like he wanted to tear me apart for daring to touch his woman."

She shook her head. "It isn't like that. We're not...involved."

His smile was wry. "I can't tell if you're really that naive or if you think I am."

"We're not," she insisted. "Until last week, I hadn't even seen him in more than sixteen years."

Rafe looked unconvinced. "I always figured you were still harboring feelings for the man who'd fathered your daughter, but I also figured, with time, you'd get over him. Of course, I never expected that he would turn out to be a prince."

"What difference does that make?"

"Maybe none," he allowed. "Maybe your feelings have nothing to do with his title and everything to do with the fact that he was the first man you ever loved—the man you still love."

She shook her head again, refusing to acknowledge that it might be true, refusing to even consider that she might be so foolish as to harbor any feelings for a man who had proven years ago that he'd never really cared about her.

But Rafe only lifted a hand and laid his palm against her cheek. She closed her eyes, savoring the warmth of his touch, and wishing she could feel more.

"I can't make you love me," he said, as if reading her thoughts. "And I can't accept any less." Then he dipped his head and kissed her softly. "Goodbye, Gabriella."

She watched him drive away, as she had so many times before, but this time, she knew that it truly was goodbye.

Chapter Seven

The morning of Sierra's sixteenth birthday was sunny and bright, and the only thing that put a damper on her spirits was the cast that still weighed heavily on her broken arm.

Her grandmother brought a tray to her bedroom, preserving the "breakfast in bed" tradition that had been a birthday ritual in the Vasquez household for as long as Sierra could remember.

She sniffed the air, hummed her approval. "Fresh chocolate chip waffles?"

"They are your favorite," Katarina said, settling the tray across her granddaughter's lap.

Sierra took in the glass of orange juice, the bowl of fresh fruit with a dollop of yogurt, the small pitcher of warm syrup, the plate of waffles—already cut up, in deference to her injury—and the vase with a single white rose, and smiled. "You spoil me."

"That's what *abuelas* are supposed to do."

"If I eat all of this, I won't fit into the dress I was planning to wear tonight," Sierra warned, spearing a piece of waffle with her fork.

"Then you should have bought a bigger size," Katarina said, with only the slightest hint of disapproval in her tone. Though they didn't often battle over Sierra's wardrobe, the teen knew that her grandmother didn't favor the figure-hugging fashions that were currently in style.

"What if I share my waffles with you instead?"

"You're just like your mother at your age—with an answer for everything," Katarina said, shaking her head in what Sierra took to be a combination of exasperation and affection.

"Where is Mom?" Sierra asked, popping another piece of waffle into her mouth.

"Right here," Gabriella said, carrying an enormous vase overflowing with tropical blooms. She set the flowers on the table beside the bed and leaned over to kiss Sierra's cheek. "Happy Sweet Sixteen."

"Where did those come from?" Sierra asked.

"Rafe sent them," Gabriella told her.

"Is he coming for dinner with us tonight?" she asked.

Her mother and grandmother exchanged a look, and then Gabriella shook her head. "Rafe went back to New York."

"Oh." Although Sierra couldn't deny her disappointment, she was more concerned about her mother's apparent reluctance to share the information. "Is everything okay with you two?"

"Yes. No." Gabriella sighed, then lowered herself onto the edge of the mattress as Katarina hustled away on the pretext of cleaning up the kitchen. "Rafe and I… We're not seeing each other anymore."

Sierra felt her jaw drop open. "But…why?"

"He wanted more of a commitment from me than I was ready to make."

Though her tone was casual, Sierra knew that her mother's

feelings for the American were not, and that knowledge only baffled her more. "You're not going to marry him?"

Gabriella shook her head.

Sierra narrowed her gaze. "Is it because of Prince Cameron?"

Her mother's head shot up, her eyes went wide. "Why would you ask something like that?"

"Because you've been acting kind of weird ever since that day he showed up here."

Her mother hesitated, just long enough to convince Sierra that her suspicions weren't unfounded.

"I was just surprised to see him after such a very long time," Gabriella said. "But even before Cameron showed up, I knew I couldn't marry Rafe."

"So I guess that means we won't be going to New York City, either," Sierra said, aware that she sounded like a spoiled child.

"There's no reason we can't go for a visit on our own sometime," Gabriella promised her. "If we save our pennies."

Sierra sipped her juice and tried not to resent the fact that they wouldn't have had to worry about pennies if her mother had decided to marry Rafe. He could have flown them all to New York City—and anywhere else they wanted to go—on his company's private jet.

"So it's just you and me and Grandma tonight," Sierra clarified. She knew her mother had planned a party and that all of her friends would be at the house later, but she played along, not wanting to ruin the surprise.

Gabriella fussed with the flower arrangement, repositioning an enormous pink lily. "And Prince Cameron might stop by later."

Sierra nearly choked on a piece of pineapple. "Why?"

"To wish you a happy birthday," Gabriella said.

But Sierra suspected that the real answer wasn't nearly as simple as her mother wanted her to believe.

* * *

Gabriella hated being less than completely honest with Sierra, but she wasn't nearly ready for the life she'd built with her daughter to come crashing down around them, and she hated knowing that that was exactly what would happen when the truth about Sierra's paternity came to light.

And she knew that it would eventually come to light. Now that Cameron had figured it out, there would be no stopping it. And as concerned as Gabriella was about her daughter's potential response to the news, she had more reasons than that to worry. Because when Sierra was only a baby, she'd struck a deal, and she knew now that it was only a matter of time before the promise she'd made would be broken. And though the bargain might be destroyed through no fault of her own, she knew there would be repercussions.

A knock at the door startled her from her reverie.

She set down the knife she'd been using to chop veggies and made her way to the door, expecting Beth or Rachel, who had volunteered to come by to help set up for the party while Jenna kept Sierra occupied and away from the house. She wasn't expecting Cameron, and her heart gave a traitorous thump against her ribs when she opened the door and found him standing there.

"You're about five hours early," she told him.

"I know," he admitted, unfazed by her lack of welcome. "But I wanted to show you what I picked out for Sierra before I gave it to her tonight."

"You didn't have to get her a gift," Gabriella protested.

"I could hardly come empty-handed to a sweet sixteen birthday party."

"And yet, your hands are empty," she noted.

"It's an expression," he chided. "The gift is parked across the street."

Parked?

Gabriella's stomach twisted into painful knots as she looked up and spotted the shiny yellow sports car with an enormous pink bow on its roof.

"You've got to be kidding."

He frowned. "What's wrong?"

"What's wrong?" she echoed, incredulous. "Do you really think that's an appropriate gift?"

"I can exchange it for another color, if she doesn't like it. Of course, I don't know what she likes and doesn't like, but I noticed that her cast was yellow and thought she might be fond of the color."

"It's not the color—it's that it's a car," she said, incensed. "You can't give her a car."

"Why not?"

She stared at him, stunned by his obvious lack of comprehension. "Firstly, because she just turned sixteen and doesn't even have her driver's license yet. Secondly, because it's far too extravagant a gift from someone who is supposedly only here as my date."

He frowned. "Considering that I've missed sixteen years of birthdays, I don't think it's extravagant at all."

"Of course you wouldn't," she muttered.

"Every teenager wants a car," he pointed out reasonably.

"That doesn't mean they should have one."

"Why are you being obstinate about this?"

"Maybe because I'm her mother and I know that Sierra isn't old enough or responsible enough for a car of her own, and even if she was, I wouldn't let her drive around in a brand-new lemon-yellow sports car."

"So it's the specific kind of vehicle and not the car itself that you have a problem with?"

She shook her head. "Take it back."

He frowned. "And get her what instead?"

"A gift certificate for the movies. A basket of bath products. A teddy bear." She ticked the suggestions off on her fingertips.

He lifted his brows. "A teddy bear?"

"Something casual and inexpensive," she explained.

"I think she'd rather have the car."

"She'd love the car," Gabriella admitted. "Just as she'd love an unlimited shopping allowance or a trip to New York City, but she doesn't expect to have either of those things handed to her, either."

Cameron frowned. "Why would she want to go to New York City? Did your American friend offer to take her there?"

She sighed. "This isn't about Rafe—it's about you getting that car away from here before Sierra gets home."

"All right," he finally agreed, but when he looked over at the car again, regret was clearly etched in his features. "It's too bad, though. She's a beautiful vehicle and drives like a dream."

"What is a dream to you would be a nightmare to me, because I'd worry every time she drove away from the house," she told him.

"I'm sure you've had enough worries, raising Sierra on your own for sixteen years, and it certainly wasn't my intention to add to that."

She was surprised by the sincerity in his tone, touched by his understanding. "I haven't been entirely on my own," she reminded him. "I've had my mother to help out along the way."

"And now you have me."

"Cameron—"

He touched his fingers to her lips, silencing her protest. "I realize that we have a lot of details still to work out, but I want you to know that I'm not going to walk away this time. Not from Sierra, and not from you."

Somehow his words left her feeling more apprehensive than reassured.

* * *

Cameron decided to go with the teddy bear. Of the options Gabriella had enumerated, it seemed the best choice. Or so he thought, until he began to search and realized there were many different sizes, colors and styles of bears. In the end, he found what he was looking for in a specialty children's shop down at the waterfront.

When he returned to the house, just before nine o'clock, the party was in full swing. Gabriella had suggested that it would be simpler if he came after the "surprise" part so he didn't have to explain to anyone who he was or answer too many questions about why he was there. As it turned out, most of Sierra's friends either didn't recognize him or didn't care, because they barely paid any attention to him when he arrived. Music was pumping out of speakers and many of the party guests were crowded together on the small patio and moving to the music while others danced happily on the lawn. To be relatively unobtrusive in a crowd was a new experience, but he didn't mind. It allowed him to hover in the background and observe Sierra.

His daughter.

He watched her move through the crowd, stopping now and again to talk and laugh with her friends, or swaying her hips and tossing her head in tune with the music. For some reason, he found himself thinking of Riley—his brother's daughter, and the way she'd spun in circles watching the skirt of her dress twirl around her legs. And suddenly he was thinking about how much time he'd missed with his own child—who was already a woman.

He wondered what she'd looked like as a baby, whether he would have recognized any parts of himself in her features. Had she been a shy toddler who hid behind her mother's legs whenever a stranger spoke to her, or one of those precocious children who was happy to make friends with everyone who crossed her path? And the more he thought about all these things that he didn't know, the angrier he got.

He heard a soft, familiar laugh and glanced over as Gabriella stepped onto the porch, a glass of wine in each hand. It was her fault. As far as he was concerned, she was the one who had deprived him of the opportunity to share in all of Sierra's milestones and moments—and not just the big events, like her first day of school and special occasions, but all of the ordinary days in between.

He wanted to hate her. He *should* hate her. She was the reason he didn't know the beautiful girl on the dance floor who was his daughter. But just looking at Gabriella—in a halter-style top that left her tanned shoulders bare and a long swirling skirt with painted toes peeking out beneath—he felt a complicated mix of emotions, none of which was hate.

She was somehow even sexier now than she'd been when they first met, and despite their history and secrets, he was just as attracted to her now as he'd been back then.

Lust flares hot and bright and burns out quickly. Love endures.

He pushed the echo of his sister's words from his mind. He was *not* in love with Gabriella. Maybe he didn't hate her, but he didn't forgive her, either. Which only made it all the more difficult to figure out how the hell he was supposed to deal with her.

He watched her approach. Her bare feet made no sound on the deck, but there was a rope of gold chain slung low on her hips that jangled with every step she took. She'd always had an innate sensuality that stirred his blood, and his response was immediate and intense.

She was smiling, as if she was truly happy to see him. He knew she was only playing her part, giving him an excuse for being there. And while part of him wanted to curse her for the fact that he needed an excuse, a bigger part was content to simply enjoy looking at her.

As his gaze zeroed in on her mouth, he couldn't help but remember the day of their picnic in the park. Kissing her in the shadows of the trees. The taste of her sweet lips, the press of her soft body against his, the passion of her response. As he pushed the memories to the back of his mind, he couldn't help but wonder if his feelings for Gabriella had always been more complicated than he'd wanted to acknowledge.

She offered him one of the glasses she carried. "It's a cabernet. Not up to your usual standards, I'm sure, but decent."

He took the glass, sipped, and nodded in agreement with her assessment. "Was she surprised?"

Gabriella's lips curved. "She pretended to be. But more importantly, she's with her family and friends and having fun."

"Not all of her family," he noted.

She sighed. "Tell me again why I let you come."

"Because you knew you couldn't keep me away."

"I guess that would explain it." She nudged him toward a long table that was laden down with enormous platters of food. There were hot and cold hors d'oeuvres, crudités and dips, little sandwiches and quiches, mini-pastries and assorted sweets, and an enormous bowl of punch. "But since you're here, you might as well have something to eat."

He picked up a plate. "It's quite a spread you've put out."

"Teenagers—even teenage girls—like to eat, and my mother likes to fuss."

"She did all of this?"

"Most of it," Gabriella admitted. "I was assigned a few simple tasks—chopping vegetables, cutting sandwiches—basically, things that I couldn't screw up too badly."

"You're not much of a cook?"

She shook her head. "That domestic talent seems to have skipped my generation. Sierra, on the other hand, is a natural in the kitchen."

Just one more thing that he hadn't known. But before he

could comment on it, someone lowered the volume on the music to announce that it was time for Sierra to open her gifts. Gabriella tugged on his arm, drawing him closer to the crowd that had gathered around the birthday girl.

The presents had been set on another table, and he'd added his to the pile when he'd arrived. Sierra took her time opening each one, exclaiming over every item and sincerely thanking the individual giver. There were CDs and DVDs and books and clothes, and she seemed genuinely delighted with each item. And yet, when she picked up the glossy pink bag that contained his gift, Cameron felt his palms go damp and his breath catch in his throat.

She read the card, then her eyes searched for him in the crowd. He'd signed it simply "Cameron" and she took the cue, introducing him to the gathering as a friend of her mother's without mention of his title. Then she pulled the tissue out of the bag and reached inside, making a soft sound of surprised pleasure when she found the bear. She held it to her breast, her eyes sparkling and her lips curving wide, and Cameron's heart started to beat again.

Gabriella watched her daughter cuddle the teddy bear that Cameron had given to her, Sierra's first gift from her father, and her heart simply melted.

It wasn't the casual, inexpensive gift that Gabriella had suggested. Even from a distance, she could see the tag on the left ear that identified the bear as a Steiff. But Sierra's appreciation of the gift had nothing to do with its price tag and everything to do with her pleasure at being able to add the gorgeous blond mohair bear to her collection.

"Good call," she murmured to Cameron.

"It was your idea," he reminded her.

"And thank you—for backing down on the car."

He shrugged. "You know her better than I do, obviously,

and if you say she isn't ready, then I'll respect your judgment on that."

"It's not the only thing she isn't ready for," she warned.

"You're worried about her learning the truth about who I am," he guessed.

She nodded.

"When do you think she will be ready?" He was trying to be patient, but he'd already lost sixteen years with his daughter and he didn't intend to lose any more.

"I don't know," she admitted. "I'm just asking you to give her a chance to get to know you first, before you turn her whole world upside down."

"Is it really Sierra's world that you're worried about—or your own?"

She heard the challenge in his voice, and thought she understood. Finding out that he'd fathered a child so many years ago had obviously affected him, but he still didn't—couldn't—know what it meant to truly be a parent. He couldn't know that Sierra's world and her world were one and the same, that when Sierra hurt, Gabriella hurt right along with her.

"In a lot of ways, Sierra is very mature for her age. So much so that I sometimes forget that she's only sixteen, that her heart is still vulnerable. And while I have no doubt there's a part of her that still yearns for a father as much as she did when she was ten, she's not going to be as unquestioning or accepting of your sudden appearance in her life as she would have been back then."

"Then maybe you should have found me six years ago," he retorted. "Better yet, sixteen years ago."

"Because you would have been thrilled to learn that you were a father," she said, not even trying to mask her sarcasm.

"No," he admitted. "But at least I would have known."

"I tried to tell you," she reminded him. She didn't want to talk about what was still a painful memory for her, but she couldn't let him continue to play the injured party without bearing any responsibility for the choices they'd both made. "You didn't even know who I was."

He winced. "That's not true—"

"Don't," she said, her voice sharp. "I'd heard the rumors. I knew that you were just looking for a good time. But I let myself believe that we had something special, that you really cared about me. Of course, you made sure I believed it—because you knew it was the only way you would get me into bed."

"I *did* care about you, dammit."

She turned away, refusing to listen to his lies, refusing to acknowledge that there was still a tiny part of her heart that wanted to believe him. "I'm going to get the cake."

Chapter Eight

Cameron followed her into the house.

He wasn't ready to let their conversation drop, but he realized that their daughter's birthday party might not be the best time or place to continue it. He wanted answers. There was so much he wanted to know, but he also knew that he had to be prepared to face Gabriella's questions—and Sierra's, too—to explain the things he'd said and done so many years ago, to accept responsibility for his own actions.

For now, he only watched as Gabriella carefully arranged sixteen pink candles around the elaborately scrolled letters that spelled out "Happy Sweet Sixteen, Sierra."

"More of your mother's work?" he asked.

Gabriella nodded.

"It's beautiful."

"Wait until you taste it," she told him. "Dominic Donatella has been trying to wrangle her buttercream icing recipe out of her for more than twenty years."

"Donatella—as in Donatella's Bakery?"

She nodded again, but her eyes—still focused on the cake—filled with tears.

"Gabriella?"

"Sorry, birthdays always make me a little nostalgic, and I can't believe it's her sixteenth already." She blew out a soft breath. "When she was little, she used to think really hard about her wish, then she'd squeeze her eyes shut and blow with all of her might. She was so serious about her wishes, so certain she could make them come true."

"Do you know what kinds of things she wished for?"

"A lot of the usual things—dolls and puppies and ponies. And then, the year she turned ten, she told me that what she really wanted, more than anything in the world, was to be a princess."

She made a show of counting the candles again, while Cameron considered this revelation. He was sure it wasn't an unusual wish for a little girl, and he couldn't help but wonder how Gabriella had responded to her daughter's statement.

"You could have made that wish come true for her," he felt compelled to point out. "All you had to do was acknowledge the truth about her paternity."

"I thought about it," Gabriella admitted. "Not because it was Sierra's wish, but because I wanted her to know her father, and for her to know you."

"Then why didn't you?" he demanded. "If you really wanted me to know, why didn't you ever make any effort to contact me? Why is it that the only reason I found out about my daughter is that I tracked you down and came face-to-face with her?"

She glanced away. "I couldn't get in touch with you."

He scowled. "Are you claiming you didn't know how to reach me?"

"No, I'm saying that I couldn't. Because I'd made a promise."

"What kind of promise?" he demanded. "To whom?"

"Gabriella—"

They both started at the interruption.

"—are you bringing the cake?" Katarina's question preceded her entry into the kitchen. "Oh." She glanced from Gabriella to Cameron and back again. "I didn't realize I was interrupting."

"You're not," Gabriella responded quickly. "I was just looking for the matches."

"In the cupboard over the fridge, where we've always kept them," her mother pointed out.

"Right." Gabriella moved away from him, rising onto her tiptoes to retrieve the long box.

Cameron hovered in the background, feeling uneasy under the older woman's scrutiny. He'd never had occasion to meet Gabriella's mother before. When he and Gabriella had first started seeing each other, they'd each had their own reasons for wanting to keep the relationship a secret. He wondered if Gabriella had ever told her mother that he was Sierra's father, and guessed not. Katarina looked like the kind of woman who would have tracked him down and kicked his ass to hell and back if she'd known. But he also guessed, based on the narrow-eyed stare that pinned him now, that she'd figured it out—or at least had some suspicions.

"You must be Gabriella's mother." He thought about offering his hand, but decided against it as she looked more inclined to swat it away than accept it. "I'm Cameron Leandres."

"I know who I am and who you are," she said. "I didn't come in to exchange pleasantries, only to check on the cake."

"Madre!" Gabriella chided, her cheeks coloring slightly.

"I will not apologize for speaking my mind," Katarina told her. "And while I appreciate that you are Sierra's mother and want what is best for her, I don't see how encouraging a relationship between your daughter and this man—a man who wasn't there for you, who did nothing to help when your baby almost died—could be best for her. It would be far better for her to never know the identity of her father than to know he is a man who could turn his back on the girl he got pregnant and the innocent child she bore."

He didn't respond to Katarina's outburst but turned to Gabriella for clarification. "What does she mean—your baby almost died?"

But she only shook her head, shooting an angry look at her mother. "I'm *not* going to do this now."

"Dammit, Gabriella. I deserve to know—"

"Today is a celebration," she interrupted, her voice deliberately calm as she tucked the matches under arm and picked up the cake. "And Sierra is waiting."

So he bided his time. He wasn't particularly happy about it, but he waited. He watched the birthday girl blow out her candles and eat her cake, saw her kiss her grandmother's cheek and wrap her arms—cast and all—around her mother. There was such easy affection between the three women, evidence of the solid bond between all of them.

Gabriella had given their daughter a good life—with help from her mother, of course—and Sierra was obviously happy. What right did he have to barge into their lives at this late date and upset the status quo?

Yes, he was Sierra's father, but that was an accident of biology rather than any particular planning on his part. As Katarina pointed out, he hadn't been there for Gabriella through her pregnancy or childbirth or any of the other stages of Sierra's life until now. And why was he here now?

He frowned over that question as he helped Gabriella tidy up the kitchen. She was right—he hadn't been ready to be a father sixteen years ago, and he wasn't entirely sure he was ready now. But he was thirty-six now—old enough and mature enough to own up to his responsibilities, to be a father to his daughter—even if she didn't seem to need him.

He looked through the window over the sink. Most of the guests had already gone, but a few of Sierra's closest friends had lingered, along with a guy who was—in his opinion—far too close to his daughter.

"Who's that with Sierra?" he asked Gabriella.

She squeezed out the dish cloth, wiped around the outside of the sink. "Paolo."

He didn't want to ask, but the question sprang from his lips anyway. "Boyfriend?"

She nodded. "They've been seeing each other for about six months now."

"Isn't she too young to have a boyfriend?"

"She's sixteen," she reminded him.

"Just turned sixteen," he shot back.

She only smiled. "Paolo's a good guy."

He frowned. "Are you really okay with this?"

"Let's just say that I've learned to pick my battles."

"You seem to have a really good relationship," he commented. "I can't imagine you having any battles."

"If you stick around long enough, you'll see plenty of them," she promised.

"But you don't think I will stick around, do you?"

She was silent as she carefully folded the dish cloth, then draped it over the faucet. "I don't have any expectations one way or the other."

"I guess I can't blame you for that," he said. "But I can promise you that I'm sticking around this time."

"Because you think it's the right thing to do?"

"Partly," he admitted.

"But what if it's not?" she challenged.

"What do you mean?"

Her gaze went to the window, and when she finally turned back to him, he saw the confusion and uncertainty clearly in the depths of dark eyes. "What if telling Sierra the truth about who you are isn't the right thing for her?"

"Would you be asking that question if I wasn't a prince?"

Her hesitation confirmed that his title was a concern to her. Most people wanted to exploit his royal status; Gabriella would prefer it didn't exist.

"The fact is, you are a prince," she said. "And when word gets out that you have an illegitimate child, there will be a media frenzy with Sierra at the center."

"She'll deal with it," he said confidently.

"But why should she have to?"

"Because whether you want to acknowledge it or not, she is a Leandres, a princess and a member of the royal family of Tesoro del Mar."

"I'm not the only one who might not want to acknowledge it," Gabriella warned him.

"What's the supposed to mean?"

She shook her head. "Nothing. Forget it."

"Obviously it was something," he said. "And I'm growing frustrated by the way you continually dodge my questions."

"I'm not dodging," she denied.

He lifted a brow. "Just picking your battles?"

She gave him a half-smile. "Something like that."

"If you're not dodging, then tell me what your mother meant about Sierra almost dying."

"It really wasn't as dramatic as that," Gabriella said.

"Sounds like a dodge to me."

"She was born with an atrial septal defect—more commonly called a hole in the heart," she finally admitted. "It wasn't anything that was immediately apparent. She came out crying and she had ten fingers and ten toes, but her skin had a slightly bluish tinge and she seemed to struggle a little with her breathing, something that became more apparent during nursing.

"When it was diagnosed, the doctors were optimistic that it would close on its own. But it didn't, and when she was six months old, she had open heart surgery."

"Why do I get the feeling you're glossing over a lot of details?"

"Because I am. Because I really don't want to go back to that time, even in my mind, and remember how terrified I was."

He couldn't blame her for that. And he could understand why her mother resented him. Katarina was right—he hadn't been there for Gabriella, he'd done nothing to help when her baby had almost died, and now he'd stormed back into the life she'd built for herself and her child and was threatening to turn it upside down.

"The worst thing," she said to him now, "was knowing that Sierra needed the surgery and not knowing if the doctors would do it."

"Because she was so young?"

She shook her head. "Because I couldn't pay for it. I had no medical coverage, no savings." She looked down at the hands that she'd linked her lap. "I had nothing but my baby, and I was so scared I was going to lose her."

He couldn't even begin to imagine. Even now, only knowing about his daughter for a few weeks, he would be devastated if anything happened to her. Gabriella had carried their child in her womb for nine months, she'd struggled through he-didn't-know-how-many hours of labor to bring her into the world, and then she'd been given a medical diagnosis that forced her to face the possibility that her baby might die.

"But they did the surgery," he said, trying to refocus her thoughts on the positive outcome rather than the obstacles she'd faced.

She nodded. "I would have done anything, given anything, to save my baby."

Something in her voice alerted him to the fact that there was more to the story, some other detail that she wasn't telling him, something that he wasn't sure he wanted to know. "But you didn't come to me," he noted.

"No," she admitted. "I couldn't."

He didn't understand. She had to know that money wasn't an issue for him. Not only could he have taken care of the bill for Sierra's surgery, he could have bought a hospital—and would have—if it was necessary.

Maybe, after the way things had ended, she'd decided that she couldn't count on him for anything. But by her own admission, she'd been alone and scared and desperate. It seemed to him that desperation would have trumped everything else, and yet she still hadn't come to him.

"Why not?" he demanded.

She met his gaze evenly. "Because I'd made a deal with your mother."

Gabriella's tone was matter-of-fact. She refused to feel any guilt for what she had done and the only regret she had was that it had been necessary. But she'd meant what she said— she would have done anything to save her baby. And when the princess royal had visited her in the hospital and offered the chance to do just that, there had been absolutely no doubt in her mind.

She'd wondered about the other woman's motives in offering to help. Elena Leandres had made it clear to Gabriella the first day she visited the hospital that she didn't for one minute believe that Cameron was Sierra's father, although she'd kept close tabs on her son and knew about the weekend he'd spent with Gabriella. And she'd warned Gabriella of the havoc she would wreak if she ever dared suggest otherwise.

Gabriella knew it wasn't an empty threat. She knew it didn't matter that she hadn't ever been with anyone but Cameron. The truth had no force compared to a royal decree and if the princess royal claimed that she'd slept with a dozen men, any of whom could be the father of her child, she'd no doubt find a parade of men who would support her claim.

Gabriella resented the implication, but she didn't argue.

What was the point, anyway? Why should she insist on putting Cameron's name on her baby's birth certificate when he'd made it clear that he had no interest in her or the baby she carried? So she'd claimed the father was "unknown" and the princess royal had ensured that Gabriella had the money she needed to pay for Sierra's surgery.

It was, she'd thought at the time, more than a fair trade. And if she'd had occasional twinges of doubt over the years, she'd only needed to look at her happy and healthy daughter to push those twinges aside.

With Gabriella's confession, all of the pieces fell into place in Cameron's mind, like a jigsaw puzzle finally taking shape. Since coming face-to-face with his daughter that first day, he'd struggled to understand how Gabriella could keep their child a secret from him for so many years, why she would lie to him about Sierra's paternity. But now he knew. And long after he'd left the party and begun to drive the familiar winding streets that led to his mother's home, frustration and fury continued to burn inside of him.

Elena had already settled into bed for the night, the butler advised him, and Cameron knew she would not be happy to be disturbed. He didn't care. Nor did he wait in the parlor for her, as the butler suggested. He'd waited too damn long already.

Elena was just shoving her arms into the sleeves of a robe when he pushed open the door of her suite. She glanced over, irritation evident in the furrow of her brow. "Honestly, Cameron, do you have any idea what hour it is?"

"Just after midnight on the day of my daughter's sixteenth birthday," he noted.

Her hands paused in the act of tying a knot at the front of her robe. "So you know."

He stared at her, incredulous. "That's all you can say?"

"If it were up to me, we wouldn't be having this conversation at all," she reminded him.

"How could you not tell me? How could you have known that Gabriella had given birth to my child—*your grandchild*—and not tell me?"

Elena sniffed disdainfully. "I only knew that you'd shown poor judgment in dating a commoner—a waitress, no less—who later had a baby. I had no way of knowing that the child was yours."

"And yet you went to visit Gabriella in the hospital, to see the baby."

"I was curious."

"Curious enough to have the baby's DNA typed?"

"I don't need to explain my actions to you."

He shook his head. He'd known his mother was manipulative and self-centered and yet, throughout the drive to her home, he'd dared to let himself hope that there was some reasonable explanation for what she'd done.

"You knew she was mine."

"All I knew was that you were careless and immature and irresponsible—no greater crimes than most young men are guilty of—and I didn't want you to be stuck paying for those crimes for the rest of your life."

"But it was okay for Gabriella to pay?"

"She wanted the child."

"How could you know I didn't?"

She laughed at that, though the sound was abrupt and without humor. "You were little more than a child yourself, neither ready nor willing to be responsible for anyone else."

"It wasn't your decision to make."

"You'd already made your decision, by finally ending your relationship with the little slut."

He felt his hands curl into fists. He'd never wanted to hit another human being and the fact that he had to fight against the urge now—and that the human being in question was his mother—made his stomach churn. Deliberately, he blew out a long breath and unfurled his fingers. "She wasn't a slut, she is the mother of my child, and you will speak of her with respect."

"I am your mother and you will speak to *me* with respect," Elena said sharply.

"I can't speak to you at all right now," Cameron told her. "Just thinking about what you did, your lies and manipulations, makes me ill."

"I did what was best for you and this family."

"My daughter is part of this family," he shot back.

Elena's eyes narrowed. "You've worked hard to get where you are now," she reminded him. "What do you think will happen to your image in the press and the future of your career if you try to claim that bastard child as your daughter?"

"Do you think I care?"

"If you don't, you're a bigger fool than I thought. And maybe that's partly my fault," she continued. "I let you be the spoiled prince for too long, trusting that you would find your purpose and direction when you were ready. And I thought you had found it when you joined Rowan's cabinet. But this renewed fascination with Gabriella and your sudden determination to be some kind of father to her daughter prove you're as unfocused as ever."

"Actually, I think I may have finally found my focus," he told her.

"Walk away from her," Elena said. "If you don't, you're going to lose everything."

Cameron walked away from his mother instead. Because he'd finally realized that Gabriella and Sierra were everything that mattered, and he wasn't going to give up on them and the future he hoped they could build together. Not again.

After Cameron had gone, Elena sat at the antique desk in her upstairs office waiting for the supervisor of her security detail. As she was considering the most appropriate course of action, her gaze fell on the silver tri-fold frame—a gift from her late husband that contained photos of each of their three children.

She'd been blessed with two sons, and she'd had dreams and ambitions for each of them. Unfortunately, her disappointment had been as great as her plans when first Michael and then Cameron had chosen to pursue his own path. Though she'd been frustrated, she couldn't pretend not to understand where the defiance came from. She herself had defied her father's wishes to make a good match for her when she'd run away to marry a farmer.

It had seemed so romantic at the time. And she truly had loved Gaetan, at least in the beginning. When he'd died, just a few months after his forty-seventh birthday, she'd grieved—and she'd felt released. The idealistic life she'd envisioned had been painted over by the reality of trying to build a life with a man who wanted different things than she did—and who made no secret of the fact that he disapproved of her plans for their sons.

But he'd been gone a lot of years before she'd approached Michael about making a play for the throne. Her eldest son had refused to even consider her proposition. She'd tried to make him see that he'd been meant for greater things than his little advertising company, but he'd been adamant that his career and his wife were all he wanted.

He didn't even plan to have children, a decision which Elena viewed not just as a disappointment but a betrayal. As the oldest son, he had a duty to provide an heir. He needed a son of his own to extend the royal line and carry the family name. But while Michael remained steadfast, Samantha was eventually persuaded. Unfortunately, when she finally did give birth it was to a girl, and then she'd died only a few hours later, leaving Michael alone with the burden of an infant daughter.

He'd taken his wife's sudden and unexpected death hard, and Elena allowed herself a moment to wonder if Michael had yet adjusted to the loss before she focused her thoughts on her second-born son. Cameron had always been more malleable, more eager to please. In his youth, he'd been occasionally irresponsible and frequently reckless, but for the most part, he'd fallen in line with her expectations. Aside from that brief rebellious period in college when he'd been sneaking around with Gabriella, of course, but she'd nipped that in the bud. She'd helped him see the error of his ways and convinced him that he was destined for bigger things.

She didn't regret keeping the existence of his child a secret sixteen years ago. She only regretted that he'd found out now. But far worse than his knowledge was his intention to publicly claim the child as his own—as if he couldn't see that such an announcement would be an unmitigated disaster. He'd skirted the edge of scandal too many times already, and it was quite possible that the revelation of his youthful indiscretion would be the final nail in the coffin of his political career.

It wasn't that Elena had a problem with Cameron being a father, although she'd naturally been disappointed by the child's gender. If she didn't know better, she might have thought that both of her sons had fathered daughters on purpose just to spite her. But at least Michael had been married to the mother of his child, and while Elena and Samantha had never been close, her son's wife had come from a good family, she'd been well-educated and she'd been both understanding and respectful of Michael's background.

Gabriella Vasquez was a completely different story. She'd been nothing more than a starry-eyed waitress who saw the young prince as her ticket to the easy life. The quickness with which she'd snatched at Elena's offer of money in exchange for her silence about the baby was proof enough of that fact.

And now, sixteen years later, she thought she could renege on that agreement without consequence?

No way in hell.

Chapter Nine

Gabriella was usually up with the sun, but the day after Sierra's birthday party, she slept late. So late, in fact, that she only awakened when there was a knock on her bedroom door. She lifted a groggy head from her pillow when her mother poked her head in the room.

"What time is it?" Gabriella asked, squinting to focus on her clock.

"Almost time for me to be leaving for mass," Katarina said, stepping into the room. "But I didn't want to go without checking on you first."

Gabriella pushed herself up in bed. "I'm okay. I guess I was just more tired out from yesterday than I realized."

"It was a busy day," her mother agreed. "And an emotional one."

She just nodded.

"I overstepped," Katarina said. "With your prince."

"He's not mine," Gabriella told her. "And I understand why you feel the way that you do."

"I was so angry with you, when you refused to tell me the name of your baby's father."

"I couldn't. I didn't dare. It was all too easy to imagine you storming the gates of his family's estate, demanding that he marry me and give his name to my baby."

"He should have married you," Katarina insisted.

"We were both too young to marry."

"But old enough to make a baby."

Gabriella sighed. "And don't you think I'm a little too old for this lecture now, *madre?*"

Katarina shrugged. "Perhaps. It's just that I look at Sierra sometimes and she reminds me so much of you that it's scary. She's so beautiful and willful and I worry that she will follow her heart as you did, and have it broken."

"A broken heart heals," she said.

"And yet, you have never loved anyone else," her mother noted.

Gabriella thought, fleetingly, of Rafe, and wanted to protest, but the words stuck in her throat. Her mother was right. As much as she'd wanted to love Rafe, to share her life and build a future with him, she'd never been able to give him her heart. Because she'd already—foolishly—given it away too many years before. "I have you and Sierra. I don't need anyone else."

"If I had known—" Katarina shook her head. "I should have known. I should have seen that you were in love and always making excuses to get out of the house."

"I was pretty industrious," Gabriella admitted.

Her mother nodded. "But he was older, more sophisticated and experienced."

"And I was blind and naive," Gabriella interjected. "I know, and I'd rather not go down that road again." She'd spent enough time, during the darkest hours of the night, remembering what she'd had, what she'd lost, and wondering how things might have turned out if both she and Cameron had handled the situation differently.

"He broke your heart." There was anger and accusation in Katarina's tone.

"He gave me my daughter," Gabriella said softly.

"You always did look on the bright side of things."

"And she is the brightest part of my life."

Katarina smiled and touched a hand to her daughter's cheek. "I know how you feel."

When her hand dropped away, Gabriella reached for it, held on. "I'm scared," she admitted.

"Of telling Sierra?" Katarina guessed.

"Of losing Sierra," she admitted softly. "He can offer her so much more than I can."

"Things, perhaps." Katarina waved a hand dismissively. "But he cannot love her more than you do, and nothing he can offer her now will undermine the solid foundation you have given her over the past sixteen years."

"I hope you're right."

"You believe, then, that he is planning to acknowledge that he is her father?"

"I think he would have done so already, if I hadn't convinced him to wait—to give Sierra some time."

"He doesn't strike me as the patient type," Katarina mused.

"Not at all," Gabriella agreed.

"Which makes me wonder if maybe I was wrong."

"About what?"

"About what he wants from you." Her mother's tone was quiet now, reflective, and made Gabriella squirm uneasily.

"He wants a relationship with his daughter," she pointed out.

"Maybe that's true," Katarina agreed, "but it might not be the whole truth."

"Care to explain that? Because it's too early for me to wrap my head around one of your riddles."

"It's not early at all," her mother denied. "In fact, if I don't hurry now, I will be late for church."

Then she dropped a kiss on her daughter's cheek and was gone.

After she'd taken a quick shower to clear the last of the cobwebs from her brain and tugged on some clothes, Gabriella made her way down to the kitchen, following the scent of the coffee her mother had already brewed. She knew that some of her friends and colleagues had wondered about her living arrangement—a thirty-four-year-old mother of a teenage daughter living with her own mother—but Katarina had truly been her rock, not just since that fateful day when the results of an over-the-counter pregnancy test had changed her world, but for as long as she could remember.

She'd been so scared to tell her mother that she was pregnant. Not because she worried that her mother would turn her out of her home, but because she knew she would be disappointed. She'd raised Gabriella with traditional values and morals, and learning that her unwed teenage daughter was pregnant was a slap in the face to everything she believed in. Still, she'd never wavered in her support of her daughter, and the only time they'd seriously argued was when Gabriella refused to reveal the name of her baby's father.

In fact, it was only a few weeks earlier, after Cameron's first visit to her home, that Gabriella had been shaken enough to confess the truth. Based on her mother's reaction to the news—and her uncensored comments to Cameron the night before—Gabriella had been wise to keep that information to herself for so long.

But now, the secret that she'd so closely guarded for so many years was about to be revealed. And she couldn't help but wonder how the princess royal would respond to that.

Gabriella had kept her end of the bargain—she'd never told

Cameron about his child. In fact, she'd gone one step further and denied that he was the father when he'd asked. She hadn't counted on Cameron making any further inquiries on his own, and she didn't think Elena would have anticipated such interest, either.

The doorbell rang as she was refilling her mug with coffee and she carried it with her when she went to answer the summons. Cameron was on the step, but unlike his first visit to her home two weeks earlier, this time she didn't hesitate to step back and let him inside.

"Coffee?" she asked.

"Please," he said, sounding desperately grateful.

She returned to the kitchen, pulled a second mug from the cupboard. "Cream? Sugar?"

"Just black."

She glanced over her shoulder as he dropped into a chair at the table. "You look like you had a rough night."

"I haven't slept," he admitted.

She pushed the mug across the table to him. "At all?"

He shook his head. "I haven't even been home. After I left here last night, I went to see my mother. And then I just drove."

"That's a lot of driving," she said lightly.

"I had a lot of thinking to do."

"Do you want something to eat? I could scramble some eggs."

He glanced up, the ghost of a smile hovering at the edges of his lips. "I must really look like hell if you're offering to cook for me."

"I don't cook," she reminded him. "Scrambling eggs doesn't count as cooking."

"In that case, I would love some."

Gabriella took a handful of eggs out of the fridge, cracked them into a bowl. She added some milk, a dash of salt and pepper, then whipped them until they were frothy.

"For someone who doesn't cook, you know your way around a kitchen."

"I can handle the basics," she assured him, setting a frying pan on top of the stove.

"Do you have a recipe that might make a serving of crow more palatable?"

She slid a couple of slices of bread into the toaster, then turned to him. "A recipe for what?"

"Crow," he said again.

"Are you planning to eat crow?" she asked him.

"At the very least."

Gabriella took the coffee pot to the table, refilled his mug. "Eat your breakfast first," she instructed. "Before it gets cold."

He picked up his fork and dug into the eggs. The meal was simple but delicious, and in minutes, he'd completely cleaned his plate.

"I owe you an apology."

"I appreciate the sentiment," she said. "But I'd rather focus on where we go from here than rehash the past."

"That's generous of you."

"Not really," she denied. "We've both made mistakes."

He nodded. "So where do we go from here?"

She folded her hands around her mug. "I know you're anxious for Sierra to know who you are."

"I am," he agreed. "But it might be better if we spent some time together first, getting to know one another without the father-daughter labels hanging over our heads."

"I think that's a good idea."

"Does she like boats?"

"She's never been on one," Gabriella admitted. "But she's usually game to try new things."

"Then why don't we plan an outing for Wednesday afternoon?"

"Wednesday?"

"School's out for summer break now, isn't it?"

Gabriella nodded. "Sierra wrote her last exam Friday morning."

"Good," he said. "My morning is booked solid with meetings, but I should be able to get away from the office by noon and there won't be nearly as much traffic on the water then as on the weekend."

Maybe it should have irritated her that he didn't ask about her work schedule, but the fact was that as long as she got her columns in to her editor on time, her hours were completely flexible. And the idea of spending an afternoon out on the water instead of in front of her computer was too tempting to resist. "Do you want me to pack a lunch?"

"No. I'll have my chef put something together for us."

"Well, then, I'm sure we'll eat better than tuna sandwiches."

He frowned at the obvious pique in her tone. "It bothers you that I have a chef?"

"No," she denied. "I guess it just reminded me that you aren't like the rest of us common folk." And she was glad for the reminder, because allowing herself to think otherwise could be very dangerous.

"I could fire him, if that would make you feel better," he teased.

"Yeah, because putting some guy out of a job would make me happy," she said dryly.

"I don't understand why my title and status are such an issue for you."

"Of course you don't, because you're the one with the blue blood."

"It's not quite as blue as Elena would like everyone to believe," he told her.

"Your father wasn't of noble birth?" she guessed, aware that his mother had a direct connection to the throne.

"My father was a farmer," he told her. "It was quite the scandal when they got married."

"She must have really loved him," Gabriella mused. But try as she might, she couldn't imagine the woman who had heartlessly bargained with Sierra's life caring that much about anyone.

"Or she really wanted to piss off her father," Cameron suggested.

That scenario was much easier for Gabriella to envision. It also made her wonder, "Is that why you were with me?"

"I was with you because you were beautiful and sexy and smart," he said patiently. "And because the moment I laid eyes on you, I didn't want to be with anyone else."

The words sounded good, and Gabriella wanted to believe them. She wanted to believe in *him*. But she couldn't help remembering how careful he'd been to ensure they weren't seen in public together.

At the time, she'd thought he was protecting her from the media spotlight. Later, she'd accepted that he'd been protecting himself. After all, it would have damaged his image to be seen in the company of a waitress.

Sixteen years later, not much had changed. Although "the partying prince" didn't grace the covers of the tabloids as frequently as he had ten years earlier, he was still accustomed to being photographed in the company of the world's most wealthy and beautiful women. Gabriella didn't fit into either category. She was a single mother who had obtained her journalism degree while her daughter was in diapers and the simple fact that her child was also the prince's child couldn't magically bridge the distance that separated their two worlds.

"How many staff do you have on your yacht?" she asked him now.

"Three."

"Do you trust them?"

"Implicitly," he assured her without hesitation.

"Then I guess we'll see you around noon on Wednesday."

On Tuesday, the long-standing trade agreement between Tesoro del Mar and Ardena was officially renewed. Afterward, Cameron tracked down the prince regent in his office.

"I'm going to play hooky tomorrow afternoon," Cameron said.

"It's not really hooky if you tell me," Rowan informed him.

"Okay then, I'm not really playing hooky tomorrow afternoon."

Rowan pushed aside the document he'd been reviewing. "Obviously there's a reason you thought I should be aware of your plans."

"I just wanted to give you a heads-up, in case some enterprising photographer catches a picture of me and/or my guests."

Rowan waited, patiently, for him to continue.

"I'm going to spend the afternoon on my yacht with Gabriella Vasquez and her daughter—my daughter—Sierra."

The prince regent's brows shot up. "Your daughter?"

He nodded.

Rowan frowned. "Your personal life isn't any of my business—except when it reflects on this office. And when I appointed you to the cabinet, you promised me that you were finished living the life of a carefree playboy."

"And I meant it," Cameron assured him.

"Then can you tell me how in hell this happened?"

Cameron couldn't blame his cousin for being pissed. Because what Rowan hadn't said, but Cameron knew was that when he'd named his cousin to the cabinet, it was against the recommendation of several key advisors—and probably both of his brothers, too.

"A youthful indiscretion?" he suggested.

The furrow in Rowan's brow deepened. "Dammit, Cameron, you're thirty-six years old—"

"And she's sixteen."

His cousin's face drained of all color. "The mother?"

"*Dios,* no! My daughter."

"Oh." Rowan exhaled. "Thank God."

"I can't believe you'd even think—" Cameron shook his head. "That's just sick."

"I'm sorry." The apology was automatic but sincere. "I guess the headlines about the king's daughter are still on my mind."

"I only recently learned about Sierra's existence," Cameron explained. "And Gabriella and I have agreed to keep the truth of her paternity under wraps until we've had a chance to tell her."

"How many people do know?"

"Other than myself and Gabriella, just her mother, my mother, Marissa and now you."

"How did your mother respond to the news?"

"Let's just say that it wasn't news to her." Cameron's gut still burned with fury whenever he thought about his mother's lies.

Rowan, being well-acquainted with Elena's manipulations and machinations, only nodded. "Then I'd suggest you don't wait too long to tell your daughter," he warned. "Secrets have a habit of blowing up when we least expect it."

It was a truth that Cameron understood only too well.

"This is so lame," Sierra grumbled. She'd been on the phone with Beth, making plans to go down to the waterfront. They were going to spend the afternoon doing some shopping and hanging out, and then she was going to meet Paolo when he finished work.

It was, in her opinion, the perfect way to spend a summer

afternoon. Except that her mother had kiboshed those plans because she wanted Sierra to spend the day with her. Which wouldn't have been such a hardship, really. Gabriella was pretty cool, as far as mothers went. She didn't harp on Sierra all the time about her clothes or her make-up, the way Rachel's mother did. And she was usually flexible about her curfew, as long as she knew where Sierra was and who she was with.

But when Sierra tried to wriggle out of spending the afternoon with her, this time she was completely *in*flexible. And it wasn't even because she wanted some private mother-daughter time, it was because she wanted Sierra to get to know Prince Cameron. And maybe Sierra had thought it was sweet when she'd first met him and realized the man standing in her living room was royalty, but now, it was kind of weird.

She'd Googled him, out of curiosity, and she'd been stunned by the amount of information that was on the internet about him. The basic facts were well-known. He was the second son and middle child of the princess royal, Elena Marissa Santiago Leandres, and her deceased husband, Gaetan Rainier Leandres, which meant that Prince Cameron was fourteenth in line to the throne—not likely to ever rule the country but not completely out of the running, either, which was sort of cool. He'd been educated at St. Mary's College in Port Augustine and at Cambridge University and had spent several years traveling abroad before returning home to accept a position in the royal cabinet. His Royal Highness Prince Rowan Santiago, the current prince regent, had made the original appointment and recently named him the country's new Minister of Trade.

Aside from all of that, most of the other stuff she found was gossip—photos of women he'd dated, rumors of engagements, reports of break-ups. He'd dated *a lot* of women, but not any one woman for any length of time, and even if only half the stories she read were true (because she was savvy enough to know she couldn't believe *everything* she read on the internet), she felt that she had reason to worry about his interest in her mother.

Gabriella was every bit as beautiful as any of the other women he'd dated, but she lacked their worldliness and sophistication. Sierra couldn't help but wonder how her mother had caught his eye and what his intentions were toward her. And she decided that, as much as she resented having to change her own plans, it was probably a good idea for her to keep any eye on things.

Gabriella finished wrapping the plate of brownies. "I thought you would enjoy an afternoon on the water."

"With my mother and her new boyfriend?" she asked, not even trying to hide her sarcasm.

"It's not like that," Gabriella said. "Cameron and I are just friends."

Sierra wondered whether she was trying to convince her daughter or herself.

"I may only be sixteen," she reminded Gabriella, "but I'm not a child and I'm not an idiot. You dated Rafe for six months before you brought him home to meet me, now this prince is suddenly in your life and you're pushing me to get to know him.

"So is that the real reason you're dragging me along?" she pressed. "Am I your chaperone—so he doesn't pressure you to go too far?"

Gabriella pushed her hair back off her forehead and sent her daughter a baleful glance. "Honestly, Sierra, you have the most vivid imagination."

"I wasn't imagining the way he was looking at you."

"I'm not worried about Cameron behaving inappropriately," her mother insisted.

"Because you're as hot for him as he is for you?"

Gabriella's cheeks flushed. "Sierra."

It was her don't-mess-with-me tone and usually succeeded in getting her daughter to back down. But the color in her face confirmed that Sierra wasn't far off the mark. Not that she could blame her mother for being attracted—Cameron was incredibly good-looking, for an old guy, and he was a real-life prince, too. In any event, she knew there was more going on here than her mother was telling her, and she wasn't going to let up until she got to the truth.

Except that before she could say anything else, Cameron was at the door.

Chapter Ten

Twenty minutes later, they were at the harbor. Sierra didn't want to be impressed, but it was impossible not to be. She didn't know anything about boats and couldn't even have guessed at the size of the yacht—except to say that it was huge, and gorgeous. It shone brilliantly in the afternoon sun—as stunningly white as a pearl in the sapphire blue waters, and when she stepped onto the glossy wood deck, she felt as if she'd stepped into another world.

Cameron gave them a quick tour. She had expected that the inside would be dim, but it wasn't, as natural light shone through wide windows on every side. There was an enormous saloon with more glossy wood cabinets and tables with leather stools, cushy leather sofas and an impressive home theatre system, a small office, a master cabin with ensuite, plus two more guest cabins, each with its own private bath, and separate crew quarters.

While he'd been showing them around, the yacht had been making its way away from the island. When they finished the tour and returned to the main saloon, she was surprised by how much distance they'd put between themselves and the shore in such a short time.

"Are you hungry?" Cameron asked.

Sierra shrugged, trying to act casual.

"Starved," Gabriella admitted, shooting her daughter a look that Sierra chose to ignore.

"Good." He smiled at both of them, his even white teeth flashing white against his tanned skin. "Emilio has set up lunch on the deck, if that's acceptable. Or we can eat inside, if you'd prefer."

"Outside," Sierra answered automatically, before she remembered that she wasn't supposed to care.

"Gabriella?" he prompted.

There was something about the way he said the name that made it sound like a caress, and the color that infused her mother's cheeks confirmed that she'd heard it, as well.

"Outside sounds wonderful," Gabriella agreed.

He gestured for them to precede him, and again, Sierra had to give him points for presentation. The table had been set for three, with linens and fancy crystal and silverware that was probably the real deal and not the stainless steel stuff in their own drawer at home.

Cameron and her mother chatted easily over the meal, almost as if they really were old friends, and Sierra found herself wondering if maybe she'd been wrong about their relationship. But when he reached over and casually touched the back of her mother's hand and Gabriella's fork slipped from her fingers, she knew that she hadn't been wrong at all.

"Do you like to swim?" he asked, turning his attention to Sierra.

She nodded, because the fact that she did was one of the reasons she'd thought the afternoon on his yacht might not be a total bust.

"Then you should take a dip after lunch," he suggested, lifting his glass of wine. "The water out here is heavenly."

Yeah, he'd probably love for her to take a swim—while he put the moves on her mother.

"I can't swim," she said, holding up her arm in case he'd forgotten about the cast on it. Which he probably had, because he was too preoccupied with thoughts of getting her mother naked to worry about something as insignificant as her broken wrist.

"Sierra." Her mother's sharp response warned that she hadn't missed the disdainful tone of her daughter's voice. "Dr. Granger gave me some waterproof sleeves, if you want to go in the water."

The prince, to his credit, responded smoothly. "Or you could try the jet ski if you don't want to swim."

"Jet ski?" she echoed, her interest piqued despite herself.

"As long as it's okay with your mother," he hastened to add.

Now she did look at Gabriella, trying to convey a mixture of apology and pleading in her gaze. Her mother's hesitation was a warning to Sierra that she expected her best behavior from this point on. She gave a brief nod to telegraph her understanding.

"It's okay with me," Gabriella finally said. "As long as you have your cast covered and wear a life jacket."

Sierra opened her mouth to protest, then closed it again without uttering a word.

"Impressive," Cameron said to Gabriella later.

Lunch had been cleared away and they had taken their wine where they could watch Sierra who, now properly attired, was making waves out on the water.

"She's always loved the water," she told him.

"It shows," he said. "Although I wasn't talking about that."

Gabriella looked over at him. "Then what were you talking about?"

"The wordless communication between the two of you."

"It's not always as effective as I'd like," she said. "Which leads into my turn to apologize to you. She was being deliberately difficult and I don't know why."

"Don't you?"

"She's a teenager, which is probably enough of an explanation for a lot of her behavior, but it was more than that today."

"The 'more than that' being her feelings about the relationship between you and I?"

"That's exactly it," she admitted. "She's somehow got it into her head that we're more than friends and—"

"We *are* more than friends," he said.

The hand she'd raised to reach for her glass dropped away. "We have a history," she acknowledged.

"I think I understand now why she's worried."

"You do?"

He nodded. "Because our daughter is obviously more insightful than you are."

"Cameron."

"Gabriella."

She frowned at the amusement evident in his tone.

"After the kiss we shared in the park, do you really doubt that I'm attracted to you?"

"Considering your reputation, the fact that I'm female should be enough to assuage my doubts," she told him.

He shifted closer. "If you're trying to distract me by making me mad, it's not going to work."

"Didn't I make it clear, after that kiss, that you were wasting your time?"

"That's what you said," he agreed. "But I don't think it's what you meant."

She swallowed, glanced away. "I'm not playing hard to

get—I promise you. I just can't risk getting involved with you again."

"Because of Sierra?" he guessed.

"I want her to get to know you and have a relationship with you. But I don't want her to hope that we'll end up together like one big happy family."

"Because that's not what you want?"

Because it *was* what she wanted, more than anything. But she could hardly admit as much to Cameron. He'd already broken her heart once before—she wasn't going to give him the power to do so again.

"I'm trying to be realistic here, Cameron."

"Reality's overrated."

"Said the prince from his ivory tower," she retorted.

"Being royal has given me a lot of advantages," he acknowledged. "It has also presented a unique set of challenges."

"I'll bet none of those challenges included siphoning money from the grocery fund to pay the electrical bill so that the little food you had in the fridge didn't spoil."

"You're right," he admitted. "I can't begin to imagine how difficult it was for you, struggling to hold down a job and raise a child. And while I can tell you now that I would have helped, the words don't change anything."

"No," she agreed, then reached over to take his hand. "But thank you, anyway."

"I hate knowing that you didn't come to me because you didn't trust me not to turn you away. Because I had already turned you away."

"It was a long time ago," she reminded him.

He reached out, wrapped a strand of her hair around his finger, and tugged gently. The unexpected gesture threw her off-balance, and she had to step forward or risk stumbling.

"Gone but not forgotten?"

She had to tilt her head to meet his gaze, but pride wouldn't let her step away again. "What does that mean?"

"You keep saying that there's no point in dwelling on the past, that it's the future that matters. But you refuse to consider that we could have a future together, and I can't help but think that you're reticent because you haven't let go of the past."

"Maybe I'm reticent because I've never known you to talk about anything further into the future than dinner."

"Ouch." He dropped his hand from his hair, wrapped it around her waist. "So what if I did want to make plans for dinner?"

She could feel the strength in his arm, the heat of his touch, and had to swallow before she could speak. "We just finished lunch."

"We didn't have dessert."

"Sierra made brownies," she reminded him. Not that the brownies had been made specifically for this occasion, it was just that Sierra had been playing around in the kitchen and Gabriella had pilfered half of the pan to bring on this outing. Despite knowing that Cameron had a chef, she didn't like to show up empty-handed.

"Then we should wait for Sierra to have those. In the meantime…" His head lowered toward her.

Gabriella put her hand on his chest. "Don't play games with me, Cameron."

"Is that what you think I'm doing?"

"I don't know," she said. "My brain is spinning in circles right now so that I can't seem to figure any of this out. You invited us here today so that you could spend some time with Sierra—"

"And with you," he told her.

And when he looked at her like that, his eyes burning so intently with heat and hunger, she believed him. More, she felt herself responding.

"This is a mistake," she warned him.

But even before the words were completely out of her

mouth, the hand that she'd laid on his chest curled into the fabric of his shirt.

His mouth came down on hers, hard and hungry; her lips parted for him, eager and willing. She could taste the wine they'd both drunk, and the darker and more potent flavor of the passion that flared between them. Her hands slid up his chest, over his shoulders, linking behind his head. Her fingers toyed with the strands of hair that brushed his collar, so soft and silky in contrast to the lean, hard body pressed against hers.

She felt weak and hot and dizzy, and though she wished she could blame the hot Mediterranean sun, she knew her response had nothing to do with the weather and everything to do with the man. She'd always responded to him like this, completely and instinctively. And while she'd once thrilled to the discovery of such intense and all-consuming desire, she was embarrassed and ashamed to realize that she could still feel such depth of emotion for a man who had broken her heart—and a lot of other hearts, too.

He was used to having whatever he wanted, whenever he wanted, women included. She had been one of those women once, willingly and happily, but she wouldn't let herself be cast in that same role again. Not just because she wanted to protect her heart, but because she wanted to provide a better example for her daughter.

The daughter who, even now, could be on her way back to the boat.

She pulled away from him. "I can't do this."

Cameron took a minute to draw in a breath before he responded. "I'd say we were doing just fine."

"We both know how to go through the motions," she agreed. "But it's never been just that for me. I can't separate the wants of my body from the needs of my heart."

"And you assume that I can?"

"I'd say that history speaks for itself."

"Gone but not forgotten," he said again.

She shook her head. "I'm not referring to our history but your reputation."

"Deserved or not?" he challenged.

"Cameron, I work in the newspaper industry. I know as well as anyone that information is sometimes slanted, the truth is often stretched, and headlines are frequently exaggerated. But I also know it's a fact that you've dated more women in the past year than a lot of men date in their entire lifetimes."

Cameron had never been particularly concerned about his reputation, nor about the fact that it had been greatly exaggerated through the media. He enjoyed spending time in a woman's company, and he'd been fortunate that a lot of women seemed to enjoy his company in turn.

"But not one of those women—not any one that I've ever dated, in fact—has ever made me forget about you," he told Gabriella.

"Cameron, we haven't had any contact in more than sixteen years." She spoke patiently, as if she was talking to a dim-witted child. "You probably didn't even remember I existed until the photos of you with Princess Leticia were published."

She was wrong, but he didn't know how to convince her of the truth. He could hardly blame her for being skeptical. After the weekend they'd spent at Cielo del Norte, he'd realized that he was more than halfway in love with her—and he'd panicked. He was only twenty years old, still in college and with no real direction for his future—what did he know about love? How could he know for certain that she was "the one" when there were so many women out there? So many women who wanted to be with him?

He'd decided to take some time to figure things out. He'd promised to call her, but he didn't. As anxious as he was to hear her voice, he refused to give in, refused to admit—even to himself—how much he needed her. Because needing some-one was a weakness, and weaknesses could be exploited, and those of royal blood could not afford to be weak.

The day that she'd tracked him down on campus, he'd been so happy to see her, but he'd pretended that he didn't even remember her name. He'd been deliberately cruel, acting as if the time they'd spent together had meant nothing to him. And still, she'd had the courage to look him straight in the eye and confide her suspicion that she might be pregnant. That was when the real panic had set in.

Afterward, he'd thrown himself at other women, desperate to forget about Gabriella. Eventually, over time, the memories faded. But he'd never truly forgotten her. No one else's arms had ever felt so right around him, no one else's kisses had ever touched him so deep inside. No one else had ever loved him as freely and unconditionally as she had done, if only for a short while.

He'd been such a fool. He'd missed out on so much time with Gabriella—and the entire first sixteen years of Sierra's life—because he'd been a selfish and self-centered fool. That was time that he could never get back and, because he'd so completely and effectively isolated Gabriella so many years before, it was entirely possible that he'd blown any hope for the future, too.

"I guess it's going to take some time to convince you that I'm not the man the press has portrayed me to be."

"You don't need to convince me of anything," she said. "But if you say you want a relationship with Sierra, you better mean it. She needs a father who will be there for her, even— or maybe especially—when she's pretending that she doesn't need you at all."

"I'll be there for her," he promised.

And I'll be there for you, he silently vowed. *Even when you're pretending that you don't need me at all.*

The sound of the jet ski grew louder, signaling Sierra's

return. "Why don't you and I take that swim Sierra claimed she didn't want?" he suggested. "Then maybe she'll be enticed to join us."

"The water does look inviting," Gabriella admitted.

"Go put on your bathing suit," Cameron encouraged.

While she was changing, he did the same, and they were both ready by the time Sierra had returned. She declined the invitation to join them, opting instead to plug into her iPod and blast out her eardrums. Cameron decided that she needed some time, and turned his attention to the woman by his side.

"Maybe we should just head back," she suggested. "I know this day isn't turning out quite how you'd planned."

"I have no complaints," he assured her. "Unless you renege on your promise to go swimming with me."

With a shrug, she pulled off her cover-up. It dropped onto the deck—right beside Cameron's jaw.

Even at seventeen, Gabriella had the kind of beauty that stopped men in their tracks and the type of body that inspired them to fantasize about her. And he'd spent a lot of long, lonely nights doing just that before he'd finally known the pleasure of that sweet, lush body stretched out beneath him, wrapped around him, moving against him. She was somehow even more beautiful now, her body even more lush and breathtaking. And while the two-piece bathing suit she wore was modest by current standards, just one glance and his blood—already pumping hard and fast through his veins—quickly detoured south.

Oh man, he was in trouble here. Big trouble. And he suddenly found himself questioning the wisdom of getting half-naked with a woman who had always turned him on more than any other. Not that he would tell her as much, of course. Because even if he was foolish enough to make such a confession, she would never believe him. It was going to take time—time and a concerted effort—to break through Gabriella's resistance and convince her that the feelings he had for her were real.

In the meantime, he would have to take a lot of cold showers. But a cold shower not being immediately available, he decided a dip in the Mediterranean would have to suffice.

He dove deep, relishing the coolness of the water as his body sliced through it. Kicking hard, he pushed himself deeper. He swam downward until his lungs ached with the effort of holding his breath in, then he turned abruptly and pushed hard toward the surface. He broke through and drew in a deep, shuddering breath—and felt something smack into his shoulder.

Blinking water from his eyes, he saw Gabriella was in the water with him. Her hair was dripping wet, and her eyes were huge in her pale face.

"Goddamn you, Cameron."

The relief Gabriella had felt when he broke through the surface was overwhelming, but her heart was still pounding too hard and too fast. For almost a whole minute or maybe even longer—it certainly seemed like so much longer—he'd been gone. One minute he'd been standing beside her on the deck, the next he'd executed a clean dive into the water, and then he'd disappeared.

She should have called for the captain. That would have been the smart thing to do. But she hadn't been able to think— she'd just acted, and apparently that meant flinging herself over the edge and into the water after him.

She'd gone under three times, mindless of the salt that stung her eyes as she desperately scanned the crystal clear waters for any sign of where he'd gone. And then, finally, she'd seen him. Not injured or unconscious beneath the surface, but determinedly swimming toward it.

Cameron frowned at her. "What's got you all bent out of shape?"

She stared at him as she continued to tread water beside him. "You were underwater forever. I couldn't see where you'd gone, if you'd hit or head on something and—"

"And you jumped in to save me?" His lips curved, just a little, as if he was amused by her instinctive response.

She wanted to hit him again. "I don't know why I bothered."

"I think you do," he said. "I think maybe, just maybe, all of your claims to the contrary aside, you still care about me."

"I would try to save anyone I thought was drowning."

"Hey." He moved closer, lifting his hands out of the water to cradle her face in his palms. "I didn't mean to scare you."

"Well, you did." This time she did smack him again. The violent action splashed more water, hopefully masking the moisture that swam in her eyes. "You big idiot."

"I'm sorry." He dipped his head, brushed his lips lightly against hers.

She wanted to cling to him, to hold him and feel the solid warmth of his flesh beneath her hands. But she didn't, because to do so would only prove what he already suspected—that she still cared about him. And while she might be able to convince herself that it was perfectly normal and reasonable to care about the man who was the father of her child, she knew that her feelings for Cameron weren't that simple or straightforward.

"Stop that." She started to pull away, but he caught her, tangled his legs with hers. Their bodies bumped, once, twice, and the slick slide of wet skin against wet skin was incredibly and unbelievably arousing.

"I can't." His hands slid down her back to curl around her bottom and pull her closer. "I've tried, really I have, but I can't stop myself from wanting you."

The words, the tone, and the man were far too seductive—or maybe she was far too naive, because she wanted to believe he meant what he'd said. Because then it might be okay to admit that she wanted him, too.

"This is crazy," she said instead.

"You've always made me crazy." He nibbled his way along her jaw, down her throat, as they bobbed in the gentle waves.

"I thought we were going to swim."

"This is so much better than swimming."

"Right now, I'm having a hard time disagreeing with that," she admitted. "But this isn't the time or place."

Cameron suckled on her earlobe. "So tell me when and where."

His voice was warm with desire, silky with promise, and far too tempting. But somehow Gabriella resisted the impulse to let her head fall back, to let him lead where she was only too willing to follow. Because she'd been down that road before, and she'd found herself alone at the end.

"You make it sound so easy," she said.

"It could be," he told her.

She shook her head as she disentangled herself from him. When he was touching her, she couldn't think straight. When she was wanting him, she couldn't remember all the reasons that she shouldn't. "*I'm* not easy," she told him. "Not anymore."

"I never thought you were easy," he denied. "And I always believed you were worth the effort."

"I have to get back." She started swimming toward the ladder.

Cameron matched her, stroke for stroke. "You're running away."

"No. I have a column to finish and send in to my editor."

He was right behind her as she climbed out of the water.

"How about dinner?" he asked, as she started to towel off.

"I told you—I have work to do."

"Not tonight," he said. "Saturday."

She hesitated. "I think Sierra has plans with Paolo."

"I'm not asking Sierra, I'm asking you."

"I'd have to check my calendar."

"I'm trying to prove that I'm capable of thinking long-term," he told her. "Not just as far away as dinner, but dinner three days in the future."

"Should I be impressed?"

"You should say 'yes.'"

"Don't you need to check your calendar?" she challenged, knowing that his professional obligations—and his social life—were far more demanding than hers.

"No," he replied, without hesitation. "Because even if there's something else on my schedule, it couldn't possibly be as important as taking you to dinner."

He had the right answers to all of her questions, which only made her more cautious. He'd always been a player, and she couldn't take the chance that he was playing her—again.

"I think being here with you today is enough tempting of fate for one week."

"Would it really be so terrible to be seen in public with me?"

She'd always thought he was the one who didn't want to be seen with her. But now, she was wary. "It's not you, Cameron, it's the paparazzi that follows wherever you go. And I don't want my daughter reading headlines that label me as your latest conquest just because we were having dinner together."

"Our daughter."

She cast a glance toward Sierra, relieved to see that she was still listening to her iPod and apparently oblivious to their conversation. "Our daughter," she murmured in agreement.

"I promise you, no one will know where we're going and there will be no paparazzi hiding anywhere in the shadows waiting to snap pictures of us."

"How can you make that kind of promise?"

"Trust me," he said. "I've not only lived most of my life in the spotlight, I've learned how to court that attention when it serves my purpose—and how to circumvent it when necessary."

Still she hesitated.

"Seven o'clock," he suggested.

She sighed. "Okay. But I have to be home by midnight."

"Is that your curfew?" he teased.

"It's Sierra's, and I need to be home to know that she is."

"Then I will have you home by midnight," he promised.

Chapter Eleven

Dear Gabby,

The first time I fell in love, I was fifteen years old. Maybe I was naive to believe that Carlos and I would last forever, but he claimed to love me, too, and we spent hours talking about the future. After high school graduation, we went to different colleges, but I continued to believe that we would get back together again when we both finished school. Except that when Carlos finally came home, he was married to someone else.

I was devastated, but because I didn't want anyone to know how heartbroken I was, I started dating someone else. After a while, I convinced myself that I was in love with him and, within a few months, we were married. It took less time than that for me to realize that our marriage had been a horrible mistake and that I'd never stopped loving Carlos.

A couple of years ago, our paths crossed again. I immediately realized that I still had strong feelings for him. And since it turned out that he was divorced, too, it almost seemed natural to start dating again. We've been together now for almost a year and a half, and Carlos has been starting to drop hints about the two of us getting married.

I have never loved anyone else as much as I loved him, but no one else has ever hurt me as much as he did, either. I'm afraid to give him another chance, afraid that he'll break my heart all over again.

Should I play it safe—or risk it all for a chance to live happily-ever-after?
Signed,
Still Sorting Out the Pieces

Over the years that Gabriella had been writing her "Dear Gabby" column for the newspaper, she'd occasionally found that a reader's questions and concerns reflected current events in her own life. Those were always the most difficult letters to respond to because they required not just a dose of common sense but a fair bit of introspection and Gabriella wasn't always willing to look into herself. It was far easier, in her opinion, to respond to other people's problems than examine her own.

In this case, however, the issue was one at the forefront of her mind. Cameron had been more than hinting about wanting a second chance, and Gabriella was still reluctant to even consider the possibility.

Dear Sorting,
A man who can abuse your trust and break your heart once shouldn't be given a chance to do so again.

Gabriella sat back and studied the words on the screen. It was a valid point, she thought, but not quite the response that her readers expected. On a sigh, she held down the backspace key until the screen was blank again. Because as justified as she might have felt in writing those words, they were a personal response rather than a professional one.

Don't think about Cameron, she reminded herself. *Don't think about the fact that he claimed to love you and then dumped you. Don't think about the fact that he disappeared from your life for more than sixteen years and now expects to pick up right where things left off.*

She pushed him out of her mind—or at least tried to—and focused on her response again.

Dear Sorting,

There is nothing quite as intense as first love. And nothing quite as devastating as a first heartbreak.

It's not surprising that you would still be holding on to your hurt and using it as a shield to protect your heart this time around. But you and Carlos are different people now than you were in high school. You're not just older and more mature, you've lived separate lives and had distinct experiences, taken different paths that have merged to bring you together once again.

It's time to let go of the past and look to the future—and decide if you want him to be part of that future. It's not always easy to forgive and forget, and only you can decide if you're ready to take that next step.

The only thing I'll add to that is that second chances are rare. If you decide you want this one, grab hold of it with both hands.

Good luck,

Gabby

It was good advice—objectively, she knew that was true. But did she have the courage to listen to her own guidance? Did she want a second chance with Cameron? Or was she a fool to think he was even offering her one?

Had he really changed—or was he just playing her? He claimed that he wanted to be a father to his daughter, and Gabriella had no intention of standing in the way of that.

So what was his interest in her?

There was no shortage of women wanting to be with him, and no reason for Cameron to be with Gabriella unless that was truly what he wanted.

But what did *she* want?

She pondered that question as she rifled through the clothes in her wardrobe.

She wanted Sierra to have a relationship with Cameron, but she was also afraid to acknowledge that relationship. As soon as the truth came out, everything would change. Sierra wouldn't be her little girl anymore—she'd be the prince's daughter and a princess in her own right. Her life wouldn't be her own—she would be thrust into the spotlight, her every action and word scrutinized by the media. Gabriella wanted to protect her from that, for just a little while longer.

And yet, here she was—watching the clock and mentally calculating the time that she had left to get ready for her date with the prince.

Was she making a mistake?

She didn't want to think so, but the truth was, she'd never been able to think very clearly where Cameron Leandres was concerned. There was just something about the man that affected her on a basic level, stirring her blood and muddling her brain so that rational thought was all but impossible.

But she did know that playing it safe was no longer an option. She was playing with fire and she knew it. All she could do now was hope that no one got burned.

Cameron knew he was early, but he'd hoped that arriving ahead of schedule would give him a few minutes to talk to Sierra. The first time they'd met, she'd been obviously surprised and adorably flustered to realize who he was. Since then, however, her demeanor toward him had cooled noticeably. As he'd done nothing to justify this change in her attitude, he could only speculate that it was a reflection of her feelings about his relationship with Gabriella.

He thought he could understand her wariness. He knew that Gabriella had been dating Rafe for a long time, then suddenly Rafe was out of the picture and Cameron was in. And Sierra really had no idea who he was, aside from his title, and no reason to trust him or his motivations.

He heard footsteps approach in response to the ring of the bell, then Sierra was standing in front of him. The welcoming light in her eyes dimmed and her easy smile slipped when she recognized him. "Oh. I thought you were Paolo."

Gabriella had mentioned that Sierra probably had a date with the boyfriend tonight, and apparently she did. The teenager was dressed casually, in a simple knitted tank and a long flowing skirt that Cameron could easily picture Gabriella wearing. Obviously Sierra had inherited her mother's innate sense of style and—unfortunately, at least from a father's perspective—her ultra-feminine curves.

He wanted to suggest that she put on a sweater but knew she would look at him as if he was crazy. And maybe he was crazy to think that he had any business trying to parent a teenage girl that he'd only met a few weeks earlier. But it was more than a recently developed sense of responsibility that urged him to get to know his daughter, it was—from the moment he'd learned of her existence—an instinctive and irrefutable desire to claim her as his child. To be the type of father to her that he'd had been fortunate enough to have for the first dozen years of his life.

He forced himself to ignore what she was wearing and only said, "Can I come in anyway?"

Her cheeks flushed. "Yes, of course. You can have a seat in the living room. My mom should be down in a few minutes."

"Why don't you wait with me?" he suggested.

"Why would I?"

He wanted to call her on her rudeness, but he gritted his teeth to bite back the instinctive response and shrugged, deliberately casual. "It will give us a chance to get to know one another better."

Sierra paused in the arched entranceway of the living room and turned to face him. "Look, I know you're royalty and you're used to people bowing and curtsying. And I should probably be welcoming and gracious and oh-so-thrilled that you're dating my mother, but the truth is, I don't think you're good enough for her, even if you are a prince."

She spoke bluntly, unapologetically, and he was sure that Gabriella would be appalled if she heard the words coming out of her daughter's mouth. And while Cameron wasn't thrilled by her obvious lack of respect, he couldn't help but admire her strength of character and conviction. "You're probably right."

Her eyes narrowed suspiciously. "You're agreeing with me?"

"I've known your mom a long time," he told her, settling himself onto the sofa. "Although truthfully, in some ways, I hardly know her at all. But I do know that she's an incredible woman and I enjoy spending time with her."

"So that's all this is?" She folded her arms over her chest in a gesture that was so like her mother he had to fight back a smile. "Spending time with her?"

"We're taking things one step at a time," he said cautiously.

She inched a little farther into the room. "She was dating Rafe for almost two years. He asked her to marry him."

"Did you want her to marry him?" The idea sliced him to the quick. It was uncomfortable enough to think of Gabriella with the other man, but to imagine that her daughter—*his* daughter—had approved of that relationship and maybe even looked at the other man as a father figure, was unbearable.

But Sierra hesitated before answering, and he knew that she was considering her response. "I don't want her to be alone," she finally said.

"I don't imagine she thinks of herself as being alone."

"But I'm not going to be living here forever. I've only got two more years of high school and then I'll be going away to college. Hopefully."

Her frown warned that this was a subject of much debate between mother and daughter, and that no final decisions had been made. If it was a matter of finances, Cameron knew that he could alleviate their concerns, but that was hardly a discussion he intended to initiate now.

"And my grandmother's great," she continued. "But, come on, she shouldn't live with her mother forever, either."

He couldn't help but smile at that.

"And she doesn't have a lot of experience with men," Sierra confided. "I mean, I don't even remember her dating anyone, aside from Rafe. And you've dated a ton of women."

His brows rose. "Have you been reading the tabloids?"

"I did some internet research," she said, unapologetically. "And though I'm sure some of the stories are exaggerated, it's obvious that you've been around a lot more than she has."

"You're right," he acknowledged. "And there's probably nothing I can do or say to alleviate your concerns, but I can promise that my only intention tonight is to enjoy a quiet dinner with your mother."

"Okay." Then, almost reluctantly, she added, "She likes to dance. So you could maybe take her dancing, too, if you wanted."

"I'll keep that in mind," he promised.

"Okay," she said again.

The doorbell sounded, and her head turned automatically, her eyes lighting up.

"I need to get that," she said, just as her mother stepped into the room.

Cameron's attention shifted automatically, and his breath caught. Gabriella had put her hair up in some kind of twist and fastened simple gold hoops at her ears. Her make-up was mostly subtle—some shadow to highlight her eyes, a touch of blusher on her cheeks—aside from the mouth-watering red that slicked her lips. It matched the color of her dress, a sleeveless wrap-style of scarlet silk that dipped low between her breasts and clung to every delicious curve. And her feet were encased in shoes of that exact same shade that added almost three inches to her height and drew attention to her long, shapely legs.

Mi Dios, the woman knew how to tempt a man.

And he was more than tempted.

Thankfully, after a quick smile to acknowledge his presence, Gabriella had focused her attention on Sierra, giving him a moment to complete his perusal and recover his composure.

"Twelve o'clock," she reminded her daughter.

Sierra rolled her eyes. "As if I could ever forget."

Gabriella touched her lips gently to her cheek. "Have a good time."

"Yeah, uh, you, too." Sierra glanced past her mother to him, whether in acknowledgement or warning he couldn't be sure, but he knew that she was right to be worried. Because his promise to Sierra aside, one look at Gabriella, and suddenly he was wanting a lot more than dinner.

"You look…exquisite."

Gabriella felt her fingers tremble as the prince kissed her hand, and she hoped Cameron wouldn't notice. She was more nervous than she wanted to admit—like a seventeen-year-old girl on her first date.

"Thank you," she murmured.

He looked wonderful, too. But then again, he always did. The day they'd spent on his yacht, he'd been casually attired in shorts and a T-shirt. Tonight, he was wearing a suit—dark navy in color and conservative in cut. He moved easily, with a fluid grace and inherent dignity, whatever he was wearing and wherever he went.

It hadn't always been like that, she remembered. He'd once chafed at the restrictions that came with being a royal—except when he was outright ignoring them. He'd been the rebel prince, unconcerned with politics and protocol, determined to make his own mark in the world. And often, it had seemed to her as she'd followed his escapades through headlines over the years, desperately unhappy.

He had changed. She didn't doubt that any more. He was more comfortable in his own skin now, happier in his career and with his life. And she was happy for him—and hopeful that he could now be the kind of father her daughter deserved. But she was still unwilling to hope that he could be a part of her life.

He kept her hand in his as he led the way to the door. "Did you need to check in with your mother before we head out?"

She smiled, a little, in response to his gentle teasing. "Usually I would," she agreed. "But she's at her water aerobics class until nine."

"Water aerobics?"

"She loves to bake—and to eat what she bakes—so she does yoga or water aerobics almost every day, sometimes both, to balance it out."

"She sounds very...energetic," he decided.

"She only retired a couple of years ago," Gabriella told him, pausing to lock the door. "Until then, she'd worked two jobs. Having time on her hands was a huge adjustment for her."

"What kind of work did she used to do?"

Gabriella looked at him, surprised by the question. "I

thought you knew—she worked early mornings at the bakery and then cleaned houses the rest of the day."

He helped her into the limo, then settled himself beside her on the wide leather seat. "Why would I know that?"

"Because—" she broke off, shook her head. "It doesn't matter."

"My mother," he guessed flatly.

"I really don't want to talk about this tonight."

"Dammit, Gabriella. I need to know what she did."

"It won't change anything."

"No," he agreed. "But I'm tired of the lies and deceptions. I want the truth."

"When she first came to me, wanting to buy my silence with payment of Sierra's medical expenses, I refused. I believed, naively, that my mother and I would somehow find a way to pay the bills. The very next day, my mother lost her cleaning job at the Gianninis'."

"Elena and Roberta Giannini have been friends—or at least acquaintances—for years," he acknowledged.

She nodded. "And Roberta Giannini was good friends with Arianna Bertuzzi, so if my mother wanted to keep *that* job, I was told I'd better rethink my decision regarding Sierra."

He took both of her hands now. "*Dios,* Gabriella, I can't tell you how sorry I am."

"I hated her for a long time," she admitted. "And I was scared for even longer, afraid that the day might come when she wanted more than my silence."

"You were worried that she would try to take Sierra," he guessed.

"She'd already proven that she had the money and power and influence—all I had was my daughter, but she was everything to me."

He squeezed her hands gently as the limo rolled to a stop. "You were right. Let's try to put this aside for tonight and enjoy our dinner."

"Gladly," Gabriella said, and meant it.

The driver opened the door, and Cameron slid out first, offering his hand to her again.

She hadn't asked where they were going and, looking at the elegantly scripted letters on the huge plate glass window beneath the green-and-white-striped awning, realized now that had been a mistake.

But she never would have guessed—couldn't have guessed. Marconi's wasn't even in business anymore. After a falling-out with his son, Franco, who had moved to San Pedro to open his own restaurant six months earlier, Alonzo Marconi had closed down the business and put the building up for sale.

Cameron gestured for her to precede him up the walk, but Gabriella stood frozen in her tracks. "What are we doing here?"

"We're having dinner," he reminded her.

"But—" she faltered, as she caught a whiff of the tantalizing and familiar scent that drifted on the air.

"I promised to take you someplace where no one would guess we were going and where there would be no paparazzi hiding in the shadows."

"And you thought an abandoned restaurant would fit the bill."

"Not entirely abandoned," he assured her. "Alonzo Marconi himself is behind the stove tonight."

Still, she hesitated. It was obvious that Cameron had gone to quite a bit of trouble to set this up, but she wasn't entirely sure how she felt about this turn of events. She'd told him that the past was over and done, except that a lot of their shared past was now only a few steps away.

Already, just looking at the door, she could hear the familiar jangle of the bell that would sound when it was opened. And she knew that the sound of that bell would tear the lid off of the box of memories she'd worked hard to keep tightly closed.

Memories of the day she'd first met Cameron, the first time he'd kissed her. Memories of hanging out with him after the restaurant closed, talking for long hours or dancing to the music that blared out of the jukebox. Memories of hiding out in the bathroom, fighting against tears, after he'd dumped her, when she'd realized her period was late, and finally—when she'd been fired from her job after confiding to Mrs. Marconi that she was pregnant.

The memories were both plentiful and painful, and she knew that she could avoid them no longer.

Chapter Twelve

As Cameron followed Gabriella through the door, he began to wonder if he'd made a serious miscalculation. He'd thought she would be pleased with the arrangements he'd made, instead, she seemed apprehensive.

On the other hand, she'd seemed apprehensive since she'd agreed to have dinner with him, as if she'd been having second thoughts from the very beginning. But he was hopeful that he could get her to relax. They'd share a good meal together, an excellent bottle of wine, some pleasant conversation, and maybe, when the night was finally over, a good-night kiss.

He turned the key that had been left in the lock, so that no one could wander in off the street and disturb them.

She moved automatically toward the round table in the middle of the room, the only one that was set. The candle, stuffed into a squat wine bottle, had been lit, and the gentle flame illuminated the shine of flatware and the gleam of crystal.

"Something smells good," she said.

He agreed, although what he could smell was her scent, something light and citrusy, decidedly feminine and undeniably sexy.

"My sincere apologies, Your Highness." Alonzo Marconi rushed into the dining room, stopping in front of Cameron to execute a deep bow. "I did not realize you had arrived."

"It's not a problem," Cameron assured him. "And thank you again for your indulgence tonight."

"How could I refuse a personal request from a prince?"

A personal request—and the offer of a significant sum for the retired chef's time and trouble. But it was worth it to Cameron, to guarantee that he and Gabriella would have privacy tonight. He'd made her a promise, and he intended to prove to her that she could trust in his promises.

"You remember Gabriella?" he prompted.

"Of course." Alonzo took both of her hands before kissing her lavishly on each cheek in turn. "*Bella,* you are even more beautiful than I remembered."

"And you are just as charming as I remember," she told him.

"You are well? And your mother and your little girl?" he prompted, as he held out her chair for her.

"We are all very well, thanks. Although Sierra is not a little girl anymore. She had her sixteenth birthday last week."

"*Mi Dios*—where did the years go?"

As Cameron glanced around, he wondered the same thing. The restaurant hadn't changed at all in the six months that it had been closed. In fact, it looked to Cameron that not much had changed in the past sixteen years. Even the layout of the tables was the same, as familiar as the cane-back chairs set around them, the red-and-white-checked tablecloths draped over them and the candles in wine bottles that served as centerpieces for each one. The jukebox was still in the corner, silent now.

It had never been a high-end eating place but was undoubtedly an extremely popular one, having long ago established a reputation for serving quality food at reasonable prices. Primarily marketed as a family restaurant, it had also become a favorite of the college crowd, as it was located within walking distance of the dorms.

"I have the wine you requested," Alonzo told him, hustling over to the bar to retrieve it.

He hurried back, showed Cameron the label. He checked the date, nodded, and Alonzo quickly and efficiently uncorked the bottle. He poured a small amount in the prince's glass, allowing him to test and approve the burgundy before he filled Gabriella's glass. After topping up Cameron's, he set the bottle on the table.

"There is a set menu for this evening," Alonzo announced. "Crostini with basil pesto and tomatoes, followed by linguine with freshly made pomodoro sauce, then a main course of chicken piccata, finishing off with a simple green salad with an olive oil and red wine vinaigrette. And finally, for dessert, warm poached pears sprinkled with goat cheese."

"It sounds perfect," Cameron assured him.

Gradually, as they sipped their wine and nibbled their way through Alonzo's impressive menu, Gabriella began to relax. It helped, Cameron thought, that they talked mostly about Sierra. Although garnering more information about his daughter wasn't the primary purpose for the evening, he looked at the opportunity as a bonus. And Sierra was the one topic of conversation that seemed to break through Gabriella's reserve.

She happily recounted stories of Sierra's childhood, reported on every illness and injury, and detailed all of the important milestones of her first sixteen years until he finally formed a picture, not of the young woman she was now but of the little girl she'd been.

While he smiled at Gabriella's charming retelling of her antics, he was again painfully aware of how very much he'd missed. But he wasn't angry at Gabriella anymore. There was no reason to be. He knew now that he'd missed out on sixteen years of his daughter's life because he'd been too damned selfish and self-absorbed to worry about an ex-girlfriend's concern that she might be pregnant. Okay, so maybe he'd sweated over the possibility for a while. Maybe he'd waited to hear back from her, regarding the results of the pregnancy test. But when she'd failed to contact him again, he'd assumed that she'd been wrong—or that she'd taken care of it. And he'd been selfish and self-absorbed enough to be relieved by that thought.

Gabriella pushed away her salad bowl, the action drawing him away from the uncomfortable memories of his past and back to the much more enjoyable present.

"The whole meal was spectacular," she said. "But I can't possibly eat another bite."

"You have to have room for dessert."

She groaned. "I wish I did. Really. But—"

Her protest trailed off when Alonzo came out with the poached pears. Her eyes shifted to the square plate of neatly arranged pear halves drizzled with a Reisling reduction and sprinkled with goat cheese, and he could tell that she was tempted, at least a little.

"A few bites," he cajoled, after the chef had slipped away again. "So as not to hurt Alonzo's feelings."

"I'll have to start going to water aerobics with my mother," she muttered, but picked up her dessert fork.

He didn't think she needed to worry about indulging in a few desserts, but he refrained from saying so. He knew that kind of comment would catapult them out of neutral conversational territory into the decidedly personal zone and result in all of Gabriella's barriers locking firmly back into place.

She broke off a piece of pear, popped it into her mouth. Her lips closed around the tines of the fork, her eyelids lowered, and she hummed in blissful pleasure. "Mmm."

"That sounds like a positive endorsement," Cameron mused.

She nodded as she chewed, swallowed. "Oh. Wow. It's... fabulous. It's sweet and tart, and the cheese adds a little bit of creamy texture, and the flavors just explode on your tongue."

She sliced off another piece of fruit, held it out to Cameron. It was a spontaneous gesture, certainly not one that was intended to be deliberately seductive. But when his lips parted and she slid the fork between them, they were both suddenly aware of the intimacy of the moment.

She pulled the utensil away, her cheeks flushing. Cameron's eyes remained on hers as he chewed slowly, savoring the bite she'd shared with him. The air nearly crackled with the attraction between them, proving that the illusion of neutrality had been exactly that.

Alonzo bustled in again, offering coffee or tea.

Gabriella tore her gaze from his, and turned to smile at the chef. "Not for me, thanks."

"Nor me," Cameron agreed. "But I think we'll linger for a while, to finish up our dessert and the wine."

"Of course," Alonzo said. "If it's acceptable to you, I will come back tomorrow to finish cleaning up so that you will have some privacy."

Cameron nodded. "We'll lock up when we go. And thank you again."

"My pleasure, Your Highness." He bowed deeply to Cameron, then turned his attention—and a warm smile—to Gabriella. "And it's always a pleasure to see you, *bella.*"

"*Grazie, Signor Marconi.*" She touched his hand. "*Grazie per tutto.*"

He captured her fingers and raised her hand to his lips. "*Buona notte.*"

With a last bow, Alonzo slipped away, leaving them alone.

"Do you want to tell me what that was about?" Cameron asked.

"What are you talking about?"

"I'm talking about Alonzo flirting with you—right in front of me."

"He wasn't flirting with me," Gabriella denied.

"It sure looked like that from where I'm sitting—and that you were flirting back."

She shook her head. "I've known Signor Marconi for a long time," she reminded him. "In a lot of ways, he was like a father to me. He gave me more than a job—he gave me advice and guidance and support."

Her gaze shifted away from his, her fingers slid down the stem of her wineglass, traced a slow circle around the perimeter of the base.

"Obviously there's more to the story," he guessed.

"Let's just say that *Signora* Marconi was a little less supportive."

"His wife?"

She nodded. "She fired me. When she found out… Well, she said that this was supposed to be a family restaurant and that it wouldn't do to have an unwed, pregnant teenager waiting on tables.

"Alonzo was furious with her. He didn't approve of my condition any more than she did, but he understood that I needed some way to support myself and my child. So he gave me a new job—washing dishes." Gabriella shrugged. "The money wasn't as good as working in the dining room, but at least it was something."

"I'm sorry," Cameron said. "I brought you here tonight because I'd hoped it would help you remember the good times. I didn't realize how much history you had here."

"Most of it was good times," she said, then her lips curved a little at the edges. "Aside from the occasional night when I had to wait on tables filled with obnoxious college boys."

"You can't be talking about my friends."

"You guys used to take turns paying the bill," she recalled. "And I always knew when it was your friend Andre's turn, because I would find my tip—in nickels and dimes—in the bottom of the beer pitcher."

Cameron winced. "Okay. He was obnoxious. But another one of those guys used to hang around after closing sometimes, staying late to help you clean up—and just to be with you."

She frowned, as if she wasn't sure she remembered what he was talking about, but the teasing sparkle in her eye assured him that she did.

He pushed his chair away from the table and went over to the ancient jukebox against the wall. He dropped some coins into the slot, punched in the numbers from memory. He watched Gabriella as the first unmistakable notes of "Why Can't This Be Love?" filled the air. The half-smile on her lips faded, and every muscle in her body went still.

She'd been a die-hard Van Halen fan and when she'd locked the doors after the last customers had gone, she'd crank up the music and dance around while she wiped down the tables and stacked the chairs. The very first time he'd kissed her, it was this song that had been playing. Thinking about that now, he couldn't help but wonder how it was that he struggled to remember the names of half the women he'd slept with in the past dozen years, but he'd never forgotten a single detail of the time he'd spent with Gabriella.

"Dance with me."

She hesitated.

"Come on," he cajoled. "You don't want to disappoint Sierra."

"How does this have anything to do with Sierra?"

"She suggested that I take you out dancing. I know the ambiance here isn't the same as a club, there's no flashing lights or pulsing bass or—"

"No," she agreed. "This is better." Then she finally put her hand in his.

He drew her gently to her feet. She came willingly, if not quite eagerly. She was still wary, he understood that, so he would content himself with little steps. Right now, all that mattered was that she was in his arms.

It wasn't exactly a slow song, but they'd always danced to it like this, close together. They fell into that same familiar rhythm now, and with each whisper of contact, even the most subtle brush of flesh against flesh, the sparks between them flared hotter.

Less than two and a half minutes into the song, he gave up any pretense of following the music and settled his hands on those seductively swaying hips, pulling her hard against him. Gabriella's eyes widened, but her lips curved, and she lifted her arms to his shoulders.

There was no hesitation when he kissed her this time, and nothing tentative in her response.

Her lips were soft and yielding, deliciously and intoxicatingly familiar. Of course he remembered her taste—he'd kissed her on his yacht only a few days earlier. But he'd remembered her taste even then; he'd been haunted by her scent and her warmth and her passion for years.

There had been a lot of women in and out of his life over the years. Probably too many women. But none of them had ever lingered in his mind or taken hold of his heart the way Gabriella had done.

It was more than the rush of blood through his veins, it was the rush of joy he felt when she smiled at him. It was the way his pulse leapt when she so much as glanced in his direction, the way his heart pounded when she touched a hand to his sleeve. It was the unexpected and undeniable bone-deep contentment and rightness that he'd only ever felt when she was in his arms.

Seventeen years ago, he'd told her that he'd loved her. But

even when he'd said those words to her, even when his heart had felt as if it would burst with happiness when she said them back, he hadn't fully understood what they meant. He hadn't fully appreciated the true depth of his feelings while he was with her—and he certainly hadn't anticipated the intensity of the emptiness he would feel when she was gone.

But she was here with him now, warm and willing, and he had no intention of ever letting her go again.

He combed his fingers through her hair. Pins scattered as the soft mass spilled down onto her shoulders. He'd always loved her hair, the way it looked spread out over his pillow, and the way she looked at him, sleepy-eyed and contented. The image was sharp and vivid in his mind, and he wanted her like that again. Now.

He tore his lips from hers to trail kisses down her throat. He lingered at the racing pulse point at her jaw, and she sighed with pleasure. He moved lower, tracing the deep V at the front of her dress, dipping his tongue into the warm hollow between her breasts. She shuddered but didn't pull away. He found the tie at her waist, released it. There was another tie inside, but he made quick work of that, too, and suddenly his hands were inside the dress, on her bare, quivering flesh.

A quick glimpse of the red lace bikini panties and matching bra had him groaning aloud. She was so lush and perfect and…his. He backed her up against the jukebox and curled his hands around her buttocks, lifting her off of the ground. She braced her back against the machine and wrapped her legs around him, pressing herself more intimately against him, and he groaned again as all the blood rushed from his head.

He unfastened the front clasp of her bra, letting her breasts spill free. He filled his hands with them, brushed his thumbs over the tightly-beaded nipples, and she gasped. He captured her mouth again, his tongue sliding between her lips, tangling with hers. Her hands were in his hair now, and the way she was kissing him back and pressing against him left him in absolutely no doubt that she wanted the same thing he did.

There was no one else around. Alonzo had gone, the door was locked, and the blinds were drawn on all the windows. There was no danger of anyone seeing inside, no fear of anyone interrupting them, and he needed her desperately.

But he'd been careless with her before. So focused on his own wants that he'd barely considered hers. He'd been so hot for her that he'd taken her virginity in the backseat of his car. He had more finesse now, and a hell of a lot more self-control. Usually.

Somehow being with Gabriella undermined all of his best intentions. She made him forget that he wanted to do the right thing this time and simply made him want. But he wasn't going to take her standing up against an old jukebox. Or laid out on top of a checkered tablecloth. He reprimanded himself for the alternate suggestion that immediately sprang to mind. And so, with unbelievable reluctance, he lifted his head from her breast and refastened the clip at the front of her bra.

"Gabriella—"

She pulled away from him, her fingers trembling as she pulled at the ties of her dress. "Don't say it."

"Say what?"

"Anything." She tugged at the bodice, settling the material back into place, and shook her head. "I can't believe how pathetic I am."

He heard the tears in her voice, as baffling as her words.

"What are you talking about?"

"Your mother was right—I am a slut. Maybe I've never slept around, but I've never been able to control my responses to you, either."

He stared at her, stunned not by what his mother had said but that she could possibly believe it. "*Mi Dios,* Gabriella. Allowing yourself to feel passion doesn't mean you're a…"

He trailed off, unable to even say the word. "It doesn't mean you're indiscriminate, it only means you're human."

"I almost let you seduce me in the middle of a restaurant." She had tears on her cheeks now and her eyes were filled with misery. "Is that why you brought me here?" she asked him now. "Did you figure I'd put out as easily now as I did seventeen years ago?"

"I didn't plan for this to happen," he told her.

She made a sound of disbelief as she finished tugging her skirt into place.

"But I'm not sorry. Because what just happened proves that the chemistry between us is as volatile now as it was seventeen years ago."

"It's not chemistry, it's hormones," she said derisively, but he sensed that she was more angry with herself than with him.

"Why are you so determined to fight this?" he asked gently.

"Because I don't do things like this." She swiped impatiently at another tear that slid down her cheek.

He tucked a lock of hair behind her ear. "Things like what?"

"Let myself be overcome by lust," she snapped at him.

She was trying to make the intimacy they'd just shared into less than it was, but he wasn't going to let her. "It's not about 'letting' when the attraction between two people is as strong as it is between us." He touched a hand to her face. "I've never felt this way with anyone else—before or after you."

"Are we done here?" she asked him.

He sighed. "And you're never going to give me another chance, are you?"

"Another chance for what?"

"To make a relationship between us work."

"We never had a relationship, we had sex."

"I loved you."

"Yeah, you made that clear when you dumped me after the weekend we spent together."

"I was young and stupid—"

"It doesn't matter," she said wearily. "Not the when or the why, because the truth is, the break-up was inevitable. Aside from the fact that we were both too young to have a clue about what we were doing, you're a blue-blood royal and I'm a working-class single mother."

"The mother of *my* child."

"Which might be my ticket to five minutes of fame but isn't going to lead to some kind of happily-ever-after."

"Not if you refuse to even consider the possibility."

She folded her arms over her chest, the action telling him more definitively than any words that she wouldn't be swayed, but she only said, "I need to be home before midnight."

"I'll have Lucien bring the car around."

Chapter Thirteen

Gabriella was on the back porch, watching the stars, when Sierra got home. While the midnight curfew was a matter of frequent debate between them, her daughter didn't seem to be holding a grudge tonight. Instead of ignoring her mother and going straight to her room, as she had a habit of doing when she was annoyed, she sat down on the step beside her.

"How was your date?" she asked.

"It was…" Gabriella wasn't quite sure how to respond. Both "wonderful" and "awful" were appropriate answers to the question, but either one would inevitably lead to more questions that she wasn't prepared to answer. So she only said, "Fine."

"Fine?" Sierra's brow furrowed. "Mom—if he can't do better than "fine," then you're wasting your time."

"Okay, it was better than fine," she allowed, not daring to let herself think about how much better specific parts of the evening had been. Specifically when her parts had been in close contact with his parts—

No, not going to think about those parts, she reminded herself sternly.

"Are you in love with him?"

Sierra's question startled her out of her reverie. She managed a laugh. "Love? Sierra, I've only been seeing him for a few weeks."

"But you've known him a long time, right?"

She nodded, because it was easier than explaining that she wasn't sure if she'd ever really known him at all.

"Did you date him?" Sierra prompted. "You know, when you knew him before?"

"Yes," Gabriella admitted, because while she'd never volunteered much information about her past, she'd never lied to Sierra, either. "For a little while."

"What went wrong?"

And how to answer that question without opening the floodgates? she wondered.

But maybe it was time to stop worrying about protecting Sierra and finally tell her the truth—to tell her that Prince Cameron Leandres of Tesoro del Mar was her father.

"We wanted different things from one another," she began, trailing off as she heard the sound of footsteps on the gravel driveway.

She glanced at her watch, noted that it was half past midnight. Sierra, obviously having heard the footsteps, too, was frowning. And they both jolted when a figure came around the side of the house.

Katarina stopped with her foot on the bottom step, her eyes wide. "What are you two doing out here at this time of night?" she demanded imperiously.

"I'd say the real question is what are *you* doing coming home at this time of night?" Gabriella countered. "Your car was in the driveway—I assumed you were home and in bed."

Katarina tilted her chin. "Well, you assumed wrong. As it turns out, I had a date tonight, too."

"With whom?" Gabriella demanded.

"With Dominic Donatella. Because I decided that I wasn't going to let him seduce the secrets of my buttercream icing out of me but I didn't mind if he seduced *me*."

"Go, Grandma," Sierra said approvingly.

Gabriella just shook her head. "Go to bed, Sierra."

Her daughter exhaled a long-suffering sigh, but she pushed herself to her feet, dropping a kiss first on her mother's cheek, then her grandmother's.

"Details over breakfast?" she whispered to Katarina.

"Not likely," her grandmother replied, but with an indulgent smile.

"I think I'm going to go to bed, too," Gabriella said, following her daughter toward the house.

"Have a cup of tea with me first," her mother urged. "I'm too wired to sleep right now."

Gabriella held up a hand. "Please, spare me the details."

Katarina picked up the kettle from the stove, filled it from the tap. "Obviously your date wasn't as…satisfying…as mine," she teased.

"No, I only *almost* had sex," Gabriella grumbled.

"That would explain your lousy mood," Katarina acknowledged.

"I should never have agreed to this dating charade. At first, it seemed like a legitimate way to explain why Cameron was hanging around while giving him some time to get to know Sierra. I didn't really think there would be any dating involved."

"And now you're worried that the lines between reality and fantasy are getting blurred," her mother guessed, all teasing forgotten.

Gabriella sighed, nodded.

"How do you feel about him?"

"I don't know. I don't know anything anymore."

"He's an attractive man," Katarina acknowledged. "A prince. And you were in love with him once before."

"A long time ago."

"Are you saying that you don't still have feelings for him?"

"I don't know. I mean, when I'm with him, he stirs up all kinds of feelings that I'd thought were dead and buried. I'm attracted to him," she admitted, although it made her blush to say the words aloud to her mother. Ridiculous, she knew, considering that her fifty-seven-year-old mother apparently didn't have any qualms about sharing the details of her sex life.

"But?" Katarina prompted.

Gabriella sighed. "But I don't know if I'm making those feelings into more than they are because I'm afraid of losing Sierra."

Her mother poured boiling water into the pot. "You're going to have to connect the dots for me."

"At first I was just going through the motions—letting Cameron hang around because I was sure that he would lose interest in playing daddy. But I've realized that he is serious about wanting to acknowledge Sierra as his daughter, and it's only a matter of time before he does so publicly. And when that happens, everything will change—for all of us, but mostly for Sierra. She will be a princess with royal duties and responsibilities, and I won't be able to help her with any of that. But if I'm with Cameron, well, it would ensure that I was able to stay close to her."

"Do you really think you could be that calculating?"

"Haven't I already proven that I will do anything for my daughter—even going so far as to keep her existence a secret from her own father for sixteen years?"

"Because the princess royal gave you no choice. Sierra

needed surgery, and she would only pay the hospital bills if you promised not to tell the prince about his child."

Gabriella nodded. "That's how I justified it to myself," she agreed. "But maybe it wasn't that simple. Maybe not telling Cameron about Sierra was a way of punishing him for dumping me."

"No one could blame you for being hurt or angry."

"But that doesn't justify using him for my own purposes now."

Katarina reached across the table to cover her daughter's hand with her own. "Are you really afraid that you're using him—or more afraid that you're not?"

"I can't fall for him again." Gabriella shook her head. "I won't."

"You say that with such conviction, as if you believe it."

"Because I do. Because it's true."

"Then you haven't learned anything at all in the past seventeen years," Katarina told her. "Because the mind does not and cannot control the heart."

Elena was growing weary of these late-night meetings, not so much the hour as the lack of results. In fact, she'd been more than a little tempted to cancel this one when she'd received Reynard's text message. "I think I've got something."

Elena had been as annoyed as she'd been intrigued. Her chief of security had been with her a long time, and he knew that she wanted results, not vague promises. Either he had something or he didn't—she wasn't interested in his thoughts.

Still, she was curious enough to keep the meeting, and she was waiting when Reynard appeared at the door precisely on schedule.

He knew her well enough not to waste any time on small talk, and as he made his way toward her desk, she could see that he had a small recording device in his hand. A touch of his thumb to one of the buttons and voices filled the silence.

Elena listened, definitely more intrigued than annoyed now. And when the playback finally ended, she nodded. "Yes, that should serve my purposes."

"Shall I arrange for a copy to be sent to his office?" Reynard asked.

She considered the idea for only a brief moment before discarding it. There wasn't a lot of time—with each day that passed, Gabriella was sinking her claws deeper and deeper into Cameron. Even though Elena had tried to warn her son about the kind of woman he was keeping company with, he'd refused to listen. His refusal had left Elena with no choice. She would do what was necessary to pull those claws free and if Cameron was left with scars, well, he would have no one to blame but himself.

"No," she finally responded to Reynard's question. "I'll deliver it to him personally."

Gabriella sat alone, thinking over her mother's words long after Katarina had gone up to bed.

She was right, of course. Not just about the fact that Gabriella couldn't stop herself from falling in love with Cameron again, but that the real root of her fear was the knowledge that she was already more than halfway there.

She should know better. She should have learned her lesson. But even if she didn't believe his claim that he'd loved her seventeen years ago, she did believe that he wasn't the same man now that he'd been then. And maybe, if he really did want a second chance and was willing to try to make a relationship between them work, Gabriella could make the effort, too.

She was scared, because there was so much more at stake now than just her heart. There was Sierra to think about—their daughter who didn't yet know that Cameron was her father.

There's no reward without risk, she reminded herself, and picked up the phone.

She faltered when she heard his voice on the other end. She hadn't expected him to answer, had anticipated leaving a message on his voice mail.

"I know it's late," she said.

"It's okay," he assured her. "I was still awake."

"Okay. Well, I, uh, wanted to apologize, for some of the things I said tonight."

"That's not necessary," he told her.

"It is," she insisted. "I was feeling emotional and vulnerable, and I lashed out at you."

"And I was pushing for too much too soon," he acknowledged.

"Maybe. A little." She blew out a breath. "Anyway, I thought maybe I could make it up to you, by inviting you to come over here for dinner. Tomorrow night."

"I thought you didn't cook."

"I didn't say I would cook, I said I would provide dinner. Actually, I thought I might be able to cajole my mother into cooking," she admitted. "But she's going away for the weekend, which means that I'll probably get takeout."

"Well, that's an intriguing offer," he said.

But he didn't immediately accept or decline, and Gabriella found herself babbling again. "It's short notice, I know. I should have realized that you probably already have plans. Or a date."

He laughed, although it sounded more strained than amused. "*Dios,* Gabriella, I don't have a date."

"Oh. Well."

"I was just…caught off guard by your invitation."

"It was an impulse," she admitted. "Probably a bad idea. Maybe we should just forget that I called."

"No way," he told her. "Just tell me what time tomorrow and I'll be there."

"Six? Seven? Whatever works for you," she said. "Although Sierra's going to a party with some friends tomorrow night, so if you want to see her, maybe you should come a little earlier."

"Earlier than six?"

"No, six would be fine."

"Then I'll see you at six," he promised.

"Okay."

She hung up the phone and wiped her damp palms on her skirt. She'd sounded like an idiot—worse, a babbling incoherent idiot. And yet, she had another date for tomorrow night.

She drew out a shaky breath and pressed a hand to her hammering heart. She was excited and terrified and determined. If this was her second chance, she was going to grab hold of it with both hands.

Cameron wasn't sure what had precipitated Gabriella's phone call, and he didn't care. He was just grateful that they seemed to have turned a corner, that she was finally willing to give him a second chance. He woke up the next morning with a smile that carried him through most of the day. The only snag was an early-afternoon visit from his mother.

There had been a time when he'd believed that Elena wanted only the best for him. He was no longer as trusting or naive, and he understood now that every action the princess royal performed and every word she spoke were carefully calculated to promote her own agenda. As she demonstrated with the recording she'd delivered to him that afternoon in an attempt to alter his intentions with respect to Gabriella and Sierra.

He'd been shocked to hear Gabriella's voice—and stunned by the words she spoke.

I will do anything for my daughter, even letting Cameron hang around. But I'm using him for my own purposes now, punishing him for dumping me. I won't fall for him again.

Elena claimed that Gabriella had spoken those words during a conversation with her mother, and listening to his own mother, he'd actually felt physically ill. Not because he believed what she was telling him, but because he was appalled by her actions. She insisted that she was only trying to protect him, but he saw the truth now: she was trying to control him, and she didn't give a damn about anyone else who might get hurt in the process.

She'd decided—for whatever reason so many years ago—that Gabriella wasn't a suitable partner for her son and she was going to do everything in her power to keep them apart. Apparently that included planting audio surveillance devices in Gabriella's home. When he confronted her, she neither denied nor apologized for her actions, insisting that she only wanted him to know what kind of vengeful, vindictive woman Gabriella really was.

Cameron had snapped the disk in half and told his mother to get out of his house. Then, when he'd verified that Gabriella and her mother and daughter were all out for the afternoon, he'd sent his own security team over to locate and remove the bugs. They'd found one in the kitchen, one in the living room, and one in Gabriella's bedroom.

On his way to Gabriella's house later that day, he tried to push all thoughts of Elena's lies and machinations from his mind. When Sierra opened the door and greeted him with a tentative smile, his heart actually felt as if it was expanding inside his chest.

And he finally realized that Gabriella was right—that the mistakes of the past didn't matter half as much as the gift of the present. Even though it was apparent that Sierra was ready to walk out the door as he was coming in, her smile confirmed that he was making progress with his daughter, and that was enough for now.

"Hi, Cameron. Bye, Cameron." She smiled again, then kissed her mother's cheek. "Bye, Mom."

But Gabriella held up a hand, halting her daughter's movement toward the door. "What's in the backpack?"

"My pajamas, toothbrush, a change of clothes."

"Because?"

"I'm staying at Jenna's tonight, remember?"

"I remember you asking if you could stay at Jenna's," Gabriella acknowledged. "And I remember telling you that I didn't think it was a good idea."

"Come on, Mom." Sierra cast a glance in Cameron's direction, as if to remind her mother that he was there, probably hoping she wouldn't want to argue in front of her guest.

But Gabriella shook her head. "Not tonight."

"Why not?"

"Because I wouldn't have any way of knowing what time you got back to Jenna's—or even if you did."

"I'll call you at midnight."

"No, you'll be back here by midnight," Gabriella insisted.

"You don't trust me," Sierra accused.

"If I didn't trust you, you wouldn't be going to the party at all," her mother told her.

"This is so unfair."

"Twelve o'clock," Gabriella said again.

"Do you realize that I'm the only one who has to be home by midnight?"

"Do you realize that I don't care what rules other parents set for their children? I only care about you."

"My life sucks," Sierra grumbled.

"I'm sure, from your perspective, it does," Gabriella agreed. "But for tonight, you have one of two choices. You can go to the party and be home by midnight, or you can not go to the party at all."

Sierra dumped her backpack on the ground. "Yeah, like that's really a choice."

"If you want to invite Paolo to come back here with you, I'm okay with that."

"Because Paolo's really going to want to leave the party at midnight."

"Obviously that's his choice."

"Yeah—*his* choice," Sierra repeated. "Because his parents don't treat him like a child."

"Maybe because he's eighteen years old and doesn't have temper tantrums like a child."

Sierra's eyes narrowed on her mother. She looked both angry enough and tempted to stamp her foot, but of course, that would only prove Gabriella right. Instead, the teenager turned on her heel and slammed the door as she went out.

Gabriella sighed, then turned to him with a rueful smile. "And that was the entertainment portion of the evening," she said lightly.

"Entertaining and enlightening," he said, matching her tone.

"Does it make you have second thoughts about wanting to take on the task of parenting a sixteen-year-old girl?"

"No," he said. "It only makes me admire you all the more."

"You're kidding."

He shook his head. "Every time I look at her, I'm absolutely awed and amazed to think that I had any part in her creation. But all I did was contribute to her DNA. And as stubborn and willful and downright scary as she can be at times, she's also a great kid, and that's entirely your doing."

Her smile wobbled, just a little. "Thanks. It's hard, sometimes, trying to enforce boundaries for her own protection when she insists on pushing against them."

"Do you really think her request to spend the night at her friend's house was just a ruse?"

"I know it," she said. "Because I was a teenager once, too, and I came up with all kinds of excuses to stay out past my curfew or spend the night with a friend in order to be with you."

He frowned. "How old were you, exactly?"

"Seventeen."

He scrubbed his hands over his face. "You were barely older than that child who just walked out the door."

"I was old enough to know what I wanted," Gabriella assured him. "And you were everything to me. I would have done almost anything to be with you."

"I don't think I'd ever been as completely infatuated with anyone as I was with you," Cameron confided. "From the very first time my friends and I went into Marconi's and you walked out of the kitchen, weaving your way between the tightly packed tables with a pizza tray held over your head, I was smitten."

"You were obnoxious."

"Andre was obnoxious," he reminded her. "I was just desperate to get your attention."

She smiled at the memory. "You succeeded."

"I ate a lot of pizza over the next few weeks, just so that I'd have an excuse to see you and talk to you."

"I didn't mind—you never skipped out on your bill and always left a decent tip."

"And still, you kept refusing to go out with me."

"I didn't understand why you kept asking," she admitted. "It was so obvious to me that you were way out of my league."

"You were so beautiful." He stroked a hand over her hair, let his fingers sift through the silky ends. "You *are* so beautiful."

"And you're still way out of my league," she said, sounding regretful.

"Don't you remember how good we were together?"

"Good is a valuation," she hedged. "And I didn't have any experience to judge it against."

"Then you'll have to trust my judgment, and believe me when I say that we had fabulous chemistry."

"We're not kids anymore," she said. "And now we have a kid to think about, which makes this a lot more complicated now than it was all those years ago."

"So tell me to go." He dipped his head and brushed his lips against hers, softly, fleetingly. "Tell me to go, and mean it, and I'll turn around and walk right out that door."

The tip of her tongue touched her bottom lip. "I invited you to come for dinner," she reminded him. "It would be rude to tell you to go without even feeding you."

"I don't care about dinner."

"I was going to order Thai."

"Tell me to go," he said again. "Or ask me to stay. But be sure you know what you want."

He saw the indecision in her eyes. Desire warring with caution; hope battling with fear. He understood her hesitation. They were at a crossroads, and if they went forward from here, there would be no going back.

She lifted a hand, laid her palm over his chest where his heart was beating fast and hard against his ribs.

"You," she finally said. "I want you."

Then her hand slid up to cup the back of his head, drawing his mouth down to hers so that she could whisper against his lips, "Stay."

Chapter Fourteen

Cameron's heart pounded hard against his ribs. Once, twice, as his mind absorbed her response. "You're sure?"

He couldn't believe he was asking the question. But the first time, he hadn't given her a choice. He'd seduced her thoroughly and completely, so that she'd been incapable of refusing what he wanted, what he needed.

He needed her no less now, but he also needed to know that the choice was hers and one made freely and without hesitation.

"I'm sure," she promised, and held out her hand.

He linked his fingers with hers and let her lead him up the stairs to her bedroom. The door was open, as were the pair of windows that flanked the gaslight-style double bed, and light, gauzy curtains waved in the gentle breeze. On the opposite wall, there were two mismatched dressers, with photos of Sierra hanging above. He didn't take in any other details—he was focused only on Gabriella.

She'd paused in the center of the room, and was looking

at him uncertainly. He raised their still-joined hands to press his lips to her palm, and felt her tremble.

"I feel like I'm seventeen again," she said, her voice little more than a whisper. "The way my heart is pounding and my knees are shaking."

He pressed her palm to his chest again, so that she would know that his heart was pounding, too. "I feel as if I've been waiting for you forever."

His lips brushed over hers, softly, testing.

Her eyelids drifted down on a sigh.

He took his time. Even if this was what they both wanted, he didn't want to rush. Not this time. Instead, he lingered on her mouth, sampling, nibbling, savoring her uniquely exotic flavor. When he finally slid his tongue between her lips, a low hum of pleasure sounded in her throat, and he took the kiss deeper.

It was only when his hands moved to the top button of her blouse that she started to draw back.

"I should pull down the shades," she said.

"Why?"

"Because it feels strange to be taking my clothes off with the sun streaming in the window."

"You don't have any neighbors close enough to peek in," he said, brushing his lips against hers again. "And I want to see you. Every inch of you. Gloriously naked."

"Now I'm really nervous," she admitted.

"Only because you're thinking. So stop thinking," he instructed, and kissed her again.

It was a long, deep kiss that completely and effectively wiped all thought from her mind. She wasn't thinking anymore, she wasn't capable of thinking anymore, only feeling. She could feel her heart pounding, she could feel the heat that pulsed in her veins, and she could feel the desperate, aching need that spread through her body.

This time, when he started to unfasten her buttons, she didn't even think of stopping him. When he pushed the blouse off of her shoulders, the balmy air caressed her skin, raising goosebumps on her flesh. Then he wrapped his arms around her waist, pulling her tight against his body, and all she felt was heat.

He ran his hands over her shoulders, down her arms. She tugged his shirt out of his pants, anxious to touch him as he was touching her. Her hands fumbled, just a little, as she worked at his buttons. When she had most of them unfastened, he tugged it over his head and tossed it aside.

Her hands splayed over his chest, relishing the feel of solid, warm flesh beneath her palms, and the strong, steady beat of his heart. Her hands slid lower, tracing the hard ridges of his abdomen, then lower still.

Within minutes, they were both naked, but as eager as she was for the joining of their bodies, she didn't want to rush a single moment of their time together. Cameron must have felt the same way, because he didn't immediately move toward the bed but seemed content to keep kissing her, touching her, teasing her.

When he finally lowered her onto the bed, the old mattress protested with a creak and a groan that jolted Gabriella back to reality. What was she thinking—making love with him here? He was used to being with glamorous women in exclusive penthouse hotel rooms, making love on top of sheets that probably cost more than all of her bedroom furniture combined. He was a prince and she—

The thought drifted away as his hands stroked over her, shooting arrows of pleasure streaking across her skin. Yeah, he was a prince, but he was here with her now, and that was all that mattered.

He worked his way from the top of her head to the tips of her toes, exploring and arousing every single inch of her. He used his hands and his lips and his body until she was panting with want, aching with need, and willing to beg. He took her to the sharpest edge of pleasure and then, finally, over. Her body was still trembling with the aftershocks when he drove into her, sending a whole new wave of sensation crashing through her system. Her hands clutched at his shoulders, her legs anchored around his hips. She felt as if she could drown in the pleasure he was giving her, and she gloried in it.

She cried out, her nails digging into his flesh as her body tightened around him, dragging him into the storm of sensation along with her.

He held her in his arms. As the last of the sun's rays faded from the sky, plunging the room into darkness, he continued to hold her. Her head was nestled against his shoulder, her arm draped across his belly—until his stomach grumbled, loudly.

"We skipped dinner, didn't we?"

"I wasn't hungry before," he said, his hand stroking down her back. "Except for you."

She tilted her head back to look at him. "And now?"

"Now, I'm starving," he admitted.

So they ordered the Thai food she'd promised him earlier. Then, refueled and re-energized, they went back to her bedroom and made love again.

"I missed you," he said, somehow finding it easier to speak the truth in the darkness. "I don't think I realized how much until I saw you again."

"While I appreciate the sentiment—"

"You don't believe me," he guessed.

"Cameron, I went to see you less than a month after the weekend we spent together and you didn't even remember my name."

"That's not true," he told her. "I only pretended not to remember your name."

"Why would you do something like that?" He heard the skepticism in her tone and ached for the hurt he'd caused.

"Because I didn't want to admit—even to myself—how much you meant to me. In only a couple of months, you'd gotten under my skin, wholly and completely. When I got home after saying goodbye to you at the end of that weekend, all I could think about was seeing you again."

"And I'm supposed to believe that's why you never called?" she asked dubiously.

"I know it sounds crazy—"

She didn't deny it.

"—but you have to understand how unusual that was for me. I was a royal—and I'd become so accustomed to having women throw themselves at me, I felt as if that was a birthright as much as my title.

"You were different, right from the start. I'd never felt about anyone else the way I felt about you, and the depth of those feelings terrified me. I was sure that if I just took a step back, I'd realize you weren't any different from any other girl I'd been with."

"That's flattering," she said dryly.

"But I was wrong," he told her. "The longer I stayed away, the more I missed you. And the harder I tried to deny my own feelings. When you showed up at the college that day—I was so thrilled to see you, and equally determined to play it cool. And then, when you told me you thought you might be pregnant...well, that panic was very real."

"I was feeling a little panicked myself."

He stroked his hand over her hair. "I'm so sorry."

"I'm not," she said. "I was hurt and angry for a long time, but once I got past that—or mostly past it, anyway—I was more grateful than anything else. Because Sierra truly was a blessing. I was young and alone and terrified, but I knew I had to get it together for her. She gave my life a focus—everything I did, I did for her."

"You put your own life on hold to raise our daughter while I was raising hell around the globe," he realized.

"We each have our hobbies," she said lightly.

He brushed a strand of hair off of her cheek. "When is it going to be time for you?"

"Well, I kind of think *this* was for me," she teased, trailing a finger down his chest, then beneath the covers and lower still.

She closed her fingers around him, and his eyes nearly crossed. "Yeah, that's definitely for you," he told her.

"Show me," she whispered against his lips.

It was a request he couldn't—and didn't want to—refuse.

A sound from downstairs stirred Gabriella from the depths of slumber. Her eyes went automatically to the clock on the small table beside her bed, though she had to squint to focus on the glowing numbers. When the time finally registered, she jolted from half-asleep to wide-awake in two seconds, but it was two seconds too late.

"Mom?" Sierra's voice was followed immediately by her footsteps.

Gabriella swore and pushed back the covers. Her clothes were still scattered on the floor, so she grabbed her robe off the hook on the back of her door.

"I'll just be—"

She was going to say "a minute" but Sierra, accustomed to an open-door policy, didn't wait for the rest of her response but stepped into the room.

Gabriella had just finished fastening the belt on her robe, and her daughter automatically apologized. "I didn't think you'd be asleep already."

"I wasn't asleep. Not yet." She tried to move out of the room, to steer her daughter back into the hall before her eyes adjusted to the dark enough to realize that there was someone still in her mother's bed.

She didn't know if Cameron had awakened, but if he had, she trusted that he would quickly assess the situation and stay quiet until Sierra was out of the room. She didn't anticipate an untimely phone call.

"What was that?" Sierra asked, obviously not recognizing the ring-tone.

She blew out a breath. "Cameron's cell phone."

Sierra's jaw dropped open. "Cameron's here?"

Gabriella took her daughter firmly by the shoulders and steered her out into the hall.

"Oh. My. God." Sierra stared at her, obviously stunned and hurt and furious. "You are *such* a hypocrite."

"I'm an adult," Gabriella said sharply. "And I don't have to explain myself to you."

"So it's okay for you and Cameron to spend the night banging the headboard against the wall while I'm watching the clock at the party to ensure I'm home by my twelve-o'clock curfew because *you* don't trust *me* to stay out with my boyfriend any later than that?"

"That's enough, Sierra." It was Cameron who spoke this time, and there was steel beneath his quiet tone.

Sierra spun to face him. "This is between me and my mother. You have no right—"

"I have more rights than you know," he told her.

"Because you're a prince?" She practically sneered the question at him.

He met her gaze evenly. "Because I'm your father."

Sierra felt as if all the air had been sucked out of her lungs.

She stared at him, unable to think or breathe. She couldn't believe it—it couldn't be true. She looked to her mother, silently seeking confirmation—or maybe she was hoping that Gabriella would deny his outrageous statement.

"Is it—" She had to swallow. "Is it true?"

Gabriella glanced at Cameron. Sierra had been on the receiving end of that look often enough to know what it meant—it was a silent reprimand to him, and a wordless confirmation for her.

"Oh. My. God." She had to lean back against the wall because her knees were suddenly feeling too weak and trembly to support her.

"Why don't we go downstairs to talk about this?" Gabriella suggested.

Sierra didn't want to go downstairs. She didn't want to talk about it. She didn't want it to be true. And yet, while her brain scrambled desperately for any other explanation, the heart that had always ached for a father urged her to believe.

Gabriella put a hand on her daughter's shoulder. "Sierra?"

She pushed away from the wall and started down the stairs.

While Gabriella busied herself making tea, Sierra tried to wrap her head around the possibility that Prince Cameron Leandres might actually be her father. She shook her head. It was too outrageous to believe.

She waited until her mother had brought the pot and cups to the table, then she asked, "Are you sure?"

Gabriella's cheeks flooded with color. "Of course, I'm sure. I was never with anyone else."

She turned to Cameron. "So you seduced a virgin and then abandoned her when she got pregnant?"

"I wouldn't have described the situation exactly like that," he said, "but that's essentially the truth."

She was surprised that he didn't try to paint the facts to present his actions in a more favorable light. Surprised and wary. "So why are you here now? It's been sixteen years."

"Because I want a chance to get to know you, to be a father to you."

"And how is sleeping with my mother supposed to accomplish that?"

"Sierra." Her mother's tone was sharp, and the glance she sent in Cameron's direction this time was apologetic.

"Well, at least I know now why you were always so tight-lipped when I asked any questions about my father," Sierra said to her. "It would have been embarrassing for you if I'd gone to school in the second grade and told my friends that my father was a prince. I mean, who would have believed it?"

"I've always tried to be honest with you," Gabriella said.

"If you'd really wanted to be honest, you would have told me who my father was when I asked. Instead, I got a song and dance about how he was someone you'd known a long time ago, someone you really cared about but who wasn't ready to be a father."

"All of which was true," her mother insisted.

"And suddenly he's ready and I'm supposed to be the happy, dutiful daughter? Well, you can forget that," she said. "I don't want or need a father now."

"Whether you like it or not, I am your father," Cameron told her.

"I don't like it," she decided. "And the way I see it, you weren't really anything more than a sperm donor."

His eyes narrowed dangerously, and Sierra shifted in her seat, suddenly nervous that she might have pushed him too far.

That she might have pushed him away.

"I think it might be a good idea to continue this discussion another time," Gabriella interjected. "Maybe in a few days…"

"Maybe in a few years," Sierra muttered.

Gabriella sighed. "Why don't you go up to bed? We'll talk in the morning."

Sierra wasn't sure how she felt about being so obviously dismissed, but she was grateful for the opportunity to escape.

She needed time and space to get her head around everything. But as she moved into the hall, she heard Cameron say, "I'm leaving for Rome tomorrow."

"Rome?"

Sierra hesitated, because in her mother's single-word response, she heard both surprise and suspicion.

"That was my secretary on the phone earlier," he explained. "I had some meetings scheduled for the end of the month that needed to be brought forward to accommodate the prime minister's vacation."

"And he called you after midnight on a Saturday to apprise you of the details?" Gabriella asked skeptically.

Sierra was blatantly eavesdropping now, but she didn't care.

"I told him to let me know as soon as the plans had been finalized," Cameron explained.

"Well, then." Sierra heard the scrape of chair legs on the tile floor, could picture her mother pushing away from the table. "You should be getting home to pack."

"I'm sure my valet has taken care of that already."

"Of course," she acknowledged coolly. "I should have realized you'd have someone to take care of those kinds of details for you."

Cameron finally seemed to clue in that something was up. "Why are you mad at me?"

"I'm not mad at you," Gabriella said wearily. "I'm kicking myself for being an idiot. Again."

"You think I'm going to Italy because we slept together? I got what I wanted and now I'm leaving the country to get away from you?"

"It wouldn't be the first time."

"I thought we'd moved past this, Gabriella. Yes, I treated you badly. I was a selfish and self-centered twenty-year-old who didn't think about anyone else. As a result, I missed out on the first sixteen years of my daughter's life, and it's quite possible she will never forgive me for that. But right now, I'm trying to focus on the future rather than the past—a future that I want to spend with you."

Gabriella's only response was to ask, "How long will you be gone?"

He blew out a breath. "Three weeks. After Italy, I'm going to France then Germany and Switzerland."

Sierra took a step forward. She was still hidden in the shadows but could partly see into the room, and she saw Cameron take her mother's hands in his.

"Come with me," he said.

Gabriella blinked, clearly stunned by the invitation. "What?"

"Come with me," he said again. "We could ride in a Venetian gondola and climb to the top of the Eiffel tower, catch a performance at the Frankfurt Opera and visit the Palais des Nations in Geneva."

"I thought it was a business trip."

"If you came, it would be business and pleasure."

She shook her head. "I have responsibilities here, I can't just take off on a whim—"

"If you really wanted to, we could make it work," Cameron insisted.

She didn't respond.

He made his way to the door, paused with his hand on the knob. "Maybe I am the one who's leaving, but you're the one who's running this time."

Gabriella stared at the door for a long moment after he'd gone. When she finally turned away, Sierra fled, silently tiptoeing up the stairs, trying not to think about the tears she'd seen shimmering in her mother's eyes.

Elena had a copy of Cameron's itinerary on top of her desk, so she knew that he was already on his way to Rome. He had a welcome dinner with the prime minister later tonight and meetings scheduled for the next several days after that.

She had hoped that it wouldn't come to this, but her son had left her no choice. She picked up the phone and called Reynard.

"It's time to get this started."

Chapter Fifteen

Sierra hid out in her room most of Sunday. Katarina came home from her weekend with Dominic later that evening, and Gabriella stayed awake all night second-guessing her refusal to go to Italy with Cameron.

She'd never been to Italy. Actually, aside from one trip to New York City with Rafe, she'd never been outside of Tesoro del Mar. She frowned at the thought, surprised by the real-ization that it was the first time she'd thought of Rafe since she'd said goodbye to him more than three weeks earlier. She'd thought she was in love with him, she'd even considered marrying him, and less than a month later, she was twisted up in knots over some other guy.

Okay, so Cameron was more than that. He'd been her first lover, the first man she'd ever loved, maybe the *only* man she'd ever loved. And the man she *still* loved.

She dropped her head down on her desk, banged it against the wood, as if the action might knock some sense into her. How was that possible? How could she still love him? And how could she have only realized it now, after she'd sent him away?

If she'd had qualms about her decision on Sunday, it was nothing compared to the fears and uncertainties that began to nag at her when she saw the photo of Cameron and Bridget Dewitt in the paper on Tuesday.

She waited for him to call, but he didn't, and she wasn't sure what to make of his silence. He'd invited her along on his trip, she'd said no. Maybe he felt that they'd said everything there was to say. But dammit, they'd slept together the night before he'd left. He should have at least called to explain why he was cuddled up with some other woman less than forty-eight hours after he'd left her bed.

She knew that she was being irrational. If she really wanted to talk to him, to demand an explanation, she could call him. But of course she didn't.

She was relieved when he finally left Rome on Thursday. And then she saw the paper on Friday.

This time he'd been photographed at a cocktail reception for international delegates attending the trade summit in France. There were several recognizable faces in the picture—political leaders and international financiers—but her gaze was drawn immediately to Cameron and the statuesque blonde by his side.

If she didn't know better, she'd think he was courting the press, that he was angry with her for turning down his invitation and wanted her to know where he was and who he was with. Except that he didn't look like he was angry. He looked like he was immensely enjoying the company of the gorgeous woman by his side.

She tossed the paper aside and took her mug of coffee into her office.

She tried to put the photo out of her mind and concentrate on her column, but the words wouldn't come. Every response she tried to write sounded false, and she knew why. Because a woman who could screw up her own life so completely had no business trying to advise others about theirs.

The tap at the door was a welcome reprieve, and she smiled when Sierra poked her head into her office.

"Busy?"

Gabriella shook her head.

"Have you seen this?" Her daughter held up the morning newspaper as she stepped cautiously into her mother's office.

She nodded and lifted her mug to her lips, wincing as she sipped her now stone-cold coffee.

"Aren't you mad?"

"At whom?"

"Cameron," Sierra said, as if the answer should have been obvious.

Gabriella noted that her daughter had yet to refer to her father by anything other than his given name or his formal title. Obviously she was going to need some time to accept the familial relationship between them, and she silently cursed the inopportune timing of the prince's trip. Sierra was still reeling from the news that Cameron was her father, and Gabriella believed her daughter would have benefited from having him around to answer her questions, assuage her doubts.

"Honey, I know this is all new to you, but your—*Cameron,*" she hastily amended, "has lived his entire life in the public eye. For a lot of women, being seen with a prince, having her name linked with his—however temporarily—is an enormous thrill."

"So it doesn't bother you that he was photographed with a redhead in Rome and a blonde in Bordeaux?"

Of course it bothered her. Enough that she'd taken the time to do some quick internet checking herself, which gave her the information to answer her daughter's question.

"He's on a business trip," she reminded Sierra. "The blonde happens to be an American ambassador also in France for meetings, and the redhead is an internationally-known model currently dating the youngest son of the Italian prime minister."

Sierra was silent, as if absorbing this information.

"You used to badger me with questions about your father," Gabriella reminded her. "If there's something you want to know now, just ask me."

"I guess I was just wondering...or maybe remembering. When I was little and asked you about my dad, you always told me that you'd loved him very much."

Gabriella nodded.

"Was it true?"

"Yes," she admitted. "I might not have given you a lot of information about your father, but what I did tell you was always the truth."

"Are you still in love with him?"

And because Gabriella didn't like to be dishonest with her daughter, even if she'd only recently acknowledged the truth to herself, she nodded again.

"So why didn't you go with him?"

She narrowed her gaze. "What makes you think he asked?"

"I heard him," she admitted. "When you told me to go to bed, I stayed in the hallway, listening to your conversation, and I heard him ask you."

There was no point in lecturing Sierra about eavesdropping on other people's conversations. What was done was done. So she only said, "Then you heard me tell him that I couldn't go because I have responsibilities here."

"That's a cop-out," Sierra said. "You know it and he knows it, too."

"I'm willing to answer any of your questions about Cameron but not about my personal relationship with him."

"Do you still have a personal relationship with him?" Sierra challenged.

Gabriella didn't have a ready response to that one.

* * *

Sierra hated keeping secrets from Jenna.

What was the point of having a BFF if she couldn't talk to her? But Gabriella had been adamant that she couldn't tell anyone about her father. Not even Jenna. Not yet.

But she had to talk to someone. And there was no one that she trusted more than Jenna. And she knew that she could trust her, because she'd told Jenna about the night she'd snuck out to meet Paolo, and Jenna hadn't whispered a word to anyone, not even Rachel or Beth.

So when she got home after her doctor's appointment Friday afternoon—without her cast finally—she picked up her phone and texted Jenna.

Can you get away? Need 2 talk 2 u.

And Jenna, because she was her BFF, texted back right away:

Where?

Half an hour later, they were sipping iced cappuccinos down at the waterfront.

It was only the beginning of the second week of a three-week trip, and Cameron already wanted to go home.

Usually he enjoyed the travel that was an essential aspect of his job, the opportunity to visit new places and meet new people. But in the short time that he'd been away, he'd realized that there wasn't anywhere in the world that he wanted to go unless it was with Gabriella and Sierra.

By the time he got to Germany, he was feeling edgy and impatient to be home. He thought about calling Gabriella. In fact, not a day had gone by since he'd left Tesoro del Mar that he hadn't picked up the phone at least half a dozen times to dial to her number. But each time, he'd set it down again. He wanted her there with him, but she'd refused. Of course, he'd been too stubborn and proud to beg, and now he was alone.

Well, not exactly alone. He was on his way to meet Dieter Meier for dinner. Dieter was the president of a major manufacturing firm in Nuremburg and an old friend from Cambridge, and Cameron was looking forward to catching up with him. But he promised himself that he would call Gabriella after his dinner with Dieter.

Except that when he got back to his hotel, there was a woman in his room. And not the woman he'd been missing.

"How did you get in here?" he demanded.

Chantal St. Laurent's glossy, painted lips curved. "I know the manager."

"Okay—what are you doing here?"

She rose to her feet, somehow balancing on four-inch ice-pick heels, and crossed the room to where he'd stopped, just inside the door. She'd poured herself into a short spandex dress that was the same color blue as her eyes. There were diamonds at her ears and her wrists, so that she glittered with every step and every turn. She looked good, spectacular even, but her presence stirred only basic male appreciation—and more than a little suspicion.

She ran a manicured nail down the front of his shirt, tracing the buttons. "Hoping to catch up with an old friend."

They used to run in the same circles, but he wouldn't have said they were friends. For a brief time they'd been lovers, but even then, they'd never been particularly friendly toward one another.

She slid her fingertip beneath the fabric, lightly scraped her nail against his bare skin. He grabbed her hand, pulled it away.

"I don't have time for your games, Chantal."

She pouted. "You just don't remember how much fun my games are."

"I do remember," he assured her. But mostly what he re-membered was that she had a red-hot body and an ice-cold heart. "I specifically remember that you screwed me over more than you ever screwed me, and that wasn't a lot of fun."

"Let me make it up to you."

She tried to reach for him again, but he caught both her wrists and held her away.

"You can make it up to me by leaving this room. Now."

He dropped her wrists, but instead of going to the door, she moved toward the bar. She took her time selecting a glass, added a few cubes of ice from the silver bucket, then poured a generous splash of scotch over them.

She swirled the liquid around in the glass, then looked up at him with those big blue eyes that had brought legions of men to their knees. "Please don't send me away, Cameron. Not when I came all the way from St. Moritz to be with you."

He didn't ask what she'd been doing in St. Moritz. Truth-fully, he didn't care. But he did wonder, "How did you even know I'd be here?"

"I've been following your career through the newspapers, hoping that our paths would cross again." She took a long sip of the scotch. "I've missed you, Cameron."

"Was I ever gullible enough to believe the lies that trip so easily off of your tongue?"

She set the glass down again with a snap. "You're not the man I remember."

"You have no idea how pleased I am to hear that," he told her.

"You'll regret turning me away," she promised him.

"I regret that you aren't already gone."

She picked up her glass again, tossed the last of her drink in his face.

He should have anticipated the attack. Unlike Allegra, Chantal had always been impulsive, her moods mercurial, and he'd baited her. Not because he wanted a reaction, but because he wanted her gone.

He was still blinking away the alcohol that stung his eyes when he heard the door slam. Well, he'd got what he wanted in that regard, anyway.

He flipped the security lock and went to the bathroom to shower off the remnants of expensive scotch and cheap memories.

Gabriella awakened to the sound of someone knocking on her door. No, it was more of a pounding, and the impatient, incessant hammering made her heart jolt painfully in her chest. It wasn't quite 4:00 a.m., and nothing good ever came from someone at the door at 4:00 a.m.

She pushed out of bed, yanking on her robe as she made her way down the stairs. She grabbed the phone from the charger on the way to the door, in case she needed to call 9-1-1. A flick of the switch had light flooding the front porch and revealing the identity of the late-night visitor.

She flipped the lock and yanked open the door.

"Alli? What on earth are you doing here?"

"I came to save you from the media hounds that will be on your doorstep before sunrise."

"What are you talking about?"

"The news just came across the wire," her editor warned her. "Alex saw it and immediately called me at home."

Her heart jolted again. "What news?"

"About Sierra."

"What about Sierra?" Katarina demanded.

Gabriella and Alli both turned to find Katarina on the stairs, Sierra behind her.

Alli glanced past Gabriella. "That she's Prince Cameron's daughter."

Gabriella didn't waste her breath swearing. She'd known the

truth would come out eventually and while she wasn't happy about the timing, she didn't think it was cause to panic—although apparently her editor did.

"The presses are running overtime," Alli told her. "But the print media's only part of it. The story's already all over the internet. There are photo montages on YouTube and blog posts about your affair."

Okay, so she hadn't expected the truth to come out quite like this. She swallowed, hard, as her stomach muscles cramped into painful knots.

"What can I do?" she asked.

"Go pack a suitcase," Alli advised, her gaze shifting to encompass both Katarina and Sierra in her instruction.

"I'm not letting the paparazzi chase me from my home," Gabriella's mother said.

"Hopefully it will only be for a few days," Alli soothed.

"And where are we supposed to go?" Sierra demanded.

"There's nowhere we can go that the reporters and photographers won't find us if they're determined to do so," Gabriella acknowledged dully.

"Actually, there is one place," Alli said.

"Where?"

"The royal palace."

Gabriella stared at her, certain her friend had lost her mind. "Okay," she said, playing along. "Let me just call the prince regent to see if there are any vacancies in the castle."

"No need," Alli told her. "I already did."

"You can't be serious."

"Prince Rowan and I go way back…to the beginning of June when you wrote that story about his cousin and the daughter of the King of Ardena, anyway."

"You really called him?"

"He's sending a car and bodyguards to make sure you get from here to there without incident."

"Well, then, we should get dressed," Katarina suggested, finally starting back up the stairs. "We can't go to meet royalty in our pajamas."

It was impossible not to be impressed by the royal palace. But as her daughter goggled over the marble floors and crystal chandeliers and her mother inspected the heirloom vases overflowing with fresh flowers and family portraits in ornate frames on the walls, Gabriella found herself even more impressed by the graciousness of Rowan Santiago, the prince regent, and Princess Lara, his wife, who both came to the foyer to greet them when they arrived.

Gabriella automatically dipped into a curtsy, and her mother and daughter followed suit.

"Please," Lara said, taking her hand. "It's an ungodly hour to worry about such formalities."

"It's an ungodly hour to be anywhere other than bed," Rowan added, "and your rooms are ready for you."

"Thank you, Your Highness," Katarina said gratefully.

"Hannah—" he gestured to the woman who hovered in the background "—will show you the way."

Sierra stifled a yawn as she fell into step beside her grandmother. Gabriella stayed back.

"I don't imagine sleep will come easily with everything that's on your mind," Lara said gently to her. "But you should try to get some rest."

"I will," she agreed. "I just wanted to thank you. I know those words are grossly inadequate, and I'm sorry that we showed up at your door under such circumstances, and so very grateful that you've opened your home to us."

Rowan put an arm across his wife's shoulders, a casual gesture of comfort and affection. "She's going to change her mind in a few hours."

The knots of anxiety that had begun to loosen when the driver pulled through the palace gates tightened in Gabriella's stomach again, but she forced herself to ask, "What's going to happen in a few hours?"

Lara smiled. "The kids will be awake."

The sun was high in the sky and the vultures were circling when Cameron's plane landed at the Port Augustine airport.

He was surrounded by bodyguards as he made his way from the plane to the car, but still he felt the press of the paparazzi pushing in on him. He ignored the shouted questions, the deliberately provocative comments and the blinding flash of cameras. He had only one focus: getting to Gabriella and Sierra.

He knew they were at the royal palace, and that they were safe there. But he didn't know if they had seen *El Informador*.

His secretary had handed him a copy of the paper as he'd stepped onto the plane, and after he'd read and reread the outrageous article, he'd spent the remainder of the almost three-hour flight thinking about how badly he'd screwed everything up.

As he ducked into the back of the black Mercedes SUV and the vehicle slowly began pulling away from the media mob, he accepted that Gabriella would have seen the article. It was inevitable, really. What worried him was that she might believe it.

Rowan and Lara's two sons were very spirited and utterly adorable. Matthew was six-and-a-half, William was almost four, and when the three generations of Vasquez women met them at breakfast the next morning—along with seventeen-year-old Princess Alexandria and thirteen-year-old Prince Damon—they were all immediately charmed. Prince Christian had eaten with Rowan much earlier, Lara informed her guests, so that they could indulge in a morning ride before the demands of the day caught up with them.

The boys chatted up a storm while Gabriella nibbled on a piece of toast and sipped her coffee, and for a few blissful minutes she let herself forget why she was hiding out at the palace and simply enjoyed being there.

When Lara slipped away to take a phone call, Katarina excused herself to head out to the gardens and Lexi invited Sierra to join her for a swim, leaving Gabriella with three very handsome—and very young—members of the royal family. By the time Lara returned, the boys had finished their breakfasts and gone down to the stables and Gabriella was indulging in a second cup of coffee.

"Should I apologize for everyone abandoning you or are you savoring a few quiet minutes?" the princess asked.

"I'm savoring," Gabriella admitted. "Probably because I know it's the calm before the storm."

"Did you manage to get any sleep last night?" Lara asked gently.

"Some," she said. "Enough that I'm thinking a little more clearly this morning and wondering if it wouldn't just be better to face the press and get it over with so that they move on to something else? And I think, if I was the only one who would face the backlash, I would do it."

"You're worried about your daughter," Lara guessed.

She nodded.

"I hope she doesn't mind staying here for a few days. I know kids—teenagers in particular—can be particular about their own space."

"Mind?" Gabriella smiled. "She said she feels like a princess."

"She is a princess," Lara reminded her.

"I know," she admitted. "But I'm not sure Sierra has let herself acknowledge that fact."

"Because it would mean accepting that Cameron is her father," the princess guessed.

Gabriella nodded. "It hasn't been an easy time for Sierra.

She hasn't known about Cameron very long—I thought I was doing her a favor, by keeping the identity of her father a secret. Because I knew that if anyone found out she was his daughter, her life would change." Her smile was wry. "Obviously I screwed up there."

"No one can blame you for wanting to protect your child," the princess said. "Although I don't know if it's fair—or even possible—to protect her from her birthright."

Gabriella sighed. "I know."

"But speaking of Cameron—he should be arriving here shortly."

"He's back from Germany?"

"His plane landed about twenty minutes ago."

Gabriella winced. "I can't imagine he's pleased to have his trip interrupted to deal with this media frenzy."

"I wouldn't worry," Lara said. "I'm sure Cameron is more accustomed to seeing his name in the headlines than most people."

"Does that mean... Is it in the headlines today?"

The princess nodded and passed her a copy of *El Informador.*

"*La Noticia* covered the basic story, too," Lara told her. "They couldn't very well be the only newspaper in Europe that ignored it, but they reported only the facts that had been independently confirmed."

Gabriella didn't reply, her attention already snagged by the harsh words spread across the top of the front page.

Chapter Sixteen

Prince Cameron's Mistress Exposes Truth About His Secret Love Child With Another Woman

Former international supermodel Chantal St. Laurent, recently spotted snuggling with the Tesorian prince in Germany, stormed out of his hotel room in Munich early this morning after learning that her lover is the father of an illegitimate teenage daughter with newspaper columnist Gabriella Vasquez.

"I was shocked when he told me," she later confided to a friend.

Independent investigation has confirmed that Gabriella Vasquez is the mother of a sixteen-year-old daughter named Sierra, but the prince is not named as the father on the child's certificate of birth. In fact, the official document lists the father as "unknown." Sources close to

Ms. Vasquez at the time of her child's birth agreed that she was uncertain about who had fathered her child.

Gabriella pushed the paper aside, unable to read any further. And the thought of Sierra being exposed to such ugly lies and rumors—she felt sick just thinking about it.

"It's a gossip rag," Lara said gently. "And Chantal St. Laurent will say or do anything to see her name in print. I don't know how she happened to be in Germany at the same time as Cameron, but I promise you it wasn't a coincidence."

"You think she set him up?" she asked hopefully.

"I think she's spewing venom and lies," Lara said. "I can't imagine what she thinks she'll gain from any of this, but I don't doubt for a minute that she made up the whole thing."

"Even the part about being in his hotel room?" she asked hopefully.

"No, she was there."

Cameron acknowledged the fact wearily as he stepped into the room.

He looked exhausted, as if he'd been up all night. Exhausted but still so handsome, and Gabriella wanted to rush into his arms. She wanted him to hold her and reassure her that everything was going to be okay. But she knew that he couldn't make that kind of promise and it was foolish and naive to wish that he could—especially when he'd just admitted that the woman who'd sold out Sierra to the media had been in his hotel room. With him.

"I was out for dinner with a friend," he explained, "and when I got back to my hotel room, Chantal was there."

"*In* your room?"

He nodded. "She wasn't there very long—probably not more than ten minutes. Just long enough to ensure that the photographer was in place to snap the photo of her leaving again."

"And long enough for you to tell her about Sierra,"

Gabriella said, though she was still trying to fathom why he would do so.

"I didn't say a word to Chantal about Sierra," he said.

"Then how—" Gabriella faltered, as the pieces finally clicked into place in her mind.

Cameron nodded. "I knew you'd figure it out."

Lara picked up her coffee cup. "Is anyone going to fill me in?"

But Gabriella shook her head, wanting to deny it. "I know she hates me, but this—the lies and innuendos—they're going to hurt you and—" she blinked back the tears, because she knew that if she let even a single one fall, she wouldn't be able to stop the flood "—Sierra as much as they hurt me."

"Collateral damage," he said easily. "The princess royal wouldn't concern herself with that so long as she got what she wanted."

Lara stared at Cameron. "You think *your mother* set this whole thing in motion?"

"She didn't want Cameron to ever know about Sierra," Gabriella told her.

"And since you failed to keep that information from me, she used it to hurt you."

"Wait a minute—" the princess turned to Gabriella "—are you saying that Elena knew about Cameron's child and didn't tell him?"

"Yes, she knew," Cameron admitted.

Lara shook her head and pushed away from the table. "Apparently you two have bigger issues than the paparazzi to work through, so I'll leave you to it."

Cameron sat down at the table across from Gabriella.

"Are we going to be able to work through them?" he asked softly.

She wanted to say "yes." She wanted to believe it was true. But she wasn't as naive or idealistic as she used to be and she knew that the odds were stacked against them. It wasn't just that he was a royal and she was a commoner; it wasn't even that their fledgling relationship was suddenly under very public scrutiny. It was so many different things, but mostly it was the acceptance that no matter how much she loved him, love wasn't always enough.

And so, when she finally responded to his question, it was to say, "I honestly don't know."

It wasn't the answer he wanted, but Cameron couldn't blame Gabriella for being cautious.

One step forward, two steps back, he thought wearily. Their relationship had finally been moving in the right direction, until he'd left the country with a lot of questions and uncertainties still between them.

"Are you…" she hesitated, almost as if she was afraid of the answer he would give to her question. "Is it true—" she started again "—about you and Chantal being lovers?"

"No," he said. "*Dios,* no." And it was the truth, but not the whole truth, and he knew that he couldn't hold anything back from Gabriella now. If they were going to move forward, they couldn't do so with any more secrets between them. "Not anymore."

"So you were," she murmured.

"A long time ago."

She nodded.

She didn't look surprised or even disappointed. Obviously his confirmation was no more than she'd expected, and why wouldn't it be? For a lot of years, he'd been known as the partying prince—a favorite of the paparazzi because he was always out on the town, always with a different woman, always having fun. He'd grown weary of the scene long before he'd managed to extricate himself from it, and though he'd done so more than half a dozen years earlier, the reputation continued to haunt him.

"If it was over a long time ago, why would she do this?" Gabriella gestured to the paper.

He had several theories about the unlikely partnership between his mother and his former lover. It was possible that Elena had bribed or blackmailed Chantal to ensure her complicity. It was just as likely that Chantal had jumped at the opportunity to be involved—just for fun. "Because Chantal's never as happy as when she's in the middle of a scandal."

Gabriella shook her head. He knew she didn't understand people like Elena and Chantal, people who could find pleasure in using their power to hurt others. Her basic honesty and goodness had appealed to him from the start. And even when he'd been furious with her for keeping his daughter a secret, he'd known that it hadn't been easy for her.

Elena, on the other hand, wouldn't have lost a wink of sleep over the role she'd played in the deception. More likely, she'd have taken pride in the display of her power. It was what she did—manipulating others so that she could feel important. He'd long since figured out that her behavior was rooted in her own childhood, in the feeling that she was insignificant and powerless because she was a female child born to a ruler who already had a male heir. But the fact that he'd come to understand the reasoning behind her behavior didn't mean it sickened him any less.

Gabriella turned the paper over, so that she didn't have to see the headline staring at her. "Sierra's going to be devastated when she sees this."

Cameron wasn't so sure. Oh, he knew that Sierra would be hurt, that she'd wonder if there was any truth in the midst of all of the lies. But the fallout for her would be minimal. Regardless of what anyone believed about her father or her mother or the circumstances of her conception, she was the innocent in all of this. Right now he was more concerned about Gabriella.

"Rowan suggested a press conference, and I agree that it's probably the best way to handle this," he told her.

"Why don't I just walk outside the palace gates with a target on my chest instead?"

He reached across the table to touch her hand. He half-expected her to pull away, and when she didn't—when she actually turned her hand to link their fingers together—the relief he felt was almost overwhelming.

"We're going to present a united front," he promised her. "Me and you and our daughter. We'll read a prepared statement and formally introduce Princess Sierra and we won't answer any questions."

"That won't stop them from asking."

He nodded, acknowledging the fact.

"Okay." She drew in a deep breath. "When are we going to do this?"

They decided that the press conference would be held at Waterfront Park at nine o'clock the next morning. The exact location wasn't too far from where Cameron had initially confronted Gabriella about Sierra's paternity, although that was by coincidence rather than design. Rowan's advisors had suggested the outdoor stage where summer concerts often took place as a suitable venue to ensure access to all the media who chose to attend. Cameron had some concerns about providing security for Gabriella and Sierra in such an open space, but the prince regent promised that the royal security detail would be there to look out for them.

Gabriella had hoped that the paparazzi would back off when the date and time of the conference were announced. As grateful as she was to Rowan and Lara for allowing them to stay at the palace, she wanted to be back in her own home, she wanted to pretend that things were normal. But the media vans remained just outside the palace gates, trapping her inside.

When she'd ducked out of her house under cover of darkness

so many hours earlier, she hadn't thought about what she was throwing into the bag she brought with her. She certainly hadn't packed anything that would be appropriate to wear to a press conference. She had no sooner expressed this concern to Lara than the princess asked if she wanted to make a list of items for someone to pick up from the house or do some online shopping. Though she was tempted by the shopping, she opted to make a list. She already owed the princess far more than she could ever repay.

An hour later, she was sorting through the suits and blouses she'd selected. She managed to narrow it down, but continued to waver between the taupe and the red.

"Definitely the red," Lara said, when she'd finally got up the nerve to ask the princess for her opinion. "Even if you wear the taupe, you won't be able to escape the spotlight but it'll look like you tried. Also, Sierra's wearing red. Red and white, actually, but you'll coordinate nicely. And red is definitely your color."

So the next morning, Gabriella got dressed in the red, then she went to see what her daughter was wearing.

She halted in the doorway of Sierra's room and absorbed the twinge of regret that stabbed at her heart when she couldn't see any sign of her little girl anywhere. Instead, there was a poised and beautiful young woman in front of her, dressed in a simple but elegant white sundress with red poppies dancing along the hemline, red peep-toe pumps on her feet and a wide-brimmed red hat on her head.

"It was Lexi's idea," she said. "The hat. She said it would make me look more mysterious."

"I almost didn't even recognize you," Gabriella said with a smile.

She was pleased that Alexandria and Sierra had hit it off so quickly. Lexi had been raised as a princess from birth, so she knew everything there was to know about the duties and responsibilities of a royal and had already proven herself an invaluable support to Sierra.

"You look fabulous."

She smiled shyly. "I feel strange. I mean, I like the outfit, it's just so different from my usual style. But Lexi said it set the right tone between formal and casual."

"It's perfect," Gabriella assured her.

Sierra nodded. Then she took a deep breath and blurted out. "I told Jenna. About Cameron being my father."

And Gabriella suddenly realized why her daughter had been so uncharacteristically quiet and withdrawn over the past two days—not just because she was feeling overwhelmed by everything that was happening, but because she was feeling guilty.

"She's my best friend," Sierra continued. "And I didn't think she'd tell anyone—"

"She didn't," Gabriella interrupted. She took her daughter's hands, squeezed gently. "The leak didn't come from Jenna."

"You're sure?"

She nodded. "There were…details given to the media that Jenna couldn't have known, that you didn't know."

Sierra exhaled a heartfelt sigh of relief. "I thought this was all my fault."

"Oh, Sierra." She hugged her daughter tight. "None of this is your fault, honey. If anyone's to blame, it's me. If I'd told you the truth—if I'd told Cameron the truth—a long time ago, we might have avoided this now. Or at least been more prepared for it."

"Well, I'm as prepared as I'm going to be," Sierra told her. "So let's get it over with."

The park was packed. Somehow word had got out that Prince Cameron's daughter was going to be in attendance and the citizens of Tesoro del Mar flocked to the park, anxious to finally set eyes on Princess Sierra. A lot of Sierra's friends were there, too. Aside from Jenna, no one had known that her father was a prince until they'd read it in the papers or seen it on television, and they were all curious to know if the prince's daughter really was the same Sierra Vasquez that they knew.

Gabriella wasn't surprised by the turnout. She'd known there would be more curiosity-seekers than media personnel, but she'd still tried to discourage her mother from attending, worried that Katarina would be an easy target for the paparazzi. But Katarina had insisted on being there to support her daughter and granddaughter, and Gabriella saw that she wasn't alone. In fact, she was flanked on all sides by members of Cameron's family. Rowan and Lara and Matthew and William; Christian and Lexi and Damon; Eric and Molly and Maggie and Joshua. Even Cameron's sister, Marissa, was there, with her other brother's daughter.

Only the princess royal was absent—apparently having left the country on short notice to visit an ailing friend in Corsica. Gabriella knew that explanation was nothing more than an excuse, but she was nevertheless as grateful for Cameron's mother's absence as she was everyone else's support.

As a child, Sierra had relentlessly hounded Gabriella for a sister or a brother, and Gabriella's heart had ached that she couldn't give her little girl what she wanted. What Gabriella, too, had always wanted. Because from the time she'd been a child, she'd dreamed of someday having a big family—including at least half a dozen kids running around the yard.

Of course, in that scenario she'd also imagined that she would have a husband—someone who went out to work at a respectable but normal nine-to-five job every day and came home to his wife and family every night. Falling in love with a prince had totally screwed up all of her plans, and while she could maybe forgive herself for the youthful fantasies that had allowed it to happen when she was seventeen, she should have known better this time around.

...the mind does not and cannot control the heart.

She no longer doubted the truth of her mother's words, but as she looked out at the familiar faces in the front row, she could at least be happy that she'd finally given her daughter the family that she always wanted.

Rowan's secretary stepped up to the microphone first, drawing her attention back to the purpose of the assembly. He introduced himself to the crowd, thanked everyone for coming, and announced that Prince Cameron had a statement to make.

Though neither Gabriella nor Sierra was expected to say anything, it was agreed that they would stand with Cameron, demonstrating their support of him and agreement with the official statement he would deliver.

"Over the past couple of days, the media has been inundated with rumors regarding my history with Gabriella Vasquez and the paternity of Gabriella's daughter, Sierra. I'm here today to separate the fact from fiction..."

Gabriella didn't listen to any more of his speech. They'd gone over it together the previous afternoon, so she knew exactly what he intended to say. Instead, she focused on the sound of his voice, allowing her frayed nerves to be soothed by the smooth cadence.

As he spoke, she held Sierra's hand in her own. Her daughter's icy fingers were the only outward indication of her trepidation. She had to know that everyone was staring at her, but she stood tall with her head held high, looking every inch the princess, and Gabriella had never been more proud.

There was a brief silence after Cameron finished speaking—probably not more than a few seconds—and then the real uproar began. There were so many questions that it was almost impossible to decipher any individual words, until someone shouted: "Prince Cameron, are you going to marry Gabriella?"

And Gabriella's heart actually stopped for the space of several beats.

She and Cameron had talked about this scenario and they'd agreed that they wouldn't respond to any questions or statements from the crowd. But this one seemed to linger in the air for a moment, as if everyone was waiting for an answer. As Gabriella held her breath, waiting for the same thing.

Cameron had heard the question. She had no doubt about that. And he even paused, as if considering his response. But in the end, he only said, "Thank you all for your time."

And then he turned away from the microphone.

Sierra immediately fell into step behind him, obviously eager to get off the stage and away from the endless flash of bulbs, and Gabriella followed her. There were still questions being shouted, but Gabriella was only aware of the one that had gone unanswered.

What did you think—that he'd want to put a ring on your finger? Wake up, Gabriella. You're a nobody from nowhere and he'll never marry you.

The words that echoed in her mind now weren't those of her mother but his, and the scornful tone with which they'd been delivered had cut her to the quick. Because she'd believed him when he'd told her he loved her, and she'd been foolish enough to think that a man who loved her would want to marry her.

She wasn't seventeen anymore, and yet, she'd let herself get caught up in the fairytale all over again. She'd fallen in love with Cameron and she'd trusted him when he'd told her that he wanted a future for them together. She'd believed that he was committed to her and their relationship, but his silence on the subject of marriage spoke volumes.

Behind the scenes, the security force was filling vehicles for the return trip to the palace. Sierra rode with Lexi and her brothers, and Katrina had climbed into a vehicle with the prince regent and his family, leaving Gabriella to ride with Cameron.

She settled back against the plush leather seat with dark-tinted windows and finally let herself breathe. No one could see her in here. No one could know that her heart was breaking. No one except Cameron—but he'd seen it all before.

She didn't realize the tears had spilled over until she felt the brush of Cameron's knuckle on her cheek, wiping them away. His touch was gentle but she felt as if a fist was squeezing around her heart, and the ache was both painful and real.

"Are you okay?" he asked.

She nodded. "I'm just relieved it's finally over so I can go home." Back to her own house, her own life. Reality.

"It wouldn't hurt to stay at the palace a few more days," Cameron said. "You heard the questions the reporters were shouting—they don't have all the answers they want yet."

"Yes, I heard the questions," she agreed.

"We knew it was going to be like that," he reminded her. "No matter how much information we gave them, it wouldn't be enough."

She nodded. "I know. It wasn't the questions that bothered me—not really."

"Then what was it?"

He sounded as if he really didn't know, and she had no intention of enlightening him. "I understand that the media attention is a fact of life for you, and I know it will be for Sierra, too, but I can't live like that."

"What, exactly, are you saying?"

She drew in a deep breath. "That I don't want a life in the spotlight so we should stop pretending that a relationship between us could ever work."

His gaze narrowed on her. "At seventeen, you were pregnant and washing dishes in a restaurant kitchen so that you could afford to buy a crib for your baby. After you had the baby, you took night courses and you worked your way up from the circulation desk to columnist at *La Noticia*. I think you've already proven that you can do just about anything you want to, so if you think you can't handle a few skirmishes with the media, maybe the truth is that you don't want to," he accused.

"Maybe I don't," she agreed. "Or maybe I just don't want to handle it all by myself."

He scowled. "What are you talking about? You weren't by yourself. I was right there—"

"Standing on the opposite side of Sierra." She felt tears stinging her eyes again. "As if she was the only connection we had."

"What was I supposed to do—announce to the crowd that we're lovers?"

The words were a knife straight through her heart, the final, fatal strike to her illusions. She'd thought they were so much more than lovers. She'd thought they were in love, planning a future together, building a family.

"No," she finally said. "You weren't supposed to do anything."

Cameron followed her out of the SUV and up to her room, where she immediately began tossing her things into a suitcase. "If you're going to be mad, you could at least tell me why."

"I'm not mad."

It was obviously a lie, but he knew better than to call her on it. "Okay, then tell me how to fix whatever it is that I screwed up."

"There's nothing to fix," she said. "I've just decided that I won't be your dirty little secret anymore."

"What the hell are you talking about?"

"That's how Chantal referred to Sierra, but the truth is, our daughter was simply the result of your youthful indiscretion. You have absolutely nothing to be ashamed of there.

"But it's not quite so easy to explain me, is it? And that's why you haven't even tried. That's why you're so careful not to be seen in public with me, and why, even today, you kept six feet of space between us."

"How can you blame me for trying to shelter you from the media when you said you didn't want your name linked with mine in the tabloids?"

"That was before we were sleeping together."

"Well, obviously I didn't get the memo about the rule change."

"You had a chance to stand with me today," she told him. "To show the world that you wanted to be with me, to tell them 'yes—I do plan to marry her.'"

He couldn't help it. Afterward, he would agree that was no excuse for his action, but it was purely reflexive, completely instinctive—he stepped back.

She turned away to zip up her suitcase.

"Come on, Gabriella," he said reasonably. "We've only been together for a few weeks."

She looked right at him, baring her true feelings. "I know. But I've loved you for seventeen years."

I've loved you… If you loved me… The words spun in circles in his mind, making him dizzy.

He didn't want to believe that she was trying to manipulate him. He knew that she wasn't like that. And yet, he'd listened to those words too many times, and hearing them fall from her lips now, he froze.

"Are you giving me an ultimatum?" he asked coolly, waiting for her to spell out her terms. Waiting for her to look at him, her eyes filled with pleading/fury/tears, and finally tell him what he wanted. What he needed to do to prove that he loved her.

But she didn't look at him at all. She only picked up her suitcase and said, "No, I'm leaving."

Chapter Seventeen

It was rare for Cameron to have visitors at his office. And his days were usually so tightly scheduled that he wouldn't have time to spend with anyone who just happened to drop by, anyway. But since he wasn't yet supposed to be back from his trip, he had large blocks of unscheduled time—most of which he spent thinking about Gabriella and how thoroughly he'd ruined everything.

So when his secretary buzzed through on Tuesday afternoon to tell him that someone was there to see him, Cameron was grateful for the reprieve. Even more so when he realized that his visitor was Sierra. He hadn't seen her since the day of the press conference—the day that Gabriella had walked out on him.

He hadn't seen Gabriella, either, but only because he had yet to figure out the best way to grovel for her forgiveness.

"Lexi told me that it would be okay if I stopped by," Sierra said. "She didn't tell me I'd have to present three pieces of ID and be subjected to a body scan in order to get past the front door."

"I'll make sure you get security clearance so you can come here any time you want without going through all of that again," Cameron told her.

"That might be a good idea," she agreed. "Since I've decided that I should probably get to know you a little better—because of the family connection thing."

"I'd like that," he said.

"But it would be a lot more convenient for me if you came around to the house again," she told him.

"I could talk to your mother about the possibility," he said cautiously.

"Or you could just show up," she suggested. "I know she'd be happy to see you."

"Well, I'm not so sure about that."

She huffed out a breath. "Are all guys so dense?"

"I'll assume that's a rhetorical question," he said dryly.

"Okay, answer this one—are you in love with my mother?"

"Yes."

She blinked. "Wow. Not even a moment's hesitation."

"I would have told her the same thing, if she'd given me a chance." At least, he wanted to believe he would have told her, but she'd started talking about commitment and he'd started feeling backed into a corner.

He'd lived his whole life with his mother pulling his strings until he'd finally severed them. And then he'd been both relieved and determined that no one else would ever have that power over him again.

Unfortunately, it wasn't until Gabriella had gone and he'd listened to himself pouring his heart out to Lara that he realized Gabriella had never tried to bend him to her will. She wasn't looking for a commitment at any cost. She only wanted him if he wanted her, too.

And he did want her—more than anything else in the world.

"That's good, but the words aren't going to be enough," Sierra warned him. "She needs to know that you're going to stick."

"What do you mean?"

"You've got a history, right? She fell in love with you when you were younger, you said you loved her, too, and then you were gone. Fast-forward sixteen years and some months, and you're back again, saying you love her, blah-blah-blah."

"Blah-blah-blah?"

"I'm trying not to think too much about the details," she told him. "It's kind of weird, you know, with her being my mom and you being my dad."

She said it casually, as if it was no big deal, but to Cameron, it was a very big deal. It was the first time she'd explicitly acknowledged their father-daughter relationship, and while he was tempted to haul her in his arms and hug her so tight she could barely breathe, he managed to restrain himself.

"Your point?" he prompted instead.

"It's easy to say you love her, but she needs you to prove that you mean it."

"And how, exactly, am I supposed to do that?"

Sierra smiled. "Why are you asking me for advice when you could go straight to the relationship expert?"

Dear Gabby,
I'm writing to you in the desperate hope that you can help me convince the woman I love of my feelings for her.

I'm a thirty-six-year-old man who has fallen in love only twice—both times with the same woman. The first time, I was barely twenty years old, too young to understand the depth of my feelings and too immature to appreciate how truly rare and special our love was.

The second time was much more recent. After more than sixteen years apart, our paths happened to cross again and I realized that the feelings I had for her so long ago had never gone away.

I've tried to show her how I feel, but I think she's afraid to believe it, afraid that I'll hurt her again.

I'm more than willing to put my heart on the line. I'd happily hire skywriters or put a message on the big screen at a baseball game—whatever it takes to let her know that I'm going to stick around this time… forever.

Should I set my plans in motion—or do you think a man who royally screwed up once doesn't deserve a second chance?

Signed,

Lost in Love

Gabriella reread the letter twice. At first, she hadn't let herself believe Cameron had written it, but there were too many specific details to be able to disregard. And while hope flared in her heart, she forced herself to tamp it down. Because despite what he said in the letter, nothing had changed.

Or maybe everything had changed. The princess royal had told her that Cameron would never marry her, but this letter suggested not only that he would but that he wanted to, that he really wanted to be with her forever.

With that cautious hope in her heart, she settled her hands on the keyboard and began to type.

Dear Lost,

While I believe that everyone makes mistakes and everyone deserves second chances, I'd hold off on hiring the skywriters. Your willingness to put your heart on the line in a very public way is admirable, but not every woman wants or needs such a big statement. In fact, some women might worry that a man who goes to such extremes might be more flash than substance.

Instead of shouting your feelings from the rooftops, take the time to show her what's in your heart. As cliché as it sounds, it's often the little things that mean the most. Pick her a bouquet of flowers. Hold hands. Walk with her in the rain. Cook her favorite meal. Call her at bedtime, just to say good-night.

Give her some time to see and believe that you intend to stick around forever. It's not easy to let go of past heartaches, so be patient, be understanding, and be there for her.

Good luck,
Gabby

It happened to be raining the day that his letter and her response appeared in the newspaper, so Cameron snuck out of the office during his lunch and dropped by Gabriella's house. His wipers were on full-speed to clear the water from his windshield, giving him a moment's doubt about his plan, but he didn't change his course.

Gabriella was obviously surprised to see him, and more than a little wary when he suggested that she should put her coat and shoes on. But when she finally did, he took her by the hand and walked with her in the rain. They didn't go far but they still ended up soaked through to the skin.

He called her later that night, to see if she'd managed to dry out yet and to say good-night.

The next night, he called her again. And then again the night after that. He never kept her on the phone for more than a few minutes—just long enough for him to let her know that he was thinking about her and, he hoped, to make sure that she was thinking about him.

On the fourth night, he invited her to dinner. And after only a moment's hesitation, she accepted.

* * *

Gabriella was a nervous wreck as she got ready for her date with Cameron. Of course, it didn't help that both her mother and her daughter were hanging out in her room, critiquing every outfit that she tried on. Too sexy. Too frumpy. Too young. Too old. Finally Katarina left to go to her hot yoga class, and when Jenna called to see if Sierra wanted to go out for an iced capp, Gabriella was relieved to shove her daughter out the door, too.

Cameron showed up a short while later, with an enormous bunch of flowers in his hand. There were tall spikes of lavender, cheery pink anemones, fat white lilies and bobbing Spanish bluebells. But what she noticed, after the gorgeous array of colors, was that the stems of the flowers were uneven and broken…almost as if he'd picked them.

"They're beautiful," she said, filling a vase with water. "But I'm not sure why you're doing this."

"Doing what?"

"Bringing me flowers. Taking me to dinner."

"Because I don't cook, either," he told her. "I wanted to make your favorite meal, but I only know how to make reservations."

She smiled at that. "It wasn't intended to be a checklist, you know, just a few suggestions."

"But those suggestions made me realize that we'd missed a lot of those basic getting-to-know-you rituals and I thought it was time we started following some more traditional conventions."

"Such as?"

"Well, dating usually precedes courtship which precedes marriage."

The vase slipped out of her hands and clattered into the sink, splashing water all over the counter and Gabriella.

He handed her a towel. "And marriage, of course, precedes children. Obviously, we've done some things backwards."

She dabbed at the wet splotches on the front of her dress. "Backwards implies a reverse order, but we actually skipped a couple of those steps."

"We'll get to them," he promised.

"Is that was this is about? Are you…courting me?"

"And apparently not doing a good job of it, if you have to ask."

She looked at the flowers again. She could only imagine where he'd picked them—probably from a stranger's garden—and her heart completely melted. "Actually, I think you're doing a wonderful job."

"Really?" he asked hopefully.

"Really." She set the vase on the counter, then turned to touch her lips to his cheek. "Thank you for the flowers."

"You're welcome," he said, and kissed her again.

It was a kiss filled with hunger and frustration and longing, and Gabriella responded with her whole heart.

After what seemed like an eternity and yet not nearly long enough, he eased away. He brushed his thumb over her bottom lip, a slow sensual stroke that made her tremble. His eyes darkened and, for just a moment, she thought he was going to kiss her again.

Instead, he took a step back. "We should get going. We have a reservation at Tradewinds."

She drew in a long, slow breath and nodded. "Right. We wouldn't want to miss our reservation."

But neither of them moved.

"Although we've never worried much about conventions," she reminded him.

"No," he agreed.

"So maybe, instead of sitting through dinner wondering if the evening will end with sex, why don't we start with sex and wonder if we'll make it to dinner?"

He drew her back into his arms, which was exactly where she wanted to be. "I really like the way you think."

* * *

It was a long time later that he looked at the clock beside her bed and said, "We missed our dinner reservation."

She sighed contentedly. "We could order pizza."

"Okay." He kissed her. "One question first."

"Pepperoni," she told him, belting her robe.

He rummaged around on the floor, looking for his pants. "That wasn't the question."

"Okay, what's the question?"

He found his pants and put them on. Apparently whatever the question was, he didn't want to ask while he was naked. Then he shoved his hand into the pocket and pulled out a small, square box. Her heart began to pound furiously inside her chest.

"Compared to the sixteen years that we were apart, we've only been together for a short while," he said. "But the past two weeks without you have been the longest weeks of my life and I don't want to live another day without you by my side."

She blew out an unsteady breath. "You sure moved through that courtship stage fast."

"Because I finally realized what I want. And that's to marry you, build a life and share a family with you, Gabriella."

She desperately wanted to throw her arms around him and tell him that she wanted that, too. But while her heart was already committed, a tiny part of her brain continued to urge caution.

"Your mother hates me," she reminded him. "And to be honest, I'm not too fond of her either."

"I've gone through this scenario a few times in my mind," he admitted. "And never once did I imagine you wanting to talk about my mother."

She managed a smile, though everything inside of her was a quivering mass of nerves and uncertainties. "She's not my favorite topic of conversation, but she's your mother—your family—and you have to know that she won't be happy about this."

"She'll adjust," Cameron insisted. "Because she knows that I won't tolerate her interference in my life ever again. She'll even come to the wedding and smile, because she's a princess and she understands the importance of duty."

The steel in his voice was reassuring, but she still felt compelled to ask, "Is that why you're doing this? Because you think that marrying the mother of your child is your duty?"

"I'm asking you to marry me because I love you," he said. "Because I've always loved you, even when I was too much of an idiot to realize it. And because I want you to be my family—you and Sierra…and maybe another baby."

Her heart stuttered. "A baby?"

"If that's what you want," he hastily amended. "If you don't want to do it again, that's okay. But—"

"I'd love to have another baby," she told him.

"Really?"

"Maybe it's crazy, considering that I'm now twice the age that I was when I had Sierra, but yes, really."

"Does that mean you'll marry me?"

"I haven't actually heard a proposal," she said.

So he went down on one knee beside the bed and flipped open the box. "Will you marry me, Gabriella?"

She didn't even look at the ring—she didn't need to. The love that she saw shining in his eyes was all that she needed to see. "Yes, Cameron, I will absolutely marry you."

He slipped the ring on her finger. "You realize that after we exchange vows you'll become a 'princess' and living outside of the spotlight will no longer be an option?"

"I can handle it." She wrapped her arms around his neck. "I can handle anything as long as you're by my side."

"Then that's where I'll be," he promised her. "Forever."

Epilogue

PRINCE CAMERON TO WED THE MOTHER OF HIS CHILD?
by Alex Girard

That's what everyone has been asking since the prince publicly confirmed he was the father of Gabriella Vasquez's sixteen-year-old daughter, Sierra, earlier this month. The question was finally answered on Saturday night in a beautiful candlelight ceremony at the royal palace.

The bride wore a simple but elegant Nicole Miller floor-length gown of ivory silk and carried a hand-tied bouquet of white gerbera daisies. The groom was outfitted by Savile Row in traditional black tie with royal decorations. The couple exchanged vows before an intimate gathering of family and close friends in the rose garden.

At the conclusion of the ceremony, the prince and his bride joined their hands together to cut into the gorgeous three-tier wedding cake created by the mother-of-the-bride (and having indulged in a taste of that exquisite cake, I now understand why Dominic Donatella wants to get his hands on her recipe!).

As the guests ate cake and drank champagne, Princess Sierra offered a first toast to the newlyweds, wishing them a long, happy life together—and wanting to know if they were *ever* going to give her a brother or a sister.

While the blissful couple left that question unanswered, at least for the moment, there is no doubt that their daughter's other wishes for them will come true.

* * * * *

A sneaky peek at next month...

Cherish™

ROMANCE TO MELT THE HEART EVERY TIME

My wish list for next month's titles...

In stores from 17th February 2012:

❏ How a Cowboy Stole Her Heart – Donna Alward

& The Rancher's Dance – Allison Leigh

❏ Meet Mr Prince – Patricia Kay

& Once a Cowboy... – Patricia Thayer

❏ The Last Goodbye – Sarah Mayberry

In stores from 2nd March 2012:

❏ The Doctor Takes a Princess – Leanne Banks

& Pregnant with the Prince's Child – Raye Morgan

❏ A Bride for the Island Prince – Rebecca Winters

Available at WHSmith, Tesco, Asda, Eason, Amazon and Apple

Just can't wait?

Visit us Online

You can buy our books online a month before they hit the shops! **www.millsandboon.co.uk**

0212/23